ALGORITHM

Artorian's Archives Book Seven

DENNIS VANDERKERKEN
DAKOTA KROUT

MOUNTAINDALE
PRESS

ACKNOWLEDGMENTS

From Dennis:

There are many people who have made this book possible. First is Dakota himself, for without whom this entire series would never have come about. In addition to letting me write in his universe, he has taken it upon himself to edit and keep straight all the madness for which I am responsible, with resulting hilarity therein.

A thank you to my late grandfather, after whom a significant chunk of Artorian's personality is indebted. He was a man of mighty strides, and is missed dearly.

A special thank you to my parents, for being ever supportive in my odd endeavors, Mountaindale Press for being a fantastic publisher, Jess for keeping us all on task, and all the fans of Artorian's Archives, Divine Dungeon, and Completionist Chronicles who are responsible for the popularity for this to come to pass. May your affinity channels be strong, and plentiful!

Last of all, thank you. Thank you for picking this up and giving it a read. Algorithm is the continuation of a multi-book series, and I dearly hope you will enjoy them as the story keeps progressing. Artorian's Archives may start before Divine Dungeon, but don't worry! It's going all the way past the end of Completionist Chronicles! So if you liked this, keep an eye out for more things from Mountaindale Press!

Please consider giving us five stars on Amazon, Audible, and anywhere else you'd like to spread the word!

CHAPTER ONE

"Artorian can cheat." Brianna, the Dark Elf queen, wore a proud self-satisfied smirk after dropping her bombshell. The words caused all conversation to stop in and around the huge vat that could fit ten. Every person currently relaxing or washing had a different reaction to the accusation, as the words meant something at least slightly different to each of them. Either way, the words themselves cut to the heart of the issue the group was facing.

The Elf nodded at the people now facing her. "Thank you for the trip, Tatum. Also to Chandra for not skewering me on arrival. I'm aware my reputation remains fouled."

"I believe your explanation calls for…" Artorian shot both his hands into the air, his voice rather concerned. "*More*, please? Communication is entirely based upon understanding."

Tatum glanced at Brianna, who had clearly taken the reins here, then motioned towards Dawn's patient in a very 'have at it' motion.

Before she spoke further, Brianna glanced around the room for approval. Checking in with the peer group was rather important. When she didn't receive the backlash she expected, a tiny smile grew on her face. "No comments? This is appreciated. Very well then... Perhaps this will help clarify what I am trying to explain, Administrator."

Moving her wrist with some sleight of hand, she produced a round gemstone—rather than her dagger—that rolled around her fingers before suddenly vanishing. "When I said that you have the blessing of Anima, I refer to a belief held by the Dark and Moon Elves. 'Anima' is taught to our young as a concept, an idea, to strengthen them in the future. We teach that there is no separation or difference between our mind and our soul, only that there is a difference between the rational and irrational part of it. The rational soul is structured, orderly, sensical. People strong in this soul are grounded, and those who stand steadfast in this thinking have the blessing of Persona. They know where they stand in relation to themselves, and others."

Rolling her other wrist, the same gemstone reappeared, only to make another dancing journey across her fingers and vanish once more. "The irrational soul is untamed, chaotic, and nonsensical. Few thrive in this madness, and those who do always appear to wander. Disconnected from their peers, unaware of their social status, blind to their relation with most others. People strong in this soul, who calmly stride across that path as if bouncing across leaves resting on still water, have the blessing of Anima. For that is what it means to face the absurd, and find it lacking."

Brianna dropped her open palm towards the human who liked to play king. "Let me help give you an example of your opposite. Henry, could you describe your experiences in Eternium?"

"My... *experience*? What I *do* in Eternium?" The human King was coated entirely in foam and bubbles—as he was trying to have a relaxing bath—but he replied all the same. "Die. Nothing but dying. I swap bodies, do whatever tiny task Cal wanted us to test, then usually die shortly after. I go back only because, as Brianna said, I have subjects in Eternium. When I leave Cal permanently, I am adamant that I will make the best

Kingdom I can, with the best possible rules in place. I still haven't gone through enough iterations to feel I would do well, and I certainly can't match Marie's natural sovereignty."

"They need backlash, is all." Queen Marie smirked at her husband and flexed her hands. "They're just more willing to backtalk you because you don't grab those who speak ill to your face by the back of their neck."

Henry settled deeper into his bathtub and grumbled. "You didn't *have* to dangle that chancellor out of the window."

The Queen just shrugged. "He never gave us lip again, nor did he steal from the coffers. I found that a very fitting end to a recurring problem. Let me pause this divergence, and get back to the question. I dislike going to Eternium because, aside from practicing how to rule, there is no merit to me being there. Granted, I haven't tested Cal's new improvement system. However, I'm already gritting my teeth before I even get started. I don't *want* to use it."

Marie needed a calming breath. "My enthusiasm is at rock bottom, and all the constant changes drive me up the wall. In my experience, Administrator, you take to changes like water filling a new container. Did you ever get told how many difficulties the rest of us actually had un-flubbing those broken items? That task was a *nightmare*. You think *you* didn't want to do it?"

Tatum picked up for her as she got close to hyperventilating, counting various problems on his fingers. "Aiden has… personal issues we won't get into. He was happy so long as there were Amazonians to kill, but that didn't last past those early days, before we even started implementing proper iterations. He's just… *sour* all the time."

He counted his second digit. "Odin also isn't a great example, as he didn't care about Eternium or Cal's system either way. He's pleased so long as he gets to try to drink a whole mead hall under the table. It didn't matter to him where he was doing it."

A third digit was raised. "Deverash could not be happier, and won't say a negative word about the system… no matter how often things break or how many Wisps he upsets."

Tatum nodded toward the other S-ranker rather than keep counting. "Personally, I am just *tired*. Dawn and I have never needed to sleep in a Seed Core, but we have also never gotten a *chance* to do so. We are exhausted, and want a break. I don't even know what I want to do with the break, I just know I want one. Even *my* work ethic needs a breather and, much like Cal, I just want to stick my fingers in some pies and do things purely for giggles."

He pressed his fingers to his forehead instead. "I won't get that chance. We are relied and depended upon to solve problems only Incarnates can, and many are so complicated that I can't even describe them. Not without a few years of primer."

Artorian looked to Dawn, who was currently holding the back of his left leg to mend it. He winced as she further repaired nerves. Dawn nodded at him when he glanced, but she couldn't spare the attention to do more than that. Repairing his Spirit body wasn't as arduous as fixing a true Incarnate's body might be, but it was still an involved process.

Artorian scratched the back of his head. "Well... I'm sorry you all haven't been having a good time. I can't say it's been easy for me either, though I think that has to do with Cal leaving me with some abysmal characteristics. *Honestly.* When Cal set me to have only fives for my physical stats? I know what it feels like to be bedridden, and I'm uncertain why it's so funny. Not being able to walk properly is already a running gag I'm ready to let die; I didn't need it repeated in Eternium as well."

Some nods made the rounds, and Brianna raised her hand to talk. Artorian motioned for her to just start speaking. "That brings me to the point everyone else is so deftly avoiding. Here is the lynchpin: Eternium uses a tier seven-twenty **Law**. Anyone of a tier below that, save for Tatum—who figured out how to circumvent things over however many millennia it took—simply cannot stand against Eternium. His system is absolute. All our powers are gone or negated, and we have to relearn them from scratch for them to count in Cal's system. A process we have to re-do for every new body we go in there with. It's *awful*."

4

Artorian pressed a finger to his lips, finally grasping her meaning. He could *cheat*! "So, since my **Law** is also seven-twenty, and on his tier, I am able to bypass the forced nature of Cal's system. As it is, Eternium is the one enforcing those rules, *not* Cal. I bet having **Order** as a **Law** is helping Eternium keep the 'game' straight whenever the rules change, a benefit we are sorely lacking."

Artorian ruminated on the topic. "I have, several times, done things that have forced Eternium to… deal with me. I have even gotten thrown out of his Core once. He has so far created Pylons to compensate for my actual abilities, forcing me to use those instead of my cultivation track variants. I admit I didn't care too much in my blind rush to accomplish things. Not my brightest moment, perhaps."

He winced as Dawn mended the nerves in his feet, squeezing the edge of the vat hard enough for it to fracture between his fingers. "*Eee*. That one hurt more than a little."

The Fire Soul replied matter-of-factly. "Many nerves exist in your soles. Keep talking, it's distracting you."

Artorian wasn't about to give away a free chance to gab. "Sure. I understand why it seems preferable that *I* go into Eternium and hunt some demons. Yet, if we're going to reconstruct things out here, and there are no further threats, I… uh… have a wall of Cores that's been eating a hole in my heart."

Tatum stabbed his thumb across his shoulder at said wall. "We know. We had a full meeting about them when we had to decide on decanting Yvessa. Picking her out was fun. She's probably going with you wherever you go from now on, especially when it comes to Eternium. She's fine, by the way. Currently she's with Oberon and Grace, keeping the Eternium Core safe while mending a branch. Which looks like it's going to take a few months."

Artorian nodded, though he had a thought. "What about that whole deity project Cal was harping on about?"

Chandra took that question. "The project itself is fairly easy, it's just that we currently don't care very much. I'm sorry for

Cal, I really am, but until he's back, I really have no interest. Neither do many of the others. The deity project is all work and no gain. I know he told me in a private meeting that DE points could be used to improve personal cultivation, but when I heard you needed several *million* to do anything, I just checked out."

Nods of agreement followed Chandra's statement, though Brianna stuck a finger in the air. "I was somewhat interested, but really just to show that I can do good and not become a power-hungry monster. I wish to drag my honor out of the garbage. It is unpleasant, feeling I have no friends. Dark Elf or not, total solitude wears on me."

Brianna turned slightly, looking through the wall at the Cores. "My idea for your family was as follows: when we are truly certain there are no further threats in Cal, I considered using the rebuild of the Vanaheim realm as a sort of... *copy*... of a chunk of our old world. Not just some tiny morsel tucked away in a beneath somewhere, but an entire honest-to-Cal continent, then decant your family there. I'm even willing to help set that up, since you will need time to..."

The Dark Elf paused, pressing her finger to her cheek. "Artorian, you realize you don't even look thirty now, when most everyone remembers you as 'Mr. Wrinkles'? I can tell you from experience that appearances are extremely important. If you decant your family, and you aren't what they remember... it will go poorly. If you have been advised to hold off before, then I would perhaps take that advice. We can make the place; we are rebuilding most of Cal's Soul Space anyway. Whatever it is you need to do to... fix yourself? Do so, and I will stand with you when it comes time for your family to again have a place to properly live their lives. No snide comments, I promise."

Henry came up from dunking himself under the water. He'd heard enough to be on board. "Artorian, we... uh, we don't really talk about it, but every supervisor had at minimum a small group of personal people they haven't been able to decant. We all have a wall like you do. Not as large, but I definitely have one. Marie does too, even though she won't admit it.

We have all felt awful about not being able to give them good lives, and we are all guilty of keeping our prized people in those Cores. You may so far have come to the conclusion that 'it's simply not a good time' and unfortunately, that's been the correct assessment."

He moved through the water of the massive vat to sit next to his friend, and put a hand on his shoulder. "Don't beat yourself up over a difficult decision that has, in the end, been the right decision. I wouldn't wish what we've gone through in these realms on any of my personal friends. With the wire-tears mending, the threats gone, a good heads up of what to expect, Cal heading to the double-S ranks, and a guarantee that the Soul Space isn't going to be used much... since it's all going to Eternium."

He paused for a beat.

"Honestly? I call those *good* conditions, and a great time to make this happen." Henry waggled his hand, but ended with a thumbs up. "I would be ecstatic to be able to decant my people at the same time as you do yours."

CHAPTER TWO

Artorian pressed his hand to his heart as he sat. He was touched, his jaw somewhat gritted at the consideration. "I'm not... I'm not the only one? This has been eating me up for ages! You all have people stored away too?"

Experiencing a feeling he didn't know how to describe, he watched an entire room nod. Even Brianna was guilty. His expression turned to Dawn expecting an exception, but she was also nodding. "Sunny, do you think I would put my chosen anywhere other than a safe place until I knew with certainty that I could let them live without threat of their demise? Tatum and I knew well that this was going to be a very long, and very rough ride. I may not have started with stored people, but I definitely gained them. Abyss, if I could have stored *you*... I would have."

A smile played on her lips, and Dawn leaned in to touch foreheads. "You're all healed up, and all you need is a large influx of energy. The more the better. If you're able, going through one of the steps of your tribulations track will heartily see you fully empowered. If you can't, hide and cultivate until

Yvessa inevitably finds you. Otherwise, I too like the idea of building the old continent on Vanaheim."

"Even if I know Deverash will stick his nose and influence it." She momentarily glared through the wall, peering at the wreckage of that continent. Dawn eased, and made a head motion towards the regretful Dark Elf. "I believe Brianna, and agree with her. Out of all of us who sit at the moot, you have the best chance of doing good in Eternium, with the least frustrations. Plus, I *love it* when you give that dungeon Core some stress."

She pressed her bronze finger to Artorian's mouth before he could speak. "Also... there's demons in there that need squishing, and you will never have to do anything that bores you. You can pop out anytime to come have a coconut, and tromping around in Eternium will only make you stronger. Plus... if you figure out the deity thing and game system, we would all really appreciate a solid explanation."

"I may be 'maxed out' in there, but I'm as clumsy as a foal. I am too old-school to work well in Eternium, but if I had someone to explain it to me... someone that really knows the ins and outs of how things actually work, then I would love to hear it." Dawn's smile was gentle, then a thought made her frown momentarily. "Cal is going to make us play deity eventually, and have our chosen run around as 'bosses.' Personally, I would much rather sit on the Silverwood branch to protect Eternium. Likely with Adam if I can figure out how to summon him out of that Core. When I am not out and about fixing things. I'm an okay builder, but I only truly excel at war."

Tatum hushed some words under his breath. "She might also be a *teensy* bit mad at what happened with Yasura. That S-ranked demon d—"

Dawn flashed Artorian an innocent smile, fluttering her lashes in a way that meant she wasn't going to explain a word of the *delicious* gossip Tatum had just dropped and abruptly ended.

Artorian quickly gave a thumbs up as he replied. "Well, I

like being a team player. Honestly, I still feel bad for doing such a shoddy job as Soul Space Administrator. If you all are going to take care of the place out here, and occasionally pop into Eternium, then I will do my best to unearth all of the system's secrets."

He smiled to himself with an idea, and wrenched his hands together. "I even have three *harmless* little friends that would adore mucking about with me."

"You need your reserves full before you head out. I promise that nobody will hold the first iteration grumble-grudge for too long." Dawn poked him in the cheek. The Fire Soul very gently cocked her head to glance at the rest of them. "Isn't that *right?*"

The look in her eyes and intimidating expression had everyone speaking over one another to quickly, and verbosely, agree. "See! It'll all work out fine. Now, you're clean, and all patched up. I'm going to get you a robe. I'll have Dev look at that wreck of a... palanquin? In the foyer. Like Tatum said, forget your prior position's requirements. We've always picked up the slack anyway, so you just do what you're good at. Okay, Sunny?"

Artorian nodded. People who felt they'd had their say started to funnel out. There were things to do, and they needed to discuss the details. Henry remained next to Artorian, gently nudging him in the shoulder. "Listen. I think you're great. About the Administrator thing, even without Dawn threatening to spit roast our souls over a fire: in retrospect, you did alright. Like Chandra said, that first iteration was rough for everyone, and we were all looking for someone to blame. Myself included."

Henry provided a fist bump. "Also, thanks. Especially for being alright with going into Eternium when the rest of us are... *erm*... not."

"Thanks, Henry, I appreciate it. I also understand. It's not easy, and not everyone bends like I do. You don't need to say it." Artorian fist-bumped the King back in reply. Then sank back into the water to get cozy. "I think that if I had been unable to cheat, particularly as I am able to do in that Core, I too would have been a very upset muffin. If you all have it covered out here, I'll have it covered in there. Your mention that you all also have people… honestly, that was a big step for me. I have been… I'm not sure. That guilt weighed so heavy. Like gold that burns a hole in your pocket and you can't get your mind off. I have been thinking that the longer I wait, the worse I'm doing by them."

Henry shook his head. "It was like that for all of us. The real issue is what would have happened if we'd let our loved ones out too soon, and then a shattering like earlier occurred. I believe that is what really would have killed me. Talking about this helps."

His old friend in a young body agreed whole-heartedly, sinking into the hot water until only his face remained exposed. "It does. Thanks, Henry. I think… I think I'm ready."

Henry raised an eyebrow. "Ready for what?"

Artorian closed his eyes, and after mumbling a few words, took a deep breath before dunking under. "Oh. Nothing much. Just talking to myself. I'm going to rest my eyes for a moment, my friend. I'll be back in a second."

The King could agree with that statement. He settled in next to Artorian and took a breath to go sit underwater on the bottom of the vat. Relaxing in this shared, precious moment, where the world wasn't falling apart.

Artorian opened his eyes in his bonfire space.

Scilla was waiting for him, seated upon one of the Silverwood Tree roots. "Talking to yourself? Come now, old man. We both know you directed that at me."

The twenty-two-year-old Artorian sat on the branch next to her, wrapping a comfortable white bathrobe around his middle. "I was. I just… didn't realize I needed other worries off my chest before I could admit it. I know what happens in the Phoenix Kingdom. I know why it's going to tear my heart to pieces. This time… this time I'm ready. Henry and Brianna don't realize how much they helped, but they did."

Scilla pressed her shifting cheek to her tiny fist. "As additional motivation, completing a tribulation will heal you up. Straight to A-rank four! Though that's not the point, is it? Not for you. You want to talk about why you're doing it this time? I know about the family, but overhearing what I did, you have one celestial blessing of a support team that's there for you on that front. So what's up, Merli? What's causing that burning zeal in your eyes?"

Artorian faced her properly, no longer hiding that his soul did, in fact, feel like it was on fire. "I want to *rip* Barry to abyss-blasted *pieces*. I want to turn what's left of him into a measly *dessert fork*. I don't know how I'm going to do it yet, but I know I need to be in Eternium to do it."

Scilla's grin spread from ear to ear. "Now *that* is motivation! I'm ready when you are. Oh, and Sunny, I will obviously be here for you when you get back. As a bonus, since you're jumping in headfirst... the tribulation won't take more than a few seconds. You'll wake up in that bath next to your friend, before Dawn comes back with the dry robe. Promise."

Inhaling strongly, Artorian prepared a fist-bump. "Catch you on the other side."

Scilla flashed him a proud grin, preparing her own. "Give them abyss, Merli. It's time for you to get that second name. Even if you don't like it."

He laughed, having forgotten that part. Artorian bumped knuckles with Scilla to get going. This time, he was ready when the world went dark.

Another strong inhale, and it was one of ales and ointments. His parting vision unblurred the tavern-table before him, covered with game pieces stacked on a checkerboard. It was his turn, and he was seven shots of rock-vomit rum deep into the game. No wonder his vision was swimming.

A bard squeaked in the corner, his singing stopped by the barbarian sick of hearing him yodel. Three barmaids moved about to take orders, handling the always stuffy crowd inside of the Tailfeather Brewery. The place wasn't an inn or tavern, but the owner had a thing about handing out free samples each time one of his batches was done. Gerald the Mill had arms like anvils, and a reputation for hand-cranking the milling wheel on days where there was no wind.

Everyone believed it too, but even if they didn't, who said *no* to free ale? The freebies had only made them all deathly ill once! Those were gambling odds the patrons were willing to throw dice on, and the occupants of the brewery laughed raucously as yet another bard was foisted out with an off-key *eeeee* from the establishment.

A fist smacked down on Merli's table, returning his attention to the captain of the guard. His current opponent for this complicated strategy game. "Your move, vagrant! I've got a whole silver on the line, and this time it will be me that cleans *you* out."

Merli shook his head, his senses turning back to the game. Three moves. He'd have the captain in three moves, but only if the man didn't realize his tower piece was all that was protecting his castle piece. The youth smirked, and placed his thin fingers on his cardinal. "Captain. You are not going to *believe* what's coming next."

CHAPTER THREE

Sir Bilkus Bingus Butcharrande the guard captain stormed, with a litany of expletives, out of Tailfeather Brewery. His cheeks were puffed and red. Regardless of how full his mouth seemed with all the insults endlessly tumbling forth, his coin pouch felt painfully empty. "That cheating *lout*! If I find so much as a shred of evidence he's broken some kind of law, I will see that swindler hanged or thrown out through the front gates!"

"I can't believe he would wager a silver against your clothes just for the chance to beat you." Larine, one of the girls handling orders and carrying around questionable ales, quipped at Merli when she set a fresh mug down. "That sounds like a lot of effort from our dear captain just to get your pants off."

She winked as she swayed along to the next table, leaving Merli beet red in the cheeks as he gingerly sipped the newly provided drink to cover up his embarrassment. He choked on his own words as a laughing duo settled down with him at the table, mumbling back. "It's unkind to mention such things, Larine. Please don't... y'know, kill me via embarrassment."

Hector, one of the guards for this area, swung his arm around Merli's neck. "Oh, tiny comments like that aren't going to do you in if you keep trouncing Bilkus in 'kings and castles' like that. He was furious last time, and spent weeks of his free time practicing in the barracks with us. He was solidly convinced he was going to win today. That bet with you just now? That's not the only bet he's lost today, and as a proud member of one of the people that will be collecting later, I want to be the first to thank you for the free coin! Who do you think bought you that ale just now?"

Merli moved the mug in his hand, swirling the contents. "Well, I knew it wasn't Larine, and Gerald wouldn't give me another free drink if the entire guard barracks threatened him to. Eh... speaking of. One moment. Hey, Efliva! I can pay! Come take this silver from me and clear my lodgings tab. This will get me, what, another week?"

Efliva glared from behind the bar at her longer-than-desired tenant. As the older maid of the three, she had the shortest fuse for Merli's brand of malarkey. "Boy, if you don't find some actual lodging soon, I am going to start denying your money and throw you back out on the street. You cannot keep using our brewery as your gambling location to make income, and if I see even one more girl leave that room missing so much as a *handkerchief,* I will personally beat you with my broom until I have wiped you from this establishment. Now pay up."

Merli said nothing, and looked away after dropping all his earnings into her waiting hand. She snapped at him for a moment before returning to her ledger. "You have another week and a day, and that's all you get. We can't keep housing a vagrant that doesn't have proper city registration, and don't feed me that obvious lie that you can't afford it. You just handed me two silver, *swindler boy.*"

Larine stepped half a mug-swing closer to the situation than she should, causing Efliva to shoot her a glare so sharp that Larine felt it in her keister. Turning around as if pretending she was never going to defend Merli at all, Larine hummed her way to the far side of the brewery to take new orders.

Efliva snapped at her regardless. "*Mhm.* That's what I thought."

Merli slumped back into his seat behind his game board. He stared at it listlessly. So much for this venture. Opening the small wooden game board like a box, he piled the pieces in before closing it back up.

Rubbing his eyebrows with his palms, he just watched the goings on. Looked like it was going to be his last week here as well, and bouncing around was getting... tiresome. He was gaining a reputation, his face was being recognized, and businesses were refusing him entry before he even asked if he could... Ah well. Maybe it was time to pack a bag and head out to another Kingdom. Pressing his hand to his cheek, he looked out of the open window.

Hector blocked his view with a heavy lean and nudged him. "What's wrong, kid?"

Shoving his thumb over his shoulder, Merli didn't much have a reply. He performed an 'it's happening again, so, you know. Not feeling great' shrug.

Hector understood well, as this was the eighth district he'd followed this kid to. "Listen, Merli. I will give you a copper if you tell me what's preventing you from putting some roots down. You don't need to wander aimlessly all over the place. I told you before, the guards could use a clever kid like you. You've got a serious melon on those shoulders. You'd do some real good with us. Plus you can write, and it's really pretty."

The youth rolled his head left to right, clearly conflicted. Hector just kept at it, thinking he might get through this time. "You'll have lodging you don't need to pay for, and a uniform that counts as clothes. Which might do some wonders in comparison to these ragged robes you've been wearing for years. I know you won't tell us what kind of wasteland you crossed to get here, so I won't push."

Hector pressed his luck some. "When it comes to the future though, why not, kid? The captain would stop giving you unholy abyss... probably. Plus you'd get signed into the city register as a citizen. No more vagrant status that will get you tossed out if a guard finds you without a copper to your name, even though you're trying really hard to stay a drifter for a reason I just can't fathom."

Merli's hands moved, but they were still listless and empty. "I don't know, Hector. It's nice in theory, but I'm not... I just can't sink myself into a job I know I won't care about come tomorrow. The perks are nice, but do I really need them? There's nothing in that offer I want to strive for, and it leaves me feeling just as empty as when I started. I'm a homesick soul, and I don't even know where home is anymore. Which, while it seems to be an attractive trait for the fairer sort, isn't something I really want to carry around forever. I... suppose I just contradicted myself there."

Hector laughed, and pushed the drink he brought closer to Merli's face. "You gloomy bastard. Perk up... if you keep losing yourself in your head like that, you're not going to see the flowers that grow in front of you. Or are standing on the other side of the street, pretending not to look at you."

Merli frowned, but picked up his head. "What do you mean? There's nobody just waiting around just to see *me*."

Hector leaned back, his warm grin spreading. "Oh, I don't know about that, kiddo. You may have angered your fair share of flowers by being... well, you... but I think there's one that rather misses you, and your bookish nose. Say, I haven't mentioned this before but, as a citizen of the Phoenix Kingdom, you can buy and own property, in the event you find someone to start a family with."

Merli scoffed at the thought. "I am a flake, and an unreliable schemer that people are learning not to trust because I can beat them at their own favorite games. So it looks very much like I cheat, regardless of just... figuring it out better. What are you on about, Hector? Move your head."

Hector smirked, and moved out of the way entirely. The view he saw made it all worth it, as Merli both shut up on the spot, and turned a little pink. The best part was that the person he locked eyes with on the other side of the street also turned pink, and promptly fled.

Hector *tsk'd* at him loudly. "Making a lady run off like that, I'm embarrassed to call you an acquaintance. Why are you still sitting here? Go apologize, you blunt mook. Why are you not getting up? Git, *git!*"

Artorian watched himself get up. His real perspective was already waiting near the door as he watched the uncertain, young version of himself rise from the table. Then take off after what was going to be one of the most important people in his early life. Artorian held his long beard, following right along as Merli dashed through the Phoenix markets, arrayed in their gorgeous purple and red awnings. Stalls displayed these specifically to show off just how rich and wealthy that particular merchant was. Supposedly, it meant to show they could be trusted.

In Merli's experience, the opposite was true.

Merli tripped over a carpet and stumbled hard, eating dust and dirt as he went down hard between sprawled salesman carts. So much for chasing. Groaning in pain, he curled up in place; he'd hit his face so hard that his nose bled. His vision swam, and getting up was difficult as some urchin smashed into his prone form and nicked his coin pouch. That urchin was going to be unhappy when he found it was emptier than a dry well. Still, just his luck. Now he needed a new coin pouch.

Sitting up, he looked at his red hands. He got worried when the bleeding didn't stop when he expected, so he had to rip off part of his ragged Skyspear robe in order to stifle it. He looked ridiculous holding a piece of cloth to his face, an angry welt already growing on his forehead. Fantastic, now he was robbed, ugly, and had lost the point of the chase. Ah well... given he only had a week left in this hole of a city, it wasn't going to matter.

"Are you okay?"

He tried waving off the question since he thought it was just some passerby, but the softness of the voice made him blink and turn to see who owned it. To his extreme surprise, it was Alina. The girl who had turned pink and run away earlier. Which made him feel terribly embarrassed. Especially given his current... state.

"I... uh." His sentence cut off with a hard wince, hand moving up to his forehead. "Been better."

Alina was clearly a bundle of nerves, but she suddenly reached out to grab his sleeve. Red as a tomato, she dragged him along to a well that actually did have water in it, where she made him sit while she filled a pail. "Here. Put some cold water on that rag, and press it against your forehead."

Merli said nothing as he was helped, his breath stuck in his throat now and then as he stole glances. Alina was an average-looking girl, but there was something about the braiding method in her long blonde hair that kept demanding his attention. That or the way her cheekbones stood out. Or how the curve of her ears was cute. Or that the tiny bend lingering on the edges of her nervous lips couldn't stop trying to form a smile. He couldn't place it. He just noticed his attention kept walking itself back to gawking at her face. Like some ogling child.

"So... are you Merli?" The question was weak, but his nodded response was strong. Too strong, as it forced a self-inflicted headache to bite him in the forehead.

"Ah, uh. Yes. Hi. I don't think I ever asked for your name? Though, I sort of know what it is." He extended his hand, properly this time, given his prior blunders. "Hi, I'm Merli. I... wander."

Alina took his hand, and the smile that bloomed for some reason made her sharp jaw and chin stand out all the more. "Alina. I... wish I could wander. I'm a maid of Lord Pershing, one of the many merchants I hear you have such great things to say about. I'm also the one that... lost the book you found and returned. That saved me from a few lashes. So... thanks."

She sat down next to him, clearly nervous and unsure of what to say after that. Though it was clear she didn't want to leave, even if she couldn't vocalize why. Merli, unfortunately, didn't have a nice mind. He pushed away thoughts of asking her about the lashes, as his opinion on wealthy merchants was bleak enough. "Why did you have a book in the first place?"

Alina shrugged, suddenly very interested in her feet. "I wanted to... try learning how to read. I was told it was a story-book, and I like hearing stories told, so I figure I might like it if I could just read them myself. I didn't get that far, I just lost it and... well. Lots happened, which would have been worse had you not shown up at the front gate. How did you even know where to return the book? Or why return it at all? You could have easily sold it for a full gold coin! Books are expensive."

Merli shrugged half-heartedly. The reality was a little dull. "Oh, I... I read the whole thing in less than an hour and found the address in the rim of the cover. It wasn't a very good book, and I wanted it out of my hands so fast that I just walked over and turned it in. Didn't even get a copper for it. Great start to my views on merchant reputation there."

She was smiling. Merli didn't know why she was smiling. He only knew he liked it. "Why'd you choose to be a maid?"

Her smile fell, and Merli felt like an idiot for blurting that out. "It... wasn't. A choice, I mean. Mom's a maid under Lord Pershing, so... that's where I fit. I can't leave that household without an amount of coins that I couldn't make if I worked for Pershing a solid twenty years straight. Or so mother says, since that was her plan. Then I came along, and I would rather not keep talking about it."

Merli nodded, and tried to mouth an apology. The words just barely made it out. "I'm s—Mm. Well, if I had a copper to my name, I'd have asked if I could buy you an ale. I am, however, currently poorer than the dirt we're sitting on."

A massive hand fell down on his shoulder, surprising them both. The smile present on Bilkus's face shone wide and oppor-tunistic. "Oh really... ? I think that means you're a coinless vagrant, and vagrants without papers are thrown from the front gates!"

Merli swallowed, his mind racing as he came to some incredibly snappy decisions. He turned his head, eyes meeting with Alina as he asked a question he really shouldn't have, but would never once in his life regret. "How much is it to get you out from under Pershing?"

Alina's blue eyes flicked from a very self-righteously pleased guard captain, to Merli's gaze. Which she could swear was starting to have fire lit behind them. Her mouth moved before Bilkus was able to drag Merli up and away. "Thirty-four gold."

Merli's head turned, gaze boring right into the gleeful captain's. "What is the pay for a guardsman who can read, write, do math, and keep your ledgers straight for the tax man across all the barracks in the city?"

Bilkus's expression brightened further. *Hector, you genius! Finally!* "Well, I'm sure we could discuss that in my office. Unless the front gate sound more to your liking."

Merli's eyes burned as he locked eyes with his new boss. "I'll see you in your office, Captain."

CHAPTER FOUR

Artorian gawked at what he was seeing. Merli gained a lesser fire channel, just for *falling in love*? Or was it for putting his foot down properly for the first time in his life? In that snap decision next to the well, Merli's mind had *roared*.

Choices turned into visible consequences. A spider web of events and decisions Merli could make exploded in his sight, showing the patterns of eventualities. From Alina's last few comments, he had seen a single, special thread. One that didn't lead back to the life of a vagrant, or lost soul on the road to nowhere.

All Merli had to do was grit his teeth, and put his foot down. He'd have to throw away his fleeting, airy nature. Yet there was a feeling in his chest that burned hot, burned bright, and burned deep. The heat gripped his heart during the moment he'd been so close to those delightful blue eyes, and he knew that if he gripped this fire, he could do true good by someone.

Artorian watched his younger self's center. The fire channel had flickered! Flaring for a moment as Merli aligned himself with both the principles of living in the moment and living for his passions. Not the fleeting, escapist ones he'd stubbornly stuck by. This was anger he could hold in his hand. A rage that could be gripped as the hilt of a sword. Wielded with hot blood against the awfulness of these merchants that thought they could buy the world.

This heat was the warmth of a flame that kindled from a source he didn't understand. Because suddenly he was around a person that sparked emotions which he thought were forbidden to him. The image of a puzzle, half finished, sprung to his mind in the spiderweb. In his hand he had the pieces, and if he so much as put a piece down, then this was a mosaic he could discern the full picture of.

It would be a long trek. A difficult puzzle. One that ended with merchants in tears, the captain bashing his head into a wall, and one very, very happy maid.

With maybe, just maybe, one happy Merli.

These consequences... these consequences were worth it. Even if it was a decision he did not reach from the smart part of his brain. Merli reached this option from the emotional part, and while ordinarily that would be questionable... to be honest, what were the emotions if not a driving force to go forwards? What good was puzzling out the world if he didn't have a clue where he should go? Here was a direction. A flame!

Sure, it might burn him, but if not now—then when? If not this, then what?

Artorian pressed his hands against his mouth, watching as the budding fire channel found foothold! Then, like a firework sizzling in the preparation stations, went up with bright splendor as it opened and took its new place. Air from running to freedom in Morovia. Celestial from mind breaking Skyspear. Fire... from purpose found in the Phoenix Kingdom.

Artorian mouthed to himself as he watched the spectacle unfold. "If one can't find value in the self, then don't do it for you. Do it... for them."

He stood still for so long that the scenes around him whirled into a tapestry of color and the passage of time. He blinked, and Merli was on the training fields next to the barracks. He'd been assigned a personal drill instructor, because of course that was how much trouble he was. Artorian smiled as he saw scores of troops frantically running around the barracks as it slowly turned into a military camp. The new scene found Merli hiding out to nap on the roof of the officer's quarters.

Because who would go look there?

Then the war with Socorro came, and the purpose of the military camp became clear. Still, he expected that was a regret for… later. Had he known signing up with the guard would get him converted to the army by forced conscription, he might have just walked. Still, a military wage was significantly better than a guard one.

As an additional bonus, each conscript was required to go through both physical and written tests. While his physical results were below par, his written portion was so flawless that he was accosted by several sergeants and checked for cheating. He ended up taking that written test four times, each iteration adding new, more complicated military scenarios and questions to it.

To Merli, those were just fun. He had all the time to describe where he would move people, for what purpose, and how many lives he could save with certain maneuvers given listed circumstances. The hard part was when he came to a question that clearly had no good endings.

He hated those. Deciding who to send out into the fire, knowing they would never come back. He despised those choices with a passion, desiring entirely to bring all his board pieces home.

Reality did not match up with such fleeting ideals of perfection. Reality was ugly. Gritty. Filled with accidents, and people who were obstinate. Soldiers and leaders who countered your orders and wishes, or outright conspired against you. His fourth test was so heart-breaking in difficulty and realism that by the time he turned it in, he had also chewed away half of the writing utensil they'd given him to use.

Merli was so distraught by that test, and the gory details in it, that he couldn't fathom it originated from any place other than… reality. A real commander had written up that scenario, and not because it was theoretical.

The scenario featured detailed, brutal, ugly losses. Broken chains of supplies. Crashes in morale. Ignored orders. Misunderstood orders. Flags stolen by the enemy. Poisoned meals. Just… awful.

Artorian watched Merli have a small mental break when he collapsed to a knee in the middle of the dirt street. Merli was holding his head, thoughts swimming with what the realities of actual war must be like. Was that what they were heading into? That disgusting brew of horror? Could he get out of it? At all? Was there any job he could ease into, or rather, could he even get away from the Phoenix Militarum?

No.

His spider web of visualized options bashed into dead ends. He was trapped, and spat out his anguish. *"Crackers and toast."*

"All that drama because you wanted some toast? Well, I did just get fresh bread. It's still hot. Though I've got nothing to put on it." Merli looked up to see Alina's beaming face when she spoke.

Her soft, thin hand reached down. "Hey you… it was taking you too long to show up, so I walked over to come get you from the camp. You okay?"

Merli gripped the offered palm, the new calluses on his own feeling insulting in comparison. Weapon training was hard, and he was about as good with the bow and glaive as a foal was at stumbling. That was to say, pretty decent. "I am now."

Alina snorted while helping him up, her finger pushing into his chin. "Are you an awful sweet talker, or awful at sweet talking? That was so terrible, and yet terribly sweet. That I don't know if I love it or hate it. Maybe you can convince me by reading the next chapter of the story? I snuck the book out again. Trade you for something crunchy to eat?"

Merli pulled a face. "Does it have to be *trade*? Can't I just do it because I like you?"

Alina smirked. "Oh... well. Maybe... Though *only* if you insist. Did you know I had a bard come sing for me below my window today? He said all sorts of flowery, sweet things. Yet it was all promises this, and in the future that, blah blah blah... I prefer someone who reaches out and really grabs on. Someone who sticks around and keeps me company for more than just the span of an otherwise cold night. I like the sweet words, but it's useless if I don't feel any support."

Merli's headache was clearing, his mental break fading as his mind cobbled together a priority and need for focus. Artorian spoke the words Merli was thinking. "Be firm in one's decisions. Be honest with your words. Both in matters of love, and the handling of troops."

Merli smiled, gentle at first. Then with *scheming* thoughts. Alina was much happier about this. "There you are... Welcome back, pretty boy. Was wondering where you went. Come on, let me hear the pretty words. I like hearing your voice more than some two copper bards with a one-stringed lute."

"Bards? Multiple? Your story is growing more convoluted... was there really one, or did you just say that to twist my ear?" Merli playfully rumbled as they began their walk. Intending it cheekily, he received a loud slap on his hind cheek in return.

Alina betrayed her amusement by smirking as she spoke. "Don't be a brat. Deriding a lady's honor and doubting her words? How could you, sir. Besmirching a good maid's name."

He laughed out loud, though a playful glare shushed him. His laugh needed time to stifle as they crossed from dirt paths into meadow grassland. Settling under a tree so they could snack and spend a little time with a good book, Merli held out his hand to hers.

"Hmm?" Alina placed hers in it, and something cold and round was placed within so quickly she didn't even notice the sleight of hand. Opening her fingers ever so barely, she saw the shimmer of another gold coin. "Oh... but... are you sure? Why do you keep doing this for me...?"

"How many more?" Merli cut her off, his hands squeezing over hers. "How many more until I need to see about a house?"

Alina regarded him sternly. "Merli, the last time we were here you emptied your heart about how you didn't want to stay in the Kingdom. Now what's all this about a house? Twelve, by the way. Twelve more gold coins and I can slap Pershing in his chubby face."

He nodded, and sat down. He was given a torn off piece of bread, and chewed on it as he watched a parade of flags in the distance. "Because of bad news, that is going to cut short the life expectancy of everyone currently stuck in the military. I'm not… exempt. I might be a decently respected curator when it comes to ledger magic, but nothing will make me immune to a sword to the throat."

He shook his head. "My pay went up since I was moved from guard curator to fifth-rank military curator. As they too, surprise *surprise*, don't like to have more money taken than they should pay to the taxman. Why the military pays taxes, I have no idea. I haven't even figured out *where* they are getting their money from. Though, I'm starting to piece together that the military is actually the private forces of a bunch of Noble households, who are all really unhappy about suddenly losing those people."

Merli mumbled a little too loud, as after his next comment, Alina slapped her hand over his mouth. "Honestly, I don't know much about the rulers of this Kingdom, but I know that they are celestially awful at m—*Mmm?*"

Alina shook her head no, and only then did he realize that he was about to talk serious feces about the rulership. That was a big no-no. "*Mmm.*"

She pulled her hand away at that second mumble, which meant he understood where he'd gone wrong. When he tried to speak again, however, Alina shoved a piece of bread into his face. "That'll teach you. Eat more, talk less. You're still skinny."

Exhaling through his nose, Merli dropped the topic and picked up the book Alina had nicked. Flipping to the page they left off last time, he swallowed his bread, downed a drag of water, and just began reading out loud. Or so Alina thought. The words he spoke clearly didn't match the words written.

Merli was melodic. "Twelve by twelve, coins will fall. Twelve by twelve until she has them all. Twelve by twelve will make people smile. In twelve more seasons, Pershing will have choked on his bile."

His eyes were soft, and Alina slowly pieced together what he meant. "Wait. So... Do you mean that you are honestly going to have twelve gold coins together within twelve seasons? Specifically to give to... me? I know you've been helping, but are you actually serious?"

Merli nodded slowly, and just asked his prior question to confirm. "House?"

Alina squeezed the coin in her hand. "You really took that support I mentioned to heart, huh? Yeah. House. Just... make sure you stay alive, even if it's all you do. Just stay alive. I can't imagine the upcoming war is going to be so nice as to keep you from me mere seasons at a time."

Her sweetheart nodded again, his fingers pressing into his brows. "Based on how the money is moving, and money doesn't lie, it's not just the Socorro picking a fight. The tribes in the wilds are as well. That or the Phoenix Kingdom is instigating war to expand territory. I have no idea. I just know that both are going to steal me away for years. That doesn't sit well."

Artorian stood nearby, watching the interaction. "Ah... How unexpected. Scilla, you devious little brat."

He had... forgotten about this moment. It pained him to see it again, though a smile still played over his lips. Of course there was more than *one* regret during this time.

He sighed, and watched as Alina stole poor Merli's heart. Not that he minded. Even now, watching it again. He wouldn't wish this moment changed. Not for all the world in trade. She reached over and pecked Merli's cheek, nestling into his side. How strange that such a small thing could make Merli's skin tingle and prickle across his arms and neck. The youth's next breath was drawn with certainty, even if he was already filled with deep regret in knowing that he would need to leave behind what he loved.

Artorian hung his head, jaw clenched. What an awful feeling, yet one that even back then he knew he wasn't going to be able to do anything about. Planning for a happy life was fine and well, but potholes were a grievance. Potholes you knew were guaranteed and could shred the entire plan to bits… that was the kind of uncertainty that tore lives apart. Or just outright ended lives, if circumstances took a turn for the worst.

What did he regret more? Knowing he was going to leave Alina alone for years, or that he'd essentially promised her something he didn't know he could deliver? A promise to this lovely, beautiful creature that cradled his heart. How it ached so, even now.

Artorian shook his head, another cold breath drawn to match Merli's candor. Ah, yes… this was the last day he had that name. Come tomorrow, he was going to discover the results of that awful test, and meet the grizzled veteran commanders that wrote it. They were going to be furious at him. Not because he had done something poorly—but because he'd solved the battlefield puzzle in less time than they had, with less casualties. Even if it was but one man.

Still, saving just one person can change the world.

When Merli had to sign his commander position papers that next morning, he couldn't do it with the name he had.

"Too weak," the generals had said. Merli had looked outside at the cloud-covered Sun, and decided that his new name was… Tzu.

Unfortunately, due to the specific, exacting methods and order of operations he required from his troops—particularly in order to make those excellent strategies and tactics a reality, that name was changed in the span of a year. Both as whispers behind his back, and at times angrily howled straight to his face. He was not Tzu the Strategist, as he'd hoped to be known.

Instead, he was Tzu the Tyrant.

CHAPTER FIVE

Artorian opened his eyes in the bonfire space, wringing his hands together with a dejected sigh. "There was never going to be a way around that. No matter how long I schemed, or worried, or suffered trying to find one."

Scilla sat next to him after a blob of amorphous matter shapeshifted into her. She said nothing at first, her form shifting again to create the spitting image of her mother, Shamira. Shamira did not have the overbearing pink colorations. Instead, hers were all dark green.

Her voice matched what Artorian remembered as well. "You asked me once if I would be *that person*. The one you could just speak with, without judgement. Am I still that person?"

Shamira opened her arms as if to accept a child asking for a hug. Artorian just fell sideways to wordlessly **plof** into her grasp. That by itself was answer enough. Scilla had said she'd be there for him, but at this moment, Scilla couldn't help. Shamira, on the other hand, was a personality that had no problems here.

The mother from Chasuble replied kindly. "No. There was never going to be a way around. Yet still, for those years after, you bit into meal after meal of regret at what you told her that day."

Shamira's fingers softly pet across a thirty-year-old Artorian's head. He still didn't have his old man form back, but she paid it no heed. "A pointless, recurring, empty regret that nothing could be done about. Yet it ate you up anyway. You forgot a small tree in the meadow is where that all started, but I found it for you. This regret, unlike the others, is about one that deals with the inevitable. Destiny you can rail against, while your fists can never find purchase on that which you so badly wish to hit."

Artorian nodded, but knew the lecture wasn't done. "You let it eat you up, then. Yet, I also think it was the last time you held such matters to your heart. Isn't that right?"

He sighed again, all defeated. Feeling just as listless as Merli had in the brewery as he said some words that weighed on his mind. "If nothing can be done, truly nothing, then do nothing, and do not worry as things pass. One day, it might change, but as someone that may live for an insurmountably long time... that is not a trait one can afford to keep. Something similar broke Ember, back when she was Ember."

Pulling himself up, he just sat on the tree branch, staring at nothing. "It doesn't hurt, you know? My chest just feels... hollow. Like I lost something so empty it doesn't even feel like a loss. Except that I'm keenly aware of the hole. I don't feel sad. Certainly not happy? Yet, not sad. There is just a void where once something was, and only the memories remind me of what I was railing against all those years ago. A purposeless nothing. Just... nothing."

Shamira understood. "You were going to the Wilds if you wanted to or not. You were going to Socorro, if you wanted to or not. You would. You will. You did. You have those coming up next. Do you want to jump into regret number five right away? Or is this where we leave it for today? I've already noticed a difference, and I consider the regret resolved. You're A-rank four. Not that you care, even if the rank increase patched up the framework of repair Dawn put in place for your burnout."

Artorian silently motioned that he understood, though he was counting on his fingers. Shamira heard his mumbles, and realized she wasn't needed anymore. Her greens turned to pinks, and in a moment, Scilla was back. "Hmmm? What's that?"

Artorian repeated his words in response to her question. "Phoenix Kingdom. The Wilds. Socorro. The Fringe. That's the order you told me last time. That order… that order is wrong. I will go back to the Phoenix Kingdom at least one more time."

Scilla shook her head. "No, you won't. I'm tackling regrets, Tzu. Not moments of your history where your heart got torn out. That event was no fault of yours. I refuse to detail your visit to that empty house. It will do neither of us any good."

Cocking his head, Artorian looked at Scilla with nothing but questions plastered on his face. "Tzu? I suppose the naming convention follows my last tackled regret. I'll drop it. Still, are you sure? If your examples are in order, we end up at A-rank seven. Not nine? If I'm at four now, Wilds, Socorro, and Fringe pull that up to seven. I'm short three. Do I have regrets I don't know about after that? A whole *three*?"

Scilla rolled her thumbs over one another, feet kicking since they didn't reach the ground while she sat. "Tzu, as per the last version of you that we have tackled in your regrets, yes. No more Merli. Merli left us, happy and full of hope and wonder, sitting under a tree."

She shrugged. "As for the count… spoilers. I can't tell you about eight and nine until you finish up the Fringe. Want to do that now?"

Artorian's displeased sneer made her rather smug. "No? Shame… not that I expected otherwise. You have wanted to bolt for dear life after every single one. Not that that's out of the ordinary for someone undergoing the Tribulations track. As a minor, minor note: if you are supposed to be gaining cultivation progress from other sources, like whatever madness that game thing your dungeon friend is mucking about with, that's... not going to work. You know that, right? It's me, or bust."

Artorian nodded in response, not feeling like being a chatterbox. Though, talk he must, so talk he did. "I figured, Scilla. That's not what's burdening me right now. I'm processing that this is what the regret was, rather than what I expected."

She regarded him flatly, and when Scilla spoke she sounded insulted. "I'm not *cruel*, Tzu. Not needlessly, at any rate. Regrets aren't straightforward. You can't always just point at an event that hurt and go 'that must be it.' That's not how it works. Regrets tend to happen before that, in the decisions leading up to that point of pain. Because it's rare that you stumble once and then everything goes to the abyss. A sequence of events is far more likely, and if you can find the first domino in that chain, then you can handle every domino that falls after the first."

Artorian scratched the back of his head. "Alright, alright. I'm just a student here. I'm not going to make a fuss. There's enough on my plate; arguing with the intelligent being made out of my Liminal energy isn't something I want on my docket. Anyone that didn't understand the sequence of events that led up to this wouldn't even understand what that could mean. I'm good."

Scilla nodded towards the nonexistent wall of the bonfire space. "I'm not hearing a yes when it comes to tackling number five. On with you, then, enjoy your bath. Talk to your friends. Remember that you're not doing this alone, and that no amount of pain you remember from the Phoenix Kingdom diminishes what other people might feel for you."

Artorian stood up, but paused at the last mention. "Dawn?"

Scilla's cloud swirled to stand, rather than just move so her body would get up in an ordinary way. "There's a chance after this regret that Alina is going to be on your mind for a while. I need to cut that off early. That was your past. This is your future. Don't make the mistake of choosing the former over the latter. Your past is over. Don't be a Mage that starts overthinking to the point where they can't realize that difference, because you're not exactly done with memories of her. Make sure your heart is in the right place."

The thirty-year-old youth momentarily shimmered, his body that of a long-bearded old man once more. "Oh, my dear. My heart is safe in the hands of the rising sun. That wasn't going to be a concern, though I do appreciate yours."

His form shimmered back to that of Tzu's. Artorian flexed his hands when he noticed he'd gone back and forth a moment. "Well, that's certainly positive and promising."

Scilla pointed at nothing, but didn't need to press further. Artorian just pulled himself out of the bonfire space, and opened his eyes a mere seventeen seconds after he had closed them.

He was in the baths. Henry sat still next to him.

His hearing kicked in as he noticed vibrations. The sound of Dawn's footsteps resounded on wooden flooring as she returned to the vat he was in with that promised fresh robe. Artorian stood up slowly when she entered, hand outstretched to accept it.

Oh, he could stand! Fantastic. He beamed a wide smile, instead pointing at his feet when he realized it. "Look! *No* burnout!"

Dawn gently tossed the robe over his face before glancing at his legs, checking her handiwork. The Fire Soul was pleased. It wasn't a perfect recovery, but she couldn't see much evidence of the burnout she couldn't fix. "*Yes,* burnout. You don't just get rid of an injury like that."

She waved her hand, drying him up so he could just get that robe on rather than fumble like a C'towl with its head stuck in a sleeve. "Burnout, much like merging Aura layers into Presence before the Mage ranks, is lethal. Didn't you get told before? If that wasn't a Spirit body mimicking a Mage variant, you would be crispier than burnt toast. S-ranked bodies can endure so, so much more. Don't let that allow you to think, even for a moment, that you got off without so much as a sear on the crust. You have burnout damage, and I would need a two-year discussion with Tatum to figure out what that actually means for you."

Artorian wiggled the right limbs into the right holes of the robe, then held his own hands as he was expecting a lengthy lecture. Instead Dawn just stepped in, cupped his face with both her hands, and left a big lingering kiss right on his cheek. The smooch even sizzled, momentarily leaving a red mark. Henry saw when he got up from the vat, but strategically decided to say nothing. That was something to tease their sort-of-Administrator with later.

Dawn touched foreheads with Artorian, her tender hands holding his face firm. "You be careful. If that acts up, you let me know. I don't care what you're doing, where you are, or what the social situation is. If you need me, you better call for me regardless of what Core, realm, continent, box, or layer you may be in. I don't care, you hear me? You send me that fire bee. Promise me."

Artorian nodded, their foreheads still touching. "I promise."

His face was pulled into the side of her neck, and he said nothing to the contrary in complaint as she held him. "Good."

Henry started to turn a little pink from the display, rather than the amount of time he was spending in the baths. Granted, Mages didn't turn pink from hot water to begin with. It was harmless, innocuous, and sweet. It was the amount of sweetness that was starting to give Henry the skin-crawls. Was he jealous? Well then, it seemed he needed to spend more time with Marie! He hadn't taken her somewhere nice for a while… Maybe he could convince Chandra to help set up a nice dinner date. Just for the two of them. He wanted to see her smile in the same way Dawn did, just from holding her person.

Henry looked away when he realized Dawn was looking at him, rather directly. He turned around in the vat, sinking beneath the water's surface to pretend he wasn't there. It hadn't mattered, Artorian was already suffering a series of giggle fits in her arms. "Oh, poor Henry. We're being awful to him. Or rather, anyone that might be stealing glances through a wall. I know from experience they mean nothing to even a B-ranked Mage, much less the posse of power gathered nearby."

Dawn agreed, but refused to let go of his hand as they walked to the dining room. Some papers were strewn about on the table, including the unexpected company of a few Wisps. Each with some kind of yellow hard hat on. Artorian blinked at the scene. "What's going on?"

Dawn just nudged her nose over at the temporary plan of action on the wall. "They're figuring out where to place Seed Cores, from the areas that wire-tear damage was irreparable. Nothing fixes perfectly."

She let him go and, like a small child, he zipped his way over to the Wisps. He was looking for something very specific, and pressed his finger down on the spot he wanted to see. Dawn hovered close, looking over his shoulder. "What's that?"

Artorian beamed a smile. "That? That's *me*."

CHAPTER SIX

Once at the location, Dawn covered her mouth to prevent herself from laughing out loud. Artorian just stood next to his Core. The real him. The source keeping his current body to be as functional as it was. He was gawking at it in disbelief. Was this a prank? Someone's idea of a joke? His voice boomed, hands shoving outwards as he spoke with them just as strongly. "Why is it so *tiny*!"

Dawn couldn't help herself, and turned away as her snort destroyed the gathered cloud layer entirely. No grayscaling, as that would have been even more of an obnoxious giveaway that she was devolving into a state of weak laughter.

Two citrine Wisps hovered nearby, not sure what to say. They'd brought Artorian to the site his Core was at, and were ready to start moving it. All he had to do was pop over while someone took care of the empty shell of the body he'd leave behind. Instead he was kneading his temples, unhappy about something. It was a perfectly good Seed Core. Did he think these things were supposed to be large? They were called *Seed Cores*; how big did he think they were?

Dawn managed to compose herself. "Mm. Let me guess.

You were expecting something along the size measurements of Eternium, or the massive orb that Cal is. When we saw him outside in the real?"

"Yeah!" Artorian turned, motioning right back to the tiny orb that appeared to contain his actual cultivation technique. "Look at it!"

Her fingers pressed to her lips, but it failed entirely to contain the following smirk. "Mhmm... I see it. Tell you what. Why don't you complain about it after we move you? I'll be along for the entire ride, and the body you're currently in will be nearby when you're awake again. I may even try to see if I can't make further repairs, now that it's topped off on Mana at a very sturdy A-rank four. Well done with that tribulation... even if I don't know what it was."

Artorian dropped it, as there was no point in being upset. This was pride talking, and he didn't have a use for it. "Let's just say I'm very glad you're here, and call it good."

One heavy exhale later, he walked over to Dawn and just raised his arms like a baby wanting to be picked up. "Alright. Let's do this."

She nodded, and picked him up like one. The Wisps said nothing, completely ready to add this to the gossip mill as Artorian was held like a two-year-old. A short moment later and his frame went limp in her grip as he checked out. The Seed Core hummed loud with celestine blue coating the edges, then shone bright with loving pink light from within now that all true components of him were in it.

Done with pleasantries, the citrine Wisps got right on with the job. They knew their task, even if it took multiple slow, draining hours to safely disconnect Artorian's Core. The orb rose from the branch, safely hovering between the two Wisps as they began the transfer. Dawn didn't like that they didn't move right away. "What's the hold up?"

The citrine Wisp on the left spoke in a serious mutter, as if he had a thick mustache and liked working with wood. "Well, according to the manifest, we've got two possible locations this nut can go to, and we don't have a sign-off on which location we're supposed to crack it into. Looks like there was a late addition, but the new option is going to be the cause for delays."

Dawn inspected the citrine orb of light shrewdly. He wasn't lying, and that upset her. "There was only one approved location, so why suddenly a new one? Are there any notes? This is not a piece of information I wanted dropped on me last minute. What about-to-be-crushed newlight just did this?"

The sound of papers unfolding rolled out of the citrine light. "Here it is, signed off on by a Wisp named Invictus. Must be a fella that thinks highly of himself. That's some flowery script. Doesn't appear to be a reason why."

"Oh… that's alright, dear. A *name* was all I needed. Take Artorian to the original location." Dawn's smile twisted into a gentle facsimile of hidden evil. After the citrine Wisps shared a quick glance, they got a move on with Artorian's orb and body as the Fire Soul's clawed grip rose and extended.

To them, her aim reached out to a random direction. They hurried away faster when void and gravity coiled around her like a twisted, burning kaleidoscope. They knew better than to be around that! Off to location one they went!

When Dawn squeezed her grip, an unpleasant teleportation sound cracked between her fingers. As if lightning had just been bottled. *Crack*! A forcibly teleported Invictus popped into existence right into her closing grasp.

The silver Wisp was squeezed instantly, his silvery light peeping like a crushed rubber duckie. Dawn's eyes had returned to being oppressive black holes, corona flame roiling within them as she locked gazes with the captured troublemaker. "Hello, Invictus. Do you know *why* I'm angry?"

Invictus learned newfound fear, and yelped. Something had just gone terribly wrong.

Later, when properly installed in his new Silverwood Tree spot, Artorian felt groggy when he woke. His hands flexed as his senses returned, feeling Dawn's heated arms around him as his blinking vision slowly cleared. Going into his Core was akin to a nice nap, but he was still never fond of waking up early. Was it early? He couldn't tell.

Dawn's warm, chipper voice greeted him with delight. "Morning, sunshine! Sleep well?"

It took him a minute to really get his bearings, but he managed to stand after some wobbles. "Yes? Yes, I think so."

Looking at his feet, he didn't notice any differences, in the event that Dawn had attempted repairs. He did notice the silver bark of the tree, and noted they were in a different location entirely. "We're up higher."

Dawn agreed with his comment. "We're up *highest*. Your Core is exorbitantly bright when you're in it. Warm too... Paradise for any lizard that loves to lounge and bask. Also a minor bonus perk to tell the others they're safe from rampant shenaniganry."

Artorian's lip drooped. "I'm not *that* much trouble..."

She stuck her tongue out at him, plenty aware he was being dramatic and entirely joking. He huffed, his ruse as effective as wet salt. "Crackers, saw right through me. Well alright. I miss anything? No mysterious eons that have passed during my little nap? It's always impossible to tell."

The Fire Soul just shook her head no. "Nothing interesting happened. A very boring transfer. Very boring set up. Very boring waiting for you to wake up. It's been about nine days, give or take. Your Wisp has asked me to bring you over when you woke up. Something about needing to finalize some branches. Though I bet it has far more to do with shoving you into Eternium."

She pointed at Eternium's current location farther down. "Now that he's back on a branch, repairing what he can. He heard you, by the way. When you said everything was going to be alright. Really helped put him at ease with the whole 'being covered in demon tar' thing."

Artorian started doing stretches out of habit. Then stopped when he realized he was getting looks. "Well, I'm glad that helped. I didn't realize he could hear me. I don't really remember how the mechanics of dungeon Cores work when they're held items. It's been ages since the Scar Core, and given that's Zelia now, who is very much in my good books, I'm not a fan of digging."

He clapped his hands together. "So! What's on my to-do list? Am I being hurled into Eternium immediately?"

Dawn squeezed her lips into a line. A scheme? A scheme! Oh, he couldn't stop himself from being interested. "Well now… I don't know what you're planning, but I'm dying to find out."

The Fire Soul moved her head sharply in a 'come along' motion. Artorian didn't hesitate, kicking his flight into action. Dawn filled him in shortly after they were in the air, a nice safe distance away both from branches and opportunistic ears. "No. We're going to drop by your Wisp. First is finalizing the branch so Oberon is happy. Then we're taking a few days off. We're going to spend some time with your chosen. Including the people who are out and about, which you previously have not had the opportunity to relax around."

Dawn slowed down to match his flying pace. "Eternium needs a while to sort out his 'importing,' since I have already made it clear that we will not accept Spirit bodies of his make. That will give him absolute and total control of your limitations. And since we're relying on your cheating ability to get around the nightmare we all hate, that's not acceptable. You'll be going in with your current body, because I don't want to hear anything about additional difficulties. Cal's mess of a game is annoying enough, and I want explanations. Not more confusing complications."

Artorian wasn't going to argue that point. "Fair. I can't say I'm not happy about the opportunity to check on Halcyon. I missed her last go around, and more Zelia is always good. Even if I think she's inherited far too much of my secretive nature. I always think she's up to something that she's just not telling me. Though, I suppose that's fine. I know she keeps my well-being and interests close to heart, so when she doesn't tell me something, I just go ahead and figure it was for the better. I always find out about these things later anyway."

Dawn squeezed her face in discomfort, but cleared her expression before the reaction was noticed. She zipped ahead, instead flashing him a challenging motion as she formed rings of fire before them. "Agile enough with flight to make it through these?"

Artorian snapped back at her challenge. "*Ohoho!* Bring it on, burny!"

She stuck her tongue out, and created the obstacle course for sheer entertainment. By the time they arrived at Eternium's location, Artorian was solidly singed. His new, plain robe was already in dire straits. The end of his tiny mustache was still on fire as he coughed out a small gray cloud, hand reaching up to squeeze the flame, stifling it with a sizzle. "Never mind. I got burned."

Yvessa's green glow hovered nearby, voice already accusatory in tone. "Pride get to you, old man? Get over here and stand on this bit of the branch. I need a little more Mana to finalize this. The big work is done, but we needed to make some channel changes for Eternium to realign."

Artorian didn't really know what that meant, but he reached out with his Mana and handed it over regardless. "Sure, got plenty. Did repairs go well? No nasty surprises after I dragged Ghreziz's face over a celestial grater?"

Yvessa's glow turned grass green. "Well, you scared me half to death, but no. After you and that demon vanished into thin air, I had all the time in Cal to calm down. Took days and days to replenish the branch, but overall it was worthwhile. I was provided plenty of help. A fresh branch is better than a corrupted one in every respect."

Her voice dropped, gaining concern. "I've been getting periodic updates on the local happenings. It sounds like we won the battle, but are in a lull where the war is concerned. I hear you're the poor sap going into Eternium? Tell me something I don't know."

Artorian sat down. "I really hate demons. In particular, the source responsible for making them exist here. Eternium gets a pass, Barry does not. So, I'm the vanguard. I will likely need to start over from nothing since I don't get to begin in the child body I left behind. That's fine… This will only slow down the hunt, not stop it. That aside, do you need me for anything? I'm not jumping in right away. Dawn has an itinerary for me."

Yvessa just bobbed to say she understood. "No, you're all done here. Go take some time off. You're going to have me glued to your shoulder as soon as you import."

Artorian got back up, not feeling like flying after he looked himself over. "I'll see you when I'm back in Niflheim then. Dawn, can we take the quick route this time? I don't feel like arriving even worse for wear."

Dawn's arm curled around his shoulders. With a silent wink, she teleported them both out with a *vwumph*, leaving a pleasant, dancing little flame in her own image behind. The tiny effigy shot Yvessa a thumbs up. Excellent teamwork!

Yvessa just fussed to herself, doing the work on the added channels. "As if I was going to say *anything* after what you did to Invictus…"

CHAPTER SEVEN

Zelia was, as always, expecting them. Not even Dawn could pull a fast one on her. Not when the fire Dreamer used Zelia's **Law** to get around. Fully humanized, the kimono-clad secretary held her sun-blocking umbrella in one hand. A robe identical to the one she'd given Artorian previously hung nicely folded across the arm of the other. If her Dreamer thought she didn't know about said creation not living particularly long, he didn't know her very well.

Artorian threw his hands up when they ported in. "Zelia! You clever nugget! It's like you just *know*."

Her response was to slightly tilt her head, and run a single digit across the edge of her ear. Information was her thing, so that comment had been a sweet compliment hidden in the guise of a quip. "What? Oh, no, I'm here by complete accident. I was just passing by with this robe design you most certainly didn't wreck once before. I see you've been provided a backup specimen of... well. It can be called a robe, but do replace it with this one in short order? You look like a vagrant."

Dawn nudged him to take it.

Zelia's design and clothing material were better than the spare she'd found in the archives in every respect. Now the outfit was singed and somewhat toasted from not quite making it through the gauntlet of consecutive fire rings. Flight needed to be practiced to keep on top of. Unlike riding a rowdy palanquin, you could forget how to use certain techniques if you didn't keep them in daily rotation.

After requisite greeting hugs, and some technical difficulties with re-robing, Zelia took them on a minor sight-seeing trip. First stop, the Jotunheim Beneath. Artorian frowned when they arrived, his hands pressing into his cheeks. "It's gone!"

Zelia nodded sagely, motioning at the bit of the water where her and Halcyon's Skyspear recreation used to be. "I wanted you to see this example first. All structures of the old world are being moved to the floating wreckage that is Vanaheim. Once we piece the place together, every bit of old-world material is going there. It won't be a flawless recreation, but long-kept undecanted people shouldn't be able to tell the difference unless they pay attention to the sky."

Artorian dropped his hands. "Well… alright then. I take it you already know I won't be around for that."

Zelia's nod was short and curt. "That decision came to pass? Good. I helped consult on the matter and was a strong proponent for having you see to the tasks you were good at. Rather than the most exciting task of watching grass grow. On that matter. On behalf of your chosen, I would like to relay the message that we have inherited your… distaste… for the more infernally inclined. Yuki in particular has a… what did she call it? A big mad."

The Dreamers held back their short giggle. Though Artorian had to know. "Are you telling me that the lover of tales, writer of stories, and luminant of histories used language that curt? Oh, I feel bad for Asgard. Those poor mead hall boys."

The spider secretary agreed. "It's on the schedule. First, we go pick up Halcyon from her nap cave. Please do know, she's not sick, or in need of attention. She only needs a full iteration of sleep. Much like Odin, though with his ego, he's coined it 'Odin sleep.'"

Unlike Dawn's teleportation, Zelia's slipspacing felt a bit better. Artorian knew it was essentially the same thing, but Zelia's was always just better. He wasn't going to mention it with Dawn in close earshot. He was fairly certain that the scrutinizing look in her eyes meant she'd noticed, and was trying to figure out how the non-actualized had gotten a leg up on her. Higher technique efficiency was always of interest to Dawn.

Halcyon was an adorable bundle of blankets when they arrived. The decor seemed to be the interior of some large fortress, with sliding doors that were lined with rice paper. Fancy! The partially bouncy floor underneath was pleasant to step on. It was firm, but with some serious give. Likely to compensate for weight differences. Again, not something to mention out loud.

Artorian didn't have to glance at Halcyon more than a second time on his approach to feel something was abysmally wrong. His slow tourist walk turned into a concerned jog. Upgraded into a straight-shot blitz to be at her side. "Cy? Zelia, what is this? I thought you said she wasn't sick. How is this *not* sick?"

Zelia turned to face Dawn before answering him. "Is he still an Administrator?"

The fire Dreamer crossed her arms to make an 'x', indicating that was a negative. Zelia closed her umbrella when she understood. "Good. That means there is no longer a ridiculous laundry list he needs to attend. I can tell him now."

Artorian fussed. "Tell me *what*? Zelia, Cy is definitely ill! Look at her. She's pale, her breath is shallow, and even with these blankets she's shivering!"

His starlight Aura flickered on to full blast. The radiance was invisible to all but Dawn, who winced since she could very easily see the light spectrum he'd dumped all the brightness onto. An alteration of her senses allowed her to ignore it.

Zelia was at her Dreamer's side when Dawn's vision cleared, kneeled right next to a sleeping Halcyon and concerned Artorian. "All is well. Her condition looks unpleasant, but this is just the way of things. Here is the short of it. Nobody is immune from needing sleep. Not the Dreamers. Not the chosen. Not the wandering creatures. After iterations were implemented, we suffered additional strain. Some of us could remain healthy and awake for one iteration, sometimes two. If absolutely necessary, three. Though it was an unpleasant experience. That I can tell you with certainty."

She gently brushed her hand over Cy's head. "So we had to come to some well-planned compromises. We needed sleep, or we would crack. Yet, sleeping meant we could not fulfill our roles. So while one of us slept to recover, the other would pick up the slack. To be informed of happenings when passing the baton."

Zelia curled close to her resting friend, cradling her jaw. "This is what it looks like when we sleep, and either do not have a Core to rest in, or cannot go to our Core to rest. I would consider it a kindness, my Dreamer, if you didn't ask me about that particular problem. We have solutions in the works, but they will take time. You have the penchant to miss important events. Just know we do not hold this against you."

Artorian felt his stomach twist. He gritted his teeth, but leaned forwards to touch Halcyon. His Aura wasn't doing a thing to help. Anything it could fix, Cy wasn't lacking in. This was… something else. "Very well, dear. I hope this isn't another behind my back whisper to limit my tasks, but if you say you have a solution coming. I'll only muck it up by involving myself."

Zelia smiled, pleased with the concession. "Good. Then also don't ask about this."

Her Dreamer didn't know what she meant until Halcyon stirred, her eyes slowly opening while her face contorted in the configuration that screamed she had a migraine. Her voice was music to the ears of her guests. Whiny as it was. "Zeliaaa, I'm tired. Let me sleep."

Zelia said nothing. She just foot-nudged her Dreamer. Artorian was more than happy to say hello. "Well if you want to be tucked back in, we can do that too."

Blankets were flung across the room. Pillows bashing to the walls from the sheer speed Halcyon moved from her laying position to an upright sitting one. Her sheer strength was impressive, even when so visibly diminished. "Dreamer!"

Artorian chose to be tackled to the ground, following the natural momentum of an overly excited orca-sized outburst. Halcyon's arms wrapped around him, her cheek mushed and shoved to his to rub up and down. Just in case this was a dream and this wasn't actually real. She rolled over the floor, but Artorian did his best to skillfully navigate the roll so Cy didn't take any hard falls or hits to the head.

No matter her rank, he wasn't going to let so much as a scuff mark mar her knee. She was withered in comparison to what he recalled. The blankets had hidden much of her weakened, slumbering state. He said nothing of it, and gently ran his hand over her head to soothe his chosen. "Hello, Halcyon. I'm sorry to wake you up. I came to spend a little time, though I can let you rest."

Cy's face vigorously ground a decisive set of 'no' responses into his shoulder, though she held her head after from the pain it caused. Her Dreamer was patient with her, moving nice and slow. "You'll be alright, dear. When it gets to be too much, and you need to go back to napping, you make sure to let us know. Alright?"

She nodded, and went incredibly quiet, trying not to move while she was being held. Artorian rose his head to address Zelia. "If the plan was to go to Asgard to see Yuki next, I think that will be difficult. Any chance we could gather people here?"

Zelia said nothing, and pulled the physical copy of today's to-do list out from the inside of her kimono. That, or she cleverly made it look like she did, while teleporting the item from elsewhere. She turned it around, and pointed at the next item down on the list. She read it from the list without looking at it. "Gather in Halcyon's Daimyo Fortress in Jotunheim."

The clipboard was teleported back to the place she'd pulled it from, her hands neatly folding over one another. "I am *very* good at this, my Dreamer. Everyone awake will be here shortly."

Artorian's mouth hung open, but his attempt to clap fell short since he was holding Halcyon. She, on the other hand, made a very high-pitched pathetic sound, then giggled as if affected by delirium.

Zelia closed the distance to bundle a blanket back around her chosen sister. "That's going to keep happening. Cognitive dissonance tends to run rampant when we're awake over our limit."

Her Dreamer squinted at her in confusion. "Co-what now?"

The secretary teleported in a wet piece of cloth, and folded the warm silk over Cy's forehead. "Cognitive dissonance. It's what we're calling one of the effects. She's having thoughts and beliefs that are inconsistent, and clash with both reality and her own decisions and attitudes. You're holding the equivalent of a toddler, my Dreamer."

She moved her hand into Halcyon's grip, who clamped down on it. "She may not seem it, but she's happy to be held. After she has rested enough, she will feel better over the course of a meager few days. Her frame will fill back in and her color will clear up. Until then, Cy is a baby. Just like we all are in that state."

The rice-paper doors to the room slammed open, a cold front passing through as Yuki had managed to approach them entirely unnoticed. "Then give her to me. I am the best match when it comes to handling oversized babies."

Artorian smiled wide, his tone delighted. "Yuki!"

The cold look on her face didn't crack an inch. "Yes, my Dreamer? I was talking about you. Clearly."

His smile faltered, feeling disheartened for getting slapped down on greeting. His warmth returned when Yuki smirked at him afterwards. "Oh you… cheeky! Cheeky, *cheeky* lady!"

CHAPTER EIGHT

The supposed 'few days' of downtime turned out to be a sneaky three whole *months*. Solely because installing Eternium didn't go smoothly, as the Silverwood channels had to be redone several times. Artorian didn't exactly know how Silverwood Trees worked, but figured the process was more complicated than it seemed. Dawn sure wasn't willing to tell him any details beyond, "Actualize and see for yourself."

Cryptic, but *enticing*!

On the plus side, Artorian enjoyed incredible quality time with his people, since his nook became *the* location for supervisors and chosen to go when they were on break. He helped transform the entire top floor of Halcyon's Daimyo castle into a relaxation hotspot. No more being cramped as a group in his comparatively tiny archives in the sun. Have a castle? *Use* a castle!

He also finally got precious parenting time as he took care of Halcyon. Zelia had been right: she was just a big baby. Still, Cy's was a mind he very much liked, and she was going to get his utmost care. Even if that care came in the form of bottled milk, and scrubbing her down every day with hot water to keep her skin hydrated so she could be awake for a few hours. That was all she got every day; just a few short hours.

Artorian wasn't going to let that time go to waste. He put on plays, told stories from Yuki's books, interpreted tiny dances, and contrived gorgeous fireworks when the big group sat on the balcony. Those turned into competitions with the other chosen more often than not, as specifically Karakum and Surtur used the hot spectacles to double as a method for fighting off the cold.

On quiet days, he played strategy games with Zelia—who shouldn't have been kicking his butt as well as she was! It was like she had eyes hiding in the back of his head, secretly looking at his planned moves. Even kings and castles, one of the games he'd been spiffingly skilled at. Artorian could not finagle a single win out from her threads of strategy. How times had changed. That or he wasn't facing self-confident unskilled guard captains with fat coin purses. "*Heeheehehe.*"

On days where Halcyon really needed to spend the entire time sleeping, Artorian tried his hand at fencing practice with Karakum, or glaive maneuvers with Surtur. A few days of this, and he felt entirely cheated as they tore through his lessons like Cy consumed Chandra-crafted buffets—even the table ended up having bite marks. "Dawn! Your chosen are ridiculous! Is this what gifted cultivators look like? They're picking these skills up so fast I ran out of things to show off *yesterday.*"

Sensing he was actually irritated, Dawn put down her caviar snacks and seamlessly hovered from her rich lounger. Silk blankets fell away as she slid free, moving over to press her hand to his forehead. "Temperature is fine. Why so worked up? Too many losses in a row is something that gets to everyone. Even you, patience boy. Tell me what you want to do to relax."

Artorian rubbed the part of his forehead she'd touched. "I don't know, dear. Maybe I just need to go shoot some arrows at an iceberg."

Dawn took his hand and softly pulled him to the balcony. Stretching out her fingers, a burning bow of carmine flames burst into existence. She created the entire weapon in a fraction of the time Artorian had cobbled together Decorum's fencing blade, and from far better materials. "Here. Damocles won't burn you. Just pull the string back, and an arrow will form. Don't identify the ammunition, the arrows are surprises."

He gawked at the complicated-looking craft. Sure, this cross-stringed harp could function as a bow, but it sure as crackers didn't look like one. More of a gnomish contraption. Were those *wheels* on the edges? Which of those strings was he supposed to use? He touched foreheads with Dawn a moment before graciously accepting the weapon.

"Thank you, dear." He looked puzzled while turning the device every which way. The lack of weight threw him off nearly as much as the orchestra of strings. "Maybe... that one? Yes, that string looks like the one I pull."

Dawn moved out of the way, sitting down in a balcony seat as some interested eyes came to peek. Curious at what the bright light was about, Valhalla and Manny—who were visiting today—peeked their heads around the corner.

Manny came by more for Zelia than anything else, while Valhalla checked on Cy. Brianna was also present, though it seemed only a scant few people present noticed she was lurking in the shadowy corners. That and sea fish snacks kept disappearing from a nearby stacked table.

Artorian felt the carmine string that appeared to be a line of solid fire. As Dawn had said, his touch did not burn. He smiled while reminiscing. "Just like that broadsword in the grove."

Drawing a deep breath, he looked at the snow-covered mountains in the distance. The fresh air tasted crisp, and he shifted his stance so his feet formed an 'L' shape. His bracing arm kept straight as he bent sideways, allowing the string to pull back without touching his robe. His fingers pulled back on the string, though nothing occurred even as he pulled it back all the way to his short moustache. The string slowly slid by the side of his nose until it was in the same position he always kept it.

His anchor.

To Artorian, the world slowed down. Not due to dilation or a power, but in an experience similar to relaxation. Snow fell slower. Breath became loud. The wind sang rather than howled when breezing by. This calm state of Zen felt familiar, and a soft golden sheen coated his entire being without his notice.

Dawn likened it to a kind of battle trance. A state of being formed from pure focus. Artorian had lost himself in concentration when an arrow conflagrated into existence. The miniature spear twisted from the burning void, nocking itself to the string as the ethereal color-matching projectile solidified.

Odd trepidation hung in the air as the wind ceased its whistle. Artorian didn't release his arrow, causing onlookers to fall quiet as they tried to discern what was taking him so long.

To Artorian, all was still. Only his breath made sound, and only the arrow existed. His fingers released right as his exhale began, though he didn't stir from his position. He saw the gleaming arrow flex and bend, grinding against the burning bow to shoot forwards and begin to twist. The projectile turned like a screw, straightening both itself and its flight path. Influenced by the flame, his shot altered from a naturally curved one to a pure and straight one. As if the arrow was locked between rails during travel.

Artorian felt free.

The world sped back up after the fletching of the arrow whistled away past his fingers, followed only by the concordant *boom* of an incredibly cylindrical hole being punched into the far mountain he'd aimed at. Or was that more of a cone? Rather than puzzle that out, he was more interested to see that it wasn't merely one mountain he'd put a hole though before the arrow's journey culminated, erupting into a cascading set of color-changing fireworks. Make that seven mountains.

"Whistling mountains." He said the words without much thought, but just as the cold wind made large wind chimes ring, so did the holes in the mountains sing. Each being of a slightly different size, the new natural features added their own melodies. The combined song was... surprisingly serene. "Zelia?"

"My Dreamer?" Not expecting to be called, Zelia slip-streamed into existence next to him. Her clipboard was at the ready before the flutter of her kimono had time to settle.

Her Dreamer sounded somber. "Could we not add that to Cal's game world? I like the sound. This serenity would make for a nice difference between out here, and in there."

Zelia grew concerned. "Of course, my Dreamer. Are you well?"

Artorian said nothing, his bow once again drawn with a new gleaming arrow. Dawn nodded for him. "He's fine. Can't hear you at the moment, I think. That's the kind of concentration that makes him get lost in his own world. I think he's coping with difficulties in his own way. After all, a lot did happen, and this is decompression time before he gets stuck in Eternium. We don't even know how long that will be."

The secretary noted it down on her clipboard, then walked back inside to give the updated orders to some of her hidden spiderlings. She paused to glance at a shadowy corner. Brianna wasn't exactly hidden to her anymore, though it didn't appear the Dark Elf was putting much effort in. Like she wanted to be found? Zelia huffed, handing her clipboard to a spider-child dressed in a sharp Modsognir suit. He vanished into the slip-stream web, and Zelia laced her fingers before approaching the dark corner.

"If I can be cordial with Dawn, I can certainly put in the effort with you." The arachnid lady snapped to the point. "Are we going to glower at one another for the rest of eternity?"

Brianna dropped the shadows around her, her arms crossed as she leaned against the corner. "I prefer we didn't. Though I don't have a say in the matter, given I'm responsible for a great many... grievances."

Brianna didn't move when she spoke, though some of the

other chosen thought it best to make themselves scarce, and listen from the other side of a door or wall. Karakum instead sauntered his way over to Dawn's side, standing nearby like an attendant. He didn't care in the slightest for this drama, unlike Surtur... who had joined the bandwagon with her newfound love of all things gossip.

Zelia squared her shoulders. "I would prefer we didn't either. What would you say to a cup of tea?"

Brianna's eyes momentarily flicked to the door hiding several not so sneaky listeners. "I would say a cup of tea is wonderful. Particularly if we could share one."

Zelia released her resting hand, moving it towards the next room over. "Then let us share one."

The exchange remained tense regardless of the surface kindness. When the arachnid hostess and the Dark Elf moved away for what was going to be a drip-fed conversation, the hidden chosen funneled back into the room. Including a previously hidden Henry, who poked his head in with a low whisper after having arrived while things were tense. "Is it safe?"

Dawn made a hand motion for him to come over. "It's safe. Just don't be too upset if Sunny doesn't notice you. He's being one with the bow."

Henry pulled up a chair next to Dawn, dressed in one of the cozy robes that were freely available here. "Oh, no problem. I was just popping in for a snack. While I'm here, though, I wanted to ask: Do you think Brianna is being serious about the whole good person routine? I want to believe her, but I'm very much aware of what happened after reading the logs."

Dawn kept quiet until Artorian released his arrow, drawing another. These new arrows were just fireworks, rather than mountain-piercers. When he dipped into deep concentration again, she chimed in. "I think people feel guilt, regardless of whether they are a cultivator or not. Her pride devoured her, thinking that the first iteration was going to be her new forever. Who wouldn't want to hold on to every last scrap of time, if they thought there would never be an after? Even Mages are afraid of death, and I can tell you from experience that Incarnates aren't immune either. Not being able to perish naturally does not mean you can't be killed."

Karakum didn't know how to feel with the news that his Dreamer could be killed. So he said nothing, and began conjuring protection plans.

Dawn continued since Henry was attentive. "When Brianna realized that this was in fact a cycling process until Cal can let people out, the guilt of what she did, and specifically how she acted around what was essentially going to be the only matchable social group around, ate her alive. As someone who has spent centuries of her life alone, I too would rush to the opportunity not to be."

She parted her fingers palm up, allowing Karakum to set a glass into it. Suddenly quite pleased with himself since he was able to be helpful. After taking a drink, Dawn handed it back. "I think when Brianna says she wants to turn over a new leaf, she is serious. It must pain her down to the bone to let herself be seen as vulnerable as she's keeping herself. Not a single hostile ability of hers has been active when she's around us lately. She put painstaking effort into making sure her blade Aura was off before Tatum brought her into the archives. Her reputation is, like she thinks, not doing great. Or you would not ask what you just did under the hush hush cover of shade. I can't give you a clear conscience, Henry. I can tell you that when Brianna acts genuine about wanting to mix in with us, she *is* genuine. I hope that helps soothe your concerns."

Henry bit his thumb. "Would you feel safe if she was alone around Artorian?"

The temperature in her vicinity frosted unpleasantly, but returned to what it was a second or two after. "My initial reaction is… quite upsetting. On thinking about it, yes. It would be fine. If Brianna wants what I believe she wants, working against Sunny and his interests would only stab herself in the foot."

The regent dropped it, his thumbs pressing together as he clearly had a more difficult question. Dawn just gently laid her fingers on his wrist. "What is it? You're sweating."

Henry swallowed. "Can we talk about Invictus?"

CHAPTER NINE

Her tone chilled. "What *about* the silver cube?"

Clearing his throat, Henry just rambled. "Well, why is he… a cube? I couldn't even find anything about what he supposedly did. The Wisps are sealed tight on gossip, and he's on a rather prominent display."

Dawn warmed, understanding that his question didn't concern undoing her binding on the Wisp. "That's a stronger response from the Wisps than I was expecting. My apologies for feeling like the edge of a knife. Let me explain and set you at further ease."

Henry shakily accepted an offered glass from Karakum, drinking the whole thing in one go. "That… that'll be nice. Thank you."

The Fire Soul gently patted his wrist. "I'm sorry, Henry, I very frequently outright forget that I am what I am. I know that sounds strange, considering I'm not nearly far along enough in my Actualization for it to be stable and comfortable. It's like this. Sunny swindled information out of the Wisps that he shouldn't have gotten. Invictus, the slighted individual he pried it from, was essentially scorned by his brethren."

She dropped her hand while explaining. "Given he was the kind of Wisp he was... In his resulting treatment, Invictus tried to apply Fae trickery. Specifically in order to inconvenience Sunny, without him knowing, in a situation he couldn't control. Because Fae rules respect that kind of trickery, especially the court he's in."

Henry downed a second glass, but was feeling much better since Dawn was opening up rather than cubing people out of sheer ire. It was nice when the powerhouses shared like they were on an even level.

Dawn spoke softly. "Sunny needed to transfer his Seed Core, because the branch he was on suffered residual damage that wasn't going to be repaired for a while, given that new channels are needed for far more than just Eternium's branch. In case nobody told you yet, channels are the paths of power inside of the Silverwood Tree that allow it to grow and keep all the Cores connected to one another. The difficult part with channels is that only the tree can mend them. The best even the Wisps can do is create the space and provide the Mana. They're not happy about it, and they will refuse to tell you. That doesn't mean an Incarnate can't just see it."

She pointed in the direction of Niflheim, even if it was nowhere in view. "The damage inside of the tree is invisible, and nasty. Luckily nobody has really asked why we've needed to move Seed Cores, so we've gotten around that. This is one of those Incarnate-only matters, but I am not specialized in healing or mending. It's a backup skill for me. I can't begin to help aside from being an energy source."

Henry's look made her realize she was getting off track. "Invictus. He secretly changed, without letting anyone know, the destination of Sunny's Seed Core. I didn't need to know that the new location was going to be inconvenient. When a Fae tries to backstab you for any reason, playful or otherwise, it's not going to end up in your favor. So I was livid instantly, because it is excruciatingly important that our best method of making progress isn't hampered."

She opened and closed her hand, energy crackling between her bronze fingers. "So I forcibly bent space, and snatched the culprit within my grasp. After his confession, I told him something very, very simple. Then I squeezed my Spirit power around his form, cubing him as a message to the other Fae. I understand they have their own social rules and methods of resolution, but if those methods clash with my goals, they will know that I will not hesitate one igniting spark to drag them into the tribunal of my rules, and judge them accordingly."

Henry frowned, more confused than anything. "You make it sound as if the Wisps think that their society stands above all others, and that their ways of doing things usurp or mean more than those others. Such as a Kingdom's established laws and rules."

Dawn was taken aback in surprise, her smile proud. "My my, Henry… get any smarter and you'll start giving Sunny trouble. That is the exact measure by which they think. Most courts don't see any action taken against them as offensive, or something as silly as an attack. Actions against them are invitations for them to engage in a clever rebuke. The more unnoticed and inconvenient it is for the recipient, the better. They love long cons with big payoffs if they can get away with it. This is why Fae are considered conniving. It's just how they do things. Tell nobody that red Wisps secretly love a good fistfight."

She motioned over at Artorian, who was completely lost in concentration. "Sunny's prying of knowledge was an affront not to a specific Wisp, but to the rules of Wisp society. Fae are prideful, and all the blame fell on Invictus. He is a cube, not because cubes are harmful, but because it is one of the only measures that other Fae will fear. I didn't take from him his health, I took from him his ability for action. Which, to a Fae, is far more valuable. Imagine being immortal, but trapped and unable to engage while you are entirely aware of your surroundings. Exempt from goings on, unable to add your two coppers."

Henry didn't feel so great. "In my Kingdom, I doubt there

is a judge in all the land that wouldn't condemn such an action as outright evil."

Dawn considered it, but agreed with a far too casual nod for his liking. "That's because it is. If you want the ethical retort, ask Sunny. He'll be happy to pontificate. If you want an effective retort, you have me. I'll be happy to be laconic. Even if life around Sunny has made me horribly wordy. I never used to talk this much. Now I feel like it's a waste to stop."

Henry decided to just let it go. "Well... alright then. So Invictus is actually... unharmed?"

Dawn calmly satisfied him with a positive response. "He's just fine. He'll be healthy as he was if my cube is undone. I simply refuse to. Though now that you've mentioned it, and my eyes have had some moments to look at the Wisps and their reactions..."

She put her hand up apologetically. "I know you can't see it, dear. I just want you to know you're right. They're all cowed by the cube. I wanted to instill the lessons that their rules are not above all else. That just because they are Wisps aligned under Dani, they can get away with everything. For they cannot, and I refuse to let them in on matters close to my heart. From what I can gather, the Wisps see the cube not as the deterrent of 'don't upset Dawn.' They see it as... *Mm.* That's fear. Definitely fear. On second thought, I don't like this, and perhaps I've gone overboard with my actions."

Henry honestly felt good about the sudden change of heart he was seeing. "I'm rather surprised you changed your stance. Not unhappy. Just surprised."

Dawn grumbled a little, making a so-so motion with her hand. "It's easy to be powerful, and think that the way you see the world is not just right and correct, but the only way it's right and correct. It's easy to stumble into that pitfall. As someone with a little oomph up her sleeve, I'm not immune, and I realize that it doesn't put me in a great position when I, much like Brianna, just want some friends. It's rough to tell someone more powerful than you that they're wrong. Especially if you know they have difficulties being receptive, or in my case, having a very one-track mind."

She motioned to Invictus, even though he wasn't remotely nearby. "Wisp society seems to think that if they cross me on *anything*, I will bind them out of fury and rage. I have become an oppressor, rather than a reminder that we're all in this together."

Her orange nails tapped on the end of her seat, mulling it over. "Should I uncube him, Henry? You want to be the best King there ever was. If someone came and brought this to your throne, what would be your verdict?"

Henry felt put on the spot. "I... would ask for Marie to come attend since that's not something I would want to decide on alone. While yes, cubing a living Wisp and excluding them from everything their society is about is, undoubtedly, evil. You have some merit with effective results, as it will completely prevent similar occurrences from leaking out again. Invictus invoked his society's rules to commence a great transgression. One that in ours, especially given that we need Artorian for Eternium, isn't seen in a great light. Could we go visit Marie? I would honestly like to chat this over with a larger peer group."

Dawn nodded, rising from her chair. "Actually... about that. Brianna? I know you're listening. Would you like to join us for this talk? I think your unique perspective on the matter could help with insight on how to resolve this."

Brianna unsheathed herself from the shadows, opening the door to the room she was in with Zelia. Who had also stopped her teatime with the Dark Elf to listen in. "You know? I can't be surprised. Yes, I would very much like to be included."

Her Elven gaze drifted over to Artorian, ignoring that the non-Jotunheim chosen were shuffling out to return via the beacon system. "Will he be fine? He hasn't moved in minutes."

Dawn replied, already walking into the room. "Tatum will be here soon. He will bring Artorian to Eternium."

She had a quick look at the Silverwood Tree, noting that the channels were in fact good enough to continue on to the next step. Several months of downtime had been nice. She'd like to do this again sometime, with people and creatures of all sorts popping in to visit. "Yes, all ready. Zelia, you're welcome to confirm it, but we're on item seventy-four of the list."

"I have confirmed it with one of my children. Best wishes on your trip, Fire Dreamer." Zelia gave a surprisingly cordial bow during her response. "I will have the realms managed as we have prior."

She then also did the same for Henry. "Beast Dreamer."

Finally, she turned to Brianna. After pausing for only a moment, Zelia performed the bow for her as well. "Blade Dreamer."

Brianna had difficulty expressing how happy she was to be included. She returned a small cordial movement with her hand pressed to her chest, then joined the other supervisors to be winked away via teleport. Zelia waited, then looked at her own Dreamer. "How long must you continue to pretend, my Dreamer?"

Artorian lowered the bow, turning to share her expression of a broad, scheming smile. "Oh, about that long? Well, was I convincing? What do you think?"

Zelia placed her fingers in front of her smiling face, only to realize they had become claws. She had done her best with Brianna, but it had required more concentration than she had to stay tip top on everything. "I think your ruse was splendid, my Dreamer. Perhaps the Fire Dreamer knew? I lack the skill to have discerned it."

He performed a little dance jig, the carmine bow vanishing from his grip once he released it. "Oh, it's fine if Dawn knew what I was up to. I'm fairly certain my awareness of the conversation had something to do with her change of heart. She's a Blade of War deep down. Efficiency is king. Repercussions are just another thing to stab. She wants to try better, and if I happen to be the reason for her desired improvements, I will simply do my best to be there, even if helping directly would be detrimental. It's important Dawn does things at her own pace.

Who am I to scold her for mistakes? Learning opportunities, I say!"

Pressing his hands to his hips, he enjoyed a firm breath. "How's Brianna?"

Zelia brought him a plate with some food to eat, and a decanter of water. "Better. I believe she will likely join you in Eternium if Vanaheim reconstruction languishes. She is also very serious about protecting your family and ensuring their safe decanting. She considers this act a meaningful method of proving her words. You will not have concerns while you venture into the depths of Eternia. The name Eternium has for his version of Cal's game."

Artorian ate what he was given, then went to sit down next to a snoozing Halcyon. "Wonderful. That brings relief. What about this one? I'm starting to really believe recovery will take the entire iteration."

Yuki entered without a break in stride, warm silk cloth in her hands. "It will. Recovery always takes at least an iteration. The sleeping rules keep changing. Very inconvenient. Except for Dreamers it seems. Your ten-to-one sleeping needs have remained the same. In the event that applies while you are on your adventures, keep the time limit in mind. You may need to rest when you return."

Artorian jumped out of the way out of surprise. "Whoa! You're harder to notice than Brianna. I suppose you're happy about that?"

"Enough to write a story about it." Yuki kneeled down, giving Halcyon her daily hydration wash. Her actions slowed, then stopped. "I like that you took the time to stop everything and spend time with us."

Artorian began to mumble a reply, but Yuki cut him off. "Do it again. Preferably soon."

Silently, he made the hand motions that he would try. Given he was very much aware the Eternium trip would be a long one. "Zelia, do you think I'll be able to come and go from Eternium as I please?"

His spider chosen shook her head no. "I suspect you would be better off planning to be stuck, and then to be pleasantly surprised if that turns out not to be true. We will run things as we have. You see to your new tasks, and just come back to us when you can. This was lovely, my Dreamer. It was incredibly nice to feel like a little family again. I hope that, when your old family is decanted, we can all become a big family instead. I, for one, deeply desire to meet those souls on your wall, that you have protected since before our time. If they are anything like Yvessa, the stories Yuki could gain alone would make all the patience in the world worth it."

Yuki smirked, but said nothing. Her eyes instead shifted to the left, as Tatum had silently arrived in Halcyon's castle. The remaining chosen performed the cordial greeting, and returned to background duties. "Artorian! Hey! Great news. Eternium is all set to import you. Are you ready? Yvessa is waiting on you."

Nodding, Artorian folded his hands behind the small of his back and said his goodbyes to his darlings. Then returned to address his friend. "I know I can't take anything with me, and I think events have wrapped up nicely. Fold me over, my friend."

Grasping each other's wrist, Tatum did just that.

Artorian blinked a few times to realize Tatum's version of moving around wasn't always a teleport. His whole void-shifting weirdness was unique. Honestly, with Tatum, transportation felt like moving through nothing.

Yvessa's glow sharpened at the edges when they arrived. "There you are! Good. Press your hand to Eternium's Core so he can import you. I'll be right behind you, so don't go anywhere when you wake."

Artorian and Tatum shared a high five for a job well done. "Yes, yes… on my way."

Not feeling like dallying today, he leaned over and pressed his hand where he was indicated to. Moments later, he was gone in a *vhwop*.

CHAPTER TEN

Yvessa hovered in place at the entry zone in Eternia. The green around her edges deepened in hue as her impatient hover shifted to a menacing one. How Wisps were able to seamlessly do that was impressive. Unfortunately for her, it didn't acquire her charge's attention.

Artorian was just standing there. Still as a statue on the welcoming dais in one of the special import introductory areas. He looked fine, but his eyes were still closed. His beginner's robe provided as starting equipment moved in the soft breeze, even if the rest of him didn't. Yvessa would scratch the top of her head if she could. Maybe there was a delay when a new body was loaded into Eternia?

There shouldn't be, but since she had a minute to herself regardless, Yvessa decided to have a look around and get her bearings. They were on a promontory, a point of high land that jutted out of a large body of water. Or just a long rock with a gazebo carved into it. Though a piece of carved rock didn't have a status sheet. Why did a gazebo have a status sheet?

Hovering out of the carved construction, Yvessa accessed

the information with less effort than it took to be upset at Artorian. "Huh."

Dread Gazebo. Level: 25

Hidden spawn point and monster, activates on being pointlessly badgered. This Dread Gazebo is named Elric. It has chosen to relocate to this promontory to be left alone, as it was tired of being called short and tiny. The Dread Gazebo takes damage as an ordinary stone building unless awoken via badgering. If woken, a Dread Gazebo will immediately gain the following status effects: Enraged. Jaws of Hate. Tentacles of Hate. Increased natural attack range x2. Howling Pit. Gnash Master.

Yvessa cautiously dismissed the status sheet rather than continue to its actual statistics. *"Huh."*

"All done just hovering in place over there, my dear?" Artorian's voice calmly carried over the breeze, the very much active and moving charge already busy prodding his fingers into the gazebo's pillars. "Curious."

Yvessa borderline turned red from having the situation turned upside down. "You were waiting on *me*? No sir, I was waiting on *you*. Also stop prodding that pillar. It's not what you think."

Artorian blinked and rose from his half-hunched position, questioningly pointing at the carved pillar. He scratched his chin a moment. "Status."

Information filled his vision, but it was his own. "Oooh, well look at that. Right! That means the correct spoken locution was... Inspect?"

From the tilt and move of his head, Yvessa could see he'd successfully pulled up the exact same information she had just dismissed. That, and it now said: 'Inspecting Dread Gazebo status sheet' above his head. That was likely a Wisp-only function, or so she hoped.

"Oh dear." His hands pulled back from the pillar, fingers curling in somewhat as his face pruned at reading the informa-

tion. A backhanded wave of his hand dismissed the gazebo's sheet, and Artorian instead pulled his own status back before him. "That was more interesting! Even if the numbers were… odd. This is terribly organized."

If Yvessa hadn't clearly seen his activity change into him checking his own status screen, she'd have been sure both of his statements would have been about the gazebo. Having a look herself, she couldn't say she blamed the man. "I see it now. All those broken Pylons in Cal must have carried over? Nothing would work if Eternium didn't have backups. I'm seeing several fields that simply don't exist where they should, and at least half of this sheet is functioning erratically. The attributes are mostly being calculated correctly, thanks to the Pylon backups Eternium did have in place."

Artorian burst out laughing, his left hand holding his stomach while his right pointed at something on the screen. "What is this ridiculous title?"

Yvessa wasn't amused when she saw what he was pointing at. Artorian had five assigned non-removable, non-combinable titles. Right at the top, in a bar of a truly upsetting red. His first entry read:

Title: 'Observer Wisp'. Dani assigned. Cannot Combine. This user has a WISP assigned to follow them. Keeping track of their actions, and keeping them on task. This title cannot be deactivated or removed. The WISP determines if 'Administrator' and 'Deity' titles count as active or inactive.

Artorian wasn't laughing for long, a little confused about a few things. "Why is Wisp in all big letters? Also why am I being referred to as a 'user'? That's both very impersonal and a little… *Mmm.* It doesn't sit well. I hope that's a broken Pylon problem and not the final product. That needs to change. What about 'person,' or my name. The way this is written feels as if the title could apply to anyone, and it just happens to be plastered onto me."

Yvessa bobbed. "That was exactly the intent. Most titles

can be acquired by anyone, so long as they meet the conditions. I'll change the wording in yours, but I can't change anyone else's. That needs a big Pylon update, and they grow slowly. They need to be done growing before Dev can start doing anything with them, so I expect that Eternia-wide changes will come as big sweeping updates. Dev and Eternium will have to make entire batches of Pylons activate at the same time to make things like that work. Even for an alteration this small."

Her charge understood, trying very hard to tap on the WISP word with his digit. He was visibly becoming frustrated at it simply not working. "Oh, come on. Just show me why this is in all big letters, I just want to *select*... oh. Oh, this *also* works with special wording!"

Artorian's face dropped when the new information screen just came up blank. There clearly should be something here. "Well... crackers. Never mind then."

Dismissing his curiosity, he noticed Yvessa was adapting into her menacing hover, clearly impatient about something. "What's wrong? You're all edgy and sharp."

Yvessa grumbled. "Are we ready to go? I'm eager to go and... I don't know. Do something. All I'm doing is observing, and sending in updates and improvements as we encounter them. Yet you're just standing... sitting there. Why did you sit down? Looking at your status screen like it's an academy paper."

Seated in the gazebo on a rock bench, Artorian rested his chin on his fist as he tried to figure things out. Much felt different. For starters, he felt *mortal*. In the sense that the experiences he had with the breeze alone were reminiscent of when he was still a normal person. Or... up to a C-ranker?

That was a good comparison. He didn't feel like he was an extremely dense A-ranked Mage, or an invulnerable B-ranked one. This feeling was distinct, and closely familiar with being in the C-ranks. He could get hurt, he just knew it. Easily, as well. Granted, he had never felt this capable as an unempowered C-ranker, but the detail that he felt vulnerable ached under his skin in a place that couldn't be itched.

He looked up a moment to regard his assigned Wisp. Given the title, this was a permanent arrangement. "I'm not. In fact, I think it would be foolish to do so."

Yvessa had to admit she was curious, even if that didn't diminish her drive to get up and go. "Elaborate?"

Artorian calmly nodded, pointing a digit at certain lines on his status sheet. "The numbers are different from when the group and I did testing. I can guess a balance change is in effect, but the numbers are so vastly different from then that I'm not sure I know what I'm looking at. I also can't seem to change this 'Mana bar' into an Essence or Spirit bar like Marie could. So either that's a change, or a missing Pylon. Yet that's not what's twisting my beard into a knot."

Yvessa landed on his shoulder so she didn't need to look at his sheet from an odd angle. She verbalized a rundown of what she saw. "Numbers are high for what they should be, but they originate from a verifiable source. So they're correct. You've got five titles, two of which are hidden from you since I have proprietary access. According to this, you have no skills, no abilities, no class, and no profession. Ah... the introduction didn't start up right away like it should have. I'll have to elevate that issue. Give me a moment."

Artorian went quiet when Yvessa did, content to read over his sheet to make sense of it. He was aware of a distinct difference between existing in Eternium, and existing in Cal. In Cal, that was the real you. As much as it could be when you were borrowing a body. However, in Eternium, the world was made of numbers. Nothing but numbers. So while he felt mortal, and knew he could get hurt, the entire system worked based on what your numbers were, versus what everything else's numbers were. He might get stabbed by a pokey stick, but it wouldn't damage him the way he thought it might.

Instead, the damage would be taken off his 'Health Point' bar. HP for short. This number was entirely responsible for how damage on his 'body' was represented. He knew that much. His health currently was... Why was it so high?

"*Hello again!*" A bright orange light popped into being, exuberant with mirth as Oberon whisked around the gazebo. He borderline skated the edge of 'badgering' with his loud noise and unbridled enthusiasm.

Artorian's arms shot up, his smile wide. "Fine print boy! Good to see you. I was hoping you were alright. I figured since I entered Eternium safe and sound, you were also in good health. How is my favorite mandarin light?"

Oberon burst out laughing, and took a few seconds to compose himself. "Oh, I missed you. So few souls have the orbs to talk to me without deference, I love it."

The Wisps' attention looked at some list Artorian wasn't privy to. "Oh, hey! That's you! Congratulations on that. Not even done with character creation, and you're already in Eternium's top four most wanted list. Right next to Discord, if I recall. Ah *ha!*"

Yvessa hovered dangerously close to the orange orb, forcing him to gag on nothing as his remaining giggles sputtered away. Oberon knew a Dani glare when he felt it. "Right, right. I read the message. The introduction Pylons didn't fire, so we'll do it manually. I've got Dev on standby near the backups. We'll have to grow brand new ones to fix this. It's good to see you as well, Yvessa, kindly cease trying to pinball me with your glare. It *does* distract me."

The green orb hummed, as if to say she was keeping an eye on him. "Not so tough without your champion, *huh*. Why don't you stick around for a while? I think Dani would be very happy with a report on *both of you*."

Oberon's hue paled. "Now, that's really not necces—"

Yvessa's orb hummed again, causing Oberon to turn on a copper and hover right towards Artorian as he changed his tune. "About those introductions!"

CHAPTER ELEVEN

Information screen after information screen populated within the gazebo's interior. Oberon spoke swiftly, knowing Artorian could keep up, and not at all to make it seem to Yvessa that he was on board with the program. He may be older than the lot of them, but sometimes changes in management were both unforeseen and inevitable. While Eternium resided in Cal, Dani was the big boss. She could, and *would*, scold his orange keister.

"Welcome to Eternia! The game world version in Eternium that Cal has been putting together. With lots and lots of help. Ordinarily, there's a long reading scroll that opens first. Consisting of thorough terms, conditions, and a question that asks: *Do you want power?*" Oberon made his voice deepen and reverberate on that last mention. As if he were a large creature speaking in a hollow cave.

When he continued, his voice was normal. "We're thinking of giving some bonus if a person actually reads all of the conditions. They're terribly dull, and I've had more fun watching paint dry and grass grow. So far, not even the Wisps have wanted to chew through it all. It's *so* boring. After the introductions, we are going to hold trials. These trials happen in separated pocket spaces where Eternium and a few Wisps filter through some scenarios to see what your actions and reactions are. This helps us with deciding initial statistics."

The orange Wisp took a breath for Artorian's sake. "In this case, the Pylons needed are beautiful shattered shards. Some are *still* on fire. Dawn does *not* hold back when she's angry at something. Just to set you at ease if nobody told you before. All the demons in Cal are handled, the rest are... uh. *Here.* On second thought, that wouldn't put someone at ease."

Oberon's worry faded when he saw the vigor and virulence swirling in Artorian's eyes. The man's voice rumbled tense, carefully controlled as his anger bled through regardless. "I look forward to personally meeting every single *one* of them. Please continue."

The orange orb bobbed in lieu of nodding. "Instead of running you through the situations, since we have plenty of information on you, we were thinking we could use Dev's suggestion, and just roll some of his dice. All your attributes start as a base of five. Then we roll two six-sided dice, and add each roll to one of the attributes until we have a bonus for everything except Karmic Luck. In fact, don't even look at Karmic Luck. That's a toy Cal uses to mess with people, one that I have so far kept Eternium uninterested in."

The human gave a thumbs up, then held up his open palm. "Hand me the dice then."

Teleportation sounds *bwipped* from above as tiny versions of Dev's brethren appeared for him to catch. A large coin also appeared, but for the pure purpose of hovering nearby and serving as a rolling surface. Artorian smiled, patting the makeshift table. "Thanks, buddy, good to see you too. Even if you're not directly here. I take it you're watching from somewhere? Well then, watch these rolls!"

The heavy dice made delightful click-clack noises as they bounced over the flat surface. One of the dice fell from the edge, but swung around underneath the table and came back up on the other side as if trapped in a tiny gravity field, ending on the coin table regardless. Overall, he rolled an eight, seven, nine, three, eight, four, another eight, and another seven. "Just add them in that order from top to bottom, to all the fives."

Oberon was glad to oblige. "Great. Next is a big decision, your starting class. You'll find or unlock more of them as you play. While you play and grow, the class you choose determines the type and kind of abilities you unlock. Or what kind of system lenience you get from Eternium when you try to make an ability, if outside the theme of what that class is supposed to be about. The main merit is that almost every class gives you a bonus for choosing it. As an example, the cleric class doubles your mana pool. Or mana bar. Whatever we call it when we settle on a name."

"I'd rather not that one…" Artorian grumbled. His noises were cut short when Yvessa looked away to snicker. "What's so funny?"

Oberon said nothing so Yvessa could answer. "You, specifically *you*, cannot take the cleric class, even if it's available. There's a mechanic present that requires a cleric to be bound to a specific deity, and well. Uh… you work for Cal and have a hidden title that may… have to do with that."

Artorian flatly regarded her. "No need to play coy. I promised Cal I would help test deity functions, so it makes sense that I have a title that leans to such. Which likely comes with hidden bonuses that I currently don't have active. Per this class business, it would be narcissistic and wholly unpleasant if I were to play a class that allows me to select *myself* as the deity in question. Even without the nudge, I'd have declined. Though I can't say I like what I'm hearing. It sounds like any class would force me into a corner when it comes to thematics. If I want to make sure things work, I need a class that lets me do and learn anything. I don't care much if that comes at a penalty."

Oberon was already flipping through lists at the mention. "I recall there being a few, but at least two of them require you to have things unlocked before you can pick them up. Let's see.

The Monk class allows for a facsimile of other abilities to be implemented, though they will be heavily re-flavored."

Flipping to the next list, he found something else. "There *is* the Generalist, which I normally don't recommend since it does come with a nasty learning penalty. This class allows you to pick up any abilities or skills, from anywhere, at the cost that developing and learning them is a full fifty percent slower. There are also no bonuses for taking this class, and you won't gain abilities just from leveling. Save that you won't need to pay cross-class mana or stamina costs. Monk at least changes your mana bar into a chi bar and gives you the concentration and meditation skills for free. There's a few more, let me find them."

Artorian just held his hand up. "No need, my friend. You already found something that fits my criteria. Tell me more about the Generalist class. Also, if you have a moment, why don't I have the skills or abilities I did when I performed testing? It's like this body is a brand-new person."

Yvessa cut in to answer that last question, since it was easy. "That's because as far as Eternium is concerned, you *are* a new person. You have a young version of your body lying in stasis in a Midgard domus, which holds all those tester abilities. The body you're currently in actually isn't even human. It just looks human. Eternium uses Pylons to remember your information based on what state you enter in. The actual race listed on your sheet is 'Long.' You have a title called: 'Additional Nature' that allows... Let me just show you."

His Wisp pulled up a screen and made it visible.

Title: 'Additional Nature'. Tatum assigned. Cannot Combine. This user can have an additional base form, so long as that form is not of the same species as an existing one. This additional base form does not incur an upkeep cost, regardless if the additional form is used as the primary basis.

Artorian grumbled. "Again with the 'user' thing. Honestly, that grates."

Yvessa had a quick reply ready. "It's already flagged and

elevated, remember what I told you, about how updates work. Changes are going to take a while. If you want something minor changed on your sheet, Oberon and I can do that. Though we won't be touching any of the mechanical effects. That's against the rules, and please do remember where we are."

He waved it off, plenty aware the **Order Law** was in full effect here. "Yes, yes. So far, I only have more questions, but let's do them in order. There's much I wish to know. Class first?"

Oberon was long since ready. "Generalist is a slow grower. Unlike ordinary classes, which give you some attribute points relevant to the class every *even* level, this class only gives you attribute points once every *five* levels. You also don't receive any skills or abilities for choosing this class. Generalist heavily demands and expects you to figure it all out on your own. This class theme connects and refers to a person who is competent in many skills, but is not outstanding in any of them. Thus the growth penalty. This honestly isn't a class for cultivators coming to play, as much as it is one for residents who couldn't decide and want to figure it out eventually."

Artorian raised an eyebrow. "So can I take it or not?"

Yvessa sighed and slotted the class in. "You can. There you go. I've added it to your status sheet. Your level now also says one, instead of zero, since you have a class and the system can start keeping a proper track. To make that number a two, you need one thousand experience points. From two to three, you need two thousand plus the one thousand points of level one; three thousand points in total, and so forth. I'll explain how to get experience in a bit. You wanted this in order."

Appreciative nodding followed, and Artorian's gaze returned to Oberon. "What's next?"

Oberon seemed to be trying to bash one of the screens. Ha! Didn't work for him either. Or did it? His was starting to show cracks. "Well, you *should* have received a prompt when your class was slotted. However, I didn't see it come up. So I will just pull the text up and read it out loud to give you the mimicked experience. Or I would if I could *find it*!"

The other two snickered at Oberon's difficulties. It looked like they were all in this half-functioning mess together. Yvessa turned to Artorian. "What do you need explained next while he's looking for that?"

Artorian rose a finger to point at his status screen. "There are more attributes here than last time, and I honestly don't know what they all mean. Could we go through them?"

Yvessa began at the top, working her way down. "Name is self-explanatory. Class is what your ability and skill-gain theme is while you gain experience and increase in level. Profession is something you'll pick up as you play, and refers to something you do for work in order to gain currency. Or just because it's your calling. You unlock your first slot at level five. Overall level refers to your level total, based on all the class experience you've gained. Which is why it says zero. Specialization is…"

She mulled it over, wondering how to word this. "So, you can have multiple classes, but only one specialization. You could have the Cleric class, the Monk class, and the Pirate class. However, only one of those can open up into a Specialization, and those will never change. Once you pick one, that's it. Specializations will grow from then on into ever more specific variants, and I believe you can evolve a specialization when it reaches level ten. This is separate from your overall level, but comes with its own bonuses. Increasing your specialization level will give you attribute points, and abilities or skills specific to that niche thing."

A list appeared in front of her, clearly stating 'Wisp Access Only' at the top. "As an example. Campfire Cook can specialize further into Chef. Chef can specialize further into Exotic Chef. Though this is only if your class is set to Survivalist, otherwise those are all individual professions that unlock once you've done the previous one enough. We have some duplication going on that we still need to sort out. We don't want our professions and classes to exist in the same lists when it's all up and running."

Artorian pointed at his attributes, hoping she'd continue.

Yvessa zipped right to it. "Health Points are... you know what? We have a list we're supposed to read from that involves some truly terrible puns and tomato jokes. I'm going to skip that and give it my own flavor in a way I know you'll understand."

The human just smirked wide as Yvessa launched into a semi-tirade. "Health is your scream holder. Run out of screams, and you're dead. At which point we will... figure it out from there. Try to avoid this. There's also a hidden health rejuvenation stat that works only if you have the right abilities, otherwise you slowly heal over time when you sleep. The natural way. If you want to speed it up, use the scream rejuvenator. You'll figure it out."

Artorian was already laughing, and leaned back to keep listening. "Mana is how long you can grunt, in magical. Mana regeneration is how quickly you recover magical grunts. There's a hidden mana reserve statistic, for keeping the smoke in the bottle to keep other abilities powered. Such as Shield, which while hidden, is next. Shield is an ability to create temporary health that takes damage for you, before your actual health is impacted. You need the ability first, but I recommend it. Then there is stamina, which is how long you can grunt in physical. Stamina recovery tells you how swiftly you get grunts back per second."

Artorian's laughter turned to weak howling, needing to hold his ribs. "This is gold. Tell me you have the same pizzaz for the attributes."

Yvessa bounced herself on the ground like a rubber ball, did a spin, and got right on with the performance. "Strength is your *OOMPH*! It determines your physical output, and has a direct impact on melee damage. Dexterity is your *hiyaah*! It determines your nimbleness and grace of action. Dex has a direct impact on success to hit. Constitution is your *ungh*! It determines your solidity, rigidity, and overall wellbeing. Con has a direct impact on HP. Intelligence is your *aha*! It determines processing capacity and problem-solving power. Int has a direct impact on mana."

The luminous smiles she got only made her ham her speech up further. "Wisdom is your *abyss*! It determines internalized experience. Wis has a direct impact on mana regeneration. Charisma is how pretty your scream *sounds*. Perception is your *hmmm*. It determines your ability to adhere to important information, details, and what might otherwise remain hidden. Perception has a direct impact on noticing the obvious, though we're not sure if that last bit actually works."

She smirked. "Luck is your *Oooh*! Sometimes the universe just feels like it. Luck determines what kind of random rewards you find. Luck heavily involves loot roll checks, and generally isn't something you control. Since regardless of that score, if what you'd find is unreasonable, then you find nothing."

Yvessa then became quiet for a moment, looking at the number he had in that stat. "Why is...? Oh. Right. If luck wasn't balanced with the rest, you would be incurring significant penalties. Try not to let your attributes deviate from one another too much, there are some serious repercussions and negative effects. We heard Cal cackling all the way to Niflheim when someone handed him that penalty list."

She wanted to skip the last attribute, but sighed. "Then there's Karmic Luck. Which... well. I want to say it does nothing, because by itself it doesn't. However, it keeps track of your good-boy deeds. If it's positive, you might lose a number when Cal intervenes to keep you alive where otherwise you should have just died. It has other uses, but that's the only one I cared to remember."

Oberon turned around, which made Artorian and Yvessa provide him their attention. "It's blank. I found it, and it's *blank*. It's not fair that you get to have fun while I was sifting through this mess. So I'm going to make it up as I go as well to fill this back in. Behold, me! Explanator grandiose."

Artorian smiled, folded his hands, and leaned back for an encore of Wisp-tertainment.

CHAPTER TWELVE

Yvessa and Artorian laid on the grass on the other side of the lake, away from the promontory. They screeched with laughter from the dubious performance Oberon had started. Stopped. Restarted. Then finally serenaded to the heavens in such a sharp pitch that the gazebo couldn't take it anymore.

The green Wisp and assigned human continued laughing helplessly, because while they had managed to beat a hasty retreat, Oberon was currently trapped, entangled, and being accosted by one very unpleasantly awake Dread Gazebo.

His yelps and yowls for assistance were cut short by howls of verbalized attacks, as the gazebo utterly refused to let the orange Wisp go without giving him a good thrashing. With its teeth! Each time Oberon narrowly managed to zip free and escape, a tentacle lashed out, latched on, and pulled the screaming victim back in for further lessons on respectfully keeping quiet. There was even a sign! Why did nobody ever see the sign! Or did they see it and just choose not to read it? The answer was simple. More gnashing!

When Artorian sat up and wiped a tear away, his jaw hurt from how much giggling he'd done. "It has been ages since my jaw has hurt. Definitely a C-ranked body. I really do feel every-thing as if I were a common crop human boy again. Not simu-lated like in the Mage ranks. I can feel my lungs burn, my heart beat, and my neck hurting all around my lower jaw. Odd how you don't notice what you give up as a Mage. It's the tiny things."

He swiped his hand a few times, pulling his status screen to the forefront. "Alright. I've had a lovely breather. Now could you tell me why these numbers are so high?"

Yvessa composed herself, revealing a title Cal had assigned him. "This would be why. Try not to have a heart attack."

Title: 'Cultivator'. Cal assigned. Cannot Combine. Gain ATB based on personal Cultivation Rank. F-rank: 1. E-rank: 2. D-rank: 6. C-rank: 24. B-rank: 120. A-rank: 720. S-rank: 5040.

Note: Dani, remind me to settle on ATB or ATTB. I've been using both and that acronym just means 'attributes.' I'm going to confuse people at this rate. That being myself. I know for sure, because it just happened. Thanks, love!

Artorian would have choked on his water and spit it out in a misty cloud as if spritzing a potted plant if he'd had any. He gawked at the message and tightly held his chest. "You must be joking."

Yvessa turned a softer green. "No joke. Apparently someone got upset at Cal once for not including cultivation gains in the game system. Made the experience… poorer for it. I also have a log from Cal noting there was a *strong* suggestion to combine the gain systems of cultivation, game, and deity functions. So people wouldn't feel like they were being short-changed. So, cultivators from our old world all get this title slotted by Cal. So if or when they enter Eternia, they gain attribute bonuses based on their progress."

"Seven hundred and twenty points as bonus, per attribute? I'm guessing that's what Cal meant by the big-text ATB. Since it comes up blank again when I select it. Would have been lost without that extra note."

Yvessa bobbed affirmatively, temporarily distracted by combat noises from Oberon. She shut him out in short order and returned to task. Artorian momentarily looked when the sound from the gazebo faded, dropping down in volume as if it came from the other side of a wall. When he turned back to Yvessa, he questionably pointed at Oberon.

She set him at ease. "He'll be fine. Wisps count as Immortal Objects in Eternium, so we can't come to real harm. We can certainly still feel pain, though. Your guess is correct, which is why your attributes are so high. You're an A-ranked cultivator. So that title adds the appropriate bonus. Don't ask me how the numbers were decided on. Factorials or something."

Yvessa made a section glow verdant. "You also have four attribute points still to spend, just for starting the game."

Artorian smoothly ran his hand over his head, still surprised to feel short brown hair. How old was he after that last regret resolution… thirty something? His facial hair felt trimmed to the Phoenix Kingdom standard military cut. He could accept that for now. "Two in intelligence and two in charisma. I want to try to keep them decently even until I actually grasp what they do. Your explanation was lovely, but I need to play with things."

Yvessa added the requested points, and Artorian followed up with his next question as he lay flat on the grass. Slowly making snow angels without the requisite snow. Yvessa felt confused, and just asked what he was up to. "What are you doing? Do you need a pail of water to splash into your eyes next?"

Artorian nodded. "I may, actually. Yes. Let me explain. I've had several bodies now; from entering the Mage ranks, to monstrous ones, to… well, this. Since I essentially have to re-learn how to walk each and every time, I've devised a set of methods and actions to test what the limits of the current body are. Including how to use it. It's very embarrassing to keep stumbling all the time, but there's nothing wrong with that. You do things wrong for long enough, and you'll start to find nuggets on how to do things right. It's alright to take the time, and work with patience. Also, since I'm already on the ground, I can't fall!"

Yvessa snorted. "Unless there's random holes in the floor. *Again.*"

Artorian twisted himself into awkward poses for stretches. "Those still exist? Honestly, after all this time I was certain they'd be patched over with some nice, real grass."

His green Wisp just shook from side to side. That was a negative. "Nope. Still colossal structural failures just lying around, waiting for someone to step on them."

"Great." Her charge sighed deeply, calmly closing his eyes to just exist and be still for a moment. "I suppose I'll just run through my checklist then. Do let me know if something happens that isn't supposed to."

If there was a reply, he didn't hear it. He effortlessly calmed himself, beginning with his senses of awareness. A small notification popped up, though without an audible cue it went unnoticed. Yvessa saw it, but the skill gain was within the norm.

Skill gained: Calm Mind. By actively doing nothing, and choosing to simply be, you've discovered a state of tranquility! This skill belongs to the Monk class. Calm Mind provides a 2% bonus to resist a status effect that would alter your mind away from a state of calm. This skill provides a 10% bonus once at the Beginner ranks, increasing by 10% each subsequent rank.

Once content, Artorian did what he usually did. Sinking into himself to the cultivation layer, so he could see what had become of his refinement technique. To his great disdain, he found a terrible emptiness where a raging gyroscopic system should have been. He squeezed the bridge of his nose a moment, opening his eyes after a deep breath and a harsh sigh. "Well, that's disheartening."

Skill gained: Meditation. This is a general skill. Meditation allows the user to delve within themselves. Furthering the discovery of the self. While in meditation, the user is unaware of the outside world. Meditation causes a 1% increase in mana recovery for the duration of the skill being in use. This skill provides a 10% bonus once at the Beginner ranks, increasing by 10% each subsequent rank.

Yvessa pointed at the skill he gained. "Looks fine to me?"

Artorian noticed the prompt after the notification was pointed out. He read it, nodded, and dismissed it with a wave of the hand. "So that's how that works. Interesting. No, I meant that my cultivation technique is missing."

Oberon burst onto the scene, digging himself into the grass and dirt like a cannonball fired from far away. "It's in your Seed Co~o~ore! Yes! I'm free! Aha!"

He left quite the ditch, but shook himself off after rising back into the air as a clump of sticky mud. "Your cultivation technique isn't stored in your Eternia body. It's in your Seed Core where the real you is. I'm guessing you tried to cultivate just now?"'

Artorian smiled and welcomed Oberon back by wiping away some of the missed grass. "I just had a look. I was going to, but the technique being missing entirely put a deep pit in my stomach. I'm very used to that being in place."

Oberon glowed a proud orange once clean. "Much better! Yes, we figured. Though the lack of cultivation spiral is intentional. We have our own mechanics on handling abilities and skills that deal with mana, mana quality, and such. Though the process is honestly much the same. Easier if you already know how."

"I'll try it then." Artorian held his chin, then sat back down. Oberon was going to ask him what he was trying, but mana was already thrumming around Artorian's form as uncontrolled notifications began to populate over his head. Oh no. No, that wasn't allowed. That was messy! While the Wisps rushed to fix this mess and log the problem for a future system update, Artorian resided in his center.

He had the mana bar. Therefore he had mana. It was just… loosely around. Undefined. Unshaped. Unfocused. Within his center, he formed himself as a forum mote, temporarily losing about a thousand mana from his bar before it ticked back to full over the course of a few seconds. He mused to himself, even if nobody heard it. "So my mana refills at a prodigious pace? How pleasant… Right. Yvessa did say 'per second' when it came to grunt recovery. A different system. No pulling and refining to get mana, you just *get* it? Cheeky!"

He began as he always did when working with Essence. With a loving welcome. His mote developed arms and hands, just so he could extend them as the dot took on his old, grandfatherly form. "Hello, my old friends. Come home. I've missed you so."

There was no headache. No pain. No discomfort when he pulled this mana towards himself with a warm beckon. The energy gathered between his hands, unruly and unfocused. Spasmodic and wild. Like a puppy jumping all over the place because it could not properly express how ecstatic it was to see you.

Skill gained: Coalescence. You have taken the first steps on the path of the mind! By collecting your mana in an orderly form, you will be able to pack more mana into a single usage, with far greater effect. +10% spell efficiency and +10% mana regeneration per skill rank, once this skill is at the Beginner ranks. This skill belongs to the Mage class. Wisdom +1. Increase your wisdom to coalesce your mana to a higher degree. (Maximum 50% spell efficiency.)

Notice: Attribute increase withheld due to region limits. Due to your attributes being above 150, further increases will not be possible while in your current realm.

Notice: Backup version. This skill will be improved in the future to calculate for every skill level, rather than merely the overall skill rank. No difference will be noticeable after the Beginner rank until this skill achieves the Apprentice rank.

Artorian smiled as his thoughts formed the rogue mana into a tiny three-headed dog. Ah, yes. Just like ordinary mana, this version was also eager to find purpose and solidity. He brushed his hand over the tongue-lolling pup's head, and nodded approvingly. The puppy was boring its gaze into him with unspoken questions. Seeking direction.

Artorian spoke to the energy as if it were alive. "You wish to know what to do? Well, my sweet, I think… that is a question I have asked myself as well lately. I believe I would do you a disservice if I did not share my answers in kind. I feel like I have been asked some impossible task. Yet, with love, I will make it possible. So why don't we do that? Let's make the impossible possible."

He smiled, and the mana puppy wagged its tail right back. "I have memories of a list I was once shown, by a creature I'd rather not remember. Yet the lessons… I must admit so far the lessons ring true. I am going to put forth an idea, my little sweet. I will be here to guide you, and hold your paw. Don't be concerned if it doesn't work. If we fail, we can always try again later."

His solar gyroscope had been a high-tier technique. However, he firmly remembered that the Blight had shown him what the worthy tier looked like. Those mind-bending impossible shapes. He was uncertain if he could manage one, but here perhaps the story was different. With an empty canvas ready for paint, and a system that needed tending and testing. He imagined the 'Penrose Triangle,' and began his work.

Skill gained: Mana Manipulation. Where others are content to throw unseemly amounts of power into a spell—swiftly fueling their own destruction—you use a lighter touch. This skill belongs to the Mage class. -30%

mana. Starting at the Beginner rank, you gain +10% mana and +5% spell efficiency per rank. (Maximum 30% efficiency). Intelligence +1.

Notice: Attribute increase withheld due to region limits.

Notice: Backup version. See the Coalescence skill.

Crafting took hours, but Artorian danced with the energy as a seasoned performer. He lovingly threaded and wove the mana. Hands waning and waxing different densities of energy that molded to his ministrations like the thinnest fabric, painstakingly folded. For a moment, Artorian felt again what he had experienced when Rosewood granted him her memory of artistry. There was a peculiar freedom found only in the pursuit of a passion.

He indulged freely. Unaware of the utter abyss he was causing out in Eternia, as both Wisps scrambled to correct errors from the sheer amount of mana moving and flowing through the region. Notifications populating above his head endlessly increased as the system became burdened from the influx of activity.

Skill gained: Mana Affinity. You have aligned with mana in a way that allows for a smoother transition and flow. Having reached the Expert ranks in both Mana Manipulation and Coalescence, your mana will regenerate 30% faster!

Notice: Bonus additive, not multiplicative.

Skill gained: Magic Knack. You are gifted with mana. It speaks to you like a muse to bardic music. Having reached the Master ranks in both Mana Manipulation and Coalescence, your spells and abilities know what you intend, lowering the failure chance of spells and abilities powered by mana by 50%!

Skill gained: Mana Consciousness. Mana has a mind, and you have connected with yours. Having reached the Grandmaster ranks in both Mana Manipulation and Coalescence, your maximum mana amount has doubled!

Notice: Doubling occurs after all additive effects are calculated.

Skill gained: Mana Mastery. The secrets of your energy are unveiled, and hidden from you no longer. Having reached the Sage ranks in both Mana Manipulation and Coalescence, you now shape all your magic free of cost! The shape of mana abilities will no longer be considered in the mechanical cost calculation.

System notice: Sage system currently shattered. This advance will currently not count toward progression once mended.

When Artorian was done, he didn't leave his center. Not right away. He was mesmerized by the object in his center, so steady and stable. Yet somehow impossible at the same time. A functional Penrose Triangle turned in place, yet didn't appear to move in the slightest. No matter where he moved as his mote, he only ever saw the triangle as if he faced it straight on.

System notice: For creating a complex cultivation technique and proving your absolute mastery to the system, you gain the title: Mana Loved.

Title gained: Mana Loved. You have moved as one with the will of mana, and it adores you for it. While you have this title, your mana regeneration is doubled.

Artorian smiled wide, utterly delighted. "Magnificent."

CHAPTER THIRTEEN

"Are you pleased with yourself, Mr. Broke-the-sky?" Yvessa drummed very human fingers on a very human bicep. She'd gone through the trouble of using a humanization purely to scold Artorian when he came out of meditation. "You have no idea of the work you just gave us. I had to send Oberon out to delegate *other* Wisps, just so we have enough Fae power to coordinate this repair effort."

Artorian stretched once back on his feet. "Yvessa! You look marvelous! Just as I remember you. What a lovely—*please put the spoon away*."

His hands shot palms up to surrender, while a dangerous mana spoon hovered a bare inch away from his nose. Sure, it *looked* like a spoon. Yet he felt there were more damage numbers hiding in that tiny object than he had in his entire health bar. "I didn't do anything major!"

Yvessa's spoon thunderously sputtered emerald sparks as she moved, but didn't make contact. "Didn't do anything m—*Boy*! You just power-leveled two skills so hard using imported knowledge—proving to the system that you *could* do it—that Eternium had to slot them all the way into the Sage rank. Do you know how high that is?"

Artorian pursed his lips, attempting to look as innocent as possible. "...No...?"

Skill gained: Speech. Talk your way out of things, talk your way in! This skill adds a bonus equivalent to your rank onto your Charisma. When attempting to convince another person or group of people to do something they normally would not. A rank counts as ten points. Only activates via talking. Chance for new or unique access to quests has increased!

"*You* behave!" Yvessa pulled her spoon away from a very nervous nose, and intimidatingly levered it right at the sky. As far as Artorian could see, there was nobody there. Given the sudden skill gain, she must be snapping at Eternium. Though... he was likely just doing his job. The spoon was right back in front of his nose sooner than he liked. "What do you mean *no*?"

He cleared his throat. "Well... that wasn't in testing. What's 'Sage'? The thing you burn to make the house smell awful?"

To his great relief, the spoon was traded in for an informative screen. "I'm letting you off the hook this time, old man. Don't think I don't know you're an ancient longbeard, even if you're hiding out in that strapping body."

Artorian couldn't help but smirk. "Strapping, you say..."

Thunk

"*Ow!*" A notice blared. While his vision turned horribly wonky, he remained cohesive enough to see his health bar be reduced by a whopping *five thousand* points. "Yeowch!"

Yvessa narrowed her eyes at him. "Don't you dare smirk coyly at me like that, you codger. I can and will smack you well past the point of needing to drag you back to a Fringe medical cot for forced bedrest. Dani and I spent lots of delicious gossip time hashing out how to deal with you, and she gave me all the **oomph** I need to get the job done."

"I yield, I yield!" Artorian swiftly protected his head from another soft pop of the doom spoon, already wondering how he was going to get that health back. One problem at a time! "Please just teach me about the Sage thing…"

With a huff, Yvessa pulled the screen close. "Every skill and ability has an individual leveling track. Some are affected based on your statistics. Some are not. Most abilities will be tied to your overall level, and their personal track, rather than your attributes. The ranks are divided based on how well you understand the skill or ability you're using, which translates to how *well* you can use it. In easy terms: higher rank, better numbers."

Rubbing the wound, Artorian nodded to convey he was following. Yvessa went on with the list. "The rankings are as follows: Novice, Beginner, Apprentice, Student, Journeyman, Expert, Master, Grandmaster, and Sage. Normally when you first gain a skill, it begins at Novice I. Gain some experience in the skill, and it levels up into Novice II. Once at the point where it increases to level ten, it will instead increase its rank and reset the count to one. This being Beginner I. If you suddenly see a zero in any of your skills, let me know because that improvement isn't supposed to be ready yet."

Artorian frowned a touch, but was informed before he could start with questions as Yvessa continued. "There are two ways to gain experience. The first is to import it. Which involves showing the system you had skills in what you are doing beforehand. Eternium will then do its best to match the real skill you have, to a number equivalent of what the game skill should reasonably be. It's impossible to properly and fully quantify knowledge to numbers, but that's what we're trying regardless."

Yvessa created the image of a tome. "So if you spent your entire life studying a few books, when you enter Eternium you'll notice you have no skill in it. Because the system has no clue that's what you did. When you start talking about it in detail or begin scribing the knowledge down, Eternium will rush to catch up and give you the proper level equivalent to knowledge shown."

Her hand moved to the second column over, dismissing the tome. "The second method is to practice the skill and learn it from the ground up while here. As one would normally. Learning through this method generates a number known as experience. Get enough, and you level up. This includes swinging pokey sticks around and sticking them in things that want to eat you."

A piece of the column highlighted. "As you level, you can slot gained skill points into a skill, and be granted the knowledge equal to one level per point invested. Up to a limit where the system won't let you anymore, which I think is currently the Master rank. Gain enough experience to pass where Eternium has set the numerical threshold, and pop! Up a level or rank you go. Just like that."

Artorian motioned at the 'modifier' numbers next to the chart, wondering what that was about. Yvessa's spoon tapped the number next to Novice. "This? This says zero point two. Meaning that at the Novice rank, the skill or ability is one fifth as potent as it should be. This modifier goes up by point two until Journeyman. Which is one point zero. Journeyman is the basic level of a skill or ability. When someone talks about the average, Journeyman is it."

She changed the highlighted content to this new chart. "Note that the numbers you see here are only for skills or abilities that aren't individually specialized. If you read the descriptions for Mana Manipulation and Coalescence, you'll notice this isn't mentioned. That's because they've been tweaked and individualized to have unique effects. For all other skills that we're still working on, this is the current math."

Her charge nodded, and pointed down to the number two next to the Expert rank. "So does that mean an Expert ranked skill is twice as good as the Journeyman one? Master three, Grand four, Sage five?"

Yvessa dismissed the panel. "That's right. We also use this for skills that are so general, we don't know what to do about them yet. Such as running or jumping. The skills exist, but aside from altering the outcome based on the rank modifier... we're not sure."

Artorian tapped his chin, paying attention to her rather than the remaining panel. "When did you become so good at math? You suddenly have more knowledge than you should reasonably have been able to attain in the timeframe I thought you'd been a Wisp."

Yvessa quietly leered. "Memory stones. A mind can take in an incredible amount of information when they're motivated enough. Particularly if it's to stoke a fire under someone's keister."

He dropped the topic like a hot potato, conveniently finding something else to point out by pulling up his character information and making it visible as a public panel. "Speaking of modifiers, what's this odd fifteen-point-something next to my attributes?"

Character Panel—Base statistics only view:
Name: Artorian
Character Level: 1
Class: Generalist
Specialization: N/A
Profession: N/A
Hit Points: 2290 / 7290
Mana: 21900 / 21900
Mana regen: 366 / second
Stamina: 7285 / 7285
Stamina regen: 371 / second
Characteristics:
Strength: 733 (15.33)
Dexterity: 732 (15.32)
Constitution: 734 (15.34)
Intelligence: 730 (15.30)
Wisdom: 733 (15.33)
Charisma: 731 (15.31)
Perception: 733 (15.33)
Luck: 732 (15.32)
Karmic Luck: 0

His Wisp had a look, but shrugged. "That's the modifier that tells you how many times more powerful you are than the average human. The additional number is likely good for new minds that have no idea how to orient themselves, but aside from that it has no use. I'm sure it will confuse the abyss out of a few truly invested people who can't figure out why it's called a 'modifier' when it doesn't modify anything. I'll hide the number on your sheet for you so it's not a distraction."

"I appreciate that." Artorian gave a curt nod, then hopped in place after closing the distraction panel. "So, jumping and running, you say? Odd. I don't appear to be getting the Jump skill."

Yvessa shook her head. That wasn't how it worked. "No, not like that. You unlock skills by actively wanting to improve them and putting effort in, or performing a feat that would make the system assign it to you. I don't recommend it, but you may get the Jump skill just by falling from the edge of the world with a hop or skip. Nasty fall. Luckily nobody is crazy enough to do something like that willingly."

That seemed reasonable, so Artorian nodded along. Since small little hops in place weren't doing a thing, he figured to take her advice. Pressing his hands down to the ground, he hunched and took a firm breath before launching himself up. Keeping in mind that he specifically wanted to practice jumping better. "Hwhoo!"

Skill gained: Jump. Your desire to go places most would not has paid off! Honestly, who jumps at random in their daily life? This skill is normally given out to children! This is a general skill. Jump more often to improve this skill!

Recording it, Yvessa noted Artorian had jumped straight up about two hundred and twenty inches. Or roughly eighteen feet. That was a lot, but his strength statistic was the kind of ridiculous that lent itself to such measures. He landed hard, but remained stable. "Not bad for a C-ranker!"

Keeping quiet at his outburst, Yvessa just sighed. "Your attributes are just too high for Midgard. The limit here is one hundred and fifty. You can't gain attribute points over that number, even if you can be here with higher ones."

Artorian had a thought, and pulled up a previously dismissed notification. "Is that why Mana Manipulation said that a plus one intelligence gain was saved for later? Where do I need to be for this to properly tick?"

Not knowing off the top of her head, she dug around for the relevant chart. "Here it is. Maximum ATB per location. Can be increased to the next cap by stepping foot on the soil of another continent, after crossing the correct Bifrost bridge."

Yvessa hissed a sucked breath through her teeth at reading that last line. "That's going to hurt."

Artorian grew instantly concerned. "…Why?"

She shook her head. "It's the crossing the bridge part. You need a second specialization just to attempt it, without being squished by unopposable gravity that otherwise turns you to paste. You may be exempt from event requirements for advancement, so you don't need to complete Cal's tutorial. Though, just getting that second specialization is going to be difficult. The system only saves up to fifty points per attribute for you, to be attained later. Past that they're just wasted."

Her human mumbled some, but rolled his wrist for more. "Which realm do I need to be in then, and what are the requirements?"

Yvessa just made the list visible for convenience, verbally addressing each item. "Midgard has an attribute cap of one-fifty. Crossing to Alfheim or Svartalfheim requires a second specialization. Their cap is three hundred. Vanaheim's cap is four-fifty, no additional crossing requirement. Jotunheim's cap is six hundred, and requires you to have your third specialization. Muspelheim and Niflheim both have a cap of seven-fifty, but you need to find the hidden bridges in Jotunheim to get to them. Please remember these are just the current numbers. There's been some argument about swapping the Jotunheim and Vanaheim requirements due to some problems with skyland positioning."

She had a quick look at his attributes. "Given you're a scant ten to twentyish points away from Muspelheim's limits, it may be best to aim for Asgard. Asgard's cap is nine hundred, but requires you to have a fourth specialization just to cross the bridge. Normally you also need to also defeat all prior realm bosses in the places you've been, and most of them are roaming. This is why you can have higher statistics in a lower realm, because Eternium expects you to go back for them in order to get to Asgard. You're exempt from this, and you'll see why when you meet one of the bosses."

Artorian just waved it off. "I already know my chosen are filling those roles for at least Jotunheim. I fully understand why I'm exempt here. Though I may try to find them just to see them, if they happen to be in Eternium. I yearn for the days when everyone I know and love can be bundled together in a single location."

Exhaling hard through his nose as he thought of Zelia's words, he cracked his knuckles and rolled his shoulders. "Enough reminiscing. I'll make it happen one way or another. It sounds like specializations are my hold up for true progress. How can I attain those?"

Yvessa sat down and moved her mimicked priestess raiment so it didn't get in the way. Artorian went ahead and plopped down next to her on the grassy knoll. He rubbed his hands together at the next screen while Yvessa motioned at the relevant lines. "Like we said before: Your character level needs to be at least ten. Then you should get an automated list of options, based on what you've done up until that point. The system isn't going to offer you a Pirate Captain option if you've been neither a pirate, nor a captain, as an example. Only what you've done with your theme. The sooner you know what you want to do, the easier it will be."

His Wisp highlighted a column that made Artorian stop rubbing his hands together. Those were some painful looking numbers. "Leveling specializations isn't simple. You really need to focus on them, and that can come at the cost of time and resources. So far, your generalist class has nicked Mage and Monk skills, so you're probably going to get offered something along those ideals if you beeline it."

Artorian raised an eyebrow. "Probably? Don't you already know with a list somewhere?"

She shook her head firmly no. "Assumptions are terribly dangerous. If Eternium doesn't have hard facts, the options will default to no or not available. If you didn't go after it, it won't get offered. Freebies are rather frowned upon, which is odd since the system will give you free attributes for gaining skills or accomplishing feats. I think it's trying to give you motivation to continue? Either way... to unlock a specialization, you first need experience. That means completing quests, absorbing Beast Cores, fighting the wildlife, removing area bosses, or performing feats of note."

Artorian leaned back, his fingers steepling. "Hard no on the wildlife... I know what they really are, and I don't want to harm them. They're all sweethearts who don't know any better, wearing a skin that isn't theirs. I refuse. I'll figure out how to gently handle them, but I won't kill wantonly. That's not me. Are there any other w—"

An idea twinkled in his eyes, and his smile broadly grew. Yvessa pulled a face. "Oh no, now what did you think of?"

He grinned at her, happy as a clam. "I have a *wonderful* idea."

CHAPTER FOURTEEN

"Hello th—*what* is he doing?" Oberon winked back into Eternium to a truly odd sight. He'd started off joyful, since his prior problems had been properly accosted and tackled to the ground. The Pylons were now in the skillful hands of some zealous triangular Gnomes.

Yvessa didn't answer him, just standing nearby with her human hand covering her face. Her elbow was held by the other arm, as the hand covering her face dropped away to sharply chop toward her charge.

"Just... just watch." Yvessa sounded defeated, and that piqued Oberon's curiosity. He hovered closer, but cleared his throat at her first. She glanced at him before catching his meaning. "*Hmmm?* Oh. Right. Now that you're here, this is improper. Let me just..."

Yvessa popped back into a luminous green orb, her human guise dropped in order to acquiesce to Wisp social rules. Complicated things, those Wisp rules, but minor in the face of one Artorian's unit in shenanigans. He was currently laying stiff as a plank on the ground, face down and wiggling from side to side like a boat that was gently being rocked by the ocean waves.

Oberon watched, but slowly turned himself to face Yvessa for answers anyway. Yvessa dimmed. "He's... figuring out skills. Let me go ahead and translate that. He's trying to give Eternium a headache, by attempting the most obscure of... things. I'm not sure I know the words."

Artorian pressed up from his planked position, grinding his balled hands knuckle-down into the dirt before pulling in one leg as if he were on a starter block. The Wisps thought nothing of it until they saw the blink of a skill gain notification pop up, then spin in place as Artorian ran right the abyss past the sign with enough velocity to make it whirl.

Yvessa fumed. "That little..."

Oberon looked between the spinning notification—which he dismissed since a mere moment afterward he was alone with it—and the vanishing ball of green light that zipped off into the distance. Chasing after a person who was going... *how* fast? He pulled the notification back up just to look at it.

Skill gained: Run! Why go slow when you can go fast? Take off at speed and get to where you need to be! This is a general skill. Running drains stamina at a flat rate, multiplied inversely by your rank modifier. At Novice rank, running will cost five times as much Stamina! Base stamina drain for running: ten per second. Run more often to improve this skill!

Making the notice disappear, Oberon vanished in a flash. He caught up mere seconds after scooting off from where he was, displacing enough air to cause a vibrant sonic boom to quake in his wake and bend his surroundings. When Yvessa realized it was okay to go that fast, she caught right up to the both of them while Artorian hauled butt at the full running speed he could muster. Which was... a ridiculous seven hundred and thirty-three feet per second. Or around five hundred miles per hour, if he could sustain it for long enough.

That number didn't seem right, so Yvessa quickly checked

the rank of his running skill. How was it already all the way up to Journeyman? He should have started at Novice and been a fifth as fast! Oh... he *had* started at Novice. Eternium had fixed up the rank via memories. "Well... alright then."

Artorian was halfway and a bit from breaking the sound barrier! Based on the smile plastered on his face, that was exactly how fast he was hoping to go. Though when he realized he was far away from achieving it, he began to slow down and hop in place.

Artorian had left his spawning point in the dust. The gazebo location far behind him as he finally came to a standstill by digging his feet down into the ground and skidding to a dirty halt. Enough earth was displaced to cause a small avalanche, creating a new hill. "That was fantastic!"

Jumping into the air, he punched the sky before landing hard once again. He needed to do something about his landings, but boy oh *boy* did he have ideas for that! Though... that was odd. Didn't these skills level up with use? He pressed his hands to the sides of his robe. "Say, Yvessa. Should I have received a ding or notification about a skill up by now?"

Oberon pulsed a sharp orange to cut in. "About that! I was going to tell you, had you not sped right off. In order to fix some latent issues, we had to turn off some of your Pylons. You're going to get notified if you gain a new skill, but not if your skills level or rank up. If you want to see what they currently are, you'll need to manually check your status screen. We absolutely cannot afford another cascade event like with your double Sage-rank gains. That was a nightmare. You broke the *sky*, Artorian."

"It got better." Artorian provided a sly thumbs up. "So are you going to tag along as well? I know Yvessa is stuck with me, but I didn't think you were."

Oberon calmed his strong coloration. "I... I'm on the fence, as you humans say. You see outside there's Dani, and the courts. While I'm on good terms with the former, I am tired of the latter. I *yearn* for fun. I *ache* for something other than procedure and work. I might be part of the development team for this game, but I haven't actually gotten to play it. Nor does anyone else really... *delve*. So while you are *technically* 'work' if you break something, you're also delicious entertainment."

Artorian didn't need to see Oberon's teeth to know he was smiling like a cheeky little snoot. "*Mmm*. Well alright then. I'm doing the jog test next. I doubt it will be as fast, but that's what's on the docket. Also, are either of you going to point me in the direction of some civilization, or am I wandering until I run into some? I guarantee you I am excellent at enthusiastic walks."

Yvessa made an unhappy sound when recollecting the stories concerning these supposed harmless outings. "I'll slot you in a quest to find a nearby town so I can give you a clue."

Oberon physically bashed into the screen she pulled up, actually shattering it to pieces. "Now now! That won't be necessary! We just can't tell anyone about certain world details, but if we were to accidentally point out that very interesting looking common malus tree over there. Yet not tell you that if you walked in the direction of where the one behind it is, for about a half a day, you'd run into a town... well, that's just happenstance, isn't it?"

"Fix. My. Screen." Yvessa glared at him with seething, sharp colors. Oberon made the sound of a finger snap. The pieces of her shattered field reconnected without a fuss, allowing her to angrily dismiss it with a sharp flick of mana. "Don't. Again."

Oberon, the cheeky orange ball of fine print, moved over to Artorian with tiny bounces, giggling to himself. After the orb had passed him, Artorian looked back at Yvessa and moved his hands up with a 'nothing to be done' motion. He turned on his heel to jog after Oberon as the notification for the relevant skill appeared.

Skill gained: Jogging! Health is important, and so is pacing. Won't get there on a walk? Make it a jog! This is a general skill. Jogging drains stamina at a flat rate, multiplied inversely by your rank modifier. At Novice rank, jogging will cost five times as much Stamina! Base stamina drain for jogging: one per second. Jog more often to improve this skill!

Yvessa zipped up next to Oberon while Artorian practiced jumping from both jogging and running starts. A jogging jump took him seventy-three feet forward, while a running jump doubled it. Not bad! Though she could tell he knew it was the Novice skill modifier stifling his true distance. "Alright, explain. Why did you bash my screen? Before you showed up, Artorian already had a clearly terrible idea in mind that he was going to put into action, but breaking my work tools was uncalled for."

Oberon slowed, putting some distance between their human and themselves. "Listen, newlight. I understand that the hierarchy is a mess between the obligations of social rules and… how things stand while Eternium lives in Cal. Given I also have no love for it, I won't mention much more about it. Though when it comes to my boredom, I will break oaths to be freed from monotony. The quest you were going to give him involved the boring old tried and tested starter town that we are sort of forced to send him to. *If* he's given a location quest. Instead, he's now going to a far more interesting place that hasn't been tested, and I don't know the outcome of every quest by heart."

His tone turned more serious. "If I had given you as much as a second longer, that quest would have been active. That means it would have gone in the log. The log is immutable, and law. Plus, you saw his reaction when we mentioned demons. I want those things dead as much as he does. They're in my dungeon's Core, and I am *royally miffed*. I fully understand that the true place and direction I'm leading him is *infested*—that's clear from as much as a minor glance at the map—yet so long as I am restrained from harming anything here, I cannot personally indulge in the satisfaction of killing those things. In the kind of imaginative and inventive ways that would be considered revolutionary by the Abyss's standards."

Oberon's tone darkened further. "I cannot verbally express my utter distaste and raw seething hatred for the things trying their utmost to take control of my bonded dungeon, and the heinous actions they clearly want to take with it. I want to wipe every single one of those tar-oozing, charisma-mooching stains on the underpants of society off the map and burn them to the last crisp and cinder that allows their souls the very idea of a scream."

His every breath was sharp. "I have been given a very high-profile tool and I will not sit idly by. Not when I can instead direct that human, who very much falls in step with my line of thought, to jump right into the pit and get to *smiting*. There is no rule in the book and no law in heaven that I will not use every last drop of my significant sneaky skills and Fae trickery to circumvent, if it means I get to feel the catharsis of those. Things. Dying. Screams and ignored pleas for mercy *very much desired*."

Oberon ceased his dark tone, instead shining bright and sounding fresh as a fiddle. "So I happily look forward to your unobstructed assistance! I am so glad to have you along…"

When the orange ball zipped along ahead of her, Yvessa turned pale. Her coloration baby-vomit green while her feelings felt twisted. Oberon bounced up along next to Artorian as if he'd never had his momentary dark outburst, and the two merrily laughed at some quip that was cracked.

She'd not expected this, and was suddenly very concerned there were events in motion that were very much happening above her head. Artorian? That old codger she could handle. Artorian *and* Oberon as a team? That was like mixing a person who would do anything to get the job done with one who had all the details meticulously planned out. She couldn't even tell who was who.

This was going to be a problem.

CHAPTER FIFTEEN

Half a day's journey must have been something Oberon calcu-lated if traversing at walking, or otherwise ordinary expected speed. Not the laugh-while-zooming-along journey he and Yvessa were keeping up with as Artorian took Midgard by storm. His running skill had already ranked up to Expert from his newfound love of speedrunning. The zooming blur wondered to himself if everyone with this speed would do this, because the skill description had been so on the copper. "Why go slow when you can go fast!"

Artorian only stopped because he shoulder-checked some-thing before crashing through a stone wall. He tumbled through a field of wheat, functioned as a plow for the field behind it, and finally came to a face-first standstill in a turnip patch. Coughing out some mud, he got up and felt dirtier than a soiled rag. He also hadn't taken care of that damage from earlier. Perhaps in his rush to do things, he'd overlooked something important. Also, why was he covered in plumage?

"Bahaha! That was great!" Oberon was of course a warm glow-ball of laughing pleasantry. "I am sharing that with the other Wisps later, I recorded that entire tumble. You smashed through a chicken coop and sent them all flying!"

Artorian slapped his forehead and spat out a piece of muddy turnip. "I was trying to *avoid* the wildlife!"

Yvessa made a side to side motion. "Technically you did. Not everything in Eternia is recycled from something else, and not all creatures have a true mind. Those were facsimiles. No actual animals are ever harmed here. Definitely not when they're meant for eating."

Their human pressed his hands to his hips, popping his back. "So did I hit chickens or not? I'm fairly certain the turnips, mud and feathers makes me rather culpable."

Oberon was too busy snickering and watching the recording once more, so Yvessa picked up the slack. "Animals meant specifically to further the continuation of something else weren't allotted the ability to feel or perceive harm. They can act harmed, and due to the rules in place they will, but they never actually will be. Those creatures have a false life effect on them that makes it seem as if they have more hit points than they do. Those chickens really only had one health, didn't notice you killed them, and felt as if they just went to sleep. Those minds are going to wake up later as other chickens, never being the wiser. They only get the good chicken life. To answer directly: yes. You fried chickens on impact."

Artorian nodded, and looked at his dirty arms. "I never had this problem in the past. Though I reasonably should have. Why didn't...? Right! Aura!"

He plopped right down on the ground, and didn't hear what Oberon said as he dropped right into meditation. There was crafting to do! "Alright, let's see here."

Since he had to do it all from scratch, he could risk rebuilding a Presence field. Perhaps best to see if he even had separated Aura layers to begin with? "Yes, check your building blocks before putting up a house."

Funneling some mana, his inner, body, and outer Auric layers bloomed when fed. He unconsciously rolled his shoulders when the balms of power misted out of his skin. C-rankers felt it far more vividly since they had real skin, while this was a seamless process as a Mage. As a whatever-he-was-now, it mimicked a C-ranker the best. More proof for his theory.

He waited a moment, but nothing happened. No skill popped up?

"That was odd."

Ability gained: Auric Field. You have merged your mana with your body! In doing so, you have found you can affect yourself and others, by investing a flat percentage of your total mana in order to sustain certain desired effects. Due to the myriad uses of this ability, costs will stack if you attempt to use multiple fields at once! You may use the inner field to affect your vitals. Your body field to affect yourself and your statistics. And your outer field to affect everyone else!

"There it is! Fantastic." Though this one called itself an ability. Not a skill. He should ask Yvessa about the difference once out of meditation. On second thought, why was he aware of a notification he couldn't see? He just sort of... knew. That hadn't happened earlier, so Dev must have been playing with Pylons.

Should he attempt to combine them right away, or perhaps leave them and see if he could use them better as they were? Mulling it over, he mentally shrugged. He knew what he was doing with Presence, yet had no clue concerning the divided ones. If anything, he guessed that one effect would affect all three zones, rather than each zone being slotted individually?

He was speculating. "Let's just give it a whirl!"

Condensing his mana and reshaping it without effort—a feat that left him pleasantly surprised—he recalled that a side effect of Mana Mastery was at play. That one mana notification had mentioned something of the like. Good enough! His attention back on the task, he recalled how his Presence felt as an A-ranker, and re-molded his fields to match.

Or he tried to. They didn't budge.

"What the abyss?" Was he missing something? "Oh you old fool, you forgot to *build* your Aura! All this reminiscing about C-rankers and you forgot entirely what you're supposed to do in that rank."

Exhaling a physical sigh, he pulled some mana from his bar and began to loop, twist, loop. Just like the old times.

A few minutes in, and the mana began to sputter. That was new. What was going on? His entire work faltered, falling to pieces as strips of thinned mana. "Oh, come on!"

Mentally tapping his fingers on his knee, he went over his attempt. Perhaps he was doing this wrong and skipping steps? He would take it from the bottom. Gathering Essence? Not needed. The system fed mana like a grandmother who thought her grandchild was starving. Creating a cultivation technique? Already done. Then it was rebuilding time, via imbuing the body and building one's Aura. Was it a requirement that it happened in that order? "Would it hurt to try?"

No, no it would not. Though if he was in a Spirit-quality body, mimicking a C-ranker, while using mana… this was all sorts of confusing to begin with. That was going to hurt his head, so perhaps he should take a page out of the book of his old apprentice. "What would Dale do? Dale would just jump in headfirst and care not for the consequences!"

Artorian rubbed his hands together and pulled a Dale. His mana bar shook in place, the contents plummeting. A pleasant discovery occurred! Not only did the replacement process not hurt, but the effort was ridiculously easy. Replacing a real, physical body made of meaty bits with Essence was… painful, slow, taxing, and arduous. Imbuing a Spirit body was just like adding a pitcher of water into the space of an empty pool. The spirit form was already prepared for the influx, and would laugh at his attempts.

Ability gained: Empowerment. Not strong enough at the moment? Trade one power for another! By investing a percentage of your chi bar, you can increase your base physical attributes. This ability belongs to the Monk class.

Notice! You have mana, not chi. The Generalist class will allow mechanics of the existing math to be kept the same.

Notice! As a cultivator importing this knowledge, know this. Permanent increases to power other than those established by the system will not be allowed or tolerated. Attempting to breach the Mage ranks will be circum-vented. A temporary power boost via an X to Y trade will be unlocked instead.

Eternium had made a way around his shenanigans? Nobody would be a Mage-quality being in Eternia with that active! Drat! This also severely hampered his prior attempts. Though the prompt did explain why his efforts had fallen apart in his hands.

"Though... *hmm.*" If Empowerment was the replacement to imbuing, did that mean he just needed to have it active to build his Aura, or merge them? "Dale it!"

His mana built up again, only for his bar to squeeze into itself and be reduced by ten percent in both its represented size and maximum value. He felt a tad stronger, but that was just numbers at play. Numbers were unimportant for now. Currently it was vengeance-o-clock! Fun vengeance. For fun.

Artorian smirked and flooded his Auric Field with undi-rected mana. When he felt the amount was sufficient—even if there was currently no effect—Artorian then added the identity portion, after which he had to hold onto his proverbial hat as changes happened rather quickly.

Ability gained: Presence. Fielding not good enough? Don't like having a high Karmic Luck stat? If this triggers I know exactly who is responsible for it. Fine! You have discovered the advanced function of Auric Fields. Why affect one zone at a time when you could do them all at once! Presence func-tions similar to Auric Fields, except that you spend a flat percentage of total mana in order to sustain a desired effect. You may choose for Presence to affect all three zones at once, two at a time, or just one, at your choice. This is an Imported ability without class bonds. Karmic Luck -5!

Notice: Each time you do this to my well-ordered system, I will dock you another 5 Karmic Luck.

Artorian broke out of meditation because he couldn't contain his laughter. "Hahahaha! Great success! On both counts!"

A few deep breaths later, and he wiped his face only to realize he was horrendously dirty. It also dawned on him at that moment that he was surrounded by... people? They looked like people, but there was something odd about their coloration. Also were those animal ears? He blinked up at the tiny crowd of four farmland-attired people, and shot his hand up in greeting. "Hello there! Terribly sorry about your field. I'd love to help fix the damage I caused. I stumbled fairly egregiously."

Artorian looked around for his Wisps, but they were nowhere to be seen. He then opened the sheet of the person his hand was aimed at with a whisper. "Inspect."

Name: Ruffle
Race: Red Panda (Humanization)
Character Level: 2
Class: Farmer
Specialization: N/A
Profession: N/A

Oof. Level 2? Likely without his particular bonuses as well. Life must be tough on Midgard. His offered hand was grasped, Ruffle pulling him right up from the ground only to realize he was a full two feet shorter than Artorian. He made sounds akin to language in return as a reply, but just as Ruffle hadn't understood a word of what Artorian had said, the human equally had no clue how to speak Red Panda. Or should he have been counting himself as a Long?

Dismissing that consideration, he remained quiet while the people around him talked amongst themselves. One of them was a touch louder than the rest, so he must have been in charge. Sure enough, the skinny adult male with long red hair made one of those 'come along' motions. Artorian smiled, answered with a nod, and did just that. How fortuitous! He'd found people! He considered it strange to call them people, but then again in their eyes he was likely the weird one.

Best to drop it.

A very awkward set of meetings later where he felt like both the subject and silent participant. The ever-growing Red Panda group eventually arrived a few hills further down at a structure that anyone could recognize as a longhouse. The doors had some childish art carved in, and in hindsight he noticed that it wasn't childish at all. That art was just the best they could manage for now. So… a *new* civilization trying to crop up?

Before entering, he turned to look behind him to take in the haphazard town layout. A city planner would have a heart attack at seeing this sneezed sprawl of shelters and buildings. Also, was the entire south side… destroyed? Yes, there was wreckage there, including signs of larger structures than the current longhouse used to occupy the land. This longhouse must have been a new one, and the Pandas had their own problems. Good to know.

Entering the longhouse, he was instantly accosted by the smell of cooked fish. That and whatever blend of berry mead they had cobbled together. The wafts were thick and strong, and they should really open a window. Speaking of, no windows in this longhouse? Odd. Though he supposed some of the construction was so shoddy that the holes allowing light in would suffice.

At the very end of the longhouse, a Red Panda with far more scrutinizing eyes and a crown of chicken feathers narrowed his gaze at the newcomer. Panda-speak was thrown around, and wooden spears with sharpened stone heads were leveled in his direction. Well… he couldn't say he was surprised, so he just smiled and casually waved back a hello.

His interest shot up when the chicken-crowned one managed a few words of a language he understood! Unfortunately… that language was *scree-scree*.

"Abyss."

CHAPTER SIXTEEN

Artorian pulled the Red Panda chieftain's status sheet up with an inspection immediately. He instantly didn't like what he was seeing. Artorian also felt something plink off his... skin? Strange to describe. The sensation was akin to someone tossing a crumpled paper ball at his face. The feeling didn't do anything aside from being slightly insulting, and that's what resisting someone else's *Inspect* felt like.

Name: Woffo (Possessed by: Krikirshin, the Ripper)
Race: Red Panda (Humanization) (Possessor: Demon)
Character Level: 5 (Possessor: 22)
Class: Chieftain (Possessor: Psychomancer)
Specialization: N/A (Possessor: Inhabiter)
Profession: Tribal Leader (Possessor: Spy)

What the abyss was a Psychomancer? A level twenty-two at that. He attempted to tap the class for more information, and tried not to smile when a new screen came up with a functional explanation.

Class: Psychomancer (Restricted). A being that inspires fear into the hearts of foe and friend alike, the Psychomancer works to directly control others. Unlike a Bard who evokes reaction through emotion or a Necromancer who controls empty bodies of the dead... a Psychomancer controls the living, easily being able to turn groups into puppets at higher levels.

Artorian's smile dropped like a rock, his tone turning dark. He spoke in his normal language rather than scree-scree, not particularly caring if he was understood. He was still missing a few puzzle pieces when it came to what was going on with this town, but that was sidelined in favor of a chance to strive forward onto the main goal: *extermination.* "Oh, so *that's* how you're playing it?"

Rolling his shoulders hard, Artorian inhaled to flex and get a feel for himself in a state of combat readiness. Though that awful mud was still all over him, and his health bar had that... *dent.* He should do something about both. *Right now.*

The demon possessing Woffo knew something was wrong. His scouts had been noisy about some crash, but the lack of events after had caused Kri to simply not care. Just another Panda being an idiot. Somewhere between three to four decanters of mead later, his doors had opened. Some farmers who were dragging in their latest problem or offering, no doubt.

Krikirshin's interest rose from bored, to surprised, to interested when a creature two feet taller than the average man entered his longhouse. It wasn't important it had been rebuilt a third time, given he'd torched the first two for insubordination. The creatures under his control were... properly passive now.

Downing another swig of berry drink, Kri wondered for a moment if this dirty gutter rat they'd hauled in wasn't another demon in disguise. Their echelon had strict rules for expansion, but if this was a messenger then he needed to confirm it first. Because if it was a usurper...

His voice was that of the Panda's he was possessing, but the words spoken were his. "Under which torturer's banner do you serve?"

The reply he received made him frown. Words and language? Yes. Proper Demoniac? Abyss no. So had the creature understood him or not? It didn't matter. Without a proper reply in Demoniac, this was none of the things he was worried about. Yet for some reason Kri felt unsettled, and he realized what it was when his casual Inspect procured no results. No handy little information box floated over the tall man's head.

That was cause for suspicion, but Kri felt secure in his position. He was, after all, hidden away inside of a gentle Panda. If anyone wished him harm, they would have to deal with the demerits that came with killing an innocent, while at the same time he remained entirely unharmed, since this wasn't actually his body. Just borrowing... oh, who was he kidding, he loved the word *steal*.

All would be well, per the status quo, with business working as usual, unless the world *changed something*. He'd only been subject to observing such a jarring event once, but the sudden occurrence of malus trees covering his entire status sheet had been outright bizarre.

Before the event, he'd noted a cat meow in the doorway, then a moment after saw that same cat make the exact same meow. After the event, all status sheets had replaced the word 'malus' with 'demerit,' returning them to legible functionality. As if the voice of the world had come across the great works of Traviticus of Baldree, then become aware that the word 'malus' didn't actually mean 'negative,' but rather referred to a species of tree.

Was it getting brighter in his longhouse? For that matter, why was it suddenly so hot? Kri didn't feel great, and pulled up his own status to—*why was he losing health points*? Panic filled his borrowed heart as cold chills ran down his otherwise on fire spine. He frantically threw perception checks all around the room, but couldn't discern anything except for the mysterious bright spots appearing in his vision. Like holes were being carved out of the canvas of what he could see.

The strange human the farmers had brought was also losing

dirt by the second as it either just fell off from him to leave him spotless, or vanished from his being entirely as he cleansed and freshened up. It was slow, but noticeable enough for Kri's attention to be drawn to it. The demon also noticed that the injured in his longhouse were suddenly feeling much better. Invigorated. Refreshed. Topped up on health? How had their health recovered?

Quickly checking his own again while trying to maintain the ruse that nothing was wrong, he felt sickened. He was at half health already! His host was at full hit points, and feeling better than ever even with the possession demerits. It had to be that human! He needed to swap his possession targets right now and shut that down, or he was going to burn out and be nothing but a husk! Kri didn't even understand how he was taking damage. He felt as if he was in a field that was slowly whittling away at him just for being in it.

Forget the ruse! He was in a fight and hadn't realized it. He was under attack, and needed to abandon his Panda prison immediately! Kri burst from Woffo's mouth in a grievous dark purple cloud.

Woffo was freed! His eyes momentarily turned starry and dark, before clearing up and regaining their original luster as Woffo's own voice found ground to stand on once again. He gasped, mumbling some words in Panda while pointing at the Caligene. After which he passed out on his seat from the exertion of being used as a medium.

The pointy sticks in the room were confused for a moment, but changed their orientation away from the self-cleaning man. They instead turned to the very obvious danger cloud hovering ominously above the rectangular fireplace in the middle of the longhouse.

Artorian indulged the touch of pride he felt. His ability worked outside, so it worked in here! He hadn't received a new ability notification, so to see what he'd done he needed to pull it up. "Let's have a look!"

Ability: Presence.
Utilization: Resplendence field.
Zones affected: Inner, Body, Outer.

This is an imported function. Explanation: The Resplendence field is a derivative of the original cultivator ability known as starlight Aura. This field performs multiple functions in a lesser capacity, and requires a constant flat percentage of a mana bar's maximum to be invested in order to sustain its upkeep.

Flat cost: twenty-eight percent of total mana. Equal to four percent per active effect. This field heals, cleanses, cleans, revitalizes, restores, regenerates, and invigorates via the formula $n\%x$, where n represents the rank of this ability, and x represents the rank of each other individual ability listed.

As this is a field-based ability, this effect is indiscriminate, affecting any valid target present within the radius. The radius is determined by $30r$, where r represents the rank of this ability. Individual levels are not taken into account to calculate the radius.

Notice: Due to the individual abilities not being unlocked, their values will remain static. If the listed abilities are unlocked, their individual leveling track will increase the potency of their effect in this field accordingly.

Notice: This ability is light-aligned. Light-based creatures and their adjacents will be immune, or gain additional benefit. Dark-based creatures and their adjacents will take additional damage, or gain additional demerits.

"Well, that's a sandwich and a half of an ability!"

Easily a mouthful when biting through that juicy bit of system knowledge. Though, sweet mercy! This field cost him nearly a full third of his entire mana allotment to keep active? Eesh! The effects were static as well, unless he leveled the individual abilities? Then he would need to discover how an always-active effect improved.

That was a problem for later, as he gained a sudden

headache from an attack bashing against his wisdom score. The problem right now was what caused his next notification.

Skill gained: Mental Manipulation Resistance. This skill is a staple for the paranoid and frightened. While it might be useful in certain situations, all that you are doing is hurting yourself. Effect: Grants $10+10n\%$ direct resistance to mental manipulation where 'n' equals rank. This will help you block out effects of skills such as fear, control, and magical seduction.

Caution: Frequent use of this skill may lead to a damaged mind. It isn't normal to walk away from a fight where you were killed. By removing some of the mind-altering effects of dying and coming back, you lose experience.

Notice: Possession resisted.

Had that daft demon just tried to *possess* him? *How* was he supposed to defend against that? The skill he just gained seemed passive, and he very much wanted something active! Though he supposed killing it faster would perform very much the same function. "What does one do when in doubt?"

The answer arrived on superheated wings. "*Fireball!*"

Artorian hurled his hand forward, as if throwing a ball. The somatic component felt so natural to do that he didn't question why he'd made the movement at all. The sound of unpleasant static cracked through the longhouse as Artorian finally introduced his first true error. A silently observing Oberon had expected errors to occur much sooner than this, but his quiet Fae grin spoke volumes to the concerned, equally muted Yvessa hovering next to him.

Lacking the ability in question, the correct alignment to the element he was using, or any of the appropriate requisites, the system hiccupped as Artorian still managed to fire the effect off by importing knowledge on how *his* effect was accomplished to the tiniest detail.

The problem was one of language. 'Fireball' was a preexisting, popular, tested and true ability with a hefty log of uses.

The given method of 'fireball' which Artorian showed Eternium wasn't that established method at all. The system had to improvise as it logged its first instance of Artorian truly 'cheating.'

Blasted **Law**-bypass allotment!

Eternium didn't function in the same time frame as the game world he was running for Cal. Much like Cal, he preferred operating on the slowest possible frame of reference, so he had years of time in order to come up with a good solution for whatever problem he might encounter. While a mere second might pass in Eternia, he had oodles of noodles of time to troubleshoot.

To figure this one out, Eternium reviewed Artorian's personal history. A file that the dungeon Core had specially slotted on his quick-access shelf. On further inspection, what Artorian was actually doing was creating an all-affinity ball-shaped emanation. One with several functions, the most frequent use of which led back to a fight in a Ziggurat against some snake-bone monster known as a Vizier. Another ability with stacked functions? It had taken him a week just to make the Presence ability work with the Pylons available.

Artorian was easily responsible for Dev having about a hundred tickets for new Pylons that needed to be grown. Why wasn't Oberon curtailing this behavior? Actually, what was his Wisp doing at all?

Given the map available to Eternium, two Wisps were nearby keeping active tabs on the situation, and both were reporting events. A team of Gnomes also seemed to be paying constant attention to Artorian's activities, keeping their own logs. Dev had assigned an engineering squad? Probably for the best. Certain individuals were far more dangerous to let loose, yet at the same time Artorian was, in his own way... *benign.*

Eternium metaphorically kneaded the bridge of his nose.

Artorian was here to help, and anything he broke they could repair, improve, fix, or otherwise tend to. A grand testbed of options appeared where the inactive Administrator tread, and regardless of how irritated it could make him. Eternium had to remind himself to be thankful for the help. If he needed to, he would assign even more oversight. For now, he had a new fireball-type ability to figure out.

Before that, given Oberon's reports so far, he also had enough information to assign Artorian his initial character trait. That needed to happen first.

CHAPTER SEVENTEEN

Artorian received several screens at once, but couldn't pay attention to them yet as a glowing solar ball slammed into the Caligene's stomach equivalent. No boom? The orb was swallowed up by the demon, though that appeared to have been a mistake as the not-fireball detonated in a flash of obliterating light. Eradicating Kri from Eternia and whisking his soul away to a memory Core as the demon promptly died with a pathetic squeak.

The attacker worried for a moment that he might have hurt the Pandas, but to his surprise they were not only entirely unharmed, but extremely buff! The Pandas had gained a temporary boost to their strength from the rampant celestial affinity filling the space. Though that translated to 'light' in Eternia, it seemed to accomplish the same effect.

Partially confused, but not complaining in the slightest, the Red Pandas released a victorious war cry as they shook their makeshift spears. Upon figuring out their leader had actually been possessed, and that this mysterious stranger had just released them from servitude—given the demerits that vanished from their status sheets when they checked—they excitedly released wild cheers!

Another notification popped up, forcing Artorian to physically move them out of the way to organize them in a fashion that allowed him to read them. Why had this been so convenient when he meditated? He sort of just knew then, and now these darn things were physically in the way. This was a terrible game design choice!

Giving the matter some thought, he closed his eyes for a spot of meditation and understood all the notifications without needing his eyes to read over them.

Character trait gained: Relentless Demonbane

This character's abilities and skills are twice as effective against dark-based entities and their adjacents. Such as infernal-affinity creatures.

"A character trait?" Certainly handy, and he absolutely agreed with the listed effect. Smacking demons down? Yes please, with a cherry on top! The next notification was a *fat* one. Most likely, it was the result of what his attack had turned into after that momentary crack of nasty static.

Ability gained: Resplendent Obliterator

Sourced from: 'Fireball'

This ability functions similar to Resplendence field, with the exception that it happens as an explosive burst rather than as a sustained effect. This ability will drain 28% of your maximum mana per use, calculated as if there are no effects currently detracting from your maximum mana.

Damage is calculated based on the 'healing' ability that your Resplendence field would have ordinarily drawn from. The attack range and area of effect is calculated based on the user's rank with the actual 'Fireball' ability. If the user does not have the 'Fireball' ability, then the attack range is fifty feet, and the area of effect is a five-foot radius.

Explanation notice: If you have one hundred maximum mana, this ability will drain twenty-eight mana on use. If you have effects active that alter your new maximum mana to fifty, this ability will still cost twenty-eight mana.

Notice: This is a compound ability requiring active intent. This ability will not inflict damage on any sources the user didn't specify, and will instead function as a healing burst with the stated effects listed in Resplendence field. Specified targets will gain none of the listed bonuses, and will only be affected by the damage calculation.

Notice: This ability cannot be used if the user is incapable of clear thought. Light-based creatures and their adjacents are immune to any damage this ability might cause. This ability is twice as effective against dark-based entities and their adjacents.

Notice: Are you doing this to me on purpose? What did I just warn you about? Karmic Luck -5.

Notice: I refuse to allot you any more compound abilities that you do not have the requisite abilities or skills for, imported or not. I will strike them from the ledger! A specialization title: 'Overhealer' has been added to your options once you achieve level 10. If you wish to pursue the path of accosting your enemies by healing them into oblivion, you must take that specialization before I allot even a single ability that allows this theme again.

"Forget oof. Advance straight to *Big Oof.*"

Eternium was not happy with him in the least, and crunchy crackers it was *another* expensive one. This compound mess was equally as text thick as his field ability, and also functioned based on abilities he simply didn't have yet.

He needed to read the explanation twice before noticing an

oddity. He'd wiped that demon from the map in one go, but wasn't able to figure out exactly how much damage he had dealt to it. There was also this confusion on doubling. Relentless Demonbane doubled his damage against the Caligene Psychomancer. Based on the fireball's description, that doubled it again. However, it was derived from the field ability, which had in its text that it also doubled.

So did that mean three instances of doubling, or two? How did that work? Or was there a secret stacking interaction with the way multipliers were counted? He honestly didn't know, and shoved it to the side for now. There were more notifications to attend to.

You have killed a level 22 Psychomancy Demon (Young). Heroic feat completed! All stats except Karmic Luck +2! Exp: 3,000. Notice: Attribute increase withheld due to region limits.

Artorian felt his feet leave the ground, his body bathing in a golden light as he experienced what must be a 'level up.' Having achieved enough experience to go up a level. Maybe two? He needed to look up the experience table or something. Or he could just quickly check his level. Two. He was level two.

For defeating an opponent more than 20 levels above you, you gain the title: Legend.

Title gained: Legend. You have killed a being more than twenty levels above your own! Your name will be whispered through history; will the whispers be full of admiration or loathing? Effect: Doubles reputation gains and halves reputation losses. +25% damage against opponents who have a higher level than you. -25% damage against opponents who have a lower level than you.

Even Artorian considered this cheating, and he couldn't say he liked it. He was all for getting rid of demons quickly, but something didn't sit right concerning the pace of advance through this supposed game. Perhaps… perhaps he should pick up something basic. Build up from that instead. How long had it been since he'd picked up a bow? He should look into that.

*Reputation with the Red Panda Tribe increased by 4000! (2000*2 from title.) Having begun at reputation rank 'Neutral,' you have reached the reputation rank of 'Ally.'*

Neat! Now they'd hopefully not stab him just for existing. Though given his passive health restoration gains, he was starting to have doubts whether they could out-damage the healing taking place. It would still hurt, if his tumble through the fields was any indication of functional pain receptors.

Hidden Quest (Uncommon) completed: Red Panda Tribe Liberation. You completed a quest that no one knew was a quest by destroying a demon nobody should have known was there. Not only did you defeat the demon, but you did not allow any nearby innocents to perish! By completing seemingly impossible requirements and saving those that should not have survived, the rating of this quest increased from Uncommon to Rare. Reward options have increased!

Automatic rewards: Advance to character level 3!
Reward options: (Choose one)
Gain currency.
Gain regional attire.
Gain regional language. (new)

The golden level up glow occurred again, but its splendor went by the wayside. Artorian was angry. He did his best to repress it, but had there been an Aura on him it would be fuming with distaste. "Uncommon? What did the system mean, 'uncommon'? How many tribes, villages, settlements, and civilizations have demon problems for something like this to be listed as abyss-blasted *uncommon*?"

Taking deep breaths, he opened and closed his hands to

stretch them and release tension. He wanted to find every last one and stomp it nice and hard into the ground. It was taking him longer than expected to reach a state of calm. Even with the skill. Was his character trait interfering and keeping his blood boiling on the topic longer than it should? No, it wouldn't matter if it did. He was responsible for his actions, and if he knew he was angry, then he was equally responsible for applying additional restraint.

These Panda people were innocents, and not at all the culprits fueling his rage. They were victims, and fully deserving of every last drop of compassion he could muster. Relief washed over his spine and shoulders as he considered such things. He selected the third reward in the list so he could speak to the Pandas, and exhaled a smooth few words in their native language. "That is so much better."

Several of the Pandas were flexing at one another, showing off how strong they were in the moment as they savored a victory. The sudden addition of words they understood from the tall creature made them tense up, but the soothing feeling he was still emanating set them at ease.

Artorian smiled at them, his hands clasped together. "Hello again. I do so apologize for causing a ruckus. As I said before, though I know now I wasn't understood, terribly sorry about your field. I'd love to help fix the damage I caused. I stumbled fairly egregiously."

The Pandas didn't have a reply for him until a grunt from Woffo garnered their attention. Several of his people dropped their weapons in order to attend to him, some jumping over tables to get there at the speed of a full sprint. Artorian said and did nothing as the Pandas got their chieftain some much needed normal water. The cleanse effect in Artorian's Aura was helping, but nothing beat a cold cup of crystal spring water.

Once their chieftain was situated, Woffo assessed the situation and spoke freely. "My thanks on behalf of my people, and myself, stranger. I was unable to tell them of my plight. My people needlessly suffered while I was forced to watch from behind my own eyes. Unable to act as I wished. I felt in my heart some of my people knew something was amiss, and I will speak with them about it later. For now, I wish to bid you welcome to our tiny tribe, small and broken as it is. May we know of you, luminous one? I am Woffo, chieftain of the Red Panda tribe. I apologize that I cannot greet you properly, as even though I feel healthy, I am weakened by... recent events."

Artorian nodded, understanding that being possessed might take a toll on a person, and even his tricks couldn't fix that... yet. "Feel free to call me... Love. I believe that's the moniker I might go by here. I'm aware it's a little odd. I'm glad I could help, though I don't believe I am done. I really would like to fix the fields I damaged. If that's allowable."

Woffo couldn't help but laugh. "You come into my tribe, release me from terror, free my people from servitude, and you ask if it is *allowable* that you repair our fields? What manner of creature are you, *ally* named Love? For I know none with a mind or powers such as yours, and I have lived for a lengthy forty years."

It was one thing for the system to establish his relation to this tribe. It was another entirely to hear it spoken from Woffo's smiling mouth. Hey, even Woffo's teeth were being cleaned by his field effect? Sweet! No reason to turn it off then. Interesting how he was referred to as a creature. Was Woffo aware he was a humanized Red Panda, and thus played into the assumption Artorian had a similar effect going?

Artorian beamed. "Well, could we go and have a walk together? I'd love to hear about what's been going on, and I would be delighted to tell you a bit about myself. I may be capable of a few tricks, but to be fully honest, Chieftain, it is *I* who is in dire need of guidance."

Woffo was off his chair and ignoring his walking stick altogether as he marched to the door where Artorian waited. His people nearly fell over themselves with worry that he didn't have his stick, or any of the other needs their leader normally required. Woffo was old! Forty was a good ten years past their average lifespan!

Woffo didn't care. He felt like a youngster again, and the warmth radiating off his new ally only bolstered his confidence that they were going to be alright. "It would be my great delight and pleasure to attend this stroll."

With a scrambling mess of pandas in tow, Artorian and the chieftain went on an enthusiastic walk.

CHAPTER EIGHTEEN

Repairing the tribe's entire domain took perhaps two days. The fields were re-tilled in an hour, and raw materials were distributed with an ease and speed that left the majority of the tribe flabbergasted. A score of seven hundred plus strength was nothing to scoff at, and Love's work ethic was a thing of wonder.

At the end of the second day, their settlement had a brand-new moat dug out around the village, several tons of building materials, a small molded hill that served as the start of a wall, and enough supplies derived from nearby large animals that would let them last two whole seasons!

Artorian hadn't gained any experience from the captured animals, but then again he also hadn't killed them. More of a… gentle nudge to put them to sleep. He should invest in a sleeping field effect when Eternium wasn't miffed at him.

His Wisps had made themselves known in the forest once he'd been alone again. They'd caught up and explained that unless it was just him, they were under protocol to remain completely hidden and out of all events. They were observers first, not really allowed to interfere.

Oberon had said that last part with a devious smirk, to which Artorian responded by knowingly tapping the side of his nose. There was always a way around the fine print…

Once back in the Panda village, Artorian sat down on a foot-high stone wall the farmers were building. Since food wasn't going to be a problem for a while, the tribe could focus on other matters. It was the sight of some of the kids actually being out and about to play that made his heart drop like a bag of abandoned bricks.

Forget the experience and the skills. That sight? That sight was everything. Dumb giggling. Haphazard laughter. Just good simple fun by free minds that didn't need to fear the world.

One of them tumbled over another and exploded in a cloud of puffy smoke to become… a normal Red Panda? Artorian gawked. "You can turn *back*?"

His outburst of a statement didn't go unnoticed, and the very much animal-shaped tiny Panda children bounded up to him. They knew something he did not! It was showoff time! They spoke over one another, but Artorian got the gist of it. He kept his hands on his knees while bending forwards to listen, while the cluster of Red Pandas bundled and crawled on one another to be the voice at the top of the pile.

In short, you could 'suppress' the title allowing your humanization. That was all well and good, but he didn't have the 'Humanization' title. He had the Additional Nature title. Considering it again, didn't that mean nothing was stopping him from swapping out of that nature? He just didn't know how at the moment, and 'Dale'ing it was difficult when there was no cliff to throw yourself off.

Also, even if he could—should he? His control over that form was still fairly abysmal, and smashing into the ground when the town was finally starting to come together was not a pleasant consideration. He shelved it for later, nodding at the Pandas. "Thank you, my dears. Go play, go…"

Woffo exclaimed a pleasant natured 'ha!' on approach. He was using his walking stick again, age having caught up after the bonuses faded. "Love! There you are. I hear you've torn through enough to-do lists to put my own exploits to shame. I can't imagine our tiny village was the endpoint of your journey, so after that long chat we had, I thought it would be best if you took these."

Artorian accepted the bundle, and gave it a look through after. Inside a simple bag that was nothing special, he found two sets of altered clothes that would roughly suit his size. "Why thank you kindly. That'll be nice while passing through this region. Let me put one of these on right away. Though, my friend, even I can tell this gift is a poor excuse for what it is you want to ask me. I can see the frown creased deep on your face. Come now, what's the real worry?"

Woffo eased himself next to the human, 'oof'ing as he sat down. "There are many tribes afflicted with the problem we had. In fact, you will find... scant few locations that aren't in some way inconvenienced. I wish to convey some wisdom I gained while stuck behind my own eyes."

Love the ally nodded, waiting for Woffo to speak further. "There is a strict, exacting hierarchy amongst those vile creatures. If one of their superiors calls them, they must come. It happened twice while I was ensnared, and the trip was swift and done with great haste. While you may feel inclined to go tribe by tribe to put out small fires, I would instead ask if you would... apply your significant powers to the larger threats? Removing those would also free us of the lesser evils. Though I'm afraid I've nothing further to give or offer you past what I have. I've been informed I could make this a 'Quest' via the world lore. Those windows with text, I mean. Different people call them different things."

Love gently patted Woffo's shoulder. "It's fine, my ally. I would have done so just from the information gained. If anything, that brings relief, since it will save me a lot of time if I can rush towards the bigshots."

The chieftain nodded, and offered his small hand for a wrist shake. "Then it would be my great honor, if I could call you extended family."

Quest gained: Extended Family.
The Chieftain of the Red Panda tribe has offered you an extension of your current reputation; you may accept or decline without penalty.
Notice: This is a test of the quest system, Karmic Luck +1 if assisting.

Artorian took the offered grip, and softly shook it. "The honor is mine, my delightful furry friend."

Quest completed: Extended Family.
Your reputation with the Red Panda Tribe has increased from 'Ally,' to 'Extended Family.' You gain: Karmic Luck +1 for assisting.

Hopping off the small stone wall, he swung the bag over his shoulder to fasten the rope about his chest. He didn't want it flying off when he started his run. "Can you point me in the direction of where the biggest demon is hiding out?"

Woffo pointed north. "Can't miss it. It's a massive multi-spired castle with blackened walls and matching decor. A moat filled with bubbly hot red stuff surrounds it, and the sky cracks with lightning. The place is utterly infested with Psychomancers and Warriors. Several hundred of each. It's their big hub. You'll cross two more actual towns along the way, and an unknown number of tribes trying to do what we are with our village. Which is set up away from it all."

Artorian thought that the demon's location screamed evil villain base. It was outright trying too hard. Still, nice and recognizable worked just fine for him. He nodded. "Any idea where I might pick up a bow? Maybe some arrows."

Woffo shook his head no. "First or second town maybe, but I don't have a good answer for you."

Artorian appreciated it regardless. "Well alright then. I'm going to walk a good distance away from the tribe before I set off. I'm going to cause a bit of a gust on launch."

Woffo didn't quite grasp what Love meant, until he watched from the top of the sort-of-wall hill. When Love was a few hundred feet out, he adopted this odd, low to the ground pose. Following a push of air and a blast of dirt that carpeted the area behind where he'd stood, Love was gone. Only a hole the size of a small lake remained behind.

After gawking a moment, Woffo just raised his stick and cheered.

"About time!" Oberon winked into visibility next to a full-speed Artorian. "That took two whole days! Are we back on track for demon derby dancing?"

"We are," Artorian confirmed for the Wisp, which improved his mood. "Though I need a few things. It's been a while since I laid siege to a castle, and while I did it alone the last time as well, I had more tools to work with. I need a weapon. One that I can work toward a specialization with. I don't like that Over-healer option mentioned in the notice. I doubt I'm going to be able to rely on my mana bar to pull my keister out of the fire every time, regardless of all these pretty bonuses I'm sitting on. I need my bases covered. Tell me you know where I can get a bow."

"I know where you can get a bow, but *now* I can't tell you. That was far too overt," Oberon grumbled back as Yvessa made herself visible. "That one reported me for trying to sneak around the rules. I'm working under a sizable demerit right now."

Yvessa's green ball of light snapped right back at him. Though she enunciated her last word on purpose. "Well if you'd done things properly then I wouldn't have had to. I have to report what I *observe*."

Oberon looked to Artorian, but his only reply was a tap to the side of his nose. *Details, details…* Their human spoke up mid-run as a forest blew by his right side. "I'm just going to run to the first town I was made aware of by Woffo. That information I received legitimately. Also, I need to develop several abilities, and I need to do it in short order. I don't like my Karmic

Luck being at a negative nine, and negative fourteen doesn't sound any better if I get slapped with another penalty like that. Any ideas?"

Yvessa had a quick idea. "It's in the log. Just pick up the base abilities or skills you plan to import a derivative from, and you should be fine, though finding those may be more difficult than you may like. Fireball is classed as a spell, meaning you will need a Mage class to teach it to you."

Oberon looked affronted, his coloration half-red, half-orange. "Why can *you* tell him things without penalty? I mean I'm not going to report on you either way, but still!"

The green Yvessa radiated hummed with sneaky pleasure. "I didn't tell him anything he didn't already know. I'm just reading from the log, and repeating information he's heard or read before. I did nothing against the rules."

Artorian smirked. "Oh, you two are *clever*. I like it. Very well then, I'll try to come up with something. On top of my current schemes-in-progress. Oh, if possible, I'd like to not take quests. I don't want to deal with a confusing fat log of tasks that I will inevitably forget about. If I'm not doing it in the moment, I don't want it kept in mind. If it's important enough I'll put it in a personal note, and otherwise I want to decline both the task and reward. Someone else can test quests."

An area boss jumped out of the way of the Artorian-train, alert and bristled as whatever had just rolled past it hadn't bothered to stop or turn around in the slightest. The oversized leopard was confused, but didn't think about it again as it watched the clouds above twist in the wake of the speedy thing moving away. It was out of the ordinary for it not to be attacked because of what it was, so it certainly didn't mind that it wasn't bothered for long.

"Did I just pass a leopard?" Artorian asked his Wisps, who checked the rules before seeing if they could answer.

Yvessa got through her list first. "You did. Didn't injure it either, but so long as you're running on ground-level there's going to be a chance you either bowl over something, or run right through it and make a big splatter. You're also ripping up the landscape by going the speed you are. I know you're keeping below boom-speed on purpose, but you're an environmental hazard. Midgard wasn't built for this. In addition, your mana regeneration is so freakishly demanding. When you need to recover any, you drain the area of so many resources that other people are going to get ugly penalties to their regeneration while you're around. I also have a question."

Artorian glanced at her, but needed to return to what was in front of him or he'd smash right through a tree. "Go ahead."

Yvessa asked. "Why a bow? That weapon works very poorly with your attributes. At least a sword would add your strength to it when calculating raw damage, so long as your stamina holds up. An arrow will not."

Stabilizing his breathing, he explained. "It's that specialization thing. I don't want to build one that involves a sword. I don't quite know how the numbers work, but swords here will do what? Around ten to thirty damage? That's just a loose guess. If my strength is added onto the number, then the difference between using a sword and just slapping something is moot. The bow is an old flame of mine; something I *want* to do. That means more than picking up something I'd be good at, just because I match it well. If I don't have the passion for the task or craft, then what's the point? I'd rather be slightly worse at what I do if it means I'm doing something I love."

Yvessa sort of accepted the answer. "Okay. I'm following so far. Though classes in Eternium are vast by themselves, and specializations let you dig into almost anything you can think of. I have doubts that a thinker like you would be content with just putting a pointy stick into someone from far away."

Artorian stuck his pointer finger up. "About that! Even big thinkers need tasks that let them lose themselves for a while. It's no good to do the same thing all the time. No matter how good you are at it. When I was younger, I didn't pick up the bow because I was good at it either. I picked it up because when I pulled that string back, I was lost to the world. I heard the brush of the wind. Felt the tension of the waiting possibility between my fingers. I enjoyed the silence of the focus. No amount of being clever helped me in that moment. It was just me, and this moment of potential that made everything else fall away."

A smile bloomed on his features. "Until suddenly, the conditions were right! Then my fingers loosed, and I felt the barest moment of feathers brushing against my cheek as potential turned to action. There is a liberty in that feeling. A sameness that occurred regardless of how many times I pulled back that arrow. The feeling is raw, and real, and constant. I bet that even in this game world with numbers instead of truths, I can find solace in that sublime moment once again. I'm not picking up the bow because I expect it will be effective. I'm picking up the bow because I expect it will keep me *sane*."

CHAPTER NINETEEN

Artorian didn't get a response from either of the Wisps after that revelation. Oberon was silent because he was furiously adding psychological screening needs to his report, since that aspect drastically affected a person's time in Eternia. Artorian had uncovered a good point. This wasn't the world where he wanted to be. This was a world where he *had* to be.

The topic of cultivators being in the game had come up more than once in discussions before. Additional difficulties had presented themselves each time. These people had achieved a level of power either out in Cal, or out in the real world before Cal. That achievement, without doubt, had taken such a large chunk of their personal and development time, over the period of time they'd been alive, that being in Eternia alone was... almost an insult. Especially since it forced them to use a system they neither knew nor wanted to know.

Eternium stripped them of all they had, and traded it in for some numbers. Numbers that meant nothing. Numbers that didn't replace a Mage's invulnerability, nor several other truths of life that many Mages had grown accustomed to. Well-practiced abilities had to be relearned, and that scathed many a mind. That Eternium required them to have specific prerequisites, which were honestly a pain to obtain, didn't help either.

Artorian was being a good sport about it. Yet Oberon was convinced that had it not been for the support Sunny had outside, and the burning personal drive to eradicate every last demon so his own family would never need to deal with them, he wouldn't be here either.

Yvessa was quiet because she didn't know how to help. As a caretaker, she could do a lot. Yet when a person gave you the exact mindset they were operating under for them to remain okay, that was hard to make snappy commentary on. She was convinced he'd have been better off with anything other than a bow, but that comment was stuck in her metaphorical throat.

She'd feel dirty for saying those words, and thus she didn't. Yvessa vividly remembered him as the old nobody in the Fringe, who actually managed to pull off something as insane as stealing their little ones back from a raider pack, and came home as a Mage? That family reunion in the Fringe had nearly made her weep, and no amount of not having tear ducts in this moment detracted from that being a sensitive personal memory.

Oberon broke the silence, though only to leave some in his wake. "I need to go talk with my dungeon. I'll be back when it's convenient."

The orange Wisp winked out via teleport, leaving Yvessa to follow Artorian alone. That was fine. It was supposed to be her job anyway. When she was able to, she spoke. "You have a way with words, old man. If you want people to talk, they talk. If you want them to be quiet, they're quiet. I don't know what your Speech skill is at, but I've flagged it for review."

That got a chuckle out of him as he dodged out of the way of some trees, only to notice that the sound under his feet had changed. Oh, he was on a lake! Oh, crackers, that meant he couldn't stop or he'd be going for an unplanned swim. Please let there not be some swimming skill he needed just so he wouldn't drown... "Yvessa, on a more pressing note. How am I running on water?"

The Wisp glanced, and thought that this should be some kind of achievement. "I guess you're just going fast enough? Physics isn't my strong suit, even with the memory gifts. Personally, I want to see what happens if you slow down. Sploosh?"

Artorian refused for the moment. "Young lady, I have no idea what my current weight or density is. If I am too heavy, I will sink to the bottom like an Iridium Li, and unless there's some secret Eternium rule that allows humans to breathe water, I am just going to keep making waves and get to the other s—"

Whumm.

His gaze snapped downwards, then behind him before he was forced to look in the direction he was going again. Yvessa looked behind her as well, not needing to keep track of what was in front of her to keep glued to his shoulder. "Hmm? What? You just stopped in the middle there. That's not like you."

"Are character traits supposed to *hum*?" Artorian asked outright. He'd passed over a location that had caused his trait to... resonate? He'd physically heard some kind of chime. "That was new."

Yvessa was already several pages deep into his character information, then cleared her throat and read over her improvised spectacles. "Traits and titles may incur short, temporary resonance effects when in close proximity to a hidden object, person, or thing that it should reasonably have a sympathetic bond to. This is currently a system mechanic that will later be developed into Magical Synesthesia, when Pylons are available."

Artorian's shrewd nose smelled something foul. "Alright, now I'm with Oberon. How are you able to tell me things I clearly shouldn't be allowed to know?"

Yvessa glowed a wholesome forest green. "Who's going to report on me? *Me*? I need to make logs on what I *observe*. The last log entry is that you're running on water and we should have something for that. Otherwise, I changed my mind on being a stickler for the rules. Oberon is... Honestly, I thought he was irritating, but new details are coming to light that are making me understand certain Fae perspectives. If I can get away with sneaking in innocuous details, fine... It's not like many other people are going to have a forced Observer Wisp title they can't get rid of. I may as well find ways to be helpful in my own way. Snapping at you all the time is... Y'know, I kind of don't like it."

Her charge just smiled warmly at her, making her hover away an inch. "*What?*"

Artorian's voice was grandfatherly. "Just look at how far you've come, my dear. You're not the only one who remembers the Fringe days. From an uncertain little girl, into a headstrong woman, to a near-Matron keeping an entire camp alive with the skills of her spoon. Now a Wisp! A different *race* entirely. Through trial and tribulation, you've punched from the ground like a bouquet that doesn't know how to quit. *To bloom out of great drought,* indeed. If any meaning was right for your name, it most certainly was that one."

Yvessa felt apprehension, but pleasant afterwards. "Yeah... I'd say it was. So, do you actually speak Elven, or did you make that up, that night in the tent?"

The old man she knew smiled from behind the young face it was currently occupying. "Does it matter?"

Yvessa kept quiet a moment, then made the choice for herself. "No. No it doesn't. I made it true, and that's what matters."

Her charge nodded sagely in response, flashing a proud smile. "That's right... Let's see anyone try to take that from you again. They don't even realize the abyss they're in for. Speaking of! I think I'm going to turn around and check that resonance. The curiosity is killing my C'towl, and no amount of going fast should mean I shouldn't have some fun on the way. Life is made of detours!"

His Wisp was honestly glad for the change in topic, though the arc Artorian had to take to turn around on water was ridiculously wide. Did this qualify as a lake? Wasn't this the prototype for the mini sea? The water body lacked waves, but with the oomph Artorian was adding, that problem might just fix itself.

He also gave her work right away with another question. One that rather mattered this time. "If I'm going to go underwater, I need to create some abilities as preparation. What method would annoy Eternium the least?"

Oberon was the right Wisp for this, but he wasn't here right now. So she just threw a dart at the ideas board. "Based on the horribly little I know of Pylons, it's easier to make active ones do something slightly different than it is to light up entirely new ones. So... making new functions out of toys you already have? It might also help if I sent in a notice you were going to mold certain effects beforehand."

She flipped through a few screens. "Empowerment is a flat trade from your mana to your physical attributes. Not much to go on there. Let's see. No, no, not that one either, no. Presence? You made the obliterator out of that and fireball. Shame you don't actually have Fireball. My vote would be that building abilities out of the Presence ability would annoy this dungeon the least. So... if you know what you're wanting to do, I'll send it up."

Artorian rattled off ideas that had been tumbling around in his noggin for a while. "Sure thing. An air bubble or shell for starters. I like breathing! Some kind of sustenance ability, similar to how cultivators feed their body using Essence. I barely had to eat as a Mage, even if I loved to do so. I badly want to import flight, so I don't need to swim around down there. Though if building the effect out of Presence is the preference, well, there we have it."

He considered other ideas. "I need a method to see underwater. So I need either the thing I had as a Long that let me notice the electrical fields, or becoming flat-out able to see in pitch dark. I know abyss-well how light works, and it doesn't play friendly in deep water."

Yvessa noted it down. "I have it. Anything else for the future you already know you're interested in? Less backlash might be worth sharing."

He sighed, knowing full well that was a Fae moment if he had ever seen one. "Uh huh. You just want to know so you have less headache in the future. Well alright, I'll tell you this time. Not much reason to keep secrets. I want to import my predictive sight, even if it has been bloody useless against infernal things. The 'someone else's problem' field effect. My sleeping Aura. The original version of my Presence that I used to absorb affinity attacks and constructs, and maybe see about importing my personal brand of martial arts. The 'No' style."

His observer Wisp had it all down. When he stopped talking for a while after, Yvessa figured he was done. She sent it off as they were approaching the spot where Artorian experienced his tiny resonance event. "I thought you didn't like naming things, or styles for that matter. Actually, I don't remember you putting much value in the entire concept of styles."

Artorian shrugged, slowing down bit by bit. "I learn some things fast. I learn some things slow. I came around to the styles thing, it just happened at the latter speed. No amount of me being good at learning makes me not horribly stubborn when I want to stick to my prejudices."

Yvessa snorted, as if he'd just spoken a universal truth. "You and everyone else, old man. The report is sent. So… try what it is you're going to try."

Water couldn't break, but Artorian did use it as a launching point for his jump. Since he, for fun, decided to cannonball his way into the middle of what was essentially a small sea. Forget lake. It didn't even have a name yet.

The resulting wave from one enthusiastic boy's *skadoosh* easily reached thirty feet in height. He'd taken a nice big breath, and dropped right into meditation. Just for safety's sake, he left his Resplendence field on.

Once present in his center where the Penrose Triangle lived harmlessly, he got right to work. Technically, this counted as importing. No way it didn't. He knew how to shape and move air Essence so a nice snug ball of it surrounded him. Hopefully his active field would keep the stored air within it breathable.

When he moved the Essence like he should in order to create the effect normally, a notification came up before he was even halfway done. The effect listed wasn't at all what he was trying to do, though he had to admit the ability worked fine given what he needed it for.

Ability: Presence
Utilization: Omnibreath
Zones affected: Inner, Body, Outer.

Omnibreath allows the user to breathe air, water, gasses, or other harmful vapors in order to satisfy the user's breathing requirements. This does not protect the user from harmful effects that may be involved.

Flat cost: 12% of total mana. Equal to 4% per active zone. Only the Inner zone is required for this ability to function. Adding the Body zone removes some minor harmful effects, while adding the Outer zone extends this effect to others around the user.

If the Outer zone is active, this becomes a field-based ability. A field ability is indiscriminate, affecting any valid target present within the radius. The radius is determined by 30r, where r represents the rank of this ability. Individual levels are not taken into account to calculate the radius.

Notice: **Fine**.

Fueling some mana to flicker on the ability the cheapest he could get it, Artorian dropped out of meditation in a hurry. Right away he noticed that he was wet, cold, and surrounded by water on all sides. Holding his breath had not prevented him from sinking, so he was heavier than ordinary after all.

He didn't really want to let his precious breath escape, but he needed to know if the ability worked. Or if Eternium had just played a truly terrible prank on him. The **Order** triple S-ranker wouldn't... would he?

Releasing his breath, he hoped for the best and drew in a big one. Oh, sweet crackers and toast. Thank Eternium for not stabbing him in the kidney there. With his Karmic Luck in the negatives, he was thoroughly expecting the sneak attack. His relief lasted a delightful three seconds before Eternium turned on all the Pylons having anything to do with thermohaline circulation. The ocean now had motion, and it swept him along as if someone was holding him by the ankle while surfing on a slipstream.

Artorian's only true response was something akin to *hrmblrmlbl*!

That negative Karmic Luck had gotten him in the end, much to Eternium's great amusement. Yvessa had been right. A heads up vastly improved the dungeon's mood on the subject of ability creation. Though it had not spared Artorian from some improvised repercussions. Eternium was starting to understand what Cal had been trying to explain to him for years. Karmic Luck was a tool for *fun*!

He was required to give Artorian positive Karmic Luck points equivalent to what he was putting him through, but that was allowable while his Karmic Luck remained in the negatives. As soon as it hit zero, though, he needed to play it more hands-off. Then again... At the rate Artorian was racking up the negatives...

Oh, he'd blocked off using multiple Karmic Luck events in a row, hadn't he? Well, no time like the present to change one's mind! Eternium had to make sure the underwater currents worked, and here was a convenient system-approved target. A trackable one, no less.

Congratulations, Artorian, you're a buoy!

CHAPTER TWENTY

Artorian's undersea rollercoaster ended only when Eternium ran out of negative Karmic Luck points to play with. Still, the dungeon both made serious progress and had a good time. Confirming his sea currents worked the way they were supposed to. So, the codger deserved his break.

No longer trapped in interlocking current streams, the well-shaken and rather stirred victim broke the water's surface inside an underwater cavern. His grip clamped so tight on the rock as he dragged himself up and out that the stone shattered between his fingers.

Rolling onto the stable, non-spinning surface, Artorian just lay there for a minute and spat out water in a perfectly vertical line. Yvessa teleported in, nice and dry as she'd observed his entire trip from a comfortable distance. "Got so waterlogged you turned into a fountain?"

With a cough and wheeze, Artorian weakly rolled onto his stomach. Slowly pushing himself up with a grunt involving labored effort as his healing field gingerly patched him up, mending one horrible injury after the other. "Where...? *Why?* Oh my head..."

Curling up into a ball, the human held his skull in the hopes that it would make the awful ringing end faster. He kicked out at the notifications hovering nearby. Why did those things have to *follow you* if you didn't dismiss them? He was going to complain to the manager! As soon as he was able. Which was not right now. Maybe in five minutes. Five more minutes.

Two hours of not moving later, the last harsh negative effect finally cleared itself from his status. A deep breath punched him in the lungs when he was able to draw them in again. Even though the prickles hurt the tips of his fingers, he was glad for the feeling.

Yvessa silently hovered nearby. Both serving as the only illumination, and keeping track of how long it took for her charge to be okay again. She knew he'd be fine, but wasn't going to make a snappy comment. Not yet... "Feeling better?"

Sitting up on his keister, he weakly leered up at the green ball. "Couldn't have helped? Even a *little*?"

She bobbed in response, finally getting to make her sassy comment now that there was an invitation to. "I did. Just not in a way you've noticed yet."

He grumbled, holding his stomach. "*Mhm.* I should have asked the Pandas for food. Can you at least tell me how long I was being blindly bashed along underwater? It's rough to have no idea where you're going and not getting the chance to be of clear enough mind to drop into meditation. That was what? Several *hours* of being a tumbler?"

Checking the log, Yvessa went ahead and confirmed that. "You were used as something called a 'buoy' for one hour per point of negative Karmic Luck you had. You're back at a flat zero, and I have a really lovely aquatic map now. Which brings us to the thing you haven't noticed."

Artorian held up his pointer finger to motion for a pause. He was starting to feel better, thanks only to his field. Though he needed to dismiss these annoying notifications, preferably right now.

For traversing untold, unexplored leagues none have set foot or fin in before you, you have gained the title: Trailblazer.

Title gained: Trailblazer. You have provided so much mapping information on sea currents that you will now also be privy to current events in your area! While you have this title, you gain the ability: Mapping.

Ability gained: Mapping. Mapping provides the user with a new function known as 'Minimap.' This allows a person to pull up a map of the local area, filled in with as much detail as the user is able to perceive. The higher your perception, the better, broader, and more detailed your map! This is a general ability. Physically being in an area updates what you perceive to the global minimap! When you leave the area, your minimap will showcase that region in sepia tones in the quality and state it was observed as.

Notice: Ordinarily, you gain access to the global minimap once your rank in the ability reaches Master. However, the Trailblazer title locks this ability's rank at Grandmaster. This rank cannot be improved, and the ability will be lost entirely if the title is removed.

Artorian grumbled and dismissed it for the next one. Not in the mood.

Event notice: For taking fifty thousand consecutive points of damage over the course of multiple hours, and living through it, you have been awarded the exact amount of experience required to attain character level four.

Notice: You have been awarded a gift box for your efforts in system assistance. Please consult your Observer Wisp for use.

Notice: Several restrictions have been lifted from your Observer Wisp.

"*Fifty thousand?*" No wonder that entire trip had hurt so much. He didn't like that every notice caused its own popup. With that all nice and cleared, he felt much better about himself. That or his butt being lifted from the ground while being full-body bathed in golden light had something to do with it. Probably the latter, as his level up fully removed the residual side effects of his underwater trip.

He landed gently back on the rocky ground, and flopped purely to begin what would normally have been start-of-routine stretches. In hindsight, these didn't do much before a workout. After seemed far more useful. Lying on the ground, he poked the elephant in the room. "Alright. What happened?"

Yvessa's green glow wandered back from the cavern wall she'd been carving on. "Remember how you really irritated Eternium not so long ago? Very much on purpose? This is what happens in order for that score to be considered settled. Negative Karmic Luck lets our evil overlord, Eternium the dungeon master, toy with indirect effects that cause significant inconveniences. Nothing like directly smacking you in the face, but if a bear were to suddenly walk out of the woods when you really needed one not to... Things like that."

She made a small diagram appear using a trick he very much recognized. "Is that my Grid technique from Cal's Soul Space?"

She bobbed to say yes, and enlarged a particular square. Oh, it was the map! "Currently, we are here. Unnamed cavern fairly deep under the sea. Please notice it already..."

Given this was the third poke in the ribs that he was not perceiving something, Artorian stood up to have a proper look around. His smile shot into existence at the same speed his hands flung into the air. "My teleportation beacon!"

At the end of the cavern, which remained ever so barely visible in the dim Wisp-lighting, an unpowered beacon that Artorian had haphazardly plunked down during his Administrator days hid, tucked away in a corner. "Yvessa, if you had a body, I would *hug* you! You influenced the journey so I'd get deposited here! Though... I can't say I recognize what 'here' this is supposed to be."

"Check the name." Yvessa was right to the point, her light-providing form hovering right over the beacon now that he had properly seen it himself. Moseying right over, Artorian did so by pouring mana into the Artifact Structure. Properly fed, its lights blinked right into activity. This allowed Artorian to use his Inspect on it, and only then did he realize that Inspect wasn't an ability he had in his list. Neither was status. It was just something he could do. A topic to dig into later.

Artorian had a greater confusion when reading the information that came up. "This can't be right. According to this name and description, this is the beacon I put up for Henry and Marie to have their little getaways in my unfinished version of the Midgard Fringe. That ended up being a scrapped project. What's it doing all the way down here? I didn't put this here. I thought these couldn't be moved?"

His Wisp landed on the beacon, slowly adopting a human form so she could accept that promised hug. Watching from the sidelines while he'd lived through that harsh ocean coaster hadn't exactly been pleasant. "That's much better. So you're partially right, your beacons couldn't be moved. Everything else around them, on the other hand, very much can. Whole region chunks have shifted around across the iterations, modified afterwards."

He motioned to the beacon, his brow deeply furrowed. "How did you know this was one of my schemes?"

Yvessa stopped cold, her voice slipping and falling from the edge of the proverbial boat given the new higher pitch it gained. "I knew what now?"

Realizing she hadn't known, Artorian's mouth adopted the patented Tibbins expression. A face Yvessa knew extraordinarily well. Silently walking away without addressing it, he found some rocks that he pretended looked cozier than the rest. Sitting down in a hurry, he crossed his legs and dropped into meditation. Right as Yvessa turned just a little red and drew a massive breath to begin questioning him with.

Once in his center, he loudly hummed to himself to block out all the residual sound he swore he could still hear. He didn't know if it was his memories playing back the echoes of one of his caretaker's many outbursts or if he could *actually* hear her. Currently, he didn't want to know. Instead, he cobbled together the mana for something that would make the pain in his stomach go away.

When he looked up, a thin spherical beehive webway glowed with pristine gentle light around his Penrose Triangle. He didn't see a notification, so checked manually.

Ability: Presence
Utilization: Sustenance
Zones affected: Inner, Body, Outer.

Sustenance allows the user to replace their daily food and water intake needs by draining it from their chi instead. Allowing them to seek inwards perfection for weeks, if not months at a time. This is a Monk ability.

Notice: This ability has been adapted for use by the Generalist class.

Flat cost: 12% of total mana. Equal to 4% per active zone. Only the Inner zone is required for this ability to function. Adding the Body zone increases the beneficial effects of sustenance from 'fed and hydrated' to 'well fed and well hydrated.' Adding the Outer zone extends this effect to others around the user. If the Outer zone is active, this becomes a field-based ability. See prior abilities for the radius explanation.

Notice: Your restriction banning import abilities has been lifted. The -5 Karmic Luck penalty will apply for each instance. Now that we both know what that does. Using the Presence ability as a basis reduces this penalty by a value of 2. Informing your Observer Wisp of impending creations reduces this penalty by a value of 2 again. Karmic Luck -1.

The Tibbins expression lived strong today. Artorian didn't know how to feel about that last notice. He couldn't make all his imports from the Presence basis. He'd end up without a mana bar in no time flat!

What was he currently even at, if he used the maximum of

everything needed? Turning it all on at full blast to check, he ran quick numbers. Twenty-eight from his healing fields, twelve to breathe, twelve to not starve. Overall, fifty-two percent of his maximum mana was just gone. That was without stuffing points into Empowerment, which seemed to be limited only by the maximum mana amount he could cram into it. That didn't help him at the moment. He was going to need to pick and choose his zones more carefully, adapting them on the fly.

Checking his attributes, he saw that his Karmic Luck was at minus one. He didn't feel too good about bouldering that statistic all the way back down to the ocean floor. He now also considered that he'd gotten the event notice not out of accomplishment, but out of pity for being put through the wringer. That wasn't going to happen twice.

Event notice: Your Observer Wisp has activated your gift box.
Select one of the following three rewards:
A pouch of local currency.
A randomized piece of equipment.
A regional language.
Notice: Get back out here!

He sighed while in his center, and just cobbled together the next one after selecting the language option. Those were always useful, though it made him miss translation Bob. It didn't take very long for the next ability to be completed. Artorian was starting to get the hang of this!

Ability: Presence
Utilization: Electrosense
Zones affected: Inner, Body, Outer.

Also known as Electrolocation, Electrosense allows the user to detect electric fields. This is normally used by creatures who cannot rely on sight in order to gain information, such as sharks. This is a sea creature ability.

Notice: This ability has been adapted for use by the Generalist class.

Flat cost: 12% of total mana. Equal to 4% per active zone. Only the Body zone is required for this ability to function. Adding the Inner zone doubles the range of this effect. Adding the Outer zone extends this effect to others around the user. Follows prior field rules.

Notice: Again right away? Alright, another minus one it is. You must be abuzz with impatience. Actually, this is convenient for me. Your Karmic Luck has been set to zero, and a minus two event has been triggered.

Oh *great*. Now he *had* to drop out of meditation.

Opening his eyes, he came face to face with a very impatient humanized Wisp. She was sitting on her haunches in front of him, arms resting on her knees as she invasively leaned forwards. "Welcome back. You wanna tell me what the company is about? Or do you want to begin with fully explaining your scheme? If you drop back into meditation, I'm going to make you regret it."

Hanging his head in defeat, Artorian just moved his hand so he could be helped up. "It's not my day, is it? Though I'm doing this to myself. First things first. What company? Our dear dungeon master triggered an event; what happened?"

Yvessa flicked his shoulder after he was on his feet, sharply pointing behind him with a stern motion before disappearing. She snuck in a comment before being required to go quiet. "Not a what. A who. *Two* whos."

Artorian turned around. "We have *owls* as company?"

The two mostly humanized sharks he saw clamber their way out of the water were anything but feathery, and they looked at one another for a moment to process what was being said. The tiger shark smiled, showing off a whole big row of teeth before replying in the regional language. His voice sounded like gravel crunching. "No, but I would definitely say that we are a *hoot. Left shark best shark!*"

Pulling up their panels, Artorian decided he didn't like

negative karmic events one bit. These sharks were named 'Rip' and 'Tear,' respectively. Looking up, he wasn't sure where to even start with the twelve-foot-tall beings. His voice became just a pinch hesitant as he whispered to his invisible Wisp. "I'm going to have to wing this one."

CHAPTER TWENTY-ONE

Rip rubbed at his jaw after speaking; a crucial detail that didn't escape notice. Since Artorian already had the shark's character page up, he gave it a second glance and noticed a demerit labeled 'Toothache.' Since winging it was the programme du jour, this was the trip to Chasuble all over again, as far as Artorian was concerned. So, on with the show!

Loudly clapping his hands together, he smiled and strode right toward the massive duo. Answering them in the Aquatic language he'd just picked up from Yvessa's gift box. Artorian understood why Rip had sounded gravelly the moment he tried. This was a method of speaking one was only meant to use underwater, because his throat felt full of sand. "Well hello there! So lovely that we can converse right from the get go. Are you here to have those teeth seen to? That can't be feeling good. Come, come! Sit down and open wide."

Rip and Tear were both seasoned apex predators. Ordinarily, sharks tended to hunt alone. However, since the spike in their intelligence, they'd decided having a meal was better with company. Particularly the kind of company that helped hunt some of the tastier things deep down in the dark, which would otherwise remain unattainable if you went at it alone. For some creatures down there, that even meant you became the meal instead!

Life tip? If in doubt, bring a friend.

Their humanization increased their options, and they were both veterans in the ways of hunting. As sharks, they heavily preferred taking their prey by surprise. Following blood trails and smells wasn't their strong suit after some injuries to the nose, but there had been such a swath of it! Even when the world below had suddenly begun moving, they'd tracked the easy injured meal well enough.

With humanization, a small hurdle such as their prey escaping into an air-filled cavern was no longer a challenge, where for an ordinary shark that would have been the end of the hunt. Given their sizable girth and impressive statistics, especially since they were both a solid level twelve, Rip and Tear had few worries.

On the other fin, finding that the wounded prey was entirely unharmed, unafraid, and approaching them as if they were as threatening as a tiny yipping minnow… was a new experience entirely. That this odd creature also instantly knew of Rip's mouth pain, ordering him to open up, made both of the sharks' shoulders tense with concern.

"Well? I don't have all day. Get down here, tall boy. I don't want to have to clamber up and pry your mouth open just so I can see what's causing that abysmal cheek puff." Artorian impatiently bunny-tapped his foot in short and quick succession on the cavern floor. Yvessa may have vanished, but the soft green glow she was providing for the area had not. It was fine, he'd make some extra light for the ideas currently formulating.

Tear the hammerhead shark slowly turned to look at an equally confused Rip. This was not how things were supposed to go. Prey did not fuss at you and demand you open your mouth. Tear spoke before his brain caught up: "Why not?"

Rip slow blinked at his hunting partner, but also couldn't for the life of him figure out the danger. It was a first for food to actually want to crawl into his mouth of its own volition, but the mention of his exact pain still made it feel like he was missing something. Without reply, the lumbering shark lowered himself to a solid knee.

His mouth opened slowly, showcasing a vast cavern of pointy nommers as the weird man got to work. "Ah! There it is. Oh, my boy, you have an infection. What did you eat with poison in it? Do you brush your teeth or do these just fall out?"

Artorian's voice reverberated from the inside of Rip's mouth as he spoke. A space that also turned horrendously bright as he quick-formed a simple mana shape to make a tiny hovering light ball. He was momentarily surprised not to get a prompt, but didn't have time to think about it right now.

Rip frowned excessively hard with vast concern, his eyes darting to Tear who was making a face that clearly indicated he had no idea what in the deep waters was going on. Rip's hands motioned at the mouthful that was currently tugging on some of his teeth. Silently asking: "So do I bite down on it or what?"

Tear slowly leaned to the left without truly moving the majority of his body. More of a curious, 'I want to see' motion. His eyebrow equivalents slowly went up, hands rising to make a big x motion with his arms. Rip did not appear to be noticing that the thing in his mouth was plucking his bad teeth out. *All* his bad teeth. A feat Rip didn't even feel as the pile next to the creature's feet grew and grew.

Tear was so out of sorts he verbally replied instead of keeping it quiet. "Erm… just… stay put."

Artorian's voice reverberated from the illuminated toothy cavern. "That would be the clever thing to do. I'm almost done. I've found the culprit. You ate something overly acidic lately. Whatever that was, don't do it again. The acid is a goo and sticking to your gums where your teeth grow back in, causing them to take damage at the root. I've gotten almost all the acid and bad teeth. The last one is in the back so you keep steady while I pluck that one. It's going to hurt."

Rip motioned again, harder this time to silently ask: "*Now can I eat him?*"

Tear felt uncertain about that option, his eyes on the pile of teeth. That must easily have been *all* of Rip's teeth. "I… don't think you *can*."

Artorian's voice replied deep from within the no-longer-as-toothy cavern, believing the shark was talking to him. "No, no! I absolutely can. Let me just give this a—"

"*Ow!*" Rip jerked when the back teeth were pulled, tears welling in his eyes as that had been particularly painful. His mouth clamped down hard, but no teeth punctured the prey creature that was supposed to be an easy meal. Rip equally didn't like it when he felt hands push against the inside of his mouth, Artorian seamlessly muscling himself free.

"Alright. That's part one taken care of. Smile for me." The man seemed entirely unbothered by being smothered in shark-saliva once he hit the ground feet first. Artorian's grip pressed into his hips before lifting a hand, some kind of bright orb forming above it. "Nice and wide."

Tear quietly shuffled a step back, realizing too late that this person was a *caster*. "That doesn't look too friendly."

Artorian just waved the comment off with his free hand. "Oh no, it's fine, he's not a designated target."

Rip nervously smiled as told, his toothless expression pained. Could this entire stream of events end soon? At least the odd shiny orb wasn't for hi— *Bapf*!

The orb was hurled into Rip's mouth, causing an entirely new set of teeth to instantly develop in his mouth with a very noisy *shink*! Leaving him with a brand-new set of top-quality dentals. His finned hands snapped over his sore mouth, groaning at the sudden addition of bitey bits that he could very much feel again. Granted, no aching pain! Loved no aching pain.

Still rubbing his jaw as he opened and closed his mouth a few times to get a feel for his chompers, Tear continued backing up step by step as the caster slowly walked towards him. "Now it's your turn. Come, come. Don't make me climb you."

The hammerhead felt a chill in his tail when his back pressed up against the cavern wall. His tone sounded hesitant, the usual confidence feeling pulled from under his fins. "No, no, that's fine. Nothing wrong with Tear's teeth."

Artorian raised a disbelieving eyebrow. "Oh? Well then you have nothing to fear, my boy. You be good and take a knee."

Rip had never heard his friend whimper before. When the tiger shark looked over, Tear had clearly lost the interaction. The large creature was on a knee while Artorian illuminated the insides of his mouth, already hard at work making a tooth pile. Seeing said pile made Rip understand Tear's earlier apprehension. That was a lot of teeth...

Artorian's voice resounded from within Tear's mouth. "*Mhm*. Nothing good will come from lying to your elders, boy. You call these chompers healthy? You've got it worse than your friend over there. We're going to need to replace all of these."

Tear looked at Rip with pleading eyes, but the tiger shark was rooted to the spot. There was no way in the deep waters that this caster was *prey*. There was just no way. Physical might was one thing, but casters? Oof... Forget it. Still, Rip wanted to help his friend. Even if the resulting fate would be the same as his own. Which, granted, was one of positive repute.

He asked the caster his questions outright, his tone being a good deal more respectful than the playful big-boy banter from earlier. "What manner of creature are you, caster, that you do not fear sharks such as us? Your Humanization is so good, I cannot even discern your origin."

When Artorian extricated himself from Tear's mouth, he formed the same glowing orb and slapped it against the hammerhead's cheek. The shark's teeth grew back in with a healthy new set on the spot as well, leaving Tear to rub at his jaw. Also feeling much better about life.

The 'caster' warmed when hearing Rip's way of speaking had become friendlier. "Hmm? Oh. Nothing interesting. I'm just bumbling around looking for... a resonance. Hard to explain that. I don't suppose you know of any creatures possessed by demons? I know that's a touch specific. If not, introductions would be lovely."

Rip and Tear shared a look to get a feel of the other's reaction. As the sight that followed was the caster becoming a pristinely clean version of his prior self. Like he was using some kind of invisible power meant to clean himself. They had no clue about this demon business, since much larger problems were present. So, introductions it was.

Rip motioned at himself and his hunting brother. "We are Rip and Tear, hunters of the Octoid Authority. Our social ranks are low, so we do not have any say in larger matters. Little is demanded of us, so we tend to just eat and sleep. Uh... thank you? For taking the pain from us. My jaws no longer hurt. I am sorry that I thought you were prey; we did not know you were a caster."

Artorian took Tear by the hand, and walked the twelve-foot brute back to his friend as if he were a small child. "Oh, it's quite fine. Both of you dip your heads down a moment."

Uncertain, they both decided it was better to just not upset a caster. Those tended to come with social ranks, and that meant everything while within the bounds of the Authority. They felt sparks tingle through their noses as Artorian gently booped their snoots, and rubbed over them while allowing some of his healing effects to flow through. "All is well, my boys. You will never really know the value of a moment until it becomes a memory. I hope your lack of pain becomes your new normal; those aches can't have been pleasant. I've healed your noses; how do you feel?"

Both sharks went pink in the cheeks, entirely unaware that having their noses rubbed was a delightful, relaxing experience. They felt calmed, no longer tense and uncertain if they were the ones currently threatened in the deep. Artorian didn't get a response from either of them until he took his hands away, gently folding them behind his back.

Tear coughed hard out of embarrassment when he realized the bubbly state he was in, rising back up to full height to get a hold of himself. He rolled his shoulders, looking away to provide Rip an opportunity to compose himself as well. "Good. Yes. *Good.* I feel good."

"Excellent! Can I ask more about this Authority civilization of yours? Perhaps someone there has more information about the peculiar thing I'm looking for." Artorian clapped his hands together, happy this had gone well. He sat down on the ground, but both of the sharks were rubbing at their gills. They needed to get back into the water as just talking was starting to become pretty painful.

Artorian noticed a demerit appear on their character panels, and instead got back up. "Though perhaps that's better to do after a little swim. Let me finish turning this beacon on, and I'll be right in the water with you. Do wait for me, won't you?"

The sharks didn't think back-talk or backing out was going to lead to a long and prosperous life. Their noses being healed also gained the caster some reputation in their eyes. Nodding without speaking, they both dove back into the water. Artorian noted their demerits vanished before their panels winked out. Oh? He needed to keep a line of sight to the targets for those to stay active? Good to know. "Yvessa, still here?"

The humanized version of the green Wisp winked back to visibility, leaning against the wall next to the beacon. "Never left. Why'd you do that? I was certain you were going to just snap their necks and call it a day."

Artorian moseyed over to the beacon, shaking his head no. "No hurting the wildlife. Not even the big scary ones. They're all sweet children. Now... if I explain to you my scheme with the beacons, are you willing to help me activate them properly?"

Yvessa smiled from ear to ear. "I want every detail."

CHAPTER TWENTY-TWO

Bright and vigorous, the beacon hummed into full activity after about half an hour of mucking around. The sight made Artorian's smile match that of his Wisp, his hands wringing together like a cheap villain knockoff. "Beautiful. This won't do anything by itself, but it's the first step in a long set. Now why couldn't I do that earlier?"

Yvessa meddled with Artorian's titles, deactivating the title she'd temporarily allowed to be active. "I'm not telling you because you didn't fess up to me right away. Maybe next time. So, part one of the scheme is we're going to be looking for as many of these as we can?"

Artorian nodded, already on the way back to the water. "That's right. Now that I know how to activate and set them, it will go much faster though. This took a while. I hope those sharks are still waiting for me. If not, I'll ignore the resonance and just move on."

Hopping into the water, he was a little surprised to see both of them very much waiting for him. Though, *seeing* was the wrong word. With Electrosense on, he felt them nearby. Just like in his Long days. *Oh*, speaking of! He was underwater! It was safe to give that a try here.

Perhaps he should warn the boys? "You waited! How kind. Per your earlier questions, would you like to see the kind of creature I am, in my original base form? I would prefer you have a look, in the event it might cause issues for where we're going. I know nothing about your civilization's rules."

The sharks grinned wide, which was an imposing, toothy sight. Especially with their brand-new teeth! That was all the response Artorian needed. Though he surmised that one's base form may have an impact on that whole social rank thing. Perhaps if he was of specific fishy varieties, even the sharks might have a higher rank? That was speculation, so he just let himself sink, breathing in his first watery breath without issue. Gotta love that Omnibreath ability!

Repressing a title was difficult. Though, once he felt it was sort of like a lever that just needed to be shoved into one position or the other, he cranked it with ease and transformed on the spot. Water displaced by the tons as his form glowed bright celestine, bursting outwards in size from his teensy human silhouette to the full three-hundred-foot dragon. The size change alone induced panic in the sharks, forcing them to flee for a short while before they turned around to have a second look at what the caster had become.

Artorian tried some words. While he was horrendously loud, he found that speaking Aquatic underwater was the way to go. Rather than gravel and sand, it felt like his throat was full of gently popping bubbles! Speaking ever so barely tickled, making his dragon face contort into a constant half smile to repress his own giggles. "Oh, this is nice…"

Given that he was smiling, the sharks felt their hesitation and concern drop away. Unfortunately, his size made the duo keep a good distance between them. No wonder the caster hadn't been in the slightest concerned, he could easily eat *them*!

Artorian rolled himself in place, trying to get a feel for things since this was going to need much more practice than some human form. As a positive, he wasn't being slapped by the ocean floor at random. Bonuses! He perked up with a thought as he managed to get his serpentine sway to start moving him forwards. "I just realized I never introduced myself. Feel free to call me Love. Shall we go? I'm looking forward to seeing this place!"

Rip felt outclassed here, an uncomfortable feeling. "Erm. Certainly! We can take you as far as the gates. We're not allowed to pass."

Artorian managed to slowly wiggle his way between them, being reminded that stopping was, as usual, not something he had great control over. "Oh? Why's that?"

The trio swam along, both sharks keeping ahead of him with minimal effort since he was going slow in comparison. They didn't know if he was giving them so much leeway on purpose, or if he was actually that slow. They didn't question it while Tear filled him in. "We're required to have a specialization, or casting ability, or special title to gain the social rank that would allow us re-entry. We may have grown up in the safe coral shallows, but as soon as we could hunt on our own, we haven't been able to return."

This didn't sit well with the caster, and they could tell since his smile dropped away. "Gating entry by usefulness? *Mmm.* What would you both need to qualify for this specialization? Given I think you're both well qualified just by looking at you, I figured you'd both have one already."

Rip sighed out the sad reply. "The Great Voice of the Deep may grant them... yes. We should have gotten them two ribs ago. Oh, Tear and I are both twelve-rib ranked. One is supposed to gain their specialization once you reach ten ribs. We... did not. We were prompted for our professions at five ribs just fine, and are both hunters. After that, we only felt inadequate, not knowing what we lacked."

Artorian softly hummed in response, noting he'd understood them both. He spoke in his normal language, since he knew Yvessa was listening even if she wasn't directly present. "Caretaker, could I momentarily have that first title back on? I'd like to… do something nice."

Rip and Tear looked behind them at the strange words they didn't understand, but wrote them off as mumbles. Maybe the large caster had swallowed something by accident? Best not to ask. A thrum rolled from Love's position, forcing them both to look away and stop in place as the voice of the deep suddenly addressed both of them. Their mouths hung open, not believing what they were suddenly looking at. "T… Tear. Did… Did you just get…?"

"I did!" Tear lost control of his humanization completely out of sheer elation, reverting purely to his shark base. Even if that too was fairly massive. "I don't know how, but I have an entire *list* of choices!"

Artorian just smiled as Yvessa deactivated his title. Gosh, these boys were just oversized puppies. They were frantically swimming around one another like excited newborns, and he couldn't help but feel pleasant about that. *"Oh? Sounds fun… What did you get?"*

Rip didn't know how to make his notification from the Voice of the Deep visible, so he just rattled them off. "I have options for Stalker, Shadow Hunter, Unseen Jaw, and… *Shadowcaster?* How do I have an option for Shadowcaster?"

Tear swam right up to him. "I have the same list! I also have that odd last one! I… I don't know what to choose. How did we even…?"

His hunting brother didn't have an answer for him, but both of them perked up with the exact same thought when they noticed the caster trying his sincere best not to smirk. Rip slowed down to swim along next to Love's face. "Did… did *you* do this? Are you able to make the Voice of the Deep speak?"

Artorian made a motion similar to a shrug. "I think you should take what will make you happy. As for whether I helped… maybe a little. Don't go telling anyone now. I want it to be a surprise."

His sly wink made both of the sharks fall silent. They

wanted answers. They wanted answers very badly. Though neither of them dared pose a question. Giving each other a quick glance of confirmation that they should get back to the list and not bite that particular curiosity-tail, they scoured over their five options. Rip chose Shadow Hunter, his body momentarily recoiling from adaptation as his coloration altered to a hue that seemed to naturally blend in with darkness.

Tear was far more hesitant in his choice. "Do you think I could become a Shadowcaster? I'm not... I'm not the smartest rock in the pile."

Artorian mused back a pleasant response. "Choose what would make you happy, my boy, the difficulty thereafter is just an opportunity for growth. If you received the option, then clearly the Voice of the Deep thought you capable. Now all that's left is for you to believe in yourself, and accept you can do the same. Either way, the hurdle is not something you couldn't overcome with perseverance. If you stumble, try again. If you make a thousand mistakes before you cast your first success, you will have learned a thousand lessons."

Tear felt better after the soothing words, and selected 'Shadowcaster.' Rather than his hammerhead form altering, his eyes brightened in a sharp flash before returning to their prior coloration. "I feel... this is going to sound odd. Smarter? Like I can think a step ahead, when before I was more... reactive?"

The Long shrugged, not actually knowing how this bit of Eternia worked yet. "Life is a series of changes, my boy. There's going to be times where you encounter something new, where all you will be is uncertain. In this event, I suggest acting in the fashion you would want to be reacted to. If it was you who someone saw for the first time. You will find that a gentle fin may carry you further than the sharpest tooth ever could."

That answer was satisfactory in its own way. Tear wiggled his tail, as if he was trying something. A loud groan and sudden headache later, and he bottomed out his newly discovered mana bar right away. Though his ability did succeed on the first try! Rip suddenly had a shadowy duplicate of himself swimming along nearby. "Ow… well, that hurt, though it worked! I was expecting the… thousand failures."

Rip looked at the shadowy clone of himself, uncertain how to feel. "So… what does it do?"

Tear shook his head, trying to clear the awful buzzing. Being near the Long seemed to remove that pain more swiftly. "It does everything you do. Maybe not as good, but I have this feeling that if you went to bite something, the shadow would do the same."

Rip approvingly wiggled his fins at this idea. "I like that. I have the feeling that I can blend in with nothingness of some kind, and become much harder to detect until I strike from that position. Let me try mine."

Swimming underneath Tear, Rip outright vanished from basic senses. Instead, Tear appeared to have a shadow lingering right below him that just barely appeared to be there, with another shadow clone beneath that one! Which just hid out and gained similar bonuses as Rip. Neat!

Artorian nudged in a comment to straighten out his assumption. "This will allow you to go home, yes?"

Tear replied positively. "It will! Now the gates will not be allowed to send us away! As they so delight in doing. *Delight*? I didn't know that word before. I like it! We will soon be at the gates, as you can see the shoals of silverfish in the distance. Trying to barter for shells, no doubt. Unfortunately, the crustaceans are still terribly upset at them for being swindled last time by a group of banker starfish. They'll get nowhere while they are aligned with the Allegiance of Stars. *Shell-grubbing bottom feeders*."

Artorian snickered; he loved a good social group interplay. That's where there was fun to be had! Oh, that gave him a pleasant idea. "I'm going to hang out of sight while you two soften up the gates. I'm going to try to hold back for an opportune time to poke my nose in. I need to see some of the interactions first."

Tear understood the scheme right away, but Rip remained

slow on grasping what Love had meant. Luckily for Rip, Tear took point right away, which made the tiger shark feel better. Perhaps this was for the best. While one of them was good at being clever, the other became an even better hunter. It would improve their catches! "I will attempt to create such a situation. Is there anything specific you want to see?"

The Long mulled it over. "I'm interested in how words are used. If motions of sorts are involved when speaking. The secret, under-the-fin language, so to speak."

Tear could answer that one right away. "There isn't any such thing unless you're conversing with Octopi or the like, the higher ranks of the social structure. Everyone else is blunt and means what they say as they say it. Pod calls, size, and favor from the Octopi are all that gets you into the larger shells of society. Unless you are an octopus or squid, then you win by default. The squid pontiffs are easily the highest living ranks in the Authority."

Artorian quirked a brow. "Currently living? As in, there used to be something above them?"

Rip cut in because he wanted to say something too. He knew this one! "Orcas! Or so we're told. We've never seen a live one, only the grand statues and stories of events that might have happened ages past. All that's left is the history stuff I'm not very interested in. Can't eat a statue."

Artorian pleasantly smirked. "On second thought, that's all I needed to know. Go home, my boys, I think I'll be just fine on my own."

Slowing his serpentine advance, Rip and Tear both made a peculiar tail movement that must have meant a cordial goodbye. After a moment of being slow, they noticed the Long give a single, tender tail wave at them in return.

Artorian watched as they sped off toward gates that were… *Oooh…* Bioluminescent! The fish-city was aglow with light. Sourced from algae, coral, plants, and even… structures? How did fish get structures down here? Ah, humanization… right. One could do a lot with a good pair of hands.

A bright green fish popped into existence next to him. A minnow? He heard Yvessa loud and clear, regardless of size. "Why did you give them both a title that unlocked their mana bar and the shadow element?"

Artorian nudged his nose at the duo, currently in line for the gates. "Because no matter how scary they might seem, those are both very good boys that just happened to be stuck in a very dead end. Now that I've given them a way forward, I want to see where they go. What's the point of having those extra titles if I can't do a little *good* with them now and again?"

Yvessa didn't have a snarky reply, so she must have accepted his reasons. She winked out of being shortly afterwards, since all Artorian did was wait for the snouty boys to make it through. Which, after a noisy kerfuffle at the gates, they did, passing with glee and speed. The guard salmon at the gate was clearly not having a fantastic day.

Now one moment. Were those... starfish using flat shells as *writing* surfaces? Ohohoho... Now this was going to be fun!

His serpentine sway slowly returned to active forward motion. Since he'd discovered that making those movements in the opposite direction also meant he went the opposite way: A method for slowing down—get! The salmon stationed at the gates thought nothing of the water disturbance at first. The sea had begun moving, and that had all the pontiffs in a tizzy. They couldn't do anything about it, no matter how scary the sudden change was. This tiny little push was just a side effect.

Or so the salmon guards thought until a distinctly lengthy noodle added itself to the end of the check-in queue. The school of fish immediately in front of Artorian hastily excused themselves, having no interest in being so terribly close to a mouth that big. The cadre of clownfish in front of that school decided to promptly and immediately follow suit. Adding themselves to the back of the line, right behind the school which had gotten out of the way.

This trend continued until Artorian arrived at the front of the line, having followed a line of glowing shells illuminating the path he was supposed to take in order to properly wait for the gate guards. Not that the gate had much meaning, since he'd have to swim over it in order to pass.

The pink salmons turned pale when face to face with the… guest. Though not a single one said a word until one of the starfish slapped some sense into one with a piece of conch. "I… the uh. Welcome? To. Uh. The place. Here. In the big wet. I mean. Welcome to the Octoid Authority?"

The salmon's voice peeped out the welcome more as a question, rather than the statement it was supposed to be.

Artorian just smiled warmly, and forgot entirely to dial back the volume of his voice, as his reverberating tones shook the left gate right off its hinges. "*Hello.*"

CHAPTER TWENTY-THREE

The salmon guards fainted. They turned sideways, helplessly floating in place as the starfish scribe could swear on all his shells that he saw the salmon's spirit leave from the closest fish's mouth. There wasn't a single fish in the queue that didn't suddenly decide to leave. Nothing was pressing enough to stay for. Not with the noodle lord here.

The hello had been so loud that guard reinforcements sped over along with swordfish military. There was a problem at the gate! To noses and arms! The swordfish slowed down long before they arrived at the glowing gate. As the… patiently waiting guest in question was not performing hostile actions. He was, however, so large that the swordfish thought they wouldn't even qualify as snacks.

This was… They needed someone of rank for this. After a quick huddle, they sped off to inform the higher ups while the salmon guards were left in the cold. Forced to fend for themselves as they bundled up at the gate, unable to leave with the convenience of their military counterparts.

One of them somehow found the roe to ask the proper entry questions. "C-could you state your business?"

The large dragon mused out his reply. "Visiting. I'm looking for someone."

The salmon wavered, asking a follow up. "Oh. W… would we happen to be able to direct you?"

Artorian waved it off using his claw, which was visible enough in the light with how he'd coiled himself. "I will find them. I appreciate the offer. I intend my stay to be… short."

"That's great news! We apologize for the delay in getting you through the gate." If salmon could sweat, this guard would be beading. The gate was half-destroyed from a noise 'accident,' and yet this large being was waiting purely out of respect for their rules. The guard had to give that credence and credit. "Would you happen to have a pre-established social rank we could go ahead and confirm for you? If not, we will need to fetch someone from the Authority for a measuring. We apologize as we had someone earlier due to a… strange occurrence with some sharks, but they have left already."

A cutting, nasally voice took that mention as a slight.

"You believe a loud sound like that would not hastily get my attention, guard?" An octopus—in… ha! Actual clothing and a hat!—pulled himself closer while traversing on the ground, the entire conch barracks of swordfish in tow behind him. Though they didn't seem very willing to enter in an engagement against the guest. "You there! I am Arbiter Unexpectus, of the Red Inkquisition. State your social rank instantly, or I shall take your ominous hovering to be a slight against my authority!"

Artorian just smirked. Fabulous… He could not have asked for a better prideful critter to inconvenience. Here we go! This was going to upset Eternium, but oh well. Roiling mana over his skin, he sent out a pulse mimicking the only pod call he knew by heart.

Ability gained: Sonar Pulse.

Also functionable as Active Echolocation, which is the above-ground version of this ability that works in an identical fashion. Sonar Pulse reveals hidden and obscured foes and places their relevant location on your minimap. Revealed entities will be outlined in a soft glow when not using the minimap to see. This pulse can be altered in pitch and sound to the user's direction, allowing some musical flair. This ability belongs to the bat and dolphin families.

Notice: While this functions as the pod call you intended, I am docking you -5 Karmic Luck for springing this on me. If you hit minus ten again, I will immediately unleash another karmic event on you. A proper one this time, since you somehow turned the minus 2 event around. The shark event was supposed to be a negative one. You're not allowed to turn it into a good one! Okay, nothing says you can't turn it into a good one. You were warned!

Unexpectus felt violated by the unexpected sound as vividly as Eternium. In this moment, their grievances were of one mind. Eternium found the opportunity so fitting that he slapped in the minus five karmic event right away, targeting Unexpectus the octopus as the benefactor.

While all fish in the general region were cowed by the strength of Artorian's pod call, the demerits shattered on Unexpectus's character sheet. Temporary immunities took their place, releasing him from any fear and perturbent factors that may have accosted him.

Unexpectus got ahold of himself. He was a red ink Inkquisitor! They were not phased by calls such as this, no matter the status! "Sir! Do you mock the Authority so that you dare to invoke a call of those who sit higher than the pontiffs themselves?"

"*Oho*, we have a fighter!" Artorian rubbed his claws together, rather happy that the wide-brimmed hatted one was putting up a solid front. "I dare. Take me to the pontiffs if you believe my call to lack that which is genuine. If my call is not recognized, then I challenge the Authority! Bring me, Inkquisitor. *Bring me.*"

Puffed up and full of pomp, Unexpectus turned on a tentacle and waltzed through a field of passed out swordfish as if they were nothing more than dirty litter, using only the tips of his tentacles to traverse the bumpy terrain as he hastily moved with the purest indignation. "The Inkquisition shall have you, bottom feeder of vigorous size! Come then! I accept your paltry defense. There shall be a trial, and inkspection!"

Taking that as permission to pass over the gate, he saw the other side now fell from its hinges as well. Artorian swam over the wall and through the field of knocked out salmon, who still just floated sideways in place. He supposed that was ungentle of him, and fed his Resplendence field for it to affect the Outer zone. On his passing, all the fish felt better before the last sway of his tail had passed them. He was getting the hang of swimming again, though he didn't feel like lingering. "Find the resonance. Smack the resonance. Head on out…"

Passing the Crustacean Council, the Inkquisitor was surprised to find their shells closed, boarded up, and hunkered down like locked bunkers. He didn't know enough of crab culture to understand why an orca pod call made them all tremble and hide in fear, but Artorian sure did. He snickered at the memory, and swam along to a few dozen shells that were so large, they could easily hold three of him per shell. Excellent! As a bonus, they had a nice rainbowy glow. He liked that.

When Unexpectus of maximum indignance entered the argumentative chambers, Artorian became privy to how names were being settled on. Turned out the inhabitants got naming rights, as he watched a violent spat between polifishians. On one side of the shell, manta rays argued that the sea should be named after their leader, Oddy. While the sunfish on the other side argued they weren't even in a sea—they were in a *lake*, one filled with bones! Therefore it should be called the Bone Lake.

When the manta rays noticed the wide-brimmed hat, they immediately turned on him for a rapid resolution. The polifishians didn't notice the noodle that was following behind, since Artorian hadn't entered the shell yet. "Inkquisitor, Inkquisitor! What say you? Oddy Sea, or Bone Lake? These sunfish are mad, believing we are in a lake!"

The sunfish were not going to take that lying down. "They

lie, Inkquisitor! Clearly the literal interpretation is the only correct one. What say you, Inkquisitor!"

The Inkquisitor was not the one who gave them a verdict.

"I like Oddy Sea, personally." The booming voice from above gave them pause as Artorian grasped the opening rim of the shell with his claws, so he could properly aim and poke his head in without damaging the architecture. A sight that, to the polifishian congregation, was cause for a heart-stopping fright.

Unexpectus wasn't having it.

"Silence, you bottom feeder! You are here to be judged! Not interfere in fishy policy! Councilfish! Abandon this chamber this instant, the Inkquisition requisitions it! By my power of Arbiter, I hereby summon the Authority!"

A horn sounded underwater, though the notes were expectantly garbled. Magic clouds of ink swirled in place mere seconds after, as both manta ray and sunfish hurried to make themselves unseen. The pontiffs appeared in short order out of their own ink clouds, and Artorian softly mumbled to himself. All the pontiffs must have had mana bars! "Ooh... Ink-based teleportation of sorts? Clever..."

Before Artorian could fire off an Inspect on one of them, he felt the resonance. His eyes were drawn to one of the pontiffs in particular, and upon perceiving their choice of attire, Artorian felt slighted. One must be joking. Was that a *chasuble* that squid was wearing? It looked identical to the ones he remembered. A quick count of the stripes... *Vicar. Mmm.* He knew how he felt about Vicars.

He fired off an Inspect, but... The system didn't feel like it.

Inspect resisted! Blocked by Unexpectus!

"Crackers!" That meant figuring out if that squid was being possessed wasn't confirmable... Now hold the toast. What was he saying? There was an easy way. The same way he'd done it the first time. Indiscriminate healing fields, *go!*

His smile gleamed shark-quality toothy when the squid in

question immediately recoiled into itself. From the look of it, *only* that squid was recoiling. The rest of this supposed Authority seemed to only get healthier. Except Unexpectus who was… resisting his effect? That was odd. He squinted at the writhing squid, but chose to pull up his own status sheet to see if anything was strange. "Well, well… That Karmic Luck value didn't seem correct. Eternium, you sly devil. "

The healthy Pontiffs rushed to the writhing squid's side, sidelining whatever the Arbiter needed in favor of gaining points with their highest echelon. "High Pontiff! Are you well? Is your illness acting up?"

The 'High Pontiff' was previously having a great day. He'd been pampered in his private chambers, only to be summoned to do awful work by a measly Arbiter. Ugh. Fine… It was his calling after all. How dumb could these fish be that they needed him, possessor demon Zindrat, to sort out their mess? Then he ink-warped into the council chambers, and suddenly got *blindsided*!

Zindrat didn't even notice Artorian due to the sudden awfulness he was experiencing. With all the other Pontiffs around, he tried to keep his cool. Zindrat acted as if he was fine and nothing was wrong. Though that proved difficult when he'd played the High Pontiff's condition off like an illness, and now they were all over him. To attempt to gain favor in his eyes, no doubt. *Ugh*. They were no better than polifishians.

Artorian calmly did nothing. He just lay on the edge of the shell's rim, and watched the slow cleansing do its work. He shouldn't enjoy the suffering of another being, but when it came to demons, he made an abyss-blasted *exception*. Unlike the last demon, this one did not seem to have the clarity of mind to check his own status panel. A strangely orange minnow tele-ported into place next to him, but Artorian just smirked all the more. "Oberon… Welcome back."

"Hello, hello. Don't mind me. I'm just here for the show." Artorian said nothing as Oberon indulged in the violent delights coming to violent ends. His vision was glued to the scene as if he *needed* this, and the Long wasn't about to interrupt the King Wisp. Or whatever the title was. He was spit balling for a good one since he'd never gotten the correct title out of his orange friend.

Zindrat perished in obscurity, never having been the wiser of his killer. Artorian received a notification, but it was just some experience that he didn't care for. So he dismissed it without a glance. He and Oberon instead tasted momentary catharsis at the creature's passing, and Artorian asked only the pertinent question. "Is the nuisance Cored?"

Oberon exhaled deeply in satisfied relief. "Cored, stored, trapped, and bapped. Just the way I like it. I only popped in for this moment, I'm not exactly done with my work. Didn't like my notification there? You just tossed it."

Artorian slowly shook his head no. "Honestly, if it wasn't a level up notice, I don't care what the demon's level was or how much experience it provided. Just more numbers I can't be bothered to keep track of. Likely fantastic for people just mucking about who delight in the tiny details, but I'm a Long on a mission. I was really just here to clear up this particular tiny detail. I'm going to head back up now; the C'towl's curiosity is satisfied."

Oberon thought about the notification preferences, and gave Artorian a curt nod before winking out. He could do something about that, and lessen his workload at the same time.

"The High Pontiff is dead! He's *dead*!" Artorian raised a brow at the news. Dead? The Panda had been just fine. Then again, he hadn't been able to check the squid's status beforehand. Perhaps this one was already so far gone that his persistent healing field couldn't even help? Ah well... He didn't have the resurrection ability he did during testing, so that was the end of it.

"*You*! You killed the Pontiff!" Unexpectus pointed some kind of overly lengthy needle at him. This gained Artorian's attention, but not his interest. "I know not how, but I know you were affecting the High Pontiff in some manner, the Voice of the

Deep confirmed this for me upon use of my Inquisitorial abilities!"

"Hmm? What reason could I possibly have?" The Long's response did not go over well with the octopus, who sliced the needle through the water in a skillful cutting motion.

"I, Unexpectus, accuse you of the murder of the High Pontiff! You will be judged and killed in accordance with the rules of the Authority. I sentence you to trial! So says I, by my power of Arbiter! Remain still so you may be captured for your crimes, foul fiend!" The other pontiffs in the room began to mimic the Arbiter's sentiment, just looking for someone to blame.

Artorian cared for none of it, sighed, and pushed away from the shell. "Oh yeah? Well come get me then, crawly. You'll have to chase me to the ends of all the realms to achieve something like that. Know what? That could be entertaining. Come! Arbiter of the Deep! Let us commence our game."

Now that he had a hold on his swimming, Artorian put serious effort into the motions while rocketing straight upwards. He rushed right to the surface as Unexpectus spouted a cloud of red ink out of pure rage, the expulsion propelling him forwards. Unexpectus chased Artorian at matching speeds as the Arbiter hurled strings of insults at the fleeing, guilty murderer! "I will catch you, traitorous bottom feeder! I will chase you for all time, until this arbitration is complete. So sayeth I, Unexpectus!"

Artorian broke through the water's surface after a few minutes of moving as fast as his swimming could take him. On the plus side, he did finally gain the swimming skill!

Skill gained: Swimming. Fond of the big blue? Make it a playground just for you! This is a general skill. Swim more often to improve this skill! Expend your stamina to swim faster!

Once in the air, he immediately threw the lever on his additional nature title. With a pop and squeeze, he was human again! Also conveniently in clothing, plus bag. Nice! Now how was he going to get enough footing to get going? As he fell, he saw the raging red tentacle ball shoot up from below. Well, that would do!

As a screaming Arbiter broke through the water's surface, he was met by the bottom of a shoe sole. Taking it smack to the face, Unexpectus was used as a footing platform, suffering an impact which added so much downwards force that it plunged him right back down into the depths. Unexpectus garbled out a watery insult in reply, his speech muddled as he sank like a rock.

For now, he was rebuked! "You scurvy cur!"

The gained momentum was all Artorian needed to take off at speed, advancing at a swift enough velocity that the water felt solid beneath his feet. Until he once again zipped off at a speed slightly below Mach one. Yvessa winked into being, her voice amused. "What's got that smile plastered on your face?"

He giggled while running, having a great time. "I just made and finished my own side quest. Making my own adventures is so much more fun! Also, I'm going to have random company now and then. This is going to be great!"

Yvessa looked behind her, matching speed with her charge. "*Mhmm.* Oh yeah. He's furious. He's going to cross the coral reef."

Artorian didn't follow. "Hmm? Why would he do that?"

"To get to the other tide." Yvessa smirked, living for the awful groan that erupted from Artorian. "Hehehe…"

CHAPTER TWENTY-FOUR

Dawn was lounging on the Silverwood branch when Oberon winked into existence next to Eternium's physical location. Eternium's Core appeared to be doing much better, now that the flower he was encased in had sprouted full leaves and petals. Her words were soft, even if her supernova gaze was anything but gentle. "How's he doing in there?"

Oberon shook himself to get a quick feel for his Wisp form in Cal's Soul Space. Moving between spaces was something only S-rankers did without side effects or strain. Having expected the company to be waiting for him, he deduced who she was talking about and replied in kind. "Well enough. A few days have elapsed, and he's put down two demons. He's also caused the expected turbulence, which is oh so much fun."

Dawn smirked from the sheer sarcasm oozing out of the Wisp. "I like you, Oberon, you don't mince or slather butter on your words. Most other Wisps that have come to bother me have tried some method of slimy schmoozing. Now that the Invictus matter has smoothed over."

Oberon considered what needed to happen for Wisps to

come bother Dawn, and then looked around, since he didn't see any. "So… where are they?"

"Oh… over there, over there, over there…" Dawn nonchalantly rolled her wrist, pointing at extreme directions and other continents entirely. "I gave them a tiny flick, since when I kindly asked if they would shush, as I was concentrating, they refused. I can't abide that, and if they refuse to listen to my words, then when their glowy butts are no longer burning sore, they are more than welcome to return and come tell me. I will flick them less kindly the second time. Should one be so uncouth as to annoy me a third time, then I will flick them so hard that they will spend days bouncing through the entire inside of Cal's Soul Space from the sheer force I put into the retribution."

The orange Wisp hovered in place, speechless for a moment given that he now heard how his people were being treated. "I… understand. Skip step two, advance straight to three. No need to give them so much leeway."

Dawn burned with enjoyment. "I definitely like you. Don't let me keep you from your tasks."

Oberon lingered regardless. "I'd like to hear what happened with our dearest silver ball, if that's on the table. It's strange that Wisps would flock to you when previously they'd learned to exercise extreme caution."

The Fire Soul looked elsewhere, but Oberon knew the reply was for him. She was functioning as oversight for several projects in progress throughout the Soul Space. "Marie, Henry, Chandra, myself, and Odin of all people—I know, a surprise, right?—had a gathering to talk it over. I ended up releasing Invictus on the condition that Dani and the active Wisp high echelon would come listen to why he was actually cubed, rather than just stick to their assumptions. When eventually they understood I function not as their executioner, but their boundaries. They understood."

Oberon burst out laughing. "So that's why they're flocking to you! They want to prod the wall and see how much they can get away with! No wonder you're being accosted left, right, and center."

Dawn turned to face him, curious interest on her face. "You can tell I'm being bothered right now, in several places?"

Oberon created several orange arrows, pointing in rampant directions. "Those are all the locations where I know a Wisp is lingering outside of Niflheim. I may not be an active functioning member of the leadership, regardless of my status. Though that doesn't mean I'm devoid of the perks. As an Actualized, you can, just like Cal, create Spirit bodies. The difference is that they have to be yours, and your mind is what needs to be in them. What I can't tell is how many copies of yourself you have out and about."

She was succinctly pleased. "Well done... I expected Sunny to figure that out before anyone else did, but it doesn't seem his Mage sight can outright ignore matter yet. That's fine, and the answer is, of course, my limit. As a first-step Incarnate, I currently have five thousand and forty active bodies working in the Soul Space. As still as I may appear to sit, that includes myself."

The orange Wisp created hands of mana just to applaud, though something about that number sounded familiar. He couldn't place it for the moment. "Progress on Vanaheim must be astounding!"

She nodded, but made a motion with her chin to denote he should get a move on. "Is your curiosity sated? I am expecting company."

Oberon turned harsh yellow, his attention whipping around to inspect Eternium's Core right away. "Please not of the Caligene variety."

Tatum stepped in from the void, momentarily interested in why Oberon was zipping around Eternium's Seed Core in panic. The Core seemed fine. Not a speck of tar on it. "Everything alright?"

Dawn nodded. "Just so. Oberon was just on his way out."

Catching her tone, Oberon realized the Core was fine, and

it would be of great benefit to him not to be present for their conversation. "Indeed I was! Apologies for the delay, I'll be on my way now that I'm sure my Eternium is peachy. Toodles!"

Zipping off, Tatum turned his head to quirk a brow. "Toodles? I wonder where he picked that up."

The person he was here for cleared her throat, her arms crossed impatiently. Tatum stuck his hands into the air and twisted them like cheap little hello waves. "Yes, yes, I found things. I wouldn't break from my moon and Hel work otherwise, even if I have many forms spare to put Vanaheim together. Mostly it's Dev going nuts on that one. Did you know he took his Gnome shape just to run around on sections of finished land? It's adorable."

"*Barry?*" Dawn's laconic nature threatened to rear its head. "I really need to know more. I was uncaring about it before, but if he's active in Eternium, stuck or not, I don't feel cozy not keeping this Core burdened under resolute attention."

Tatum hung his head and sighed. "I suppose today is not a 'lighten up and play while you work' day. *Honks.* Was hoping you'd be in a water affinity mood."

She cocked her head at him. "Would it help?"

He emphatically pressed his hands into his gray robes. "It would help *me*, yes. I'm tired of all the tension, and I wasn't kidding that last get-together when I said I needed a break. We can't all be an eternal vigilant fire like you. That's an amount of pressure even I crack under. There's always a problem. Something is always broken. There's always some big threat looming juuuust out of sight over the horizon."

When Tatum held the side of his head, Dawn changed her tune. She was on her feet and holding him by the shoulder less than a moment later. "Alright, Occy, water affinity mood works just fine... I know I've been the business end of a spear lately, but those blasted Wisps just won't leave me alone and it's really working my nerves."

They sat on the branch, and just did nothing for a few minutes. They didn't talk, or work, or move. They just laid back and looked at the movements in the sky. When Tatum felt a little better due to the tiny break from tedium, he sat back up. "It's always odd to remember you can just turn on a copper like that."

Dawn didn't get back up, seeing no need to. "You know where I got it from. Before we get to the work topic, are you having any trouble with your clashing natures? I'm having a ton. Cultivating as an Incarnate is terrible, and if I knew I was going to have these awful waking dreams, I think I might be happier just stopping at A-rank nine."

Tatum shrugged. "You get used to it. No Incarnate ever tells a non-Incarnate what the changes in cultivation methods entail. Though, perhaps if they did, it might deter Mages from passing that line. Why? Where are you having trouble?"

Dawn swatted the back of her hand through the air, a single burning-light diagram of herself appearing. Then multiple. Then a dozen and more all congregating around a bonfire. "This is a trick I got from Sunny. It's been helpful, but I can't keep the people in this mental space... hmm. Separate? Ever since Cal, the hard walls between who I am have gradually become more mellow. It no longer feels like I am going to be 'Dawn' forever, like when I first changed. I have become so much of Ember again, and I'm losing my grip."

Tatum mouthed an 'ah' of understanding. "I take it, compounded with Incarnate cultivation. That's rougher than it sounds on the surface. Yes, I understand where you're coming from. Did I ever give you the full explanation on Incarnate growth? Since... you're very much right. Our identities being... wobbly, is detrimental."

Dawn hovered upward and changed her angle to lie on her side. She didn't see a need to stand when she could just turn in place and lie on empty space. "You gave me the short version, but you also told me to just see and experience it for a few hundred years. Did that? Did far more than a few hundred years too. I think if we told A-rankers of the horror that awaits them, they'd self-righteously think it would be no problem for something as mighty as them! Then get swallowed."

Tatum flashed her a broad smile. "You held on to the idea of you! That's always good. I'm with you on the A-ranker mentality. So much about cultivation is viewed in terms of power and might that it blinds you entirely. The S-ranks are all about the mind. Our definition of solid bodies already counts as 'loose,' since these are our souls made manifest. I think you give them up entirely when playing baton-pass with your **Law** entity in the Tower. It's going to be odd for me. Unlike you, my floor doesn't have a Node yet. I'm going to be the first. Strange to think about, really."

Dawn made the images of herself dance wildly, just to make herself happy. "What abyss-minded soul thought it was a good idea to make Incarnate cultivation work by putting you through the lives of prior S-rankers? It's so hard to remember I'm me when I'm being... *them*. Tell me I don't have to do this for every step."

Her friend solemnly shook his head no. "Sorry, candle girl. After you get through the entire life of the S-ranker whose life you're living, you get the option to follow in their steps, which is how you get to the double-S ranks if one is available. Otherwise you have to wait. If you accept the second step. Then you have to do it all over again, now with a different person, who went through the entirety of the double-S stage.

Since they are even more sure of themselves than the first step, it gets even harder to remember who you are when pulling away. That's the difficulty of the stairway journey. If you can't pull yourself back, you get consumed. If you thought death or graduation for Incarnating was bad, I'm afraid to say it doesn't get any better."

CHAPTER TWENTY-FIVE

Dawn sat back on her butt defeatedly, holding her head and brushing her shimmering hair out of her face. "Abyss. I'm barely managing the stairway of my first step. I pull back, and until I manage to shake it, I'm still partially Kunandra."

Tatum turned to face her more openly. "Is that the name of your first step, whose life you're living through? What a naming convention. I'm guessing that's from before your Ancient Elven time?"

Dawn squeezed her hands for a moment, then dropped one toward him with her pointer finger extended. "That she is. Long before. Did you know that my civilization did not in fact do the majority of the work on the Tower, like my history classes said they did? I didn't realize I was lied to until I saw the world through her eyes. We thought our civilization was the Golden Age? We were bumbling children in comparison to the civilizations that came before. It's heartbreaking to see the foundation you built your certainty from is, in truth, made entirely of quicksand."

Tatum made a wagging motion with his hand. "Are you sure

she's from the civilization right before yours? Mine are… wibbly wobbly, very timey wimey. I'm currently stuck with someone living in a metal box. In space."

"Ha!" Dawn smiled and shook her head no. "Not even a little, it's probably much further back. The entire society is so different, I didn't recognize a thing. Is it like this for you?"

Occultatum refolded his robe around himself. "I can't say I'm going through what you are, because when I did my first step stairway, I wasn't in Cal. The walls were solid and firm, so keeping hold of yourself was considerably easier than it is now. I also feel the malleability of the walls, but I've chosen to look at it a touch differently."

Copying her, he also made an image of himself hover above his hand. "See, before… When who I was firmly had to stay a single solid thing. Trying to be otherwise would have caused both me and my world to shatter. The soul had become solid. Immalleable. Set in its ways. Now I can grow and change as a person again. That might sound odd, but it has allowed me to adapt to situations I would otherwise have stonewalled."

His image didn't dance, but it did wave. "Out in the real world, I was only ever going to be 'The Master.' Those traits. Those views. Those ideals. Now, instead of just having my name changed to Occultatum, I can also choose to be this pleasant, amusable, smiling person. Even if my workload makes me groan like a distraught autumn leaf while crushed beneath the weight."

Dawn giggled, dismissing her creations. "So you like it, even if it makes the stairway much harder to climb?"

His nodding was vigorous. "Oh yes! Cultivation may be important, but the ability to keep learning as a person? That's priceless in comparison. Being stuck in place, and stuck in your ways? That ends well neither for yourself, nor anyone else."

Tatum changed his constructed image above himself, to one showing Dawn. "As advice, I would say: rather than being worried about holding on to who you are, strive to be the person who you'd rather be seen as. Your soul will follow, even if that's completely counter to helping where cultivation progress is concerned. So rather than be worried about being 'Dawn,' or 'Ember,' just be you, and use the traits you want to comprise yourself of. The name... *eh*. The name will follow. Like a guidepost."

Dawn silently observed the construct of herself giving her a wave. She considered the greeting, then cheekily blew it a flaming kiss. The Spiritual energy traversed the distance to connect with the construct, who shyly turned away. Blushing after impact. "I understand now..."

Tatum smiled, curious. "Hmm?"

She walked her fingers up an imaginary staircase to show what she meant. "Why Barry is such a problem? You mentioned before he knew Xenocide's ability to damage a person's idea of themselves. I can grasp the kind of irreparable damage that might cause. After thinking about it some. Thanks for the talk, Occy. Are you okay to talk about work?"

Tatum moved his hands in a wiggly 'kind of sort of' way. "Barry is confirmed to exist in Eternium. His location is on the moon, in a special containment device that has obviously failed. Dev's anythingium was used, allowing him to bridge to other nearby empty Cores. Once he had access, he funneled Spiritual energy and filled them with newly summoned demons. As you can expect, they're all beefy boys. A-rank at minimum, S-rank at most."

That was unpleasant news, but at least it was information to work with. Tatum continued. "We don't know the exact amount of direct connections. However, we think that once those are severed and the demons that originated from them are re-Cored elsewhere, Barry will be vulnerable to attack. I wish we could just go in and crack the egg, so to speak, but Eternium has made that difficult since he has to abide by his own **Order Law**. In order to get to the directly connected demons, we *must* use the game system."

"That's awful. Why?" Dawn pulled a face that mixed hatred and nausea. She didn't like that in the slightest, and glanced at Eternium's Core neatly nested nearby. "I don't suppose I can just grab him, and use him as an item to get around that. Forcing him to…"

She cut her words off when Tatum was already shaking his head no. "If we forcibly use that Core, it'll be spilling out tar like an uncontrolled waterfall. The person trying is immediately going to get assaulted by whatever is allowing Barry to keep such strangely fine and tight mental control. Eternium will be powerless in that state, but what's in him won't be. So for the same reason that Barry is free if a demon grips that Core over there. We think that the same is true if anyone else does it and attempts to invoke control."

Tatum changed the construct above his hand to form a visual example similar to a haphazard spiderweb. "Current working theory: Barry has direct control of a few demons. Those demons in turn have control over a much greater amount of demons, who then do the same, via delegation. Given they couldn't win the rush during a direct assault, I think they're creating strongholds in Eternium so they have a stable foothold to try non-stop breakouts while being bunkered in. Given that in order to stop them at the source, we have to go in there."

Dawn's awful face only worsened. "That's so… just. *Ugh*. So not only can we not cleanly mop this up unless we play that horrible game where the world works differently, we also have to use the system there to do it? I wish I could still throw up. I'd go into Eternium to fulfill my end of the deal with Cal, but never by choice."

Tatum dismissed his constructs. "Does the mortal vulnerability in there make you physically sick as well?"

She nodded unpleasantly. "That's exactly what I meant. My first entry into the non-alpha state, when things were moving into Eternium were experiences in torture. I had nothing in my stomach, so I couldn't actually. Yet I easily spent half an hour prone on the ground, just feeling like I needed to hurl from the sheer sensations I was plagued with. No amount of 'hey, have some of these great numbers' made any of that better. I didn't care, I just badly needed to not be there."

Her friend nodded sagely. She was preaching to the choir and he was right there with her. "Then you tried doing literally anything, and it didn't work?"

Dawn shot up from her hunched over position, hands flung into the air. "Nothing! I couldn't make the tiniest flame appear above my finger. I just about had a breakdown from all the screaming I did. When I got out that first time, I thought I was going to strangle you and throw you through a few continents. Since you apparently had Pylon access to still do things. I wasn't warned the non-test version of the game stripped you of *abyss-everything*."

Tatum nodded more, though this time apologetically. "It was the worst for us, but Chandra didn't have it any better as an A-ranker. The longer someone has been a Mage, the worse the Eternium experience was. She cried for hours on import, and I just held her until the return limitations elapsed. Never even left the Eternia spawn-point. We went back to Cal right away when the timer clicked."

Dawn drew a firm breath, releasing slowly. "Then there was Odin, and we all thought he was the hope for a while."

Tatum smiled, but shook his head no. "Oh indeed we did. He cared nothing for the difference. Extra challenge, he bellowed! Then spent weeks getting drunk in the early taverns, accidentally slaughtered all the guards in a city because he tripped over a chicken and killed it. Turning them all hostile. He just... didn't care for the world. He was there to drink, party, and hip-check his way through obstacles without a care. He picked up some nice abilities on the way, but that man is unbearable."

His friend stretched her arms above her head, grunting lightly before she took over. "Then there was Sunny. What a difference! I'm still mad at Cal for throwing him back in during iteration one, just to slap Brianna. Those results in the test-versions, though… Fabulous."

She nudged her nose over at Eternium. "Now he's in there, has been for days, and hasn't come back out once. Oberon even said he squished two annoyances already."

"That long? I'm surprised he didn't just pop back out." Tatum delighted at this news, but his pleasant feelings slowly ebbed away. "Say… he *can* pop back out. Right?"

Dawn quirked a brow. "Oberon can?"

Tatum softly waved the Wisp topic away. "Yes, yes. Can *Artorian* come back out anytime he pleases? Before he went in, Eternium had to run the backups for all his Pylons, and a good number of those he modified. To show off to Cal at a later date. We don't actually know what all the differences are between our iteration tests, and Eternium's current version. It is entirely possible he changed things we're unaware of."

The air around Dawn turned hot. "Couldn't have told me that a few days *sooner?*"

Occultatum shoved both of his hands toward Cal's moon. "I was busy! You know what we're working on in there, and since you left progress hasn't exactly been quick. Also no, I only thought about it just now since we were talking about it. I can't keep track of millions of Pylons! Even Dev can't, and he lives and breathes that stuff with unmatched passion. Losing Vanaheim was a big blow, and the entire thing needs to be rebuilt before we can sync Cal and Eternium up. A process for which Cal needs to be conscious."

Dawn cracked with electricity as she scratched both sides of her head to work off the irritation. "*Fantastic.* So Sunny might be stuck. In a system crawling with enemies. In a world that's still growing and evolving. Using limited, obscure, and unknown Pylons. Under the watchful eye of a Core that doesn't particularly like him much. Not knowing he needs to target the highest levels of demon he can to make progress. Oh yeah, that *really* puts me at ease."

Oberon winked in at that moment. Only after he was being

compressed into the shape of a cube did he realize he shouldn't have done that without warning. His rebuttal began and ended with a squeak. Dawn held the orange cube in front of her face while her eyes whirled with novas. "*You*. You have some explaining to do."

CHAPTER TWENTY-SIX

The orange cube was more than happy to cooperate. To both Dawn and Tatum's surprise, he didn't even quip at Dawn for cubing him. Wasn't it Wisp societal tradition to return an inconvenience in kind? Oberon didn't seem to follow those rules.

When the Incarnates got a full update on Artorian's progress, relief visibly washed over them. Dawn kept Oberon on her thighs while running her hands over the light ball. A strange compromise they'd come to as recompense for his prior entrapment. She didn't mind, if it kept the King Wisp talking. "So he is already aiming for higher level demons? I don't understand, I only heard the theory from Occy recently."

A pleased as punch pink-on-the-edges Oberon delightfully lap-lounged. Forget Artorian's ideals of the most comfortable pillow. Laps were where it was at. "*Mhm…* He's trying to beeline it to Asgard. The rules are all that's slowing him down, and even then I wouldn't call what he's doing slow. His ability to circumvent the system via his **Law** tier is truly helping him out, and giving my dungeon incredible loads of work. I haven't had a chance to really meddle. Just sneak in some wordplay here and there."

Tatum crossed one leg over the other, trying to understand how Artorian's insanity would work with available Pylons. He didn't get very far. "Well, Sunny's methods are convenient in their own way. That Relentless Demonbane title is a nice touch. Given we now know he's hunting Barry. I imagine he will try to extract information from higher demons somehow. Can't say I know how you'd do that to a creature that considers torture an average social norm of positive repute."

Dawn shot him some side-eye, her hands kneading the orange-pink lump like it was putty. The lump liked it. "Any way you can sneak in and help? You secretly shoved titles onto Henry all the time."

Occultatum squeezed his chin, then glanced at the nearby core. "No. I think if all the Pylons were the same, I could. But as they are likely not, you might have better luck with your massage patient. You should be happy he's not mad at you for the Invictus treatment. Honestly, what did we just talk about with the being who you want to be thing?"

Dawn tilted her head, partially confused. "I choose the traits mysterious, otherworldly, terrifying, luscious, and exacting. I don't see the problem. Ember was the embodiment of war, Dawn was hope kindled anew. Now that war is more of a comfortable sofa to lounge in rather than a state I must exist in to live, and my rekindling has evolved from naive childishness and haphazard dancing, I have no problem with looking to the future. Since after Oberon's explanation, I know why Artorian goes around using the moniker Love."

Tatum had to admit he was curious. His expression spoke volumes that he wanted her perspective. While it seemed to him she was jumping at opportunities for stability, he saw no reason to attempt to dissuade Dawn from her path. Given it was entirely her choice on who she wanted to be. Anyone who tried to alter that for another person was a piece of abyss. Mentors should only provide helpful guidance. "Please, do share."

Dawn slowed in her motions, her anger fading as her fires turned a melancholy blue. "It might be better if you heard it from Sunny directly. I can't answer for him. The answer I have reached for myself today is one I think I have been trying not to accept. A dumb, simple truth we try to look away from. **Laws** are chosen purpose, right? What is purpose, if not the end point of what you strive for? I have lived so long, and lost nearly all my bonds to what you and I consider the mortal world. When the last tethers fade, what does a cultivator hold on to?"

Tatum closed his eyes, understanding where this was going. He'd encountered this hurdle himself when he was a first-step Incarnate. It happened to everyone who climbed so high, and lived that long. He answered since she was not being rhetorical. "You hold onto the only thing that's left. The curse of being smart is to realize that early. So you don't feel like you're about to step off a cliff, I have met my share of S-rankers who have stood at the same precipice you have."

Dawn paused, kneading Oberon like a stress ball as she listened. It was clear he had no complaints. Tatum wondered for a moment if Oberon was a glutton for punishment, but paid it no heed. "Incarnates all eventually take the name of their concept, usually with some clever twist. Your case isn't unique in that sense. When you start counting your age in millennia, your perspective changes. Of course it would. This starts with titles. Every Incarnate is 'so and so, the something.' Eventually, that falls away."

She remained quiet, but was hoping this went somewhere. Tatum recognized the expression. That and the color of her fire was giving her away, as it slowly altered to a dull teal. "During my staircase journey in my first step, the person I was in at the time knew the earth affinity S-ranker of that age. His name was Paarthax, but he began to call himself Earth. Both in the sense of that being who he was, and in the sense of where his purpose lay. When Paarthax started his second step journey, he turned and told me the following."

Tatum sat up straight, trying his best to mimic the crude caveman voice. "Friend, I not named Earth for Earth's sake. I named Earth because I *am* Earth."

He stopped his silly mimicry, hoping that example was enough. He didn't want to open his box of pain up. Sharing stories about one's staircase journey was not something he liked.

Dawn considered it. She recalled saying something similar once. Tatum was holding his commentary as if waiting for her to speak. She wanted to taste the words, and spoke them with purpose.

"I *am* Fire."

Oberon bolted from her lap, zipping behind Tatum for sheer safety when the sudden change occurred. The feeling she was emitting turned on its head. For a Wisp sensitive to fluctuations, that was akin to experiencing vertigo. His tone was hesitant, but in need of knowledge. "What just happened?"

Dawn's flames ceased all heat, the colors of her flame turning iridescent as rather than burning wildly about her being, they created formations and danced on her skin. The multi-colored flame turned into spirals, then fractals. Sticking close to her frame while unfolding in ever further variations of fractal evolution.

Tatum said nothing as he wore a tiny smile. He just stood in place and folded his hands. The Wisps may be masters at scheming, but he still had a trick or two up his sleeve. Iridescence was one of the best outcomes for an uncertain Dawn that he could have hoped for.

This was going to help her stability tremendously! His voice was borderline smug, but the warmth he spoke with drowned it out. "Helpful guidance."

CHAPTER TWENTY-SEVEN

Artorian was enjoying the gentle breeze atop a tall hill when a stressed Oberon popped back into Eternium. The Wisp was strangely quiet, but he wasn't prompted to speak when hovering close to his green counterpart. He pleasantly said nothing for a while, just catching up on logged events he'd missed since he didn't particularly feel like gabbing. It was nice to enjoy the offered silence, compared to the earlier word litany between S-rankers.

According to the logs, it appeared Artorian had moved a significant distance, but hadn't gained any new skills or abilities. Just some experience. How strange. Following his path on the minimap, Artorian had ignored both of the towns referenced by Woffo. The obvious villain castle was… behind him? Why did he just *pass* it? In fact, why were they just on a hill, doing nothing?

Looking up from his log, he dumbfoundedly dropped it to the ground. The screen even fell for effect, digging into the ground when he saw a… functional society? This part of the map should be empty. Why was there a domed palace in the middle of this valley? A busy one! Look at all those people!

There was a gorgeous smattering of oversized tents sprawled about, yet only the dome seemed to be a true structure.

Picking his panel back up from the ground, he pulled up the information on the dome. Maybe that would provide insight on why this stalking huddle was staking out.

Unique building: Ossuary Fountain.

Gathering the rogue dead who died in unnatural ways, the Ossuary periodically expels a lost soul as an undead. So they may once more walk amongst the living and properly continue the cycle. This structure gained its name from the peculiar method of expulsion, as once an hour it will spew a remade creature from its roof. The Ossuary is filled with bones that could not be removed due to faulty anti-littering Pylons. The Ossuary does not at all contain the bones of people who were not funny, or made puns.

"Did anything spew out of that by chance?" Oberon blinked, frowning as he looked above his screen. Without saying a word, both Artorian and Yvessa nodded. The orange Wisp glanced back at his panel, dismissing it as he joined the waiting game. They weren't exactly hidden on the hill, but they weren't being bothered either.

On continued inspection, those supposed people down there were all skeletons. They walked around as if part of an early age tribe, and underwent activities you'd expect of such an early society. Hunters, gatherers, the works. Except that the things being hunted and gathered were odd. Animals were brought in, but for their marrow rather than their meat. Foragers brought home baskets of bird bones, rather than mushrooms or edible goods. What a strange sight.

Oberon joined the prior duo in being captivated by this society. Which seemed to work as intended, in its own incredibly strange way. He cleared his throat when the silence started getting to him. "Are you going to off them all?"

Artorian turned to look at the orange Wisp with incredulity. "*No!* Why would I even try? Have you not been watching? They may appear different, yet look at them. They're good people. Who am I to judge them as they feed their families and provide for their community? They are no different from a human commune. I'm waiting to see the building spit out another skeleton, and then I'll be on my way."

Oberon hovered in place. "Huh. Okay. Say, why did you pass the marked locations? I just caught up."

Yvessa responded since Artorian looked back to the commune. "Ghost towns. Those places were abandoned and wrecked. When we finally got close enough to the very obvious evil castle, it turned out to be an illusion. An elaborate one, but still just an illusion that made information appear on our map that wasn't accurate."

Oberon frowned. "So, the places on our map that show demon infestations are…"

"Not real. Merely distractions." Yvessa's comment made Oberon turn red hot. That was awful news, and completely trashed his plans. If their information could be affected by counterintelligence, that made this difficult.

Yvessa noticed, and gave him something to work with. "No demons. Some wraiths and specters though… they didn't fare so well against the healing aura. Don't worry, Artorian has a pretty good plan put together already. We need to hit up a few more beacons, but the problem will sort itself out."

The orange coloration returned to the worried Wisp, but he clearly craved more information. Having overheard them, Artorian laid the details out to put him at ease. "If we can't go to them, we'll make them come to us! Since they're falsifying information, it would be silly not to assume they already know people are coming to stick a fork into them and call it done. I have ditched my plans of hunting down their strongholds, as they clearly have methods to befuddle even you. Meaning my only reliable method comes down to luck, and a resonance I'm not certain I can count on."

Oberon mused the question more to himself than to Artorian. "How do you make them come to you?"

Their human just smiled. "Be annoying enough, and they'll come in droves to shut you up! If I can't trust the map, I won't use the map. This means we have to start looking for the right questions. Such as: What kind of information *can* you trust?"

Oberon wasn't sure, remaining quiet. His continued silence made Artorian nod, just making it easy and answering the query. "When someone comes to hunt you down, they come from a direction. Pile enough bodies together, and you get a lovely line."

"I still don't know why they have to come looking for you? Why would they go out of their way to try?" Oberon felt confused until his orb sparkled with delight when he saw the glorious gem Artorian pulled from his robe pocket. Which he then held up to the sunlight.

The man himself grinned wide. "Well, I figure they want the Immaculate Core powering their illusory contraption back. This little bad boy offered to give me a frankly ridiculous amount of experience for using it, but I find it more valuable as a *lure*. I'm sure they can track a potent toy like this down. Thing is, I'm pretty sure they have *no idea* who took it."

Artorian pleasantly mused to himself, dabbling in assumptions for a moment. "As far as the demons are concerned, some nobody found this gem and ran off with it. Given there wasn't a single real guard defending it. Not that I'm particularly surprised. This Core was... obscenely heavy. I just walked through their wall, because it wasn't there. The whole place was all bark, no bite. Yvessa told me I offed a few wraiths by strolling around, but you know my preference on experience notifications. I found this gorgeous *shiny* snug in the middle of it all, stuck in some infernal contraption. I broke it, of course. The place was a crater anyway. Picked this right up, and moved on. All I have to do now is to choose a nice castle of my own to make a stand."

Yvessa cut in with a comment. "Not here, before you ask. Artorian doesn't want to drag these people into his war. They don't deserve that."

Sunny approvingly nodded. "Indeed, they do not. Thus why we've changed our focus to hunting down beacons. I have the hunch that the first few demons sent out are going to be the spy kind, hiding out in borrowed bodies. Now, you and I know that variant isn't a problem to tackle. We downright kill them by accident so long as I keep my field active. That means that they lose spies, and we gain allies."

Artorian smiled wide, and Yvessa informed her counterpart of the plan's latter half. "Eventually, they'll notice none of their informants are reporting back. They'll send real warriors. Beat enough of those down, and the boys in charge will start getting snapped at for poor performance. They'll start coming in person, and that's where we begin our sport."

Oberon was impressed, but didn't understand what sport was being referenced. "If you're being assaulted, that doesn't sound like a sport."

Artorian beamed in delight, pulling something from the Panda bag that he'd picked up from the abandoned town. Yvessa snarkily made Artorian's comment for him. "He found a bundle of bows, and all the arrows his sack could carry. Their quality isn't great, but it made him childishly happy to bounce around the ruins and dig them up from the rubble. You should have seen it. He was covered in dust, and just pushed off support beams he was under to hold a newly found goody aloft."

Yvessa mimicked her charge, including the jovial enthusiasm. "I found another one!"

Artorian snickered. He'd indeed had a lot of fun gathering those up. He looked at the Core in his hand, as his fingers brushed over it. As he did, his expression changed to become more contemplative.

Oberon gave him a small shoulder bump, but then had a question when he recalled Artorian had specifically mentioned the object's weight. "Something on your mind? Actually, how did you pick it up if the Core was so heavy it could not leave that crater?"

Artorian turned the Core over in his hand, a touch of melancholy in his eyes. "It's just so... quiet in comparison to what I remember."

He perked up a moment as he realized Oberon had none of the requisite history to draw on. "Long ago, in the first iteration of Cal's world, I was a fresh Administrator. One of my tasks was to tackle a particularly cantankerous crab, and the blasted thing even offed me once. It was such a troublemaker, roaming about unchecked. So when I finally had it handled, I was so sick of the thing that I just hurled its Core to Midgard after infusing it with my mana specifically to make it so heavy. I am the one who made the Midgard crater with this Core, and to find it just nestled away in Eternium... I'm not sure. I'm a touch nostalgic? Yet, I remember a troublemaker. This one is silent. Still I can guarantee that it is the identical Core to the one I threw."

He gave it a small toss, catching it without issue. "It dawned on me when I could freely just recover my mana from within it, and only just now put the pieces together. I was terribly confused how the castle illusion could stand on its own, but the crab from this Core did have a strange knack for obscuring the senses."

"Enough reminiscing." Pocketing the Core neatly back in his robe, he laced his fingers and observed the Ossuary some more. "Should be anytime now."

Yvessa checked her screen, and agreed. "*Mhm.* Four, three, two..."

The Ossuary collapsed in on itself, the roof deflating to press against the ground. When the dome bounced back upwards with a metallic *thunk*, a new skeleton somersaulted free. Unlike the last one, this one landed with a pirouette! It bowed for a clearly unappreciative audience, as the locals just warily stared at the newcomer. Artorian clapped loud from the top of the hill, catching the skeleton's notice.

The new arrival appreciated that greatly, responding with a stage bow directed at the applause. Aha! At least one being that appreciated a proper performance. The rest of these people were just rude. They didn't appear to be half as mindful. Actually, they didn't appear to be very clever at all.

Artorian checked the skeleton's status panel from a distance. "That's some beautiful intelligence. The others here have maybe some four and fives. That is a gorgeous eighteen. I'm really starting to think these are just normal people that died in strange ways, and this is one of the places they can end up for a round two."

Oberon wanted to comment that's exactly what the Ossuary was for, then recalled Artorian likely didn't have access to that information. Abyss, this cookie was smart. Just to satisfy his curiosity, he pulled the skeleton's information up for himself.

Name: Chiffon
Character Level: 4
Class: Cursethief
Health: 50/50
Characteristics:
Strength: 11
Dexterity: 21
Constitution: 2
Intelligence: 18
Wisdom: 12
Charisma: 18
Perception: 10
Luck: 1
Karmic Luck: 0

Oberon didn't want to look at that twice and dismissed it with speed. He instead turned to Artorian, who pensively rubbed his chin. "Something on your mind again?"

Sunny nodded. "Several things, my floaty friend. I'm noticing his statistics do not begin with a base five like mine did, because that Constitution and Luck don't look healthy. Also, that class he has is horribly interesting. I'm tempted to say hello…"

Yvessa wanted to dissuade him, but Artorian had already made up his mind. His field effects turned off so he didn't swat these infernal-based creatures by accident. Or at least he was assuming that was their basis. He might be a Relentless Demonbane, but these people weren't on his hit list. His enthusiastic stroll took him right to the performer. "Splendid performance! Might you fancy a short chat? I would love to hear of your exploits!"

His Wisp groaned, but had to go invisible since a large amount of minds were now paying heavy attention to his location. Oberon followed suit, hovering unseen while close to Yvessa. "Does he do this often?"

She just sighed in response. "No, only when he has a *terrible idea* in mind. We are in for some schemery, you mark my words. Let's hope this wraps up quickly and we head out soon. Him having that Core is giving me chills, and I just hope that off-the-cuff ploy of his works."

The budding tribe hid behind their tents, which Artorian now realized were large shimmering beast hides pulled out over cleverly arranged bones to keep them upright. By the time he was in range to shake the skeleton's hand, Chiffon appeared to have realized he was dead.

His voice, on the other hand, was the picture of positivity. "By my own bleached bones! I have become the very skeleton of my performance. Here I thought I was stabbed by a scorned lover. It appears that may have ever so slightly been more fatal than previously assumed."

CHAPTER TWENTY-EIGHT

Unfazed entirely by his own state of being, Chiffon grasped the offered hand and shook. "Why look at you! What a *steal*... I do so love meeting fans, although rarely do I meet them in such a state of questionable undress."

System notice: Cursetheft resisted. No curse active to steal.

Chiffon turned, pressing the back of his hand to his lower jaw as if to whisper. "Don't tell anyone that's how I've met most of my fans. Possibly also how I was quite rudely *stabbed to death.*"

System notice: Curse affliction resisted. Deathstab Curse not applied.

Releasing the handshake, Chiffon the skeleton pressed his fists to his hips and appeared to take a deep breath as the wind howled by. "Now that's what I call a breeze!"

Artorian opened and closed his hand while he looked at it. "Interesting. I hadn't heard of afflictions before."

Chiffon didn't budge from his pose, yet somehow looked

incredibly nervous. "My dear fan, you… uh, don't appear to be performing a dance I expected you to."

Artorian just smiled in response, moving his hands to the small of his back. "Hmm? Would that happen to be the dance of the Deathstab Curse? I'm sure it's a jolly tune, full of springing and thrusting action. I'd love to know why you'd make me want to dance to the music."

Chiffon sighed deeply. "Well *curtains*. It appears my jig is up, and I'd barely even started. I don't appear to have the means of escape, so I'll take my end with drama, and dignity. Allow me…"

Pressing his fist to his jawbone, he made the sound of clearing his throat. Artorian was dying to know how that worked without the requisite fleshy bits. "Oh, woe! In my performance of pain, the hero shalt be slain! So ends the tale of Chiffon the cat! T'went all so well until he lost his hat."

Artorian stifled his growing laugh, pressing his fingers against his mouth to silence himself while Chiffon retained an absolutely ridiculously dramatic pose. Was that what *he* looked like when he took the leaf pose? The skeleton hissed out his words. "Well, what are you waiting for? Strike me down already. I refuse to go without flair!"

The human couldn't take it, pressing his hands to his knees as he bellowed out the withheld amusement. "Oh, that's rich. You're amusing, Chiffon. I can't say I understand your class enough to know what a Cursethief does, but if it's an audience for performances that you seek then, my boy, do I have an audition for you…"

Chiffon righted himself unnaturally, pulling himself up one bone movement at a time. "You have me at a loss, sir. This is generally the part where I am smote. Where is my smiting? I just tried to murder you where you stand, to gain experience and get my acting profession back. Why are you offering me opportunities? This is madness."

Artorian's arm swung around Chiffon's neck, a swindler's smile plastered on his face. "Not madness, my boy, merely a labor of **Love**. Why don't we go for a walk? Tell me about your class a bit. I think we can help one another, unless you're not interested in the stage."

Chiffon fell in step far too quickly, his luck so terrible he didn't even get the chance to realize he'd been caught in a mousetrap. The mere idea that he would deny the opportunity of a grand performance was folly! "Good sir, you have me rattled, and I would love to be thrown a bone. Tell me then, where I might place my performance throne."

Artorian gleefully smirked. "Funny that you mention a *throne*. How good are you at goading?"

The performer didn't enjoy being speechless, realizing late he'd been had. Still, like any good actor, he would improvise his way through this. "I am excellent at goading, insulting, and heckling of all kinds. As for my profession, I hold the details a little close to heart, and no manner of intimidation will persuade me to revea—"

Chiffon squeaked to silence, held unpleasantly firmly by the coxal bone and scapula. The performer quickly altered his fear priorities when the concordant boom that followed had *him* cling onto the madman for dear undead life. The speed they went altered from a pleasant breezy walk, to *oh sweet mercy please put me down*.

Finally taking Yvessa's words about the environment to heart, Artorian built up to a comfortable running speed. Then jumped. Chiffon screeched like a tiny bird, trying ever harder to hold onto more of the madman. When Artorian's trajectory started curving downwards, Chiffon heard him mumble. "About here should be good."

Extending his foot as if to land mid-air and jump again, Artorian drew a stern breath and tried to craft an ability without dropping into meditation. The effect was immediate. A square, glowing light platform sprung into place beneath his waiting foot. To his pleasant surprise, it didn't even break when he pressed down and launched off from it. Sustaining his momentum and bringing him high enough to do it again.

Looking behind him between jumps, he saw the platforms last about ten seconds before winking out.

Since the notifications sprang up nearby, he gave them a quick glance before dismissing them.

Skill gained: Aerial Acrobatics. This is a subskill of 'Jump' and boosts the effectiveness of any mid-air movements. Description pending. Effect: Ease of movement while in the air increases by 10% at the Beginner ranks. This increases by 10% per rank. Jump around in the air more often to improve this skill.

Ability gained: Platform.

Platform creates a high-durability cube that lasts for ten seconds. This platform is stationary and may be placed anywhere within 100ft of you, even in the air. This ability costs 1000 mana per use. Platform is considered a light-based ability, and doubles in cost if the cube is called forth at double the size. Notice: Karmic Luck -5.

No snarky notice? Eternium must be waiting for another chance to slap a penalty on, so he could trigger something 'fun.' Artorian shrugged the thought away, running on the cloud layer shortly after. Or rather, bouncing.

Skill gained: Cloudstep. This is a subskill of 'Jump' and boosts the effectiveness of any high-altitude movements. Why run on the ground when you could run on a cloud! Effect: With a cloud as footing, ease of movement while running increases by 10% at the Beginner ranks. This increases by 10% per rank. Cloudstep more often to improve this skill.

Notice: Due to your Platform ability, clouds count as no-cost bounceable platforms so long as your running movement is not interrupted or stopped.

Artorian's smile was gentle, and soft, reminiscing about his days after leaving the grove. He exhaled with relaxation, and remembered he had a passenger. "So, what were you telling me about your class?"

Chiffon suffered the thousand-yard stare, certain he had in fact died and gone to a place far worse than some tiny tribe that didn't care for the finer tastes of his trade. Initially, he wanted to keep all mention of his precious class a secret. On more calculated introspection, that might be a terrible thing to do during this audition.

Information flowed from him like a councilman freshly handed a fat sack of gold. "Cursethief is a rare class I was offered when I was an actor, and developed during a few feuds. It allows me to apply a curse to anyone I touch, so long as I attempt to take a pre-existing curse away from them first. It doesn't matter if I succeed on that first one or not, I just have to try. Which then allows me to select one of the many curses I gained, and attempt to apply it. If I do steal a curse, then the rarity of that curse is added to the rarity of the curse I am applying back to them. It's fantastic for quietly dispatching of… opposition."

Artorian hummed in reply, though the response wasn't what made the performer shush. The sudden miss in jumps did! His transportation was falling. Nay, crashing down to earth! His explanation cut off, returning back to birdy peeps. Chiffon felt a harsh impact, but didn't dare unbury his vision out of the darkness of the robe. He didn't want to see. He didn't want to know. He only heard a disappointed voice coming from the person carrying him. "Hmm. No, too small. This won't do."

A gust of air later, and Chiffon knew they were once again traveling at speed. He stole a peek, seeing they were already heading back to the cloud layer. "Are… are we alive? In a manner of speaking."

Artorian casually responded. "Oh yes, we're peachy. Don't be too concerned. I have need of you, my boy. I'm just shopping around…"

Chiffon clung to the madman for dear life, like a cat who had touched the bathwater by accident and wanted nothing to do with it. Of course, it may have had more to do with Artorian zipping from one abandoned castle to another. When the man had stopped at his seventh castle, Chiffon couldn't take it anymore. He let go and just fell to the ground while Artorian was muttering about not liking the gate aesthetics.

"What in Eternia is going on?" The performer shook his hands, looking around. He was entirely unable to discern just how far they had traveled since his awakening at the Ossuary. "I told you what you wanted. Why must I be accosted so? I expected you to drop me from on high!"

Artorian grumbled at the current castle a little longer, wondering if he might just have to nab an occupied one, rather than hunt around for scraps that didn't suit his needs. These castles were nice, but they didn't seem to be built with the best strategic value in mind. A few of them were even placed so haphazardly, they had no value at all. Perhaps they were to one day serve as some kind of mini-dungeon?

He shrugged, and just picked Chiffon up. "No, I was quite clear. I have need of you. After all, it is difficult to cobble together a Kingdom, and not have someone present to play the role of the King."

Chiffon didn't know whether to be affronted or feel complimented. "I... I am to play... a royal?"

The madman carrying him nodded sagely, back in the air with a hop and skip. "Oh yes. Specifically, one with talents in annoying the living abyss out of everything and everyone. I want usurpers at your feet, councilmen with daggers ready for your back, visitors intending your demise, and an endless stream of Noblemen seeking both your favor and your position. I want you to be the most ostentatious ruler you can think of. Yet still one that runs an effective house."

Chiffon had been calling this person a madman to himself prior, because that was the only kind of person who would take trips on the clouds. Now, he thought it was far more apt a description. "You mean to slaughter me, through a royal mess?"

Artorian softly guffawed. "No, my boy! I mean for you to

inflict curses on the most annoying sods in all the lands. You know. *Bureaucrats*. I am going to put together the conditions, and the reason people will come. What I need from a skilled, professed actor, is the impetus causing the most self-serving and annoying among them to seek your favor. At which point, I intend for you to see them to their demise. Your skillset is particularly useful since you said people are unaware of the afflictions you cause. I had other ideas in mind, but this works for expediency."

Chiffon pressed his bony fingers to his sternum. "A King? *Me?* That's the role of a lifetime. Though I must reiterate my prior concerns on… mortality."

His carrier enjoyed a sudden laugh. "A trifle! So long as you can see to your task. A minor issue such as your continued good health is at best a momentary inconvenience. I don't think I see the use of one for myself, but I will be putting a shield around you. After all, I can't spend my entire day annoying every single politician that comes to the door. I have a trap to bait, and mice to catch. Oooh, that place looks nice! Going down!"

Chiffon didn't even notice when they hit the ground, only that cubes were used as a staircase to slow their descent. "I am… entirely lost. You wish to make an unkillable royal, who is the most goading, annoying, insulting, back-hand dealer he can be? Why me? I'm but a humble undead performer, even if cursing a small army of corrupt politicians is something to savor."

Artorian set him down, clearly pleased with some kind of strange sculptures they'd landed next to. Chiffon saw no castles? Just this oddly broken chunk of a gyroscopic contraption. "What's this supposed to be? I thought we were looking for structures."

The man pressed his hands to his hips. "Change of plans. Found something better. I know I wanted to look for them, but I didn't think I'd run into one so soon. Guess I'll greet my old friend, and turn this on."

Chiffon motioned his hands around, as there were no

friends, and definitely nothing to turn on. Now, had he been mortal with a meaty body, that may have been a different story. Though the cloud-jumper wasn't exactly his type. "This entire journey has been a theater of confusion. Could you elaborate?"

"Just watch." Artorian waved him off as he stepped onto the beacon platform. He was so pleased to see this old piece of wreckage again. Even after uncountable eons and iterations, the remains of Cal's original sun still littered the realms. He brushed his hands over massive curved beams, the runes glowing at his touch as some of his mana was siphoned over. Ah… Still trying to eat up energy to power its function? Perhaps he could do something with that. "Awaken, my dear."

The teleportation beacon he stood on was three times as large as it should have been. A vast disc in design, the half-buried thing was partially stuck in the remnant of the solar gyroscope. He was pleased to see that funneling mana into the beacon did not cause it to be stolen by the… He needed a name other than wreckage. Artorian thought he should choose something deliberately incorrect, just to make it seem special. Gate? This scrap did look like an ancient contraption meant to do something big and powerful. "Solar Gate it is!"

CHAPTER TWENTY-NINE

The disc thrummed to life under his feet as thousands of mana points poured into it per second. Artorian didn't even feel it, his mana regeneration currently at… Actually, he wasn't sure when he thought of it. Quickly having a check, his updated scream-regenerator came out to a very modest one-thousand nine-hundred seventy-six mana per second. Was that a lot? It seemed like a lot. Oh well… It was just a number.

When the light from the disc was so bright it came up from the buried section, Artorian felt it had enough juice. He strolled over to the raised pillar in the middle and tapped it. He knew how connecting beacons worked when he was an Administrator, but when he tried the mental command, nothing happened. Tapping the pillar made a screen come up. Convenient!

Teleportation Beacon 14
Location: Midgard
Status: Active
Connection: No
Claimed: Artorian

Artorian squeezed his chin, not sure how to proceed. "Well, let's just start tapping random things!"

He pressed Status, and received a prompt asking if he wanted to deactivate the beacon. That was an instant no. He tried Connection, and a list came up. Only one entry existed in the list. Beacon number thirty. *Thirty?* He hadn't put that many beacons in Midgard. He was sure of it. Eh, the more the merrier.

He tapped beacon thirty's icon, and the beacon he stood on thrummed, noting it had connected. Great! It was added in his listing as well. Good. Very good... Now for the next step. Dismissing the beacon controls, he pressed his hand back onto the wreckage he had dubiously named a Solar Gate. Time to see what made this thing tick!

Magical wreckage, titled: 'Solar Gate'
Location: Midgard
Status: Active
Claimed: Artorian
Effect: Absorbs loose and directed mana to power latent functions.
Function: Uncertain, original function unknown. Appears to cause a 'create heat' effect, as the byproduct of what was intended. Wreckage open for alteration to remove the unknown latent function.

Chiffon didn't like seeing Artorian rub his hands together enthusiastically while giggling childishly to himself. The performer instead stared at strange archaeological metal bones. Those were bones, right? He cautiously stepped back as the madman began talking to himself. "Alteration, you say! Well, well. Don't mind if I do! What's this cost? Just a gob-ton of mana. Are there options? I'd love some options. I mean if not I can always improvise."

The word improvise must have prompted something, as Artorian also took a step back. New screens appeared in his vision!

Magical wreckage, titled: 'Solar Gate'

Alteration option one: Replace current effects with an ability of the claimant. A Core is required to power this effect.

Alteration option two: Shift the absorption runes to power the connected beacon instead, amplifying the beacon's power and teleportation range.

Alteration option three: Shift the beacon runes to power the magical wreckage, activating latent functions by forcibly revealing them. Warning, it might get hot.

Artorian tapped his lips. Looked like Eternium knew darn well what this piece of magical wreckage did, and was just hiding it from whoever encountered it to make that third option seem more enticing. Abyss that! The thing's purpose was to become a miniature sun! Artorian would take out this entire section of continent by shifting to option three.

That... didn't seem like a bad backup plan if he ever lured a bigshot here. *Hehehehe.* For now, he pressed option one. With that in place, Artorian turned and called out to the performer. "Hey, c'mere! I've got to apply this to you now."

"My name is Chiffon! Or, if this ridiculous plan of yours has merit, King Chiffon!" The Cursethief posed as if draped in royal finery, even if not a shred of cloth covered his bones. He was already starting to play the role, and strolled over to the man currently sitting to meditate. How rude! Calling him over just to turn his attention elsewhere.

In meditation, Artorian found it to be much easier to craft abilities. The ideas just came easier, as if Eternium was secretly helping him cobble it together. Artorian moved the mana to form a shield around himself, but knew the intent was to apply it to someone else. The ability finished by itself, suddenly ripped from the tips of his fingers. What the abyss?

Ability gained: Divine Shell. This skill is a staple for any cleric that wants to be able to walk outside city walls without an escort! So long as your chosen deity does not abandon you, you can use your mana to shield yourself from harmful spells and physical attacks.

Effect: For every point of mana devoted to this spell, negate half a point of damage from primary sources of magic and one point from primary sources of physical damage.

Increase conversion by .025n where 'n' equals skill level.

Notice: Karmic Luck -5.

Notice: As you cannot use cleric abilities, this ability will not activate if you attempt to use it on yourself. For the purposes of this ability, you count as the deity!

Artorian wrenched himself out of his meditation just to yell at the sky. "You brat! You let me make an ability that I can't even use, and you dock me points for it? I'll remember this!"

A notice blipped to life next to him.

Notice: Even as a Generalist, I will not let you get away with being able to do everything. Aren't you cheating enough already? Besides, it does what you wanted. A shield for someone else. Have fun!

Artorian glared at the message, his gaze sharp. Rather than dismissing this one, he took a leap forwards and kicked it off the beacon, sending the notice spiraling through the clouds to get rid of it. "And stay out!"

A mountain of grumbles later, Artorian took out the Immaculate Core and haphazardly poured mana into it. No skill notice popped up, but Artorian had the hunch Eternium wouldn't let him just 'do that' twice. He didn't know if the core needed to be full before slotting it into his improvised contraption, but a few minutes later he could already feel the Core try to reject his mana flow. That or Eternium was giving him push back. Good enough either way.

Touching the core to the Solar Gate, he received a prompt.

Would you like to apply: "Immaculate core—Overcharged" to the magical wreckage to activate alteration option one?

Notice: Cores should not be able to be overcharged, nor charged so easily. As this is a helpful find, you will not be docked Karmic Luck.

He selected yes, and was immediately met by a basic follow-up prompt.

Please select ability and target.

Since Chiffon had patiently remained nearby, Artorian reached over and held his shoulder. "Alright, let me know if you feel funny."

The performer felt his jaw lock when a shimmering silver field tightly squeezed down over his bones. In his immobile state, he checked his status. Chiffon was glad to be unable to react, as he'd have choked to death on the air. He had a new entry on his status sheet!

Name: Chiffon
Character Level: 4
Class: Cursethief
Health: 50/50
Shield: 15000/15000

The silver glow gently faded, but Chiffon could still feel it when the ability to act returned to him. He knew it was there, even if invisible. His skeletal face fell in amazement. "I... I just... *Fifteen thousand?*"

Artorian didn't feel impressed. He didn't have a good grasp on if that was a lot or not. "Oh. That's all? Seems like an awful small number, but if that's what it is, I suppose that's fine. Even if I don't follow how or why it's fifteen thousand. Maybe cores have preset effect values?"

Artorian inspected the performer, but dismissed the screen with disinterest since nothing else of note had occurred, and he wasn't going to get any answers on his assumptions.

Chiffon silently screamed at him, making heavy handed motions at his status screen as he could not cope with that insane number. Did the madman have no concept just how much that was? He checked the source, and metaphorically frowned. "Divine Shell? You're a *cleric*? If you're a cleric, I am extra concerned as to why I wasn't smote."

"No, I'm no cleric. My class is entirely uninteresting, and seems to exist purely to *allow some brat to penalize me for no reason!*" Artorian shook his fist to the sky again, much harder this time. He was not on board with Eternium's excuses at the moment. "Regardless. That shield will stay nice and fat so long as this Solar Gate here absorbs mana now and then. Give the contraption some juice, and your shield will restore. Now that the Core is slotted, it also means that this is the location that's going to start getting attention. I might as well get started on the rest."

Chiffon pointed at the wreckage. "Are you telling me that so long as that has mana, *I* am effectively unkillable?"

Artorian replied with a harmless smile. "Yes? That's exactly what I mean. That should help you nicely in your goading. Would it not?"

The performer blinked at him. "Are you kidding me? Goading? Goading is gentle childsplay in comparison to what I am going to do to unpleasant visitors. Who did you need insulted? How often? Is there a specific curse I should apply?"

Artorian was pleased Chiffon was on board, and considered the question. "Hmmm. Got anything that makes people slowly take damage while they're out in the sun?"

The performer shook his head no. "I do not, and have never heard of such a curse. That's the kind of thing one of the long-lost Divines may have granted, but as there are currently none, that is a futile thought. I have a curse that causes the afflicted to stab themselves to death, one that causes continual grievous bowel movements, and a curse that makes you think whoever you are looking at stole all your money."

"From the Divines, you say? Hmm. Worth a shot. Yvessa, are you listening in? I would like temporary title access to craft a goodie." Artorian hadn't finished his sentence before his entire being turned resplendent. His body turned a milky cosmic—full of spinning stars—while his eyes became golden suns. "Thank you kindly. Let me just give this a whirl."

Notice! You have created an Affliction!

Affliction: Suncursed.

This is a curse! Suncursed applies an affliction that causes anyone exposed to sunlight, indirect or otherwise, to take continual true damage with the burning theme. Damage is equal to five per Affliction quality rank, per second. Determined by the skill of the afflicter.

Would you like to gift this Affliction option to eligible target: Chiffon, the Cursethief?

Artorian pressed yes, the cosmic effects he radiated ending instantly as his title was revoked. He nodded appreciatively, clapping his hands together to clean them off as Chiffon regarded him with paralyzed horror. "You... Y... You are a..."

"Accept the curse, my boy. We've got work to do."

Chiffon blinked at the momentarily Divine man's words. Madman was no longer applicable; Chiffon was dealing with forces that went far above his head. Noticing the gift screen only after it was pointed out to him, his bony finger reached over to press accept as the definitely-not-cleric spoke impatiently.

"I am a busy person! With much to do. Now... I believe that means you're all equipped. Please move off the beacon. I have to set up the coliseum and call some friends over." The minor 'scooch' hand motion from the kind-of-Divine made Chiffon turn tail and waltz right off. The time for questions was over. This had been the strangest, and yet most epic audition he'd ever been a part of. He was going to be King. A King!

Lost in his own glee, he didn't notice his patron throw his hands to the sky. Chiffon turned around when he heard the mana-infused yelling. "My friends! Love comes a calling! Are you here? I have devious plans with fun to be had!"

Artorian received a notice prompt.

Ability gained: The Senate

You have gained access to the Senate! A mental location where minds can gather to converse, regardless of physical distance involved. Remaining active to the Senate drains mana at a flat rate, equal to 100 mana per second. A sub-function of the Senate, known as a Forum, has also been unlocked. Forums are private versions of the Senate, requiring a more direct connection. No more than five minds may be active in a forum at any given time. Eventually, Forum will be its own standalone ability, as a precursor to the Senate. Forum access drains the same amount of mana as the Senate does.

Notice: Karmic Luck -5.

Notice: You're at minus fifteen, please keep racking these up. I have something special planned.

Something special? That wasn't ominous wording at all. *Nooo.* Not even a little. The minus ten event had been hours of misery; what was that dungeon brat planning that demanded more? He didn't want to know, but he had newfound company to help distract him!

From the ground swirled three clouds of roiling energy. Artorian clapped his hands together when he recognized the forms! With pomp and mystical effects, Chaos, Discord, and

Entropy appeared on the scene. "Djinn! You took the forms of Djinn!"

The three huge beings twisted out of their respective elemental clouds when they saw it actually was their friend who had summoned the trio instead of some scheming power-monger attempting trickery. Their aggressive demeanor softened quickly, showing the forms they had truly taken as they dropped the obscuring clouds.

Chaos had chosen the form of a verdant Djinn, Discord a lovely violet, while Entropy opted for vanta. A black so deep that the sun barely reflected on his being. They were each adorned in jewels both rich and plentiful, though in distinctively different themes. Likely done because they had picked different classes.

The three massive Djinn threw their arms open and bellowed their welcome in unison, Artorian triple-hugged immediately. "Love! Our dearest friend! How we have missed you! Have you truly some devious fun hidden within your sleeve? We have been bored to tears this entire age. We have such resources, yet nothing to spend them on!"

Djinn voices were deep, heavy, and so abyss-blasted loud! Artorian clapped his hands together, once again copying Mahogany. The clap shuddered the air, laying pleasant silence over the region as the noise faded. "Hello, my boys! I do! Although it happens to be one that's going to greatly inconvenience our host, and his precious sense of order. My tiny little idea will wreak celestial havoc, though it may take most of those precious resources. Interested... ?"

He didn't need to hear the verbal reply to read the abyssal grins on their faces. As if they could say no to an opportunity that would stick it to the dungeon brat. They had found their friend once more! It was time for rejoicing!

With just a pinch of scheming vengeance...

CHAPTER THIRTY

Cleaver, the ravaging butcher of the wastes—notably named for his weapon of choice, and significant lack of originality—was one of the first warrior demons to arrive at the Solar Gate. Or what had become the lands added to the region. How a region could grow so fast was lost on the demon hiding in his man-shaped guise. Not that he cared. He was here for glory, and the delicious reward boon known as a rank up. A full rank! How rare the opportunity!

All he had to do was kill a few people, and he'd be rewarded! Not that doing so wasn't a reward in itself, given his profession. Better still, onlookers would be cheering for him the entire way through! Up to the end, he figured. Maybe at the end when he stuck his cleaver through the King's clavicle, there would be gasps. Maybe some crying. Hopefully some woe?

He loved some well-earned woe.

"Couldn't go wrong with some lamenting either. *Mmm...* Lamenting." Traveling on foot, Cleaver's delusions of grandeur shattered. The first view that graced his eyes was anything but graceful. In fact, the view made him consider turning back.

Wasn't this region supposed to be just some small backwater Kingdom freshly sprouted from the ground?

Did he count not one, not two, but three grand castles? Each one of them defended by their own unique environmental feature? No wonder no army was sent, forget sieging this place! Now that he had a closer look, the coliseum he sought sat nice and visible in the middle of all other structures. Given how intense they were in size, each of the adjoining castles appeared to have a privately zoned cone-shaped territory.

From far away, the land layout all looked like some big triangle.

The verdant fortress was so well camouflaged, he nearly hadn't seen it between the tall trees. Based on the smell even this far away, the grounds where it stood must be some marsh or bog. Perhaps swamp? Maybe it was a fen. He didn't know for certain as his gaze wandered to the violet roofing of the adjacent castle. That one was situated on a very wide river, straddling the streams with uncountable arches and bridges. Finishing the third pie-slice, the third fortress appeared dark and brooding, tucked away on the tall ridge of a small mountain. Seemingly accessible only via a narrow pass that wound up through equally moody-looking rock.

Between each triangular zone, a massive set of statues held taut chains that kept bridges in place, providing both access to the coliseum without entering a fortress zone, and connecting the vacant points between them. Each leading to the center triangle, a commons zone offering a mish-mash of services, plus the grand prize saddled neatly in the middle.

The coliseum was so rowdy he could hear it all the way from the start of the valley. Six of these statue monstrosities dotted the inner triangle. Two at each point, each in the shape of a slightly different... "What manner of creature is that? A Djinn?"

As his gaze lowered to the surrounding valley, Cleaver's eyes scrutinized the fields of farmland stretched out before him. The land closer to the castles and bridges looked strange. Nested between the farmland and the actual city of Solar Gate, he saw a wide band of gray gravel where grass should have been.

"Why was space cleared just for a ring of gravel?" Activating some vision skills, Cleaver was able to discern that... oh. Ha! On that gravel, rows upon rows of soldiers stood, unmoving. They were but terracotta! A weak means of pretending there was might present in these lands for all who could not notice the statues for what they were.

"As if someone would be scared of a few dumb statues. Ha!" Kicking his step into stride to follow the convenient dirt road, the self-assured demon smirked the entire time he passed through the Solar Gate's Kingdom. On his way in, he passed angry, scorned Noblemen who were returning back to their own Kingdoms. They appeared sickly? Though their breath was fire! Keeping an ear out, Cleaver learned much. Apparently, the local lord was a real pain, a demon of a ruler who had made the presiding court laugh them out by sheer volume of insults!

Cleaver was endlessly amused any time he walked along the dirt path, just to pass another disgruntled person whose self-entitlement rivaled his own. They whined loud, yelling to the high heavens that they had been abused and treated as unrespected mongrels! The disrespect they suffered here would become legendary in the tales they would provide their bards! How dare the Gate King treat *them* like mere commoners, only to lambast and denigrate them before a vast public audience. The gall!

Cleaver burst out in laughter when the sermoning ceased. The Noble in question needed to squeeze arms around his own stomach. The pompous man quickly turned green. "Oh, celestial mercy. Not again. Not again! It is every hour I am accosted. I was poisoned, I say. Poisoned!"

Moving on, Cleaver discovered this outlook wasn't shared by all travelers. Merchants had the opposite reaction to the supposed Nobles! Solar Gate had many entrants, but few returners. According to quibbling peddlers, this was because the chance to perish was high. Most Nobles and warriors entered, but didn't leave. Their goods, on the other hand, became free game.

Anyone who came for the arena either made bank, or added to someone else's purse given the only coliseum rule was total forfeiture of assets on a loss, leaving some very wealthy contestants seeking the means to spend their gains! With the region focused on food production, they needed to import most other goods. Allowing merchants to arrive poorly, but leave wealthy. This drove them to return with full carts, and the hopes of even fuller wallets.

Commoners that Cleaver passed had nothing to say on this topic. They were instead enthralled by the discovery that the bards sang true. *Any* injury could be healed in Solar Gate. Any affliction. Any ailment. Any harm could be mended, and any curse could be removed. Missing a leg? Not for long! Blind? You'll see soon enough. The news of a healer so potent annoyed Cleaver to no end, as demon orders on healers of any and all kinds were strict and exacting.

Kill on sight.

When Cleaver slid his way into a conversation, he asked if there were any rules in Solar Gate. The answer he received was odd, and made him think that the local rulership no longer had all their marbles.

"It is forbidden to fly," the farmer had said. Theft, murder, and more all turned out to be entirely legal. With the caveat that anyone was also allowed to put a posting up in the brand-new Hall of Retribution. Where anyone could be tasked for a sum of gold to retrieve your goods, or enact vengeance upon you.

Cleaver thought these rules were convenient, but strange. A few more questions, and he found out why the rules were so lax. It turned out that in Solar Gate, unless you were fighting in the coliseum, it was entirely impossible to gain normal experience due to a region-wide arbitration spell in effect.

Unless the task you were on was put up in the Hall of Retribution, and valid per the cause it was listed for. Then you would gain full experience! False listings would net nothing. From the rumors, professional experience could be accrued normally. Still, the normal method of executing something or someone to gain in might simply didn't work here.

Cleaver wasn't so bothered about that. He was here for the coliseum! No loss on his part. What did bother him was how so many people were here. According to his information, the task he accepted couldn't be more than a month or two old. This location was supposed to be barren, not have an unknown sprawling Kingdom up and active. That's not the kind of detail a demon was supposed to miss. "Someone in the information department is going to have their head removed! If not the entire department. Ha!"

A wandering retribution agent searching for his mark had no issues filling Cleaver in on that mystery. After discovering Cleaver wasn't the mark he was looking for. "Hmm? The people? Well there was a spot of chaos a few weeks back. People received random prompts from the Voice of the World saying there was a place where anything could be healed, cured, or mended. I thought it was nothing but lies at first, but given I was missing an arm and homeless at the time, I saw no harm in going on a journey."

The retribution agent flexed his brand-new right arm. "Now look at me. Stronger than ever and back in action! I even have a room in the forest castle. Took me a fair bit of gold, but merchant tasks from the hall pay gooood. So long as I make my dues once a month, the room stays mine. This place is strange with how loose its rules are, but it gives men like me a very fulfilling purpose. Plus if I ever lose my arm again, I know where to go."

Cleaver thought this a grand opportunity to get some more information. "Where would that be?"

The agent smiled at him mischievously. "Oh, just hang around for a while. Trust me, you'll know."

That was less information than the demon wanted, but the retort aligned with his needs. He let the matter drop, and dropped the agent while he was at it as well. Swinging his weapon, he split the human open from shoulder to hip in one fell swoop. There was no notification, so he checked his status sheet. Having stepped foot inside of the region, he was now affected by something called *Arbitration of Entropy*. "Hmm. Look at that. No experience."

Cleaver received a significant amount of personal space after that public kill, his actions failing entirely to go unnoticed. Still, he laughed out loud and raised his cleaver to the sky as he just kept walking. Not one guard was coming to bother him! He could literally slaughter anyone he wanted. For no reason! That agent was right, this place was fulfilling! His blind warcry forced him to miss a small orb of light zipping by, striking the downed agent in the head.

The massive Djinn statues became more imposing the closer Cleaver got to them, but they were just statues and the demon paid them no heed. He reminded himself not to feel so on edge.

No matter the amount of eyes already on him, or how unpleasantly *hot* it was suddenly getting. He was going to have even more eyes on him in the coliseum! Ha!

Cleaver stopped after setting foot on the paved-stone path from the gravel section. He'd crossed over into the outer triangle zone and again felt strange. Throughout his earlier walk, he'd been flanked by rows of terracotta statues on both sides. The paved path was much nicer than the gravel ground the statues were planted in, but that couldn't be what this mystery itch was about.

He reminded himself, again, not to feel out of sorts about carved pieces of stone. Which was such a strange feeling to experience. Him, afraid of some measly stone. He put it out of mind, and set one foot down on the wooden drawbridge leading to the inner triangle, and his coliseum goal. He scowled in pain shortly after, as a whistling arrow shot through his foot, pinning him in place. "Abyss! Who dares attack Cleaver, mightiest of waste warriors!"

"Is that your name? What a waste that you won't be

missed." A calm, pleasant voice floated back down to him from the overhead walking path. Cleaver heard a bowstring snap when the strange man attempted to draw again, followed by an angry retort at the broken weapon when the haft itself followed suit. "Crackers and toast! Not another one."

Pulling the arrow out of his foot, Cleaver booked it down the drawbridge. He didn't like randomly being shot at. Then again, if that bowman was some friend of the agent he'd cut in twain, he supposed that was just how things worked here.

Another stab of pain struck Cleaver as a sword punctured through his back, spilling fresh black blood out from the front of his jerkin. He felt the stab, but the experience of pain muted itself quickly. "What the abyss? Now what!"

Spinning around without much concern for the sword still stuck in him, Cleaver didn't understand how the agent he'd cut in two was standing in front of him. The agent's clothing clearly showed where he'd destroyed the mortal. Yet he was whole! "Thought it would be so easy to end a retribution agent? Think again, fiend! The listed rules here aren't what's upheld. Thank you so much for painting yourself as a target! I can gain experience from you now. Also, please keep looking at me for just a *second* longer."

Cleaver spun around when the back of his neck tingled. Something was behind him, and that outright idiotic platitude from the man before him was befoulingly obvious. The agent gripped his sword once the handle came in reach, pulling it out of Cleaver's back as the demon in disguise took an arrow right to the head.

Cleaver collapsed to his knees, his vision going sideways and wonky. He was struck by several intelligence decreasing status ailments from having an arrow currently in his noggin, which didn't help matters.

He then saw the warrior from the drawbridge, except he was on ground level, cursing at another destroyed bow that now weakly hung in his hand. "What am I doing wrong here? One little arrow and the whole thing goes kaput. Oh, Bernard! He's all yours, my boy. I don't want any of his stuff. Feel free to take it! You've got the retribution effect active, so hack away! You're in the right!"

Bernard gleefully separated Cleaver's head from his shoulders.

The demon did not understand. How. *How*? There was no way Cleaver had accrued so much damage that he would be down and out already. Even as a severed head, his expression was one of disdain and disbelief. In his final moments, Cleaver checked his status sheet, seeing that his health had been steadily declining due to some regional effect he hadn't noticed before. Save as an itch he couldn't place. *Discordant Resplendence*? When had that triggered? When he crossed the outer triangle's threshold? What was—

Shink!

"Retribution, claimed." Bernard held his sword aloft, the head of the grievance shishkebabed on it. A golden light suffused him right after, announcing his level up to everyone watching. Onlookers swiftly broke into applause. Cheering loudly himself, Bernard jumped around full of mirth. He was level ten! He could get his specialization now! "Yes!"

When he turned to face the caretaker, the man was gone. Bernard's dancing stopped, but his pleasant demeanor did not. He'd been honest with the demon before, even if Cleaver hadn't truly known what the man meant.

Bernard loved this place. Evil announced itself with a swiftness, painting targets on their own backs! Solar Gate was a secret one-way trap for all things malicious and awful, and he lived for the purging. In fact, that was the specialization he should take.

Purger.

CHAPTER THIRTY-ONE

Artorian dropped his twentieth broken bow off with a bowyer he was on good terms with. Leaning against the pillar of the ground floor workshop, he kneaded his brows while waiting to see what Cra, the shop owner, had to say. Cra scratched a feather behind her ear, trying to come to terms with what she was looking at while speaking with an accent that somewhat reminded Artorian of Brianna. "Alright, Caretaker. I think I've found the problem you keep running into, even if I don't really believe it."

Pushing from the pillar, he sat down at the work desk bench next to Cra. Her weathered hand pointed at the wooden haft where he kept his grip. "At first, I thought it was a design flaw, or bad wood. That doesn't hold up when I've got twenty wrecked bows in a barrel, all with the same injuries. I just got my bowyer profession to fifteen, and the Voice of the World gave me a new skill."

Cra picked up the broken bow, speaking firmly. *"Properties."*

Wooden Bow
Rarity: Trash

Condition: Broken

Making the property tab visible to her customer, she showed him her new skill. Again, Cra firmly stated her wants. "*Inspect Properties.*"

Wooden Bow

Information: An abandoned bow, found in wreckage.

Rarity: Trash

Information: This item is broken, it will slowly vanish to the ether unless disassembled for crafting materials, or otherwise used in a consumptive manner, such as kindling.

Condition: Broken

Information: This bow broke due to exceeding hidden value: Durability. On last use, item durability hit the negatives, immediately reducing the item to the broken condition, and trash rarity.

Cra pointed at the last information tab. "They all have this. Every last one. As you can see, the bow was just fine until last use. Meaning that the force applied to the item was so high, it broke a value that I haven't seen before. It makes sense that most items have a durability, but I don't think that's something I can tinker with until profession level twenty. Now, I can repair this trash tier item back to a damaged tier item, but that's going to be very costly since the bows are currently destroyed. Triple the cost if you want them back up to the common tier. One better than damaged."

Artorian said nothing, trying to glean additional information from the properties screen while he held his face. No luck. He shook his head at her query, and scratched the top of his head. "It sounds cheaper to just buy a new bow, though I feel like I'm just going to tear through them one shot at a time."

Cra's eyes twinkled. She didn't mind one bit. That meant profit! Artorian caught her gaze and threw his hands in the air. "Well I'm stuck. Unless you can make bows that can survive my usage, I think it might just be me that needs to adapt. I'm mistreating these poor things, just look at how I've handled them. One firm squeeze, and crack! Tell me you have solutions other than bulk buy?"

The bowyer dismissed her screens, since the customer had the information. "Well, while it would make me very happy to sell in bulk, if you want a better bow, then I need better materials to make it out of. Unfortunately that means delivery work, as I can't leave my workshop with the amount of requests I'm getting. Though I don't know if it's to defend the walls, or for newly hired soldiers to shoot their supervisor in the face with. This place is a hotbed of turmoil and change."

Artorian raised a brow. "Is that a complaint? Tell me of the materials, I'll see what I can do."

Cra shook her head to mean that no, it wasn't a complaint. "I arrived two weeks ago with a sack of wood and a few strings. I set up a stall on the street since those were free, and sold everything I had that day. My work wasn't even good. The demand for weapons or… just about anything here, is incredible. I slammed through seven profession levels in bowyer in just the last two weeks alone because it's been non-stop crafting. A week after I arrived here, I leased this store location. Now I am already sitting on enough gold that I need to hire an assistant, and move locations to a two-story variant. Meanwhile, I have had fifteen neighbors in this area come and go in that timeframe."

She took a drink from her self-made mug just to cut herself off. Or she would be right back on the gossip train. "Bow materials. Anything exotic is always nice, but the rarities have to match. If you get me a string material that's rare, but a wood material that's just uncommon, then the finished bow will be uncommon when I check its properties. I've got a small percentage chance for it to turn out as a rare, but so far it hasn't happened to me yet."

She motioned with her cup. "The effects on the bow heavily differ depending on what they are. Get me flamewood, and your bow turns out flame resistant. Get me flamewood for the bow and pyre root for the string, and your arrows will gain a small bit of flame damage. So long as your arrows are at least the same quality as the bow. Otherwise there's no bonus, though that may be because the bow quality is too low. Higher rarity bows may not care."

Artorian nodded slowly. "Neat. Is it like that for all crafting?"

Cra made the 'no' motion once again. "It depends on the route you go. I make most of my bows with the Voice's help, meaning they get done rather fast. The downside is the quality suffers. If I make a work using the Voice, the item will always be of the lowest quality of the materials I used to make it. That part is true for all crafters. Now if I didn't use the Voice, and made the bow myself, the quality would skyrocket. Unfortunately, so does the time, focus, and effort I need to put in for crafting. I'd never make my current quotas, even if the product and profession experience is significantly better. That's why crafters will stress component rarity, as the making it yourself rules also apply to any crafter."

Artorian squeezed his gaze. "Why would anyone ever want to do it using the second method if the first is so much faster and can be determined based on rarities?"

Cra leaned over and picked up a red bow. That must have been the flamewood she'd been talking about. "I made this without the Voice, and finishing it afforded me several profession breakthroughs and unlocks. I can now craft with flamewood and pyre root without penalty, because I made it without help. *I* did this, and the Voice of the World recognized that."

Her customer understood, and pointed over at a barrel of common quality bows. "Well I can't gather materials without a bow to go hunt for them, right? I'll take the entire barrel please. I've got practice to do."

Cra counted the math out on her fingers. "It's seven copper per bow. When I checked the markets today, it was fifteen coppers to one silver. There's twelve bows in that barrel. Twelve times seven... uhh."

Her customer held out a hand filled with coins. "Eighty-four copper, or five silver and nine copper. Per today's market. Since you are such a sweetheart for explaining things to a slow man like me, please take these seven silver. Appreciation costs."

Cra wasn't about to say no to an extra silver, and bundled the bows up. "Sure thing. In the market for any arrows?"

Artorian gently waved her off that he wasn't here for arrows. "Got plenty of those. It's the bows I need. Got more ammunition than I do the weapons to fire them. Normally not a problem to have, but in this case... well. I'll come find you again if I can get my hands on exotic materials."

He mumbled a follow-up under his breath. "Since apparently I can't cheat them in, and the light balls won't let me use a title to get around it."

Artorian accepted the bundle with a big smile. "Thank you, my dear. Until next time!"

"Anytime!" Cra waved to the good customer, always happy to have a big spender come and go. She really needed that assistant now. There were easily another three customers in line at her door. She put on her chipper voice and got right to the sales.

"Hello, welcome to Cra's crafts! What instrument of death can I get you today?"

Artorian still heard her even though he was long around the corner. He dodged a pair of children chasing a creature that had made off with their piece of bread, easily outspeeding the duo as it ran faster than it appeared to be able to control. He mused. "Must be special bread."

The cheering from the coliseum momentarily distracted him. Someone else had changed up the leaderboards. Nice how that kept happening, and the small flow of profits from a one-copper attendance fee kept his pockets full enough to make a purchase like this when he needed to.

He didn't really need the money. The rest went to Chiffon so he could keep up the ruse. The 'King' had really hammered his performance up, but was gaining experience at a maddening rate. What was Chiffon now, level twenty-one somewhere? With his actor profession almost matching it? "Good going, boyo…"

Artorian's own level on the other hand, was still stuck at a measly four. He'd been busy with other things, but hopefully there would be good news today. He got in line behind a merchant troupe ascending the stairs to get to the third level bridge connections. Once all the way up top, he glanced around to see what castle his friends were hiding away in. Based on the flags, today they were in… Discord's place.

Swinging the bundle over his shoulder, he enjoyed a lovely walk in the sun while heading off in that direction. Glancing to the roads, he saw a few Nobles burst into flames when leaving the shade, and die on the spot. A few others looked a little green around the gills. Good on Chiffon for handing out curses matching the kind of malicious annoyance he saw in people. A perk of his profession! He was great at telling when others weren't being genuine. In addition, the actor seemed to truly possess a knack for twisting fate. Applying his trickery at just the right moment to nudge history in an ever so slightly different direction.

Artorian hoped that knack wouldn't cost Chiffon dearly one day. There were already signs of kingdom-trouble, but he was certain the King could keep a lid on matters. The outpouring of suncurses had caused a minor problem where some Nobles had shacked up in the castles, unwilling to leave since the sun burned them to a crisp. "Eh, it will be fine. Maybe some unexpected good will come of it."

Pushing open the third level gate to the violet-roofed fortress outer walls with a single hand, the new guards looked at him funny, then tried it themselves after he was through. They didn't remotely encounter similar results, since it normally needed eight of them to open or close one of these. That was *with* the use of the pulley system.

"That was the Caretaker. All's well," a more experienced guard informed the others when the topic came up a short while later. "Don't mind him."

Babel, the brand-new guard, motioned at the gate. "He pushed that massive thing open with one hand. It's hard not to mind!"

Kortin, the experienced guard who used to be a professional cow herder, just beckoned him closer before answering with some reed-chewed drawl. "Listen, kid. I've been here a week. That's two years in guard time anywhere else. You are very quickly going to get used to certain faces, such as the people on that big coliseum leaderboard over there. The Caretaker, who just passed us, is one such folk. Just let him go out on his business."

Kortin turned to motion at the Greenwood Castle. "Not even the King gets in his way. In fact, the Caretaker is the only person I've ever seen the King *apologize* to. So just accept that the man is here to help, and don't look twice at strange occurrences. If the Caretaker's around, don't... hold too tightly to the rules of reality. Folks on the brink of death have gotten back up on their feet, just because he walked in. Myself being one of them. Just remember that the listed rules aren't the real rules, and keep an eye out for evil. You see some new guy being shifty, you run to the Hall of Retribution and let the agents know."

The experienced guard smirked. "They'll have him followed in no time, and his name on the board not much later. As you've seen, you're unlikely to run into an agent. Or be bothered by one, if they don't suspect you in some way. Snooty Noble causing a fuss? Send 'em to the King. They'll be glad to think they're being recognized, when in reality they're going to be chewed out in public for half an afternoon. To the great amusement of everyone else."

"Skeevy merchant?" Kortin stabbed his thick finger to the mountain pass. "You send 'em to the mountain."

"Overzealous stranger with a hunger for the fineries of killing?" Kortin stabbed his finger to the coliseum. "You send those weirdos to go take care of each other."

Babel nodded in understanding. "Don't bother those who are good, send away the rest. I know the quiet rules. Though 'sending away' involves a lot of dead ends that get tied up rather permanently. How is this place even making money? Please don't tell me the rumor that they're stealing from the dead is actually true?"

Kortin waved that silliness away. "You know the way it works. Anything unclaimed goes to the Kingdom. Kingdom sells it to the merchants on the cheap in the special market below us on the second rung. Merchants get to resell and set the market prices, which is why the value of coin fluctuates. Down on the first rung, the brokers are keeping a tally of what currency is worth what, and how much of something else. That all goes over my head, but it's allowing multiple currencies to be used in the city without a problem. Just need to check the board."

Babel frowned. "Right, but how is it *making* money?"

Kortin thought that had been obvious. "Where do you think the food and lodging comes from? King owns all the properties, and rents rather than sells. He also pays farmers, guards, and helpful services a pretty silver, rather than the few copper we'd normally get. In turn, he owns all the food, and we buy it at a good rate that won't be destroyed if the market ever goes topsy turvy. Merchants keep bringing in new goods and coins, but mostly it circulates here and accumulates. 'No taxes' is a spicy offering for many a soul."

Babel could deeply appreciate that. "No taxes is great, and my lodgings are maybe a tenth of my wage. Food is another tenth. Two tenths if I really stuff myself like a pig every day. I thought it was odd we had to buy all our own gear. Given the wage, that still works out well for me. I also met this really adorable seamstress because of it."

Kortin smirked, punching the new blood on the shoulder. "Well you think of that while you finish your shift. Remember what it is we're *actually* looking for."

The guards resumed duties right as Artorian arrived where he needed to be. The main hall of the top rung. Time to check in with his friends!

CHAPTER THIRTY-TWO

Opening the hall doors caused a ruckus as attention flew Artorian's way. "Love, buddy! There you are! What took? You're rarely late."

Artorian high-fived Discord as he stutter-stepped by. Some new movement trick he was trying out where he only existed in reality sometimes, rather than constantly. He was angrily being followed by a litany of notifications, which told everyone in the room that Eternium had his hands full dealing with the Wood Elf. Since Discord was currently not using his Djinn form.

The amusements made Artorian smile, reminded of the grove and their parties once again. All that was missing was a blossom of the Elves to erupt from nearby foliage and hold up scoreboards. He should help bring that back somehow.

Artorian held up the weapon bundle. "Found out why I've been going through bows like they're sweetbread. Also got a firsthand view of the regional effects at play. It still hurts that those abilities can't be used while they're being diverted to the region, but our plans are in full swing. Got our first proper demon today! An actual warrior rather than a spy-brat. You were right, Chaos! He just couldn't stop himself when finding out there were no known repercussions for him just being… *him*. Didn't even make it to the inner triangle without notice."

Chaos grinned wide, downing a cup of berry wine while lounging pleasantly on a huge cat. That made Artorian miss Decorum. It'd be fine, he'd find the boy. Chaos stabilized his speech pattern before speaking, so it wouldn't turn into nine different voices. "Great! I've been having a fantastic time in this place, Solar Gate is lively and ever-changing. Right up my alley. Put that bundle down and come over here so I can check to see if the regionals are holding up."

Artorian walked up and opened his status sheet, making it visible so Chaos could inspect the special values. "Let's see here now. Here you go, Chaos, what's the verdict?"

Chaos tapped the relevant values, making them pop up as independent screens.

Arbitration of Entropy
Status: Active
Reach: Solar Gate region
Cost: Paid by Solar Gate wreckage
Warning: Original wreckage effects will be reduced while this effect is active.
Effect: Applied to the entirety of the spell's reach, Arbitration of Entropy prevents experience gain unless specific exclusion conditions are met.
Condition 1: Experience is Profession-based.
Condition 2: Experience is Specialization-based.
Condition 3: Experience is earned in the location zoned as 'Coliseum.'
Condition 4: Experience is earned by a wearer of Entropy's mark.
Condition 5: Experience is from a task vetted through the Hall of Retribution.
Warning: Entity 'Chaos' is locked out of using ability 'Deny the Rule' while this effect is active.

Chaos gave a thumbs up after reading through Entropy's regional effect, moving on to Discord's since the first one was working well.

Discordant Resplendence
Status: Active
Reach: Specified zoning in Solar Reach.
Cost: Paid by Solar Gate wreckage
Warning: Original wreckage effects will be reduced while this effect is active.
Effect: Applied to the zones listed below, Discordant Resplendence applies the Resplendence field effect in full.
Zone 1: Outer Solar Gate Triangle, marked by paved pathing.
Zone 2: Inner Solar Gate Triangle, marked by drawbridge perimeter.
Exclusion: Coliseum zone.
Zone 3: Discord Triangle.
Zone 4: Entropy Triangle.
Zone 5: Chaos Triangle.
Warning: Entity 'Artorian' is locked out of using ability 'Resplendence Field' while this effect is active.

Chaos closed the notifications. Things were working as intended. "That's good, they're stable. Chiffon likely isn't too happy with that significantly diminished shield regeneration rate, but he'll live. He only has about seven assassination attempts on his life per day lately. Much lower than what it was."

Artorian nodded. "Chiffon will be fine. It's the general region before the outer triangle I'm worried about. That demon cut down an agent outside of the healing field. I used an obliterator to get him back on his feet since I was lucky enough to see it happen. Glad I got him before he actually died. Still, keeping the field close made the demon not see the threat eating into his health bar when he crossed the threshold."

Chaos watched Discord stutter-step around some more, motioning in agreement. "Best it stays as is, although I think that was the last item on the docket? Since we can't test the terracotta army until someone actually breaks the only rule in Solar Gate. They were great as a tireless workforce, but now that we've converted them over to their second function, their show is a waiting game. I think that unties you from needing to be here non-stop. What's the plan after all these months of secretive building?"

Artorian motioned out the window, towards the coliseum. "That, in all likelihood. I need to achieve level ten so I can unlock my specializations and get a move on. I considered going out and about, but with the demons finally trickling in I want to stay close at hand just a little longer. Until I can confirm the field does them in all by itself. I also need to go and activate some beacons, now that I've gotten the information from merchants during downtime."

He held his short beard pensively. "I know where they are… roughly. I can hunt them down based on the comings and goings of the merchants, which will let me start cobbling the network together. On second thought, that should fetch me experience much faster than the coliseum might. What do you think, my friend?"

Chaos considered it, lying back on the fluffy tiger. "I think it would be more chaotic if you went out into the world. The demons might be arriving, but they're the weak ones. If you enter the coliseum, that's only going to have one outcome. Not very chaotic, that. The field will melt them, and if not, an agent will clean up. They're getting potent at figuring the unspoken rules out. Some of them even seem to just know what this place is actually built for."

Artorian smirked. "My little mousetrap project? How lucky…"

Chaos tossed his bow bundle back at him. "Go out and hunt, this place will run on its own now that the zones are set up. Even if it doesn't, Discord, Entropy, and I are having great fun in the new playground. Discord might currently be a buffoon, but he lives in the markets and dances with glee. I thrive from the mixture of it all, and Entropy is tingly at denying experience on such a massive scale. I don't even mind that one of my abilities got locked up. Shame we had to double up on casters to make the effects work. We could have had four!

Ah well, **Order** had to win somewhere, right? What would he do without us?"

Love caught the bundle, affixing it snugly to his back. "I'll go out then. What would be a nice chaotic direction to send me off in? I don't particularly want Midgard-quality threats to play with. Even if this realm is where I'm stuck."

The cat lounger steepled his fingers in contemplation. "North. Go north. Many of the demons have slunk in from there. Since you don't hunt wildlife, therefore also no area bosses, that's the best I've got. Not having your field is going to hurt though."

Artorian waved the comment off. "I've got my costly obliterator. It does the same, just... not as conveniently. Unfortunately, I am still paying the full twenty-eight percent maximum mana cost for the field. Even if I'm not the benefactor. Then again, I had a hunch I wasn't going to be able to rely on my mana all the time. So this is fine. I'll go beacon-bouncing, and rain some arrows down from on high while I'm at it. The scree-scree brats can't hide from my Inspect anyway."

While shuffling over to the window, Chaos made a *mnnn* 'you shouldn't' noise at him. Artorian stopped before reaching the opening. "Hmm? What? Oh! Right. I'm not exempt from the no-fly rule, and I don't want to check if the terracottas work as intended. Stairs it is!"

High-fiving Discord on the way out—who was still being chased by notifications—Artorian enjoyed a laugh, and closed the massive hall doors behind him. Kortin and Babel were still on shift when the gate doors they stood at opened from the inside. Kortin just took hold of the top of his helmet, tipping it like a cow-herding hat.

"Caretaker."

The Caretaker sent a pleasant nod in return, noticing the rest of the local guards copied Kortin's hat-tip motion. Artorian glibly spoke as he passed by. "Have a pleasant day, my boys... Do keep your senses at the ready. Life is going to get interesting over the next few months."

The guards felt bleak at the prospect, but Kortin slammed his fist to his chest. "A challenge! Our legs will get plenty of practice, running to the Hall of Retribution. The guard looks forward to days of activity. A pleasant day to you, Caretaker."

Artorian pulled one of the bows out of his satchel, and tossed it over to the spunky guard. "That's the spirit. You take that! I'll be going now. Toodles!"

The guards began talking over one another, also in an attempt to score a free bow. Their words fell on deaf ears. Or rather, ears that had stepped off the side of the wall. Artorian fell right to the bridges below, which the Caretaker elegantly hopped between in order to step foot on ground level.

Babel scratched under his helmet while watching the display. "Kortin. I think you were right."

Kortin was far too busy stringing his new bow to pay attention. Giving it a pleasant practice twang. "That's becoming a trend! Much more of this, and I might meet the qualifications for guard captain."

The guards shared a good laugh, their pleasantry leaving Artorian's earshot as he jogged over the drawbridge and away from the Solar Gate. This place was running itself just fine now, he'd just muck the finer details up by getting in the way. He cleared his throat, and spoke with a firmness matching Cra the bowyer. "*Minimap.*"

How nice that he no longer had to speak in what felt like brackets to accomplish that. When he'd crossed the cobblestone line marking the Kingdom's borders, he took off. A handful of platforms later, and Artorian was the skywards rocket he was used to being. When he set foot upon a cloud, he pleasantly bounced, his words equally amused and peppy. "Alright! You two around? It's been a while."

A green and orange light popped in behind him. The Wisps in sync and complaining in unison. "Finally! What took so long?"

Laughter was all the reply they got at first. "Well, weren't you watching? I put a mousetrap together with the help of some friends. Took a bit, but the results speak for themselves!"

Yvessa landed on his right shoulder, poking him in the cheek with some mana. "You know what we meant, Mr. Fourth Level. Now what's the real plan?"

Artorian scowled at her. "Why must you *assume* that just because… okay, never mind. *Yes*, fine. Do you have any way of getting in touch with Dev? Even just to get his attention?"

Yvessa didn't really talk to the R&D team, but that didn't sound too difficult. "Getting his attention is about all I'll be able to do within the confines of the rules."

The cloud runner changed his scowl to a smirk. "That will be enough."

Yvessa went quiet, Oberon landing on the available left shoulder. "So, Sunny, tell me we're going demon squishing."

Artorian's smirk widened just a teensy bit. "Oh, indeed we are, but I want to do it in style. I also thought it might be helpful to strain physics, see what Eternium can take."

Oberon went quiet, but not because he liked what he heard. Yvessa was done, and prompted them both. "He's paying attention."

Artorian funneled mana into his new Senate ability, triggering the Forum option. Oof. The cost felt… harsher? He grumbled on noticing the costs for the Forum and the Senate had stacked. His grumbles fell since Yvessa was already tackling it, having seen the inconsistency in the log. <Dev, you around, Gnome buddy?>

Garbled synthetic soundwaves filled his forum space. Tones that altered to become words as a visual outline of the gnome, surrounded by some equally gnomish friends, appeared one shiny line at a time. It took the Gnome a moment to calibrate, but he got his speech under control.

Deverash Neverdash was back, and his voice was as Gnomishly peppy as ever. <Artorian! How have you been! Breaking more things for me to study?>

The human was now having a good day. <Ha! It's good to

hear your voice. Is that something you'd like? Because I have a thought I think you might enjoy. Tell me, my devilishly smart, tiny friend. Do you have any more of those racing platforms up your sleeve? We haven't tested those in here, and the last one… Err. Got goosed.>

Artorian could hear Dev wringing his hands together, and he just knew that Gnomish face was forming a toothy smile, his mind full of experimental machinations. <Oh yes… We're actually pulling that palanquin to pieces. To figure out where all the strain was coming from. I've got a model I would love tested, but I expect you have your own plans.>

Deverash just knew his friend had equally devious ideas in mind, and Artorian didn't disappoint. <I do! Any chance you could put a… let's see… big plow on the front? I want to do some landscaping, preferably very quickly. If a flat platform could be added on the back that I could stand on, that would also be nice.>

Dev's expression became so thoroughly enthusiastic, that his floating hexagonal friends nearby gave him some space. <That can certainly be done. Getting it to you is the hard part. Any chance you can make a gate, or have a specific beacon I can import the final draft to?>

Artorian thought he could get that done. <I will ask Yvessa to give you a notice with the next beacon I touch. I found out they're all numbered, so I should be able to get you that information. I'm actually coming up on one now, if I recognized that circle in the upcoming village correctly. Keep you posted?>

Dev was already pulling materials together, his workshop clicking to mechanical life. <I'm looking forward to it! Talk when we can! It's very busy over here. One plow racer, coming up!>

The connection closed, and Artorian was certain today was going to be a great day.

CHAPTER THIRTY-THREE

The village of Oswan dealt primarily with sheep. They exported the wool to make clothing and a variety of sundry goods, and imported food by the cart. The village elder had decided on this location because he believed the local landmark would bring them luck. The local landmark, unbeknownst to him, being teleportation beacon number twenty-two.

With the sun going down, the workday for Oswan was coming to an end. Today, that end came with a loud thud, and every item not bolted to the floor springing up half a foot. Animals and people included. The animals caused a noisy cacophony while people hustled from their homes, some of which were now in a sorry state.

When the village elder stumbled from his abode, he saw a stranger standing on the beacon. How dare he! Then the stranger touched it, and the entire landmark brightened. Teal lights illuminated along the edges and pillar, some of them flickering before fully glowing as the stranger poured power in.

Oswan felt frozen to the ground as he watched the display. When the lights concluded their show, the strange man looked around, settling his gaze upon him. This unsettled Oswan, the elder who the village was named after. Still, he was in charge and he was the one who needed to deal with this. Shuffling forwards, the strange man in red clothing and a large robe offered a hand in greeting.

Oswan looked around at his slightly wrecked town, but the people seemed alright. They were mostly running around trying to calm their sheep. Oswan was a hefty sixty-four years old, and time hadn't been kind to him. Hunched, he took the stranger's hand and shook it. This made the stranger beam out a warm smile, and speak in a language he didn't understand.

When the stranger realized he hadn't been understood, he tapped his chin and helped the elder over to the beacon. Though the man may have just as easily picked him up and dragged him over. Oswan needed to see the example twice, but understood the stranger when he pressed his hand to the pillar, motioning for him to do the same.

Just stepping foot on the luminous landmark had made him nervous. To touch the thing? Somewhere between scary and enthralling. Some of his people had stopped to watch, so he pressed his hand to the pillar. Oswan's eyes went wide when the voice of the world spoke to him.

Discovery! Experience +500!

You have discovered: Oswan Village Beacon.

Using this beacon allows you to teleport to all other beacons connected to the network. Teleportation costs are paid in mana or experience, unless your Divine of choice is set to: Sunny. As you do not have a Divine of choice, you will be given the option to align yourself without cost.

Would you like to align yourself to the Divine: Sunny?
Cost: None.
Benefits: No cost on beacon use.
Boon: Minor health regeneration (constant).

Oswan's wrinkly old face turned to look at the stranger he couldn't properly speak to. Still, he didn't need to. The Voice of the World was always understandable. He had to read over the floating notice three more times before his hand hovered to the 'yes' option. He looked at the stranger one more time, but the man did nothing. Seeming to be perfectly content to let Oswan make his own choices.

There not being a cost was something Oswan considered to be 'starting off on the right foot.' He didn't really understand the beacon information, and he wasn't one for being devout. Yet there was nothing here that demanded he do anything, only that he would gain benefits for aligning himself. That health regeneration was tempting, particularly in his old age. Tiny injuries turned into a whole week of staying out of the way.

Steeling himself, Oswan pressed yes. The notice before him changed, as did the appearance of the stranger.

Alignment confirmed! Oswan of the sheep-shearing village has aligned himself with Sunny, Sovereign of the Sun. You have gained the following benefits:

Teleportation network: Your access to the network has improved! Using beacons to travel between locations no longer costs you either mana or experience, as your aligned Divine will pay the cost for you.

Boon: You have gained a constant-effect boon! This boon will remain active so long as you remain aligned to this Divine. This boon grants you health regeneration equal to one per second. Never again will inconveniences keep you down!

Notice: You are in the presence of your Divine! Your boon is currently multiplied by a factor of ten. Your Divine focuses on the well-being of others. Your demerits are being removed as a result.

Notice: Your Divine currently does not speak your language. You have gained a quest.

Not believing his eyes, Oswan immediately checked the notification after that. He was feeling better by the second. His wrinkles faded, the ache in his bones silenced. The itching of his skin stilled. The pain in his teeth mended. The vagueness of his sight cleared. The crick in his back lifted.

Quest: Language Grant.

While your Divine asks nothing of you, that does not mean you cannot show your appreciation. At no cost to yourself, you may allow your Divine to learn your language by granting him the knowledge over a period of time. The more people who accept this quest, the faster this grant will occur.

Do you wish to provide this grant?

Oswan the no-longer-falling-apart elder glanced at the stranger, who was a stranger no longer. His appearance, even if clad in shoddy clothing, was celestial. Now that he was aligned, he saw the truth hidden below the skin. Sunny was a milky tapestry of stars, swirling in a vast cosmos. His eyes might burn as suns, but their gaze was soft. Kind.

Oswan pressed yes on his quest prompt without another thought.

When the Divine offered his hand once again, Oswan hesitated. He accepted slowly, receiving his last prompt before it was clear Sunny was going to leave.

Temporary blessing gained!

You have been acknowledged by Sunny, Sovereign of the Sun.

You have gained the temporary blessing: Resplendent Soul.

This blessing will last one hour. While you have this blessing, any other people aligned to the same Divine as you will gain benefits as if they were in the Presence of the Divine himself.

Notice: Your Divine has granted you a message through the Voice of the World, as he does not speak your language.

Message: <I apologize for landing so roughly in your village. Please, take this blessing, and see to the health of your people and flock. I cannot repair your homes, but I can give you the means to live strong, and live long. I thank you, my friend. For trusting me when you had no reason to. I must go, but I wish you and your village well.

To use the beacon, merely touch it. I suggest Solar Gate for any goods you may wish to sell. It will not work while others stand upon the platform, but you will be added in a queue for when it is safe to transfer. Merely wait for the number to strike zero, and you will find yourself elsewhere. The beacon can take you and any amount of goods you have, though it will only be free for use for those aligned. I wish you well, Oswan.>

Some kind of oversized cart appeared on the beacon plat-form when Oswan finished reading his message. He was speech-less, the Divine giving him a gentle goodbye with a wave of the hand as he jumped into the strange contraption. The long wedge-shaped cart didn't appear to be touching the ground either? A thrumming from the craft made him step back, the odd floating cart hovering off and away, leaving his village far behind at incredible speeds.

Oswan looked at the floating messages from the Voice of the World. He stood there until his son shook his shoulder. "Father? Father. What happened? You look young, and healthy. Who was that? Are you injured? The entire village is worried sick that you met some fiend!"

The village elder blinked, but broke into a smile before he faced his son, who he now looked younger than. "No, my boy. That was no fiend. That was a blessing in disguise. Do you remember when I told you decades ago that this landmark was lucky? I was right, my boy. I was right!"

Oswan's son was nearly squeezed to death with the hug that followed. "F… Father! Your strength!"

"My strength is back! I..." He let his son go, checking his own arms. His gaze steeled, determination filling his soul. "My boy. Gather the village. I have wonderful news, and even better tidings to bring. The damage to our village is unfortunate, but we have gained far more in turn. Tell all to come to me and touch the beacon. The Divines are *back*, and they are *loving*."

Artorian was unaware of the goings on in Oswan's village.

He was trying to figure out what all the new control levers on this new racing platform did. One of them turned out to be a handbrake. While the platform had stopped on a copper, he hadn't! Artorian had flung forwards and tumbled over so much grass that he needed to slap himself with his healing orb to be okay. "Physics hurt! Eternium must be *laughing*."

Sitting up, a new notification blinked into being to his right. He rubbed his head, grabbed the edge, and pulled it closer.

Event notice!
Deity: Rank 2.

Congratulations! You have taken the first steps as a budding, active deity in Eternia. You have crossed your first follower threshold, and twice in a row at that! Thresholds occur in multiples of ten, starting at five. Once you reach five hundred followers, you will reach the third deity rank. You will now begin to gain DE points, short for Divine Energy.

First Rank merit: You may now gain Divine Energy from followers. Followers generate up to 25 DE a day.

Second Rank merit: You may now gain Divine Energy from Altars. Altars generate 50 DE a day.

Third Rank merit: You may now gain Divine Energy from Shrines. Shrines generate 100 DE a day.

Fourth Rank merit: You may now gain Divine Energy from Temples. Temples generate 250, 500, and 1000 DE daily in order of rank.

There may be other places of power that can be converted, but you will need to find that information yourself.

Current follower count: Fifty-seven.
Altar count: Three.

Artorian brushed himself off, pushing his hands to the small of his back to get the crick out. Dismissing the screen after the second read over, he knew enough. It was similar to what Cal had talked to him about at the table in the archive. Was a similar version tucked away in this sun? A curiosity for later since Yvessa finished her trek, having hovered up next to him. "Had a nice fall?"

He cleared his throat and pulled his status up, pointing at something for her to read. "I'm really not fond of this saying Sovereign. I'm very anti-ruling."

Yvessa didn't know why that wording was used, so she *hmm'd* at him and hovered back to Oberon. Who was enthralled by the racing platform, indulging in a sea of menus and screens. This was a brand new, untested Dev toy! His interest was piqued, but he still heard Yvessa ask her question. "Obi, do you know why Sunny's Deity title has the word 'Sovereign' in it?"

Oberon was far too quick with his answer to think that this hadn't been done on purpose as some kind of cheeky ploy. "He owns the sun in Cal's realm via a technicality. The archives, right? That's why. He's the ruler of the archives, so a bit of wordplay was enjoyed at his expense... Is he upset?"

Yvessa bobbed with uncertainty. "I expected greater backlash, but he's not even grumbling about it, so I think he may have let this one slide. For now... Find anything interesting in there?"

Oberon brightened! "So much! Is he back yet? There's a lever I want him to pull. It's meant entirely to bring this thing up to maximum speed, and based on all of these charts I want to feel what that's like. Knowledge is one thing, experience another!"

"How right you are, my shiny orange friend!" Artorian had made his way back swifter than expected, but he hopped into the racer without another word on the matter. "A hefty difference between knowledge and experience, indeed. Much like I enjoy being both lucky and fortuitous, I find it better to be both knowledgeable and experienced as well. Even though I can be quite the sloth."

He winked at Yvessa, and settled in to try the racer controls again. "Alright, let's see. These are left and right. These are forwards and backwards. These seven are what I don't recognize. Well, six now. This one causes sudden stops. My poor nose…"

He tugged the lever Oberon was vehemently pointing at and impatiently hovering around. Artorian slammed to his seat as the racer shot forwards. The plow on the front carving a straight pathway right through a hill as he felt glued to the controls. What was he, the Scar? Didn't matter. This was zippy and fast. He liked it! "On to the next beacon!' *Wheeee*!

CHAPTER THIRTY-FOUR

Artorian calmly practiced racer operations when another notice came in. His craft was currently causing some waves as he floated at half his running speed across a small sea. The notification informed him that his follower count had risen to one hundred. Artorian turned his head to his Wisp. "Yvessa, why did I just gain more followers? I could swear there weren't more than sixty folk in the place we just left. Where's this new forty from?"

That was curious, so she looked up his log. "Looks like they're from people stepping on the beacon platform in Solar Gate, since that platform doubles as a coliseum ring. I just realized that might interrupt the events there somewhat. Which is only going to get worse as more beacons are linked."

She didn't get a reply, so continued. "You've actually had twice that amount of people step on the beacon. Your numbers are fluctuating. It seems that each combatant receives the prompt, and that the health regeneration boon is what's selling it. Since only one fighter tends to leave that arena alive, that accounts for why the numbers are rising and falling."

Artorian *mmm'd* back. "What can I do with Divine Energy

these days? Also I need to update that boon. If a demon accepts it, I want it to do the opposite of what it currently does. Not that I want the description to reflect that. Does everything still cost millions? What's my daily gain currently?"

Yvessa pulled up some information on a side screen, so Artorian's vision wasn't blocked from racer operations. "Found it. Take these with a grain of salt. These numbers are going to spike now that people in Solar Gate know they can get a free bonus from that beacon. Hope your mana regeneration is up to snuff when it comes to balancing those beacon costs out, or it's going to start eating the costs out of your experience."

Current follower count: One hundred and two.
DE gained per day: 2550
Altar count: Three.
DE gained per day: 150
Total DE Gained per day: 2700

Artorian thought that was a pleasant start, but those numbers were meaningless if he didn't know what they translated to. It wasn't like he could conveniently check the boards in the market. Those signs were easily one of Solar Gate's core features that appealed to him. He didn't need to ask a follow up question, his clever Wisp had it at the ready. These new screens replaced the gain information.

Divine Energy Shop:

This shop is under development. Please send a query to establish the cost of an item, event, or alteration. So it may be added to the list. As there have been no queries, this list is empty.

That soured both the Wisp and driver. Oberon pulled his sleeves up. "One moment, I think I can help here. I have access to the superior version of query. Artorian, what kind of things are you looking for from this service?"

Artorian thought it odd that Oberon was calling it a service, but played along. "I need a way to update or improve my boon. If possible, buying abilities would be great. Otherwise if I could buy a map improvement that shows me where all my beacons are, regardless of state, that would save me an incredible amount of time. Though, if I can really be creative, then I can let you in on the plan I told Yvessa, when it comes to gaining general experience."

Oberon looked up from his screen, scanning between Artorian and Yvessa. "That being?"

Yvessa informed her orange counterpart, having been eager for this topic. "How much DE equals one point of experience?"

The orange Wisp dismissed his screens just so he could directly address Yvessa. "That is *blatant* cheatery... I love it. Let me figure that out. I'm going to wink out. Will be back with answers when convenient. Though you should see the store populate with options if you just keep the screen handy. Actually, just do that. Let me work my magic, but ping me if a demon derby starts to occur."

He teleported out before either of the travelers could give him confirmation. That was fine, there was work to be done. Yvessa turned to face her charge. "Alright, Artorian. He's gone. Anything I should know? Like why you asked for the platform on the back of the racer, or that oversized iron-painted mithril plow. I wasn't going to say anything, but it's hard to ignore. That paint job fools nobody."

His surprised expression told Yvessa that her charge had, in fact, been fooled entirely. "He made it out of mithril? That absolute mad lad! I love it! That alleviates many of my worries about accidental crashes. It's a shame Oberon left. Now if there's a demon I've got a brand-new idea!"

Yvessa put two and two together. "Plowing through them?"

Artorian repeated her words with excitement. 'Plowing through them!"

Yvessa sighed loudly, but was swiftly distracted by the new text which had appeared on her shop screen. "I don't want to know. Let's look at what Oberon is doing. I'll read the new options out loud until you can bring this rig to a standstill that isn't in the middle of a sea."

Divine Energy Shop:

Option one.
Experience conversion: DE can be traded out at a 100:1 ratio. Meaning 100 points of DE becomes 1 experience point. This conversion can be activated to function passively, trading in all possible Divine Energy when the day timer ticks over.

Option two.
Altering alignment requirements: When a person aligns with you, thus choosing you as their deity and becoming your follower, they must follow your rules to retain that connection. You are allowed to set requisites they must follow to retain that alignment. Failure to follow this requirement will remove their connection to you.
Notice: The first alteration is free.

Option three.
Altering Boon benefits:
Your boon currently causes: Minor health regeneration (constant).
Notice: The first alteration is free.

Option four.
Divine Sense improvement:
A Divine Sense can be an extended function of any skill or ability that deals with gathering or gaining empirical information. That is, the information gained via your normal senses. Such as sound, touch, taste, or smell.
Cost variable depending on the sense desired.
Notice: The first Divine Sense is free.

Option five.
Divine abilities:
Cost variable depending on the ability desired.

Send a query per specific ability.

Option six.
Divine skills:
Cost variable depending on the skill desired.
Send a query per specific ability.

Option seven.
Title assignment:
Cost variable depending on the title granted.
As a Divine, you may grant titles to anyone you see fit. The cost, complexity, and effect of the title will change depending on the factors involved. No query is necessary, the cost will simply adjust to fit the desired effect.

Yvessa needed to take several breaths between reading those options over. That was a lot right away! Oberon sure knew how to do work when he felt like it. "If I had a jaw, it would hurt. Do you want to nudge some of these right away?"

Artorian pulled his platform up onto a beach, hovering it over some dunes before rubbing his eyes. "Any chance the cost of goggles is in there as well? Otherwise, all the free changes are what I want to address right away. Let's go through them from top to bottom."

His Wisp double checked, but saw no item listing on the shop just yet. "Doesn't look like it. First up is experience conversion. It does take everything, so maybe not the best option?"

Her charge wasn't dissuaded. "Flip that lever, I want it on. It may not be a lot, but a little is better than nothing when I'm moving from place to place."

Yvessa did as requested and pulled the lever. A noisy *kronk* was heard, but they couldn't discern the origin. Must be a system effect. Yvessa just moved on. "Option one is all done. Option two lets you add requirements. More of an 'if you do this one thing, you're not getting my benefit anymore' kind of idea."

Artorian sat back in his stationary racer, kneading his brows to think of something. "Any chance I can skip? I don't have any bright ideas for limitations in the current moment. I'd prefer to eventually kick the bad ones out. For now, more is better. Let's leave that one be and come back to it when I can afford to be picky."

His Wisp moved on. "Option three lets you alter your boon. You said something about hurting demons with it?"

He sternly agreed with that statement. "As much as possible. There isn't much I would apply such a blanket effect to, but demons certainly fit the bill. It's just not possible to let even a single one slide."

CHAPTER THIRTY-FIVE

Yvessa paused, moving the screen aside for a bit. "Say, question. Why is it that demons specifically have you by the beard? You have a level of ire for them that's simply not matched. Not even the raiders you offed in the Fringe medical tent dug this kind of one-sided hostility out of you. Why them? Can't they grow and learn like anyone else?"

Artorian pressed his hands together, lacing his fingers. "That's one celestial cake of a question. It actually isn't too much different from those raiders, if you were ever privy to what I told Hadurin in the meeting after. The difference between a demon and those raiders, is that the raiders are sufficiently 'of the kind of thing' that would allow them to apply to the requirements of your statement. They can change. Given time, will, and effort."

He tried pulling up his own screen to draw on, but failed spectacularly. Instead, he just wasted some mana and started drawing in the air. To his surprise, no skill notification. That or Eternium was working on it. "So it goes like this. Draw a big square, and then cut it into four sections. This is a good to evil chart, but we're looking at specific entries when it comes to the evil side."

Making the chart, he filled pieces in and then pointed. "This applies to both sides, but it goes like this. You've got only two variables you're looking at. Willful and caring. Which, in short, comes down to: did you mean to do the thing, and did you care about the thing you did. Then you have this bubble I call 'didn't have another choice.' Which is separate from those two. Most of the raiders knew what they were doing. They chose the life-style to pillage, harm, and such. Some of them didn't make that choice, and were just along for the ride because that's where they were stuck."

He started at the top left. "Willful and caring. So you both intended to kill, and cared about getting it done. In most King-doms, this is just called murder, but then they run into problems defending what their army is for. Those soldiers are fully intending to do some harm, but think they're doing it for the right reason. A complex mess, that. Let me not deviate too much."

He pointed at the top right. "Willful and uncaring. So you fully intended your kill, but you didn't care that you did it. These people are monsters, because they want to do whatever it is they're going to do, with zero interest in consequences or repercussions. They're going to kill, and you can't talk them out of it."

He pointed at the bottom left. "Unwillful, but caring. These people are remorseful about what they've done. They didn't want to kill. They just had to for whatever reason. Unlike the prior, they cared about it. Their act eats away at them. They had a choice not to, but they followed through. Hypocrisy is a powerful human trait."

He pointed at the last corner, the bottom right. "Unwillful, and uncaring. These are broken people. They didn't want to kill, but their apathy is so strong they simply can't, or won't, bring themselves to care. They silently do what they're told, and slave away for all to suffer. They have lost their will, and their way. Give these people a way out, and you'll be surprised at the kind of spirit they find."

Artorian drew a raider stick figure. "Now, a raider from our old world is nearly always human. A human, with all their physical limitations and ways to learn, can change to better suit the environment they live in. Unfortunately, this happens regardless of them seeing it or not. So the raiders…"

Artorian drew a stick figure in each corner. "…can be anywhere. It just so happens to be the case that all factors which have led up to their current point of being, leads to them being… unpleasant. Not all belong in the top right, but those that do get no mercy. That was the majority of people in the tent that day. Being judge and jury on a person's psyche is a heavy burden, as you can never truly be certain if you made the right call. You must make yourself unyielding and unbending to your beliefs to carry yourself through. The boy I let go belonged in the bottom left."

He poked the stick figure. "There was hope for him. You could tell from his voice that he belonged in the bubble."

Artorian picked up the stick figure, and placed him in the circle. "He didn't have a choice in his situation. With those raiders, you did what they did, or you were on the menu yourself. In addition to being unwillful, but caring. He was stuck in that situation, forcing his cycle to continue. If it brings about your demise to break from what's around you, that's a hard cracker to chew. So I give that leeway."

Artorian drew a new stick figure. A dark one with fat, thick lines. "This is a demon, and demons only belong in one place."

He slapped the figure squarely in the most extreme spot on the top right that he could. "It's important to make some starting distinctions. First, demons might look like people, but they're not people. I mean that in the most egregiously offensive manner possible. I don't have a full grasp on how the layer shifting works, but I just don't sit comfortably thinking that it is only human souls that end up in the abyss. That just can't be true. I equally can't accept that each layer doesn't have its own brand of local denizens."

He shivered unpleasantly. "I was in the Abyss by accident, and only briefly. It is something I never wish again. I can't recall for certain, but I do not think there was air to breathe. There was certainly no ground to stand on, nor a speck of natural light. It was a place of darkness, terror, horror, and grief. A human mind that ends up in that place has no hope, except to become just like that which resides there."

Squeezing his hands together, he leered at his own dark stick figure. "When I said earlier that a human is sufficiently the kind of thing that can change, I meant it. We're pliable. We're adaptive. We're amazing in every respect. Yet that malleability can be our downfall. We rely on the senses of our body to tell us if something hurts, or otherwise… Once you lose that, it is much more difficult to feel at one with the world. This is also a common Mage problem, much for the same reason if the amount of power in their fingers goes unaccounted for."

He cleared his throat and kept going, on a roll. "A human relies on this information to grow. As just a mind, we lack something that made us what we were. End up in the abyss, and your mind is exposed to what we call horror. However, to the Abyss, it's what they call their normal. That's the big lynchpin. Our suffering? Their normal."

Yvessa motioned for him to continue, but nudged her attention at his waterskin. He was forgetting to drink. Doing as instructed, Artorian had some water, then got to the point. "A demon is not sufficiently the kind of thing that can be anything other than an entity that exists in the top right of this measurement. They will never care. They will always enjoy killing. They will always want to. They will never look back. There is no hope of changing this around, on a level far worse than the raider example."

He motioned back at the raider stick figure. "The raider is

human, and moved away from what 'he could have been' in order to reach that point as a person. A demon can never be otherwise. They will all always be awful bastards. Their normal is just being murderous hate machines. Their deviancy is just a more extreme version of this, and they build their society on the extremism of these aspects. I don't know what their currency is, but I'd hazard a guess that screams and suffering of others isn't too far from the mark. Otherwise 'Torture Savant' wouldn't be a title of high repute."

He was upset, throwing his hands up. "Just think about that! Torture Savant. What kind of a monster does one need to be for that to be considered a positive, proud, upstanding reference? They're all like this. Every last one. For the sheer reason that they cannot be otherwise. There isn't a demon in existence that could ever hope to be something along the lines of a 'good person,' because they can't even begin to scrape the prerequisites together. There is no such thing as 'a good demon.'"

Artorian felt rather angry, definitely fuming. He had another draw of his water, and dismissed his mana with an angry wave from the back of his hand. "That is why demons, specifically demons, have me by the beard. Yes, I have a vendetta against them for involving themselves with my family. Above that, I have something even more pressing. A moral duty to keep them off this plane, now that I nearly have the power to. I may be jumping ahead with my spear, but I can't think of this topic and not feel a burning rage build inside of me. If our way of life is to exist, theirs can't."

He took some slow, deep, calming breaths before speaking to himself. "Priorities, old boy. Sort the game. Sort the family. Then, when we need more purpose afterwards, we can see to the great cleanup. The janitor slide will live to see another day."

A moment of silence later, and he turned to regard Yvessa's green glow. "Sorry about that. I get into it when questions like that crop up. Shall we sideline this and get back to shopping?"

Yvessa bobbed to motion that yes, more shopping would be lovely. Her question had been thoroughly answered, even though she didn't know what this janitor slide was. 'I hate demons' would have honestly sufficed. His Relentless Demonbane title seemed well earned after that long explanation. She pulled the screen back in front of her, more than happy to continue shopping.

CHAPTER THIRTY-SIX

Artorian woke when the sun rose from the west. He got out of his racer just to stretch, not caring if it did nothing. Eternium seemed to have decided he didn't agree.

Skill gained: Flexibility!

Dynamic warm-ups are good! Do those stretches! Preparing your body before and after heavy activity is a great way to prevent injury. For 1 hour after warm-ups, you gain a 10% increase in stamina regeneration. This skill increases by 10% per rank. Take good care of yourself before activity more often to improve this skill!

Ha! Look at that. He stood barefoot in the sand for a while, just watching the water rush. The breeze was nice, the smell of it a touch salty. When he turned and walked back to his racer, he noticed the Wisps were nowhere to be seen. A quick glance at the minimap didn't show them either. They were never invisible when it was just him.

Artorian had another look around, but found neither a threat, nor another living thing. So did that mean he was...

unsupervised? The smile on his face slowly developed. Devious thoughts sprang to mind, his palms rubbing together. So many options! He just couldn't choose! He could cobble together anything! He...

...stopped. There was a downside to being alone. The smell of salt, sounds of water, and painful silence were no longer pleasant now that he was alone. His hands stopped rubbing together, falling at his sides. His fingers twitched, while imagined sounds of sproutling laughter rang in his ears. He looked over his shoulder, and saw the outline of children in a distant fog. Their images broke and formed with every movement of the permeable cloud, but Artorian saw them regardless.

Even imagined, the children stopped their game to face him and wave. The sight brought a pained smile to his face. Their forms vanished on the breeze, and a stark coldness replaced the warmth in his heart as they did. He gazed aimlessly at the distance, his eyes no longer kind. Of all the things he could do when he was alone, there was only one path he could tread. A path meant to be walked alone, outside of the warm glow of the sun.

It wasn't good for him to be alone, without a task to keep him busy. He knew that. Still, he chose to remain as such. Without so much as a word, he climbed into the racer and took off once settled. His expression remained heartless the entire drive over endless grassy plains, headed in the direction of the next beacon.

He found it sticking vertically from the ground in the grassy plains. The beacon must have tilted at some point, looking like a giant coin stuck in the landscape. Once close to it on foot, he picked it up with limited effort, and came to the conclusion that one of his titles must allow him access to modifying their placement. Artorian left after linking the beacon to the rest of the network. An area boss had been nearby, but they had locked gazes and called it a day rather than engage one another.

The look alone had been enough for the venomspine honey badger to care, and call it quits. Giant snakes and iron-taloned birds? No problem. The honey badger would fight those all day, every day. The man-shaped thing out in the fields? Abyss no. Forget it. This monster's gaze alone had pierced its protections, and the unseen grasp of the creature already tightly squeezed around the badger's heart.

The honey badger felt the terror fade when the strange creature sped away on a chunk of shaped wood it didn't know the words for. Good. The thing was gone. *Good.*

A few hours later, Artorian arrived at the next closest beacon. This one was snuggled in a mountain pass barely wide enough to fit his racer. He found that this time he wasn't alone. Someone had put up a fire, and from the ash strewn about he could tell it had been here a while. The oddity was that he saw no camp, just a man in ash-covered armor poking at the flames with a stick. He inspected the man, who turned out not to be a man.

Name: Prattle
Race: Demon
Guise: Elven
Character Level: 29
Class: Warrior
Specialization: Ashcaster
Profession: Carver
Hit Points: 2200

Artorian said nothing as he got off his racer. He just brushed himself off and walked towards the man, who began addressing him in Demoniac. "Who are you? My relief? I'm sick and tired of waiting in this rocky crevice."

Prattle got up, his heavy armor grinding against itself as it was poorly sized and in terrible condition. He didn't like that he hadn't gotten a reply from the man currently power-walking towards him, so he fired off an Inspect. Prattle frowned when the Voice of the World told him it had been blocked.

The silent man extended a hand, which Prattle took to

mean his relief was equally as disgruntled as him to be stationed here. Why here? In the middle of nowhere next to some pointless pillar. The demon extended the stick he'd been using to poke the fire, but the quiet replacement gripped his wrist.

In perfect Demoniac, the man finally gave him a one-word reply. "No."

A moment later, Prattle was upside down, the bones in his arm snapped from an unexpected twist. Prattle's scream came second only to his surprise when his face crashed onto the rock below. He barely had the time to breathe in before his arm was ripped right from his shoulder, armor and all.

A notification Artorian hadn't seen before popped up, but the prompt was in terrible condition. Like the Pylons had barely been cobbled together and the runes on them remained woefully incomplete. Was this a damage log? That was helpful, though he didn't like that it appeared in such a distracting manner. He'd have to ask one of the Wisps to turn it off.

You have attacked the target: Prattle, with surprise!
Your grapple on the target's wrist has succeeded.
Unarmed attack has dealt 1d10 plus 733 strength damage, for a total of 740.
Target qualifies as a demon, title triggered!
Relentless Demonbane increases raw damage dealt to 1480.
Target's heavy armor set bonus reduces raw incoming damage by 25%.
Total damage: 1110.
Target's heavy armor reduces incoming damage by a flat amount of 100.
Total Damage: 1010.
Warning! Damage has exceeded the target's localized endurance, and the target's arm has been severed. Other status effects bypassed due to limb removal.
Target: Prattle, is now suffering a bleed effect of 1 damage per second.
Notice: Title: Legend, has failed to activate. An inquiry has been logged. This notice will not appear again until the inquiry is resolved.

Prattle had time to scream again and attempt to scramble as

he was struck by a litany of status demerits. He managed to shuffle roll back to his ashy fire, kicking up a cloud of the stuff as he grasped a handful in order to satisfy the component requirement of the spell he was about to cast. He howled the spell out in Demonic to activate it, very aware this was a fight. "Ash shard burs—"

Baf!

The demon's spell concentration shattered when he took a roundhouse kick at full force to the side of the head. His helmet shattered on impact even if it saved him from some of the damage. Unfortunately that busted both his heavy armor set bonus, and his hidden flat mana pool bonus. He needed that extra five hundred mana!

You have attacked the target: Prattle!
Your unarmed attack on the target's head has succeeded.
Unarmed attack has dealt 1d10 plus 733 strength damage, for a total of 734.
Target qualifies as a demon, title triggered!
Relentless Demonbane increases raw damage dealt to 1468.
Target's heavy armor set bonus reduces raw incoming damage by 25%.
Total damage: 1101.
Target's heavy armor reduces incoming damage by a flat amount of 100.
Total Damage: 1001.
Warning! Heavy armor has been shattered.

Prattle smashed into the rock wall from the force behind the kick alone. He was getting demolished! Another spell would just lead to his demise, so even though his vision swam and blurred red, he staggered to his feet and drew his blade. Prattle charged the unknown stranger with a warcry. The warcry buffed his strength for five seconds, which he hoped would be enough to remove this grievance in a single blow.

As the weapon came down, it failed to find purchase. Artorian moved as water, only repeating his prior statement to the demon as the side of his palm knocked the blow off course, which was enough for the elbow of his other arm to spin into place and crack the demon's forehead. Since he'd been kind enough to just run into his fist like that.

Artorian's damage notification frazzled with static, sputtering out numbers so discordant it forced the entire notification window to wink out. The unfortunate result was that regardless of how hard the blow had been, Prattle took no damage save for the concussion status effect. The demon had several negative status effects stacked now. He fell into a pile of his own ash, trying to find another weapon since he'd let go of his sword.

When his hand gripped his spare, he looked up through blurred vision only to see the bottom of a shoe come down. With a loud crack, Prattle's life bar hit zero.

Artorian pulled his foot free from the demon's smashed skull. A wet sucking noise from doing so became the grinding of ash as he cleaned the bottom of his shoe off on it. It didn't work so well. He sighed and shot an obliterator down at his foot, cleaning both his shoe and the rest of the stains on his clothing. He supposed he could have tossed one at the demon to get started, but that didn't suit his current purposes.

A golden glow surrounded him shortly after, bringing him up to level five. He flexed his hands and jumped in place to see if anything felt different. It didn't, but he did get several new prompts. He read them over as he walked to the beacon to activate it, ignoring the fallen foe entirely.

Congratulations! You have reached level 5.

Profession slot unlocked! You will unlock another profession slot at level 15, plus every 5 levels thereafter. Would you like to choose a profession now?

Artorian selected no, and moved on to the next one.

Skills gained!
Unarmed Weapon Mastery:
This skill applies specifically to unarmed combat, providing a small boost

to combat prowess. Unarmed Mastery adds an additional 10% damage dealt per rank.

Note: Reminder to self - 'Rank' refers to Novice, Beginner, Apprentice, and such. 'Level' refers to individual steps in that measurement. 890% additional damage was not supposed to happen during testing.

Martial Arts: 'No' Style.
Specific style: Denial
This is a Monk ability. Some people flail around, use tools or tricks, or even try improvised weapons if a real armament isn't available. Not you! You can't leave your weapon behind, because you are the weapon! Unlike brawling, fighting, or weapon mastery, you advance on your targets with grace and power.

Martial arts unlock special maneuvers, usable only by the specific style of arts you are a part of. More offensive styles will gain damage bonuses, while defensive styles may mitigate the harm they take.

Your style school is Denial. The Denial school is focused on neither offense nor defense, but the specific purpose of negating, denying, or preventing an opponent from succeeding in their attacks or defenses. This school's color thematic is blue mana.

Your rank in the martial arts skill determines what bonus percentage is applied to your maneuvers, in order to succeed in them. At the Novice rank, this bonus is 10%. This bonus increases by an additional 10% every subsequent rank.

Martial Arts Maneuver: Deny the Blow.
By striking the opponent at an opportune moment in the midst of their attack, you have a chance to knock or veer that attack off course, preventing it from striking you entirely. On a critical success, you may redirect the attack entirely to a nearby melee-ranged target of your choice. This includes the attacker.
Deny the Blow costs one hundred stamina to attempt.

Martial Arts Maneuver: Flow Like Water.
When engaged in combat, you may alter your movement method to this
maneuver. Flow Like Water changes your method of movement, causing you
to flow over the field rather than haphazardly step in and out as if you were
in a fencing duel. You may approach and retreat from an opponent using the
numerical bonus of your overall Martial Arts rank, and ignore attacks of
opportunity outright.

These dodges are modified by your perception, as you do not get a chance to
avoid something you didn't know was impending. Flow Like Water works
only against opportunity strikes, however they function against any number
of targets. Including those you are not directly engaged with.

Flow Like Water costs twenty stamina per second to upkeep.

Martial Arts Maneuver: Breathe the Air.
When engaged in combat, you may alter your breathing pattern to this
maneuver. Breathe the Air prevents you from missing a breath by being stag-
gered, or when suffering a concussive blow. You will be immune from being
winded by destabilizing attacks while this maneuver is active, and will not
suffer a demerit if an opponent 'knocks the wind out of you.'
Breathe the Air costs twenty stamina per second to upkeep.

Martial Arts Maneuver: Impeccable Focus.
This maneuver may be engaged in combat. Impeccable Focus allows you to
block out unneeded information to focus solely on your task or target. This
maneuver, while active, makes you immune to being disoriented, and applies
your Martial Art rank bonus against any distraction based attacks or events.
Impeccable Focus allows you to know the rough location of any opponent
you are engaged with during a melee, regardless of your ability to see them
or not.

Note: If Impeccable Focus and Flow Like Water are both active at the same
time, this maneuver gives you a chance to apply Flow Like Water against
attacks that enter your melee range, which you otherwise could not have seen
via perception alone.

Impeccable Focus costs twenty stamina per second to upkeep.

"Hmm." The small noise was Artorian's only response as he read the maneuvers over. He finished activating the beacon, then strolled back to his racer. His eye caught something on the body of the fallen's belt. Arcing an eyebrow, he tugged it free from the dead demon to inspect it. "What's this? *Inspect.*"

A notice popped up right away.

Disguised Orb of Tracking.

This orb doubles as a means of once-a-week communication, allowing a message consisting of no more than five words. When the message is sent, the orb will alert the recipient of their location. This item is disguised as a piece of coal.

Pocketing the item with a devious scheme in mind, Artorian saddled up in his racer and took off to the next location. With the threat gone, the local denizens of the pass approached the large pile of ash with newfound interest. Particularly, the chunky morsel that had just been left behind by the swift thing.

Meat was on the menu tonight!

CHAPTER THIRTY-SEVEN

Even with the racer, it took Artorian a full two days to arrive at the next beacon. He was starting to get worried about his quiet Wisps, plus he was getting more than just a bit hungry. The cold glare had faded from his eyes when the first tummy rumble made itself known. He'd left his sustenance ability off since the demon fight, the hunger having snapped him out of his one-track mindset.

He reactivated the sustenance field, and exhaled a sigh of palpable relief as the aches went away. He had stopped his racer atop a hill to provide himself a reprieve. When he felt better, he leaned over to have a look at the place built around the beacon he was near.

Didn't want to bowl over any innocent parties.

The people looked like average humans, but it was another humanization effect. These people had ferrets as their core creature, though that didn't explain their behavior.

Taking the racer to the edge of town, not a single curious set of eyes or sniffly nose came to greet him. The village looked to be in decent condition, but the people were hampered, heads held in their hands while suffering heavy purple lines beneath their eyes. An Inspect or two later, and Artorian found these people were terribly sleep deprived.

That was not a demerit he expected to see in Eternia.

He hadn't found any big, obvious threats this commune might have. No area boss in sight, nor scary things lurking in the woods. The status made no sense. Hopping out, he momentarily lamented his lack of a Resplendence Field. That might have helped. For now, he paid the extra cost for sustenance to fuel the field zone. At least that would alleviate some demerits.

It did less than he would have liked. As per usual, a brand-new language barrier was in his way. The people here barely seemed to notice him, treating him as if he were nothing more than a part of their bad, endless dream. It took an hour, but after inspecting every single villager Artorian had come up with bonk. Not one demon among them, just a pervasive deprivation demerit which they all had.

Nobody so much as blinked when he turned the beacon on, at which point he definitely felt bad. "Alright, this can't go on. Demerits have a source, especially here. I'm missing something, so what question am I tackling poorly?"

Pressing his hand to his forehead, he just stood there a while to think. "I checked their statuses, no cause was visible. Well, what if the cause isn't a visible one? They're having problems slee—"

He had a quick check around, but found that wasn't the case. People had no issues sleeping, but they were twitching erratically when they did. A nightmare? Upon closer perception, the people here were afraid not just of sleeping, but of going to sleep at all. "That won't do. If there's a threat I can't see, that has to be tackled while I'm here, and right away."

Finding the person that was so afflicted with bad dreams that his humanization was coming undone, Artorian just sat meditatively next to the afflicted tiny ferret, and held its paws between his fingers gently. He looked ridiculous, but that didn't matter.

Dropping into meditation, he extended his mana to try to

take the ferret with him. That ended in failure, and broke his meditation at the same time. New plan. Shaping his mana and letting significant chunks of it roam free, he bubbled both the ferret and himself in an energy-rich space. Mana did what was needed, given direction. It might be cheating again, but if that karmic penalty came around to whack him, he'd just bite the arrow.

Within the bubble of mana, the ferret's discordant thoughts started to form above his head. It was running. Out of breath, and running. The ferret was being chased by something it couldn't recognize, save that it was large, and hidden in the darkness. The thing had many eyes, and many teeth, but no discernable shape that remained solid for long enough to make any kind of coherent animal.

No matter what the ferret did or tried, the thing chasing it would swipe, snarl, and bite. Coming within a deadly hair of killing the ferret each and every time. If the ferret so much as stumbled, it would perish, forcing the poor little thing to develop extreme tunnel vision and see only routes that might lead to a path of escape.

The darkness followed it regardless. The ferret could feel the acid breath on the back of its neck. Artorian began to hear the snarls, and the cutting of claws on a piece of fallen wood the ferret had hopped over moments before.

This sequence was endless. Looping. Repeating. Drawing a deep breath, Artorian extended his hands and grasped the vague semblance of a dream with both his hands. Mana poured from his grip, stifling the activities in the dream as the ferret looked around, and saw another darkness had assailed the first one.

Artorian, seeing both perspectives occurring at once, arched a brow. Twisting his grip to squeeze the unknown dark part of the dream, he relayed his will to the surrounding mana. He could meddle, so meddle he would! To keep track of results, he looked left to see the new original dream the ferret was having instead.

It had broken free of the loop.

The ferret looked back again, and no longer saw two sources of darkness attack one another. Now one of the sources was bright, sun-bright, as it took the darkness apart like a piece of paper being angrily ripped and shredded. The ferret stumbled over a hazelnut and smashed face first into leaves and dirt. Oh no! The ferret heard a ripping, but then silence. When it rolled over itself and looked again, the bright luminance was... him?

A massive glowing ferret had taken the darkness apart, and smiled with kind eyes when it noticed the dreaming ferret look. The glowing one sat, calm and pleasant as tasty eggs appeared between his paws. Delicious treats... The dreaming ferret swallowed, suddenly hungry as saliva dribbled down its tiny chin.

The glowing one said nothing, and rolled an egg down the tiny incline towards him. The dreaming ferret grabbed it, and gobbled it right up without a second thought. A second egg bumped into its foot before it was done, and that one went down the hatch as well.

Without visible threats to run from, the scene around the dreaming ferret changed. The dark, damp, claustrophobic nature of the forest ended. The trees thinned, canopy and all. Sunlight poured down from above, illuminating both the green of the grass under its feet, and the blues and reds of berries that grew in nearby bushes. Still, the glowing ferret just sat there, patient.

Seeing the pile of eggs, the dreaming ferret cautiously approached. The glowing one didn't seem to be after him, nor mind him at all. Instead, it just picked up an egg and leaned down to hand it over. Like it was nothing. The dreaming ferret accepted the egg in its tiny paws, but dropped it in favor of dashing forwards and plowing headfirst into thick glowing fur. It was warm. So warm and comfortable.

Still, the glowing one didn't seem to mind. Instead it just licked over his face when the dreaming ferret exposed his nose. The glowing one was grooming the tiny thing. The dreaming ferret calmed from this act, heartbeat slowing as its shivering finally ceased. Realizing how absurdly exhausted it was, the tiny thing held its own paws and curled up. Fast asleep without another care in the world in its own dream.

Artorian thought this good progress, even if it was costing him oodles of mana. *Bah.* Who cared about the mana? There were minds to save. Closing his eyes, he let free his reserves. The small bubble around just him and the small ferret expanded rapidly. When it encased the entire village, the abundance of mana put them right to sleep. No sleeping effect needed.

With all the tiny ferrets asleep, his arms reached out. Snatching up dreams as they began and pulling the creatures close. Artorian found that it was the same dream for all of them. The unknown dark chasing them down. Perhaps… if he tackled them all, he would find the source. The ugly thing responsible would come peeking its head from its hiding hole, wondering where all its food went.

That was worth the attempt, but Artorian paused before getting started. An interesting prompt had appeared.

You have discovered a Legendary, hidden profession: Dream Weaver.

Having grasped and molded the dreams of another, either from nightmare to dream, or vice versa, you have uncovered the secrets of dream weaving. The thoughts of the sleeping are stories in their own right; stories that affect their waking days. You have uncovered this profession without having been specialized as a Witch, Jinxer, Hexer, or Cursemaker, but via sheer force of will and fine mana control.

Dream Weaver is a profession that molds the dreams of others, allowing you to give them bonuses, or demerits, depending on the dream shaped. This profession is required in order to continue the modifications of another's dreams as anything more than a novice dabbler.

Would you like to slot this profession?

Artorian was confused. Wasn't a profession something you did in order to make currency? Ember's profession was War, as an example. On second thought, bad example. Cra! Making her bows. That was a profession. Actually, he wouldn't mind learning how to do that properly himself, in this system.

He stared at the prompt for a few seconds longer, then remembered the professions prompt had told him he would be getting multiple slots. Oh well, no problem then! He tapped yes, and immediately gained information as if by memory stone. He knew how to weave dreams as more than just a shoddy twister of thoughts.

Wasn't this putting him dangerously close to Psychomancer territory? He chose not to think about it. He wasn't going that route regardless, and got right to work with his newfound profession. Charge money for this? No. This was a benefit service, and he was here to make things better. It didn't matter if these people survived the iteration wipe or not.

They were suffering now. He could help now. And help he would.

The first thing he did was mush all these dreams together. They were identical, and all that changed was that the ferrets now dreamt of each other as well. Again, the glowing ferret dealt with the unknown dark. Again, it waited patiently for them. Again, they found solace in its thick, warm fur. When he looked over his shoulder, Artorian smiled. None of the people were twitching, or otherwise having terrible nightmares.

He knew he wouldn't be around to do this again, so molded their joint dream after tying the original ferret in. The golden ferret faded, his translucent being stepping into the teleportation beacon that rose from the ground. Displacing dirt in order to arrive. The dreaming ferrets began to worry. As the glowing one entered the beacon, it burst with teal light, dispelling the darkness and pushing it far away. Sunshine poured from above without a cloud visible in the sky. The luminance of the beacon keeping it at bay. The same luminance that the real beacon currently had.

Artorian added his own ferret, one that stumbled from the weary pack just to touch the pillar. A screen opened before it, and after accepting the prompt, a golden light suffused the ferret. Which stayed warmly coated across its fur. The visuals faded, but when the ferret turned to face its family, there was a light in its eyes.

Artorian thought that sufficient, and removed his influence from their dreams. His mana bubble… he let it go rather than pull it back in. That was a lot of mana to release, but he'd regenerate the loss quickly enough. Some of the energy siphoned right back towards him from the draw of his regen alone, while the rest seeped into the ferrets and the beacon.

Artorian didn't consider it a loss.

He was gone by the time the ferrets woke, back on that same tall hill he'd parked his racer on before ever having entered the ferret village. He watched them come to, lacking the normal pain and fatigue. They'd slept nearly a whole day, but Artorian had kept watch to see if the source of those nightmares would pop out.

No luck.

He watched as some of the first ferrets connected to the beacon, and aligned with him. That follower number just kept climbing and climbing as the days went, and he thought that was fine.

The ferrets would be fine, and that satisfied him. He didn't know some of the ferrets saw him leave in a glowing flash, far more keen now that they were awake.

They didn't know exactly what had transpired, but they all remembered the dream of the glowing ferret. That was enough. The last ferret to touch the beacon crackled with golden power when accepting his boon, having fulfilled a hidden quest. His attributes shot up by ten points in every statistic.

Villagers ran up to him in their human forms as the stricken man fell to a knee. True, the person in question, clutched his chest. Newfound intelligence swirled in his eyes, followed by a momentary blip of light. He suddenly knew of the status command, granted to him via the Voice of the World. Staggering to his feet with help, the humanized ferret read the new notification.

Congratulations!
You have met all the conditions to unlock a special profession: Beacon Sentinel.
Requirements: Beacon in a village of 100+ souls.
Target has a mana abundance.
Target has martial prowess.
Target is aligned with the owner of the beacon.
Target places personal value in protecting a family beyond their own.

Out of the 121 members of your commune, you are uniquely suited in defending your people. Your way of life and methods of being make you suitable for protecting those you care for. In addition to gaining combat bonuses when enacting your profession, Beacon Sentinel may call upon you to protect other threatened beacons in need.

Would you like to accept this profession?

Upon accepting, a new notification sprung up with similar fanfare.

Congratulations!
You have met all the conditions to unlock a Unique specialization: Soulblade.
As a Beacon Sentinel, you have sacrificed your profession to see to the defense of others. However, all Beacon Sentinels gain access to this powerful, unique class. The Soulblade!

A Soulblade draws power from both their mana and stamina in order to imbue their attacks with a variety of effects. More than simply a class that slaps effects upon their weapon, a Soulblade may imbue their very being into their attacks, greatly amplifying their output at a cost to themselves. Beware not to empty your entire health bar in this venture, or you will die and become one with your weapon! This will turn you into a soul weapon for another protector to pick up, allowing two Beacon Sentinels to work in tandem.

Would you like to accept this specialization?

The ferret didn't hesitate and slammed the accept button. His humanization broke entirely, and he popped back to his red ferret form on the spot. He stood on his hind legs, confused and looking at his paws. His best friend, currently in human form, picked him up. "Having trouble, True?"

The tiny red ferret flicked both his paws to release the claws! He didn't know why he thought that was the right thing to do, but it freed his new ability like a blade from the sheath. Dozens of new notifications populated nearby.

Above True's ferret claws, a larger set of burning red claws hovered as mana constructs. They moved along with his individual digits, making him smile up at his friend. "No. No trouble. I think... I think it's my turn now."

His friend put him on his shoulder as True dismissed the claws, asking what he meant. "Turn for what?"

True just looked into the distance. His gaze steeled as responsibility became a mantle that he flung across his tiny shoulders. "It's my turn to keep the dark away."

CHAPTER THIRTY-EIGHT

Artorian's next few beacons were an adventure in sightseeing. Sure they were tucked away oddly, but that was the problem. The beacons were sort of in the middle of nowhere, so not much save for wildlife was around to serve as distractions. He craved distraction.

The wildlife did keep him on his toes, but it was usually cause for a good laugh rather than any sort of problem. A leopard had tried to attack him from above when he'd been rummaging through a tiny jungle, but he'd caught the kitten and put it down on the ground without a second thought. The leopard had stood there a moment, questioned its decisions in life, then *mrowled* at him before it ran off. Adorable.

By the time he had ten beacons activated, he thought it a good opportunity to check if his follower count had gone up a few points.

Deity: Rank 3.
Current follower count: Three-thousand forty-four.
DE gained per day: 76100
Altar count: Ten.

DE gained per day: 500
Total DE Gained per day: 76600
Conversion experience gained instead: 766.

Artorian wasn't sure what to think. That both seemed like a lot, and very little at the same time. He dismissed the screen, and looked up at the slope of the mountain he was next to. This current beacon was located in a small, cozy glen. "I wonder if the racer can go up that angle."

"No time like the present to try!" Once in the racer, he turned it to face the slope, and just pulled back on the speed handle. He shot forwards, zooming up with a gleeful "Wheeeee!"

The cold of the heights didn't bother him. That his racer couldn't get him all the way to the summit? That did. Darn thing had a height limit! Artorian couldn't tell exactly how high he was that was making the racer stall out, but it was information for Dev to play with later. Leaving the racer parked safely, he trekked to the mountaintop on foot. Just for the view.

The sight ended up being very much worth it. While his minimap expanding was a minor boon, it was the pleasantness of the sight itself that sold it for him. Even if this place was fabricated, it was celestially pretty to see while up so high. He could see now how Wo'ah the Wise could handle living his life on one of these. The experience was serene.

A few red dots on his minimap stole his attention. They were far away, but within his visual range. The height difference was allowing him to see them with clarity, even if his targets had no hope of seeing him.

He wondered. Could he use inspect from this far away? He just needed to have line of sight, right? "Inspect."

Name: Scozzari
Race: Demon
Guise: Hat
Character Level: 9

Class: Psychomancer

That was less information than last time. Did distance have something to do with it after all? It must have, in some way, so he dismissed the information. He'd found a roaming target! Based on the directions the dots were moving... Their heading was Solar Gate. Definitely. He *hmm'd* to himself, wondering if he could do anything from this far back.

The effort was likely fruitless, but he unfolded one of the bows and strung it. Drawing an arrow, he dropped right into his comfort zone. The sound of the sharp shearing wind bled away, their movements slowing. During the lull of the winds, his arrow released. Artorian just about broke his bow from laughing. Not remotely close! That arrow didn't even land in the same Kingdom; it was just lost to the world.

Wiping away his amusement, he looked at the bow in his hand. "Maybe Yvessa was right... Anything would work better than this. Ah well."

His mana shaped freely, forming around the next arrow he drew. When it released the arrow, the bow instantly snapped from sheer backlash. Artorian was once again holding a chunk of wood on a string. Crackers. He tossed it and prepared a new bow, then checked to see where the arrow had gone. He should have done that first, as he didn't see it anywhere. "Smart, Artorian. Smart. Good thing nobody saw you perform that embarrassing flub."

He felt a little chilly when the second bow was strung, so he popped himself with his healing orb and called it good. Had the bow snapped because he'd wrapped the arrow in mana, but not the bow? That only seemed sensible. Wrapping both in his mana this time, he doubled the amount invested. A thousand for the arrow and a thousand for the bow.

Releasing the arrow, he saw it went... decently straight! Adding a mana coating was definitely helping. Imbuing the arrow might work better, but he thought he might shatter the thing if the limits were anything like he remembered them.

An orange light *bwipped* in, interrupting his next arrow draw. "Hello there!"

Artorian lowered his bow. "Oberon, you sly fiend! How are things?"

Oberon beamed, speedily circling around the bowman. "I saw you were hunting! Not very effectively, but after seeing in the log that I had missed you roundhouse kicking a demon in the head, I felt left out. Now you're trying to pick them off from a distance and I'm not invited? I'm wounded…"

Artorian was amused. "Ha! Well, as you can see, I'm not doing a great job. My arrows don't have a chance from this height and distance."

He lifted the bow to make the point, nudging his nose over at his obvious misses. "I'm not getting any prompts either, so no system help. I might be spending all my arrows here trying to figure this out, but I'd be fairly proud of myself if I could make one strike land. Just think. One arrow? From all the way over here? Mighty impressive."

Oberon stopped zipping around. "What do you mean you're not getting a prompt? I very clearly saw you wrap mana around that last arrow. That's Mana Binding, and that ability has existed for a while."

Artorian softly shrugged, not having an answer for the expert on the topic. He was the dabbler here. "Well, you sorted the Divine shop out near instantly last time. Any chance it might be the same story?"

Oberon filled Artorian in on a tidbit he seemed to have forgotten. "That took me months, my human friend. I was working on a different frame of time. For you that might have been instantaneous, but for me that was half a year. Regardless, as unpleasantly brief as my visit was, you're right. Those Pylons need inspecting, you should have gotten that ability. Actually, I don't see normal archery on your skills list either. Strange. Continue your pot shots, you'll get notifications when I've figured it out. Oh! If they're orange, they're from me! We figured out colors! So exciting."

His Wisp friend blinked out, leaving him alone on the mountaintop once again. How pleasant sudden company could be. He'd been starting to feel alone. The red dots moving on his map caught his attention a second time. He really could just zip down on the racer, but he drew and nocked another arrow anyway. "Lets try a two thousand mana wrapping this time."

Having a quick check, his mana bar was limited a bit too much for his liking. He modified sustenance to affect the inner and outer zones for eight percent of cost total. He couldn't touch the Resplendence Field, so that was a flat twenty-eight in the can. Thirty-six percent of his bar locked off... quick math here. Current total mana pool? 43,800. Dwarven math said thirty-six percent of that was 15,769. Leaving him with 28,031 total mana as his maximum pool.

So if he was splitting mana evenly between the bow and the arrow, that meant he capped out around fourteen thousand maximum to apply on each. Would it come to that? Actually, what would happen if he wrapped the arrow in that much mana to begin with? He wasn't sticking the mana in the arrow regardless, so it wouldn't kersplode. At the cost that the wrap wouldn't last long. Energy investments needed containment, or they poofed.

"Did the mana do anything, other than being a transportation assist?" Now he was curious. He'd have to go slow, and move patiently. Though that was fine. He preferred his archery this way. The task took four whole minutes, but he had both the arrow and bow wrapped in the ridiculous four-teen-thousand mana amount. He was confused when he saw his pool was still full. "My mana regenerates even if I am actively using it? Well, celestial heavens, that's neat! Forget the limit then!"

He released his arrow like it was a shooting star, his energy bright and luminously white from the sheer density of raw energy packed around the projectile. The mana allowed the arrow to cut right through the wind and stay on course. Even seeming to course-correct the arrow as it *fwokked* from above into the demon hat. The mana was mostly expended by that point, having added nothing to damage.

Artorian punched the sky with both his hands, his surprised face bellowing out a whooping cheer. A hit! His mana had let the arrow hit! The crackling static screen popped up again, but he only caught a detail before it died and winked out. That still didn't work well. The detail Artorian had seen made him double over with laughter. "Ha! *Nine*? Nine damage total? That's a hoot!"

He considered doing it again, but the bow was turning to dust in his hand, entirely overburdened from the pressure it had been forced to deal with. Artorian calmed himself and stopped his outburst, opening his fingers to let the particles fly away on the wind. "Ah… looks like this was a dud. Time to pack it in."

Static cracked all around him. Notifications appearing only to break and disappear again. Artorian stopped for a moment, but moved on when it didn't immediately happen again. Must have been Oberon trying to get things to work.

The static occurred again when he was cleaning off his racing platform. Louder this time, but still without tangible results. He checked his status sheet to see if anything was different but so far it didn't appear like it.

When he was all set to leave, having turned the racer in the direction of the demon hat he needed to tear to pieces, an orange notification appeared. Oberon got his messages to work! He could have just used the Forum? Ah it was fine, this worked too. "Sunny! We found the problem, and it comes in the form of an entire Pylon field being missing. As a heads up, your attribute increases haven't triggered properly either, those are broken too."

The message updated live in front of Artorian, showing a 'two out of three' marker. "Every threshold you should have gotten either a flat, or growth-based increase depending on the core statistics of your class. As an example, at one hundred intelligence you start getting fifteen points of mana to your total, for every point of intelligence. Instead of twelve point five.

You were set to fifteen right away, but for some reason you're also getting your intelligence accounted twice? We're not sure what's going on there yet. You should only be getting it once."

The message updated again, finalizing with a 'three out of three' marker. "In short, the archery and Mana Binding lines are currently kaput. We have a backup set tied up in one of the specializations for the archer, but we can't get to it. For a reason that is annoying rather than impossible. If you happen to specialize in an archery-based tree, we will be able to crack the vault open. You won't be gaining anything bowmanship-related until then. Expect a small flood if you do. Eternium has been approving the gains, the Pylons just... yeah. Best of luck!"

Artorian slapped his forehead. *"Fantastic."*

CHAPTER THIRTY-NINE

Artorian picked up speed so fast going down the mountain, he was starting to have trouble keeping track of the surroundings. The racer adjusted once there was no more mountain to zip down, but they were easily crossing the Mach four mark. His perception couldn't keep up, which caused him to grumble.

It was a temporary moodiness as he angled the forwards-facing mithril plow right at the demon duo. Trio? Oh, it was a trio! A demon was wearing that hat, and another was following. He shot an inspect off just so he had a more accurate assessment of where to aim. Then grinned when the hat-demon's information popped into place right above it.

Name: Scozzari
Race: Demon
Guise: Hat
Character Level: 9
Class: Psychomancer

Perfect. Not remotely interested in slowing down, he quickly spent some mana on a Forum connection. Just to tap Oberon rather than try to talk to him. The orange Wisp winked into the racer not a second later, wearing racing goggles and a bright red scarf with golden-trimmed edges. A Wisp didn't need racing goggles, so Artorian just quipped a short laugh as the racer 'cleaned up.' *Squish*! Satisfaction lived in his grin when the plow turned three demons into paste.

The demons didn't even have a chance to do more than wonder what that odd thumping noise and rising cloud in the distance was. They didn't even understand the danger when Artorian bowled into them somewhere around three thousand miles per hour. The trio was gone in a splat, causing him to glow gold and increase to level 6. He'd never even seen what the other two demons were. Not that it mattered. "See a demon, squish a demon!"

The hat's status sheet didn't appear to have gotten the memo. Hovering in place all confused over a long black streak that smeared hundreds of feet across the ground. The prompt just called it quits and updated, reflecting the health value to show zero so it could wink out.

Artorian finally slowed the racer down to a non-insane speed when the racer began to make some unpleasant sounds. It took a while, but he and Oberon giggled like little children the entire way. When the racer hovered to a standstill, Artorian popped the racer with his healing orb to clean it up and mend whatever the problem was. Removing those terrible stains from the front of the plow without ever needing to scrub them. He extended a finger towards his friend, which Oberon high-fived with a movement of mana.

The orange Wisp was mightly pleased. "*Ahhh*. That was good. Really *hit* the spot. I wondered at first what the poke for my attention was about, but when I saw the trajectory and speed you were going, I just had to come enjoy that smashing event live and in person. Tell me we're doing that again."

Artorian flipped back his seat, needing a moment to just be. His hands were shaking from handling the controls at those speeds. His constitution was high, but controlling a Mach four object was no joke. His biceps hurt!

Notice: You have completed a feat of endurance. Constitution +2. Bonus withheld due to regional limitations.

Notice: Your Cultivator title provided you a workaround against the regional limitation of 150. Glad to see the limiter on new gains still works.

Artorian frowned at the notice, then pointed at it. "What's this? This is new."

Oberon looked over, not bothering to move the goggles. "That's not new at all. You just haven't been getting bonuses because Eternium is a sourpuss when your name comes up. If you haven't noticed, you haven't been getting attribute bonuses for most anything you've done since the start. You were supposed to, but negative Karmic Luck can prevent it. Eternium has been going hard on that little rule to get his frustrations out, even if petty.

The Wisp made an orange mana arrow to point at the entry. "Anytime you do something that strains and pushes your current limitations, or that goes beyond them while you survive, you're supposed to get a system bonus reward for the according attribute."

Oberon removed his arrow. "Keeping this racer on track for so long was a strength and constitution measure. From what I can tell, you strained your muscles long enough for them to tear a little, allowing for new growth. So you got a bonus on constitution, since it's your endurance that you 'tested.'"

Artorian heard something odd in the Wisp's voice, and prodded it. "You don't seem happy that Eternium did something petty, out of all of that."

Oberon sighed long and slow. "He didn't used to be like this. He was sure of himself, never petty, on top of the world. Back out in the old world, I mean. He doesn't do so well in Cal. He did at first, but his need to do well by his **Law** is obscuring his… well. Can't call it humanity when it's a dungeon. Nothing human present there. Same idea? The game is nice to have, for Eternium to have something to do. It doesn't change that he feels out of place. Out in the old world, another few hundred years unbothered and he'd have become a Heavenly. He was *that* close. Then the rules changed in Cal. They changed again, and again. You don't need to be tied to the **Order Law** for that to sit poorly. The constant upheaval was just worse for him."

The Wisp let his scarf and goggles fall right through his body, as if it wasn't there. "Take those. I accidentally lost them, or something. I'm tired of seeing you wince your eyes shut in every log I see where you're piloting the racer. We should honestly have a skill just for this, but then there's the Pylon limitations… It's all so frustrating."

Artorian tried to lay a comforting hand on the orange ball. He hadn't expected it to work, but it did. Oberon felt solid, most likely by choice. "My friend, things are eating away at you. It doesn't appear you've had a chance to vent your frustrations. I'm not going anywhere. What's nagging? Did Yvessa's spoon get stuck in one of the gears or spokes down below in mechanics land?"

He smiled while he said it, but Oberon knew it was his poor attempt at a joke. "No, Yvessa is busy with the Matron. Work in Cal that needed tending. You're missing a lot out there, but you'd find it all terribly dull. Also heard about the gazebo. I'm fairly certain that's my fault, so expect a mystery gift box in the future, when I can sneak it by the all-seeing eye. I don't know, turn over a random rock somewhere and wipe some dirt away. Accidental gift box. Or poke a pigeon. It'll spit out an entire treasure chest. Pretend that doesn't horribly break physics when you see it."

Artorian nodded, but softly patted his hand to prompt the Wisp to continue gushing about what was eating him. Oberon failed to hide his relief at the chance. "It's the Pylons. They don't grow at any speed other than the one you're going, and that's with doing everything we can to make it go faster. Most of the finished Pylons we immediately need for crucial functions, and that's not allowing a lot of leeway for the things that players need. That would be you, by the way."

The human mused, thinking out loud. "Any chance you can repurpose unused Pylons?"

Oberon made it clear that wasn't an option. "No. There's a strict no-cannibalization rule. It sounds nice as an idea, but it's a nightmare in practice. When it comes down to it. It's better to leave an unused, finished, whole Pylon able to do its thing in the event it ever becomes active. Rather than needing to remake it on the spot because it's suddenly needed, and it's gone. Making a Pylon is headache-inducingly difficult to do right. If you think just rifling through a few menus on pre-made items was bad when all you had to do was look for what was out of place, making a Pylon would drive you mad."

Artorian dropped the hot potato and didn't try to slide in more ideas. "It be like that sometimes. Can't grow the Pylons fast enough then?"

Oberon nodded. "And sometimes like that it be. Essentially, yes. Then there's misfires, bad connections, and Pylons that should work but don't. Then some that shouldn't work at all. Except of course they do. Dev has been tinkering with a Pylon without any runes on it. No script whatsoever. Yet it perfectly calculates the rate an acorn falls to the ground. *Baffling.*"

The orange wisp threw some mana tethers to simulate throwing his arms up into the air. "The last reading we got out of it was how a single squirrel holding but one measly acorn could crack the entire frozen northern ice-flow in half. A clean split right down the middle. It's mad. *It's mad.* Anything with acorns, and that Pylon has your back. But *only* acorns. It's like the Beast Core we grew it from had the most obsessed squirrel of all time in it."

That was news, and Artorian had to be sure he heard that right. "Pylons are grown from... Beast Cores?"

Oberon made an unpleasant whining noise. "Only some. Honestly, we're making them out of anything we can get our tethers on. We're that desperate. If you see a lack of bugs or creatures normally necessary for the ecosystem, that would be why. We just can't spare the materials right now, so we're optimizing what we can. As you've seen, our damage calculator is... uh. On the fritz."

Artorian lifted his hand away, scratching at his chin. "Shame you can't just count damage in acorns, and make the squirrel do it."

Oberon's light dimmed before brightening significantly. That random little mention brought on a flood of ideas. Because... why couldn't they do that? "I... I need to go."

The orange light winked out with a bright flash, forcing Artorian to wince and look away while partially covering his eyes. Needing to rub them, he blinked until all the spots went away. Since his friend had 'accidentally' left some things behind, Artorian didn't see a reason not to borrow them. Fastening the goggles and snuggling the scarf around his neck a few times, he flicked the racer back into forward motion and squeezed the controls. "I love it when a plan comes together."

CHAPTER FORTY

Artorian was driving away from beacon twelve when his pocket vibrated. Fishing the source free, he pulled out the orb of tracking. He'd forgotten about this little nugget, and slowed the racer so he could fiddle with the oblong shaped chunk of coal. How did one operate a chunk of coal? He smacked it against the side of his racer, which made the vibrations stop. Must have worked?

A *ding* appeared on his minimap, garnering his attention. Artorian had to zoom out several times before a green location dot appeared on a section of the map he wasn't remotely close to. It would take a few days to get there on his racer. Why had that shown up? What was it?

A voice erupted from the oblong chunk in his hand in scree-scree. The message made a cold, but pleasant, expression cover Artorian's face. "Prattle, report in."

Prattle was... *hmm*. Must have been the name of the stain he wiped off the map in the rocky crevice. That's where he picked the orb up. He couldn't be expected to remember every demon's name! He wondered how to reply, and if it would give him more information. He just squeezed the coal chunk, replying in Demoniac with detached chill. "I'll see you soon."

He remembered a moment later that it was the recipient who got your location, but shrugged and pocketed the rock. Not that it mattered. He knew where to go to play janitor now. His broom wasn't quite ready, but that wouldn't halt the sweeping. Or if he needed to... *plowing*. Tugging a lever on the racer, he spun around in a quarter circle, now aimed squarely in the direction of the famed green dot. "Exterminator, on the way."

The demon, who had received the message in the swamp fortress named Triplicate, didn't know what to make of the message. Prattle was coming back? That wasn't allowed! He needed to stay put until he was relieved. Them's the rules. Hjarl the Hurler tossed his vellum with complainant outcry. He was going to write Prattle up for this, right away! That abyssal worm.

Hjarl was four sentences away from finishing the report before his rage subsided to the point of realizing it hadn't been Prattle's voice speaking. Setting the diminutive imp tied to the end of a stick back down in the ink pot, he paid no attention to the bubbles rising to the surface. If someone had gotten a hold of their tracking orb, a different form was needed. That needed a demon bureaucracy form under the classification TR-7, not a TPS report. He still needed to submit it three times, but the majority of minutiae within Triplicate had gone the way of the healer.

That being: completely slaughtered down to size.

No more needing six seals on a document just to pass it over to the next paper-pusher! That was cause for rejoicing. He'd rip the head off of someone to celebrate when he had the chance! With the proper vellum on his desk, Hjarl pulled the stick with the half-drowned imp from the well. Dragging the creature right across the page to start writing.

It took two days just for the end product to end up in a pile on Lord Pencil's desk, with another two passing before he got to it. At that point, strange sightings were making the rumors around the castle. Hushed voices spoke of spirits in the wood that ate their kin. For many had boasted to slay whatever had those large, bright eyes. This lurker in the green. Not a single demon who had huffed and glorified his pomp returned from the foliage, and that was concerning.

One or two demons going missing a day was nothing special. Murders happened all the time. Sometimes you just needed to rip the head off a supervisor or lackey. It happened. It happened often. Twenty demons a day going missing was cause for actual worry. Triplicate wasn't replenishing the numbers quicker than they were losing them, and the cause being unknown was irritating for the higher ups.

The random golden flashes in the woods were what escalated the matter all the way up to Lord Pencil. That effect only occurred when someone or something was increasing in power, and they could not have that right next to their castle. The demon mouse lifted the freshly delivered vellum, his glowing lime green eyes reading it over. "A forest critter? Must be some area boss that got lost and wandered in. Take the garrison and have it served on a roasted spit."

The vellum, and the seven others related to it, all went into the fire. Pencil's pyre mimic was being fed well today, the creature lapping up the treats like they were brined turkey skin. It belched a flaming burp, sated for now.

Pencil's orders made the rounds, and Triplicate's garrison got all geared up to carve up a lost area boss. What else could it be? One of the warriors voiced a thought while getting his greaves fitted by some imps. "Hjarl, I think it's a snake. We've been steadily losing inmates for a while. At a rate of one at a time. Definitely a snake."

Hjarl, who was less than pleased to have been recruited to the garrison since there hadn't been one before Lord Pencil gave orders, spat on the ground. "Phah! It's not a bird. Nothing above the canopy. I think it's one of those blasted half-humanized ants. Those bitey bastards terrorized whole squads of Lashers."

Kreach, the talkative demon, shrugged. "What can you

expect from Lashers? Second-tier nobodies. They're not Butcher class, like us!"

Hjarl weighed his throwing axes, checking to see if they were appropriately serrated. "Butcher class is still just third tier. Jodiff was lost yesterday. He was also a Butcher class, so don't think that lost boss cares about how strong we think we are. Just kill the thing if you see it. The sooner the better. I don't want to start reporting overtime and get Ragemouth to start howling at me. If we had more inmates to throw in first, I'd have enjoyed their screams. If just for locating the beastie."

Kreach snorted. "Tier ones? Useless garbage. You'd get more success throwing an imp in, and they don't even get a rank. Besides, it's just a lone area boss, and there's twenty of us. How bad could it be? We'll have the thing slaughtered in no time."

The demon garrison shared some vibrant laughter, and left to go bring in the meat. It would be easy!

When the time for the evening grill-feast finally came as the sun fully dipped under the horizon, Lord Pencil was in a foul mood. Pencil was short one area boss, and all twenty demons in the garrison. Impromptu garrison, yes, but a garrison none-theless! So where were they?

His green gaze turned to watch the woods. As if right on schedule, one of the garrison members broke through the brush and continued his mad dash towards the front gates. It was Hjarl! The panicked demon was screaming at the top of his lungs to open the gate. "Drawbridge! Lower the bridge! Let me in! We need reinforcements, we nee—"

Thwock.

The gate guards didn't even get to the pulley mechanism before Hjarl died out on the lawn, a mundane-as-abyss arrow sticking from the back of his head. This infuriated Pencil to no end. "Arrows? The area boss uses arrows? That's not a wild beast at all, that's an adventuring party or a small army hiding out and playing us for fools! All demons! Mobilize and slaughter! Kill the hidden!"

A call for murder was a great, supervisor-sanctioned break from all their vellum work. They loved it! Axes, blades, maces, and destructive measures of all kinds made it back into the claws of creatures that had very much missed them. Some even kissed their much-missed tools of demise before enthusiastically hauling it to the now open gate. The drawbridge went down, and their forms morphed out of semi-humanization. Since they didn't have to be in a cramped space, the demons returned to being the horror shows of claw and fang that they were.

Rushing out of the castle and towards the forest's edge, they all passed a person waving them on. Yelling information at them that added to their focus. "In the forest! Get in the forest! They might be masquerading as a demon so trust nothing you see! Go, go!"

Triplicate demons howled as they shoulder-checked into the greenery, wildly slashing and beating their weapons around to wantonly destroy to their black heart's content. None realized the robed creature they passed wasn't a demon. He was just someone else's problem, because they had killing to do!

Artorian enjoyed an amused smile as the last loud batch of demons roared past him. Content with keeping them busy outside, he strolled in through the front gate without a care in the world. Making his way to the first guard tower, he opened the heavy door like it was made out of cardboard, then hummed to himself while looking around for the pulley system.

A few hapless imps were left behind to guard it, and he swatted them from the air as if they were no more than mosquitos needing a clappin'. Artorian wiped the back of his hand off on his robe, then rubbed them together while single-handedly turning the contraption to pull the weighty draw-bridge back up. He didn't want any surprise visitors coming in from outside. They were busy looking for nothing in a forest after all. No reason to give them ideas.

When Artorian turned, a screecher demon entered the pulley room to ask why the bridge had been retracted. He saw the dead remains of imps on the ground, and a person he didn't recognize that wasn't his problem. Until said person had him by the throat, squeezing hard enough to snap right through his spine and disconnect his head from the rest of his body. It didn't kill the screecher instantly, but the monster was silenced. As for the rest of the health bar, status effects dealing bleed damage over time would handle that problem all by itself.

Artorian had come to love status effects. Also hate? Love and hate. That was a good description. He had a love-hate relationship with status effects, as they could affect any creature regardless of stats, so long as the effect took. In turn, that meant he wasn't immune to drowning, bleeding, or a whole host of other unpleasantries. Who needs damage when you have status effects! Now if only he could do something more with them.

Just to make sure the trick he gained from Ember's old armor was still going strong, he gave it a quick check.

Ability: S.E.P. Field.

This is an imported function. Explanation: Someone Else's Problem field is an ability that does not make you noticeable, so much as it makes those who notice you not care that you are there. By using this ability, you become an issue someone else is supposed to deal with. This ability has a chance to work on anyone who can perceive you, but can be broken free from with requisite concentration or high enough wisdom. It is also broken if you engage in combat with an affected target, or otherwise make a nuisance of yourself to the point where others are forced to pay attention.

This ability is mind altering on a they-notice-you scale, therefore the cost is 1000 mana drained per second while you keep this effect active.

Notice: I did not enjoy putting this together. I kept thinking someone else was going to finish it. I am docking you the full -5 Karmic Luck regardless. You are at minus twenty. I have enough! I'm giving you a bit to prepare. Make it count!

That had been nearly a whole day ago, and Artorian felt he

had perhaps an hour of time left. Maybe less. The robed man dismissed the ability description since his suspicions had been confirmed. One thousand mana per second was a hefty drain, but the results didn't match up when he watched his mana bar. Watching it again now, the problem seemed to have corrected itself. For a few days, spell efficiency had affected this field, reducing the cost by eighty percent. Now it was taking the proper thousand mana a second it should.

Why was it always the beneficial matters that got patched first? *Ugh.* This game... He squeezed at his right wrist, massaging it some before deciding to start stretches right here. No time like the present! He didn't know what Eternium's negative twenty karmic event was going to be, but he wanted all the bonuses he could have active and running when it triggered.

With his field on, even if a demon remaining behind in the castle noticed him doing stretches, it went ignored and unreported. Until one didn't.

Pencil's mousy brow dug a deep furrow as he asked a pointed question, directed to the local higher echelon around him while he stood at the window of the council chambers.

"Who is *that?*"

CHAPTER FORTY-ONE

Pencil's scathing tone had several demons who were previously B-ranked come and have a look. They still received the cultivator bonus if it applied, so some of this flock considered themselves omnipotent in Midgard. A free one hundred and twenty points to each attribute was *power*. Fungris the Fury stepped forth to be in front of another window, seeing the interloper now that the man was pointed out.

His pending answer was replaced with the shattering of glass, including an arrow that went through his eye and stuck out the other side of his head. It didn't kill the council demon, but that was a fate easily worse than being offed outright. Status demerits flooded his status sheet. Fungris was a sputtering, shrieking wreck, so another councilman cut his throat just because the sounds he made were a nuisance. Not fun at all!

A golden light bathed Artorian on the council demon's death, and all the higher ups at the window could see him taking steady breaths while he hopped in place on his toes. Bow in hand. Correction. Broken bow.

Pencil didn't care about the details; they'd found their problem. His mousy voice oozed with acid. "Kill it."

Artorian received a prompt when he finally achieved level ten. About celestial time!

Congratulations!

You have gained enough experience to reach level ten! Now that you have reached level ten, you are able to specialize into a more powerful version of who you want to be! You can look at specialization options at any time!

Artorian saw no reason to wait. Hand over that smorgasbord!

Here are the higher classes you have attained the requirements for. Some simple details are provided; tap on them for more explanation.

Athlete: Like using your body? Get more out of it!
Brawler: Like punching? Punch more! Punch harder! Use that chair!
Elemental: You are loved by mana, love it back.
Elementalist: The elements are toys. Control them, use them.
Eristic: Don't agree with the way things work? Never feel a need to again.
Disciple: Advancement from normal Monk, uses chi mysteries.
Fool: Why master anything when you could dabble in everything?
Ghost Monk: Abandon your form, feed on the chi of others!
Magus: Might and magic belong together. Combine them and flourish.
Overhealer: Able to heal allies or damage enemies with healing power.
Psychomaster: Change the minds of others. By force.
Qinggong Monk: Master your chi to its true potential.
Sensei: Why learn when you can teach? Mastering all basics.
True Wizard: Evolve from mere Magehood, get true use out of your mana.
Inkcaster: Write with magic? Draw your imagination to life.
Zen Archer: By patience and virtue, you and the arrow are one.

An enticing list! Unfortunately only one option worked with his passions and continued sanity. He tapped Zen Archer, allowing more information to come up.

Notice! A primer on specialization rarity. Rarity is tied directly to how many people in the world have, or have had, the particular specialization you are selecting. Any 'Unique' specializations will become 'Special' after it has been taken once by an active person in the world. Any specialization with a qualifier higher than unique is special in the sense that they cannot be acquired under normal circumstances. They must be earned.

Zen Archer (Unique). Out of all the weapons available, Monks that bond to the bow are destined for calm minds and patient draws. Rather than merely using an object, a Zen Archer mentally becomes one with their weapon when they apply their skills. This specialization seeks perfection in the pull of the bowstring. A Zen Archer gains automatic proficiency in any bow, or ranged projectile weapon that requires them to physically draw back on a string. Instead of focusing on inwards perfection, this Monk variation focuses on unity. As such, wisdom rather than dexterity is one of the core attributes for this class. Wisdom now determines the accuracy of your bow.

A Zen Archer does not care how mighty he is. Only that his arrow is true, and aim perfect. Gain per two class levels: +4 Wisdom, +4 Perception.

Artorian pressed accept, slotting Zen Archer as his specialization. When he did, several more prompts popped up right away that made him jump for joy on the tips of his toes. His archery skills! Get! An orange notification joined the pile, and he checked that one first since it was likely a message, rather than a prompt.

Oberon clearly shared his good mood, and the prompt even spoke in his voice when he tapped it. A transcribed vocal message? Awesome! "Buddy! You saved us so much headache! With the Zen Archer Pylon open, we have access to the groundwork copies of all its advanced techniques! We've got normal archery skills again! You should be getting a bunch of prompts."

"Also, I included a gift box for saving our entire team from the bowmanship Pylon nightmare. Open it last, after all the prompts, otherwise it's a roll on the random loot table rather than the... well. You'll see... I also fixed the text on your title.

Speaking of, we should have the two withheld ones coming in soon. If you see any weirdness on the prompts, like some saying n equals rank level, where some others don't, don't worry about it, that text depends on who made them. All the Cal ones have the n equals thing, ours don't. We're in a rush."

"Kill 'em all! Tap me when the show starts."

"Ha!" Artorian dismissed the message and rubbed his hands together, dropping into meditation for just a second. He quickly ate up the prompts since he wouldn't have the time to leisurely read through them. He very clearly had threats incoming! Some gargoyle-shaped demons crashed through the third-floor windows of the big building on the other side of the courtyard, beelining for their target while he seemed momentarily distracted.

One second in meditation was enough for Artorian to absorb the entirety of the information. The first message immediately made his knuckles itch pleasantly.

Relentless Demonbane

This character's attacks, abilities, and skills are twice as effective against dark-based entities and their adjacents. Such as infernal-affinity creatures.

Attacks were properly counted as well now? *Good.* That fight with Prattle hadn't been a fluke then. He wiped away all the 'new skill gained' nonsense when pulling notifications close, wanting only the juicy bits.

Bow Mastery:
This skill gives a small boost to the use of all bows in combat, or other weapons that qualify. Accuracy, damage dealt, and armor ignored when using bows increases by a bonus of $+10n\%$, where n equals your rank level. Bow Mastery also determines how many arrows you can fire over the course of five seconds, equal to one arrow per rank. Time between shots will increase due to draw, nock, and pull penalties.
Firing one arrow has a flat cost of 10 stamina.

Notice: You may at times see references to a 'round.' A round is a time measurement referring to five seconds.

Close Range Tactics:
This skill provides an additional boost to Bow Mastery, focusing on improving damage if within thirty feet of your target. Close Range Tactics adds an additional 10% damage per rank.

Point Blank Tactics:
This skill provides an additional boost to Bow Mastery, focusing on improving damage and accuracy if within ten feet of your target. This skill stacks with Close Range Tactics. Point Blank Tactics adds an additional 10% damage and accuracy per rank.

Longshot:
This skill reduces the distance penalty of a projectile by 10%, and increases the maximum unaltered distance it can be shot by 10%. These values increase by 10% per rank.

Overdraw:
This skill trades bow strain for additional power. A bow can only handle so much strain depending on its quality. Add too much strain, and your bow will be destroyed outright and turn to dust. Overdraw works based on the archer's strength, allowing them to add a flat damage number equal to the strain inflicted upon their weapon. Strain inflicted is reduced by 10% per rank.

Multishot:
This skill trades overall accuracy for arrow amount. For each additional arrow fired in conjunction with your first, you lose 10% overall chance to successfully strike your intended target with all arrows. Each rank mitigates this penalty by 10% once at the Beginner ranks. Meaning that as a Beginner in this skill, you may shoot two arrows at once without an accuracy penalty. Multishot can fire no more than ten arrows at a time.

Luckshot:

This skill gives a small chance to turn a miss into a hit. Either on the opponent you intended, or a target you consider an enemy. Each rank increases this chance by 2%, starting at the Novice rank.

Trickshot:
This skill allows you to target something other than your target, but gives a chance for your attack to bounce, veer, or otherwise be redirected to your target. Trickshot begins with a 30% success rate, increasing by 10% each rank once at the Beginner ranks.

Flurry Arrows:
This skill allows you to draw, nock, and pull your arrows faster! Providing you more chances to shoot your bow. Flurry Arrows increases your draw, nock, and pull speed by 10%, increasing by 10% each rank once at the beginner ranks.

Notice: this skill cannot be used in conjunction with Zen Arrow.

Critical Realism:
This skill allows for critical hits to be calculated as if the damaged target was struck with true realism. A normal critical hit merely doubles the damage done. This skill improves critical hits to cause five times the original damage, rather than two. Depending on where the target is struck, an additional percentage bonus occurs. A strike to a weak point or most vitals will increase the chance by 10%, while a head or core shot increases the chance by 20%. A successful critical hit has a 10% chance to trigger this skill. This increases by 5% per rank, starting at the Beginner ranks.

Mobile Archery:
This skill reduces the penalty for using a bow while moving. Normally, shooting while moving incurs an automatic 50% accuracy penalty. Each rank of this skill reduces the forced accuracy penalty by 10%.

Notice: Unlocking Zen Archer has retroactively awarded you all the archery-based skills you should have had up to this point. Groundwork complete! You will now be awarded your specialization's skills and abilities.

CHAPTER FORTY-TWO

Artorian woke from meditation as an unpleasant feeling bristled the hair on the back of his neck: one of the demons had made it to the open door. Not interested in being interrupted just yet —as he had three new notifications—Artorian stepped forwards and snap-kicked the howling beast right out of the bridge control mechanism room, launching the nuisance away in an arc. The strike sent the screeching gargoyle tumbling like a pile of rocks to the courtyard below, where it landed with a dull smack.

One of the new notifications was large, so with another second of meditation, Artorian read through the information swiftly.

Zen Arrow:
This skill allows a Zen Archer to patiently hold the arrow, waiting for the perfect strike. This skill has a cooldown, and can only be used once per minute. A Zen Arrow doubles its maximum travel distance, and ignores all environmental factors at play that might knock the arrow off course. Every rank, starting from the Beginner ranks, maximum travel distance goes up by one point of multiplier. Increasing to three times the maximum travel

distance, rather than twice. Zen Arrow costs 50 Stamina to use per rank applied.

Ki Arrows:
This ability allows you to imbue chi into your shots. At the Novice rank, you may imbue up to 100 chi into your arrow. Energy invested directly translates to kinetic damage dealt. 100 chi means 100 damage. Each rank, starting at Beginner, increases the investment maximum by an additional 100. Notice, this is additional damage added after any multiplication formulas. Ki Arrow damage is not affected by Bow Mastery.

Soul of Zen:
The calm state of a Zen Archer, in its purity. Soul of Zen is an ability that costs 100 stamina per second to sustain. While Soul of Zen is active, you feel the flow of activity differently. For each rank in Soul of Zen, you may act in a frame of reference that lets you perceive your surroundings as if they are moving slower.

At the Novice rank; if your attribute points in intelligence, wisdom, perception, and luck are all at two-hundred, then you may perceive your surroundings as if they were occurring twice as slow. This does not mean you can act at your normal speed while engaged in this difference of perception. You will also be moving at the half speed you perceive unless you meet the conditions below.

At the Novice rank; if your attribute points in strength, dexterity, and constitution are all at two-hundred, then you may act normally during the time where you perceive the world moving at half speed. In actuality, you will be moving twice as fast to anyone else who sees you. To you, only you will be moving normally while everything else is slow.

At the Beginner rank, you will be able to act and perceive three times as fast, rather than twice as fast. So long as the relevant attributes are at three-hundred each. If even one attribute does not meet that threshold, you do not gain the benefit.

It is possible to act at double speed while perceiving at normal speed, but you will incur penalties. Using Soul of Zen differs in effect depending on the rank used, and the cost matches this output. Each rank above Novice will drain an additional 100 stamina per second.

Notice: Sustaining this Soul will cause the attributes used to be considered 'strained.' This means those attributes are not considered in any other combat formulas while actively invested here. Using this ability effectively reduces your overall statistics by the minimum rank-required attributes across the board, as they are being used purely to fuel this effect. This is done in order to balance the benefit that you are effectively gaining additional 'rounds' from Soul of Zen.

"Fantastic!" A second demon immediately got the boot as Artorian opened his eyes. In a snap, the irritant was launched right back into the third floor of the council chamber it'd window-jumped out of... although the demon broke through the wall on its way back in. Which looked considerably more painful. "A far less pleasant journey, indeed."

That's what it got for being all up in his face. With all the notifications out of the way, Artorian pulled the glow-outlined prompt to him even while rock-carving claws could be heard skittering up the wall. He quickly tapped the prompt since it was last, meaning this was Oberon's goodie!

You have received a gift box!

Would you like to open this now? If you choose to open it later, you will need the assistance of your Observer Wisp to access this prompt again.

Artorian grinned and tapped yes. Along with some orange glitter and the sounds of an out of tune trumpet, a bow popped out of the tiny box! The box reminded him of one of Dev's orbs, holding things that were larger than seemed reasonable. He'd gotten ahold of his first racing palanquin that way! Good times.

He gave the weapon a quick inspection before touching it.

Name: Poor Man's Bow
Material: Wispwood
Rarity: Special
Damage: 1–20 Kinetic
Special Quality: Brittle
Special Ability: Wispwood Thorns

The Poor Man's Bow got its name due to a Fae's insidious boredom. Buying or using this item afflicts the user with the 'Poverty' curse, preventing the user from carrying more than a single silver on his or her person at any given time. Any other monetary wealth, or currency equivalent, will find a way to remove itself from anyone who has been the owner of this bow.

As this bow has the Brittle quality, any overdraw will instantly destroy it. This also prevents the bow from being usable in melee combat. This bow cannot be used to attack or defend as a physical weapon. It will just break.

That was such a kick to the shin, Artorian almost didn't read the next bit of text attached to it. He punched a gargoyle-shaped beastie in the nose when its face showed up in the window, breaking the glass before finishing up the information on the piece of nonsense Oberon had given him. "So far, this is outright terrible! Hmm."

He grumbled, out of time since unwelcome company had arrived in spades. Most of the unpleasantness was lurking around the doorway, wary of entering since that tactic had not proven successful so far. The creature inside was, however, stuck. Having nowhere to go—save adjacent rooms where the council demons were gathering in the hopes of being the first to wet their claws—Artorian's mood lifted when he read the last bit of text on the bow's description.

Material information:

Wispwood loves mana. Feeding the bow at a rate of 50 mana per second will activate and sustain its special ability.

Wispwood Thorns:
Being cursed by poverty means that you wouldn't be able to buy arrows. So the Fae in their vast wisdom have provided you a grand blessing. You won't need to! Each draw of the string will cause one wispwood arrow, called a thorn, to automatically appear and nock itself! The arrow will be of common, non-magical quality. Nothing special, except that you get as many as you want! The arrows vanish after ten minutes.

Thorns have a special interaction with the skill: Multishot.

Notice: Due to a limitation, the Wisps will just be rolling an appropriate number of twenty-sided dice behind the scenes.

"Do I really need the money? ...*Nah!*" He triggered the curse and drew the bowstring. A perfectly nocked common-quality wispwood arrow winked into existence between his fingers. Artorian pulled it right to his anchor point near his nose to get a feel for it.

An excellent start, even though the poverty curse comfortably made a home for itself on his status sheet. Like a flock of angry birds escaping a cage too small to reasonably hold them all, money spilled from all the pockets in his clothing, leaving only one single silver remaining.

Another demon threw caution to the wind and barreled through the front door; laughably slipping on the scattered money that had barely settled on the floor. The demon lost its footing just as he took two arrows to the head; Artorian had tried Multishot so he could see this supposed 'special interaction.' He'd desired two arrows, and the one he released seamlessly split when the fletching passed his grip on the bow; forming two identical arrows with a slightly altered travel vector. Enough of these would cause *quite* the conical scattershot!

Elsewhere, working furiously in the background, Eternium

hand-cranked his catch-up mechanisms, updating some of Artorian's newly acquired skills to more appropriate levels. He was going to say something to his dungeon Wisp, but Oberon was zipping away as Artorian tapped on a forum door.

It was time for Oberon to come enjoy his show! The King Wisp must have been planning for this, because he did not show up alone. Neither Oberon nor the Wisps he'd brought were visible, but the lighting in the courtyard area drastically changed from these unseen sources.

That was Artorian's cue to get the party started.

Taking a deep breath as gargoyle claws started to come from around every door and window corner, Artorian activated a maddening litany of skills and abilities all at once. A tight field of energy clung to his skin, the glowing edge visibly serrating from the sheer density of power actively coating over and through him. The expenditure made his hair stand up ever so slightly.

The action started right as Oberon's music began. Drumsticks clicked together before the ravaging burden of sound beat the air. Artorian grit his teeth, his grip still on the bow as he heard the Wisp's voice clear as day, even *if* Oberon repeatedly whispered the words: "Let the bodies hit the floor."

Artorian's weight buckled the wood under his foot, straining it to the point of breaking as he prepared his forward lunge. He did some quick math since he wasn't going to be checking his status sheet all that much. "Field, twenty-eight percent. Sustenance, eight percent. Electrosense, eight percent. That's forty-four, might as well be half the pool. Flow Like Water, twenty stamina. Breathe the Air, twenty. Focus, twenty. Soul... *one hundred*."

The demons at the door missed their attacks of opportunity entirely when the flash of brightness burst through the doorway. Their claws swung, but bit down either on empty space, or random bits of wooden shrapnel that used to be part of the floor. Curses! Their prey must be trying to put extreme distance between itself and the council!

Braka, eighth of the council, turned his snarling gargoyle head to come face-to-face with an arrow. The notched projectile's tip was mere inches from his face, and their prey turned out to be a *man*! Though his body was gone in a flicker of speed a moment later, that arrow in front of Braka's face—unfortunately for the demon—was not. It had been released before Artorian had vanished, and the single projectile turned into ten gleaming arrows right before his slitted eyes.

For a brief second—before his health bar crashed to zero from taking ten thorns to the face fired at a distance where they couldn't have missed—Braka, the first pincushion, knew fear.

CHAPTER FORTY-THREE

Artorian's broken damage calculation flickered to life. Static snapped, crackled, and popped from the window; which brightened and dimmed erratically, its physical appearance one of shattered glass. The information screens managed to show two damage calculations out of the bunch, but didn't fare well enough to continue after that. The screen couldn't keep up with Artorian's continuous barrage while he put new skills to good use, and got right to attacking.

Multishot arrows fired: 10
Thorns will be calculated individually.

You have attacked the target: Braka, with surprise Ki Arrows!
Your Multishot triggers the Wispwood special ability!
First thorn deals 1d20 kinetic damage. Result: 17
First thorn is affected by the Journeyman bonuses from Bow Mastery, Close Range Tactics, Point Blank Tactics, user's Legendary title, and the user's Demonbane trait. Total damage bonus: 175% before being doubled. Result: 93.5
This result will be floored to 93 due to limitations.

Ki Arrows: 100 bonus Kinetic damage.
First thorn total damage: 193. Counted with 50% armor piercing.
Notice! Enemy armor will no longer be listed.
First thorn actual damage: 174.

You have attacked the target: Braka, with surprise Ki Arrows!
Critical hit!
Critical Realism skill trigger confirmed!
Your Multishot triggers the Wispwood special ability!
Second Thorn deals 1d20 kinetic damage. Result: 11
Second Thorn is affected by the Journeyman bonuses from Bow Mastery,
Close Range Tactics, Point Blank Tactics, user's Legendary title, and the
user's Demonbane trait. Total damage bonus: 175% before being doubled.
Critical Realism! Output multiplied times five after the current formula.
Result: 302.5
This result will be floored to 302 due to limitations.
Ki Arrows: 100 bonus Kinetic damage.
Second Thorn total damage: 402. Counted with 50% armor piercing.
Second Thorn actual damage: 362.

Crack!

The screens shattered right out of existence with another static clap as the numbers stopped rolling in.

Behind the scenes, the Wisp crews were in an uproar when a fire broke out in their workplace. Since the automatic calculation Pylons were out of commission—once again snapping with upset lightning—they needed to calculate all of Artorian's damage manually!

Initially they'd been very hopeful that the damage Pylon being hooked up to the acorn calculator would increase the overall yield. As soon as the acorn Pylon realized it wasn't counting acorns at all, that miffed squirrel had quit on the spot. The feedback from its sudden cessation forced all the burden back to the original calculation Pylons.

Which subsequently went up in electric flames.

There was much screaming.

It wouldn't have been such a problem if Oberon had still been around, but he'd taken his entire foreman crew and left to go *galavant*. With their oh-so-mighty orange one currently busy being lead percussionist in the twenty-Wisp skyband, they had to make do.

That meant asking the *Gnomes* for help. **Ugh**.

Several of them muttered expletives. They didn't want to, but they needed souls who liked math. Even if it meant asking the abyssal *dice*-people for help. Orb shape was best shape; who needed sides?

Deverash Neverdash the Dashingly Dapper wore a smile that went on for days when he blinked onto the scene. A cadre of Gnomes had come with him. The lot of them were painfully giddy when they'd heard what the task was. "Manually calculating damage? Well don't twist my arm too much, brighties!"

The automated Pylons had shown maybe half of the relevant arrow information. The Wisps were clear on the matter. There needed to be less clutter, information had to be more concise! Dev was of the opposite opinion. "Concise? There's barely anything there! We need to *expand* on that entry. Really show them everything when their option to check the event log goes live."

Herzog, the green Wisp currently in charge of the damage Pylon cluster, hovered forwards. The oversized hard-hat he was wearing easily covered up half of his floating body. "We need listings short! That entry was fat, obtuse, and far too burdensome to read. We don't want to see fat chunks of information like that when we check the log. I want only the final damage number to show. Maybe with what caused it."

Dev just couldn't agree with that sentiment. "That's terrible! That tells you nothing! You'd have to dig around in your status sheets and all individual's applicable skills and bonuses to see where it's all coming from. Downright awful. I want us to be able to see all the sprockets and widgets, all the knobs and nubs that make it all tick. So we get a satisfying, well explained number at the end."

Herzog began to steam. "No! The log needs to be an 'at a glance' information source. Not some 'show me your work' math assignment. Just look at that ugly clump Player 1703 saw. What was that jumbled mess supposed to tell him? That he did one hundred seventy-four damage with one of his ten arrows. That's all!"

Deverash crossed his small, Gnomish arms, his gaze iron as Herzog had said something he shouldn't have. "Artorian. His name is Artorian. Don't you dare marginalize and trivialize a person with the denigration of a mere number. That is my friend you're talking about, and I will string you up and turn you into a tool to play paddle ball with if you don't apologize."

Herzog took off his hardhat and threw it to the ground. "Are you talking down to me? I am a Wisp! My station is higher than yours, you—"

Mana wires clamped all around Herzog as a Gnomish net shot from a contraption on Dev's wrist. It captured the Wisp easily enough, much to Herzog's protests. Tugged in hard, one of the Gnomes Deverash had come with procured a human-sized paddle. A giant thing compared to the Gnome's stature. The size difference was not something that bothered the lead developer as he followed through on his threat, chiding the green Wisp as he was used in the 'ball' portion of paddleball.

"You. *Pif*. Will not.* *Pif*. Refer to. *Pif*. People. *Pif*. As numbers! *Pif*!" An extra mighty swing broke the net tether—sending Herzog away in a wide arc—only for him to land in a cluster of Pylon components. Dev's group each pulled out a small chalkboard, wrote a number on it, and held it up.

Dev *tsk'd* when he saw the scores. "A three? *Come on,* Francier. That was a pantastic paddlin' I just applied."

Francier just shook his head no. "Terrible wrist and arm motions. No finesse. No class. All brutish swings. A three is the correct verdict."

The Gnomes bickered while the Wisp foreman crew retrieved their team lead. A violet chunk of Pylon was still embedded in Herzog's side when he hovered back with assistance. "Fine! I'll call him Artorian, but I fully refuse a large damage log. If anything, give the user... I mean, Artorian... a means to expand the entries and see where all the numbers come from. Where the log is concerned, I want it to be clean! That's non-negotiable."

The Gnomes stopped their wordy arguments, a sly smile on their faces. "Optional, you say? We can work with that. Well alright then! Show us what's not working? Don't bother pointing out the fire. We could see that all the way from the other Soul Space."

Herzog picked up his hard hat, fitting it back over his glowing noggin while another Wisp pulled the last chunk of Pylon out. He grunted for effect, but the damage had never been harmful to begin with. "Good. The tables are over here. The short of it is this: Artorian's Zen Archer class has a time dilation feature, which is bothersome when it comes to his perception. That being; it functions much like the normal Mage-rank variant that he's used to. He can go faster regardless of the frame he's in, the effort is just going to cost him."

Dev and his crew walked up to the tables showing Artorian's latest activity, physically written down since the Wisps had begun manual calculations. Which was something they could do, just something they didn't want to do. Their fun ended when the dice showed their results.

Deverash just rubbed his hands together and picked up a sheet. "I can't say I see the problem."

Herzog grumbled and nudged a red Wisp to take over for him. "Rumble will explain. I have to go try to get that fire put out. *Again.*"

Rumble, a red Wisp with far more understanding and flexibility than his boss, laid the problem out for Dev. "It's not as big a problem as 'Zog made it seem. Dilation is just a pain to calculate. The issue goes like this. Because Artorian has that ability active, it's messing with the action economy and flow of combat. He's paying for fair use, but the problem is our end."

Rumble hovered over a different paper that Dev hadn't seen

yet. "We've divided our combat into a concept called rounds. Each round allows a limited set of actions or things you can do, with skills and abilities that can slightly modify that. Each round is five seconds, and a brand-new archer would get one arrow off in that timeframe. Attacks have wind-up and down time, which slows the firing rate down. That's the basic interaction, but now look at Column B. I think you can just spot the problem."

Deverash put the paper he had down and picked up the other one, his fingers moving to find the relevant column while his Gnome crew huddled up around him. "Let's see here. Eternium increased his Bow Mastery to Journeyman. Meaning the maximum number of shots he can let loose in a round is five, before that's drastically slowed down by drawing, nocking, and pulling."

His finger moved down, eyebrows slowly starting to go up. "Oh, I see. Multishot allows him to shoot multiple arrows. That accuracy penalty is horribly painful. He'd never hit with most, if any of these at range. So what if he can shoot at maximum ten arrows per pull? Most will miss. That's fifty arrows fired in… five seconds. Alright that's a lot, but if only five hit the target… Seems fine? He's still paying ten stamina per arrow, so that's five hundred stamina he just burned."

Rumble picked up a measuring stick with telekinesis and pointed lower in the table where Dev was looking. All their gazes followed it. Two Gnomes cringed just enough for it to be noticeable, but Dev soldiered on. "He did it at point blank. So currently while there's a fifty percent accuracy penalty on each arrow, before we roll it, Point Blank Tactics bonus alone cancels that out, and Bow Mastery slaps on a fifty percent accuracy bonus. *Per arrow*. We uh… we should balance this a bit better."

Rumble held up a separate paper altogether with the help of four other Wisps. Each holding a corner. "No. The balancing on that is fine, because what kind of madman archer is going to be in point blank range of his target often? It was meant more as an 'oh no! I'm in the thick of it. Shoot and run!' We wanted the archer to be useful up close, so bonus damage and chance to hit seemed applicable. Especially when you're right in front of what you're shooting. We weren't expecting Artorian to *purposefully* get in an opponent's face and unleash abyss."

Dev scratched the top of his small hat. "Alright, in that case, I'm having trouble seeing the problem. It works as intended and he's paying the proper cost. Though I'm noticing stamina and mana is regained per second, and these calculations show their cost in rounds. So this isn't costing him as much as it seems. Unless this needs to be counted in seconds? But you've got us for that."

Rumble moved the ruler to the next column over on Dev's piece of paper. "Right, which brings us to the action economy problem. Soul of Zen isn't going to stay at Novice rank long if he keeps pouring stamina into it. That was supposed to be an 'explosive couple of seconds' get out of trouble card. We weren't expecting a person that can... uh, sustain it indefinitely. All these sustain abilities are meant to be used in short bursts as a combative advantage. Not going *super*. Look at how many attacks he actually just unleashed."

Deverash handed over part of the page to his crew so he could shuffle to the right and look at the new chart. "Well so far still no problems? The bow he currently has removed the vast majority of his draw, nock, and pull penalties. So he's getting that five shots per round, every round. That's five, each affected by Multishot to turn them into ten thorns each. Soul of Zen allows him to do this twice on his round. So... one hundred thorns a round, which costs him an even thousand stamina. That's about what his gain is? That balances nicely."

The Gnome paused, some gears turning as he thought that over a second time. "That's... a lot of arrows."

Rumble could see his new coworker was starting to approach the correct problem. "Right, but we don't want it evenly balanced, we want his stamina to see actual drain. Note he did this while moving, as that's allowed and built fully into the system. His penalty for shooting on the move isn't hurting him like it should because Eternium set his Flurry Arrows skill to Journeyman. Meaning the penalty is gone entirely."

Rumble moved his ruler. "In addition, Electrosense is giving him an almost perfect idea of where his foes are. Are you aware how *fast* he can move even with two hundred fewer points in each chunk of his speed formula? Mind you that after the penalty, Zen artificially doubles because of the frame of reference he's in."

Francier pointed at the Ki Arrows column. "Boss, says here he's used this ability on every single arrow. Isn't the cost for this a flat hundred chi? Mana in Artorian's case. So one hundred arrows cost him a massive ten thousand mana! Can he sustain that?"

Dev looked at it, and shook his head no. "Certainly not. Though it will take a while before he's tapped. In this round he just completed, he has killed four... What are these things called? Gargoyles? Good title for that physically oriented demon shape. Still that's very odd, a bow shouldn't be able to do the kind of damage that eats through two to three thousand health."

Rumble moved his ruler to the chart that was being held up. "Well, our mad lad has point-blanked ten. He had the movement allotment to make the entire trip to every foe on his round. So the only thing these ten gargoyles saw was a blur, followed by a face full of ten arrows. Each of these attacks have a painfully high chance to hit with all arrows, and each of these Thorns counts as a Ki Arrow."

The ruler moved to the manual calculations some yellow Wisps were still in the process of making. "So each volley is going to do a thousand bonus kinetic damage, if the opponent has nothing that reduces it. Should we roll a twenty on his damage, and it super-crits, that's five hundred and fifty damage before the Ki Arrow bonus is added."

To emphasize, Rumble pointed at the average creature chart. "That's the current health bar of most things on Midgard. So give or take some wiggle room and low rolls, not counting the ki damage, his volley of ten arrows may average anything between five hundred to a thousand points worth of damage. Before we look to see if any of them are critical. Which is how four out of those ten gargoyles are dead in one round. Imagine how horrible it would have been had he focused his shots and clustered them all."

Dev steepled his fingers, and pressed them to his pursed lips before taking the form of a twelve-sided die. Just to drive his response home. "I have found the issue. Wisps are sour and see problems where there aren't any. Too bad you can't change the angle of your perspective. These costs are fine and would apply correctly to anyone normal."

Rumble sighed in relief when it initially looked like the Gnome had understood his point of view, starting to roll up the documents. He dropped it when Dev verbally finished his thought, evoking his namesake and starting a brawl with telekinetically held rulers and pieces of broken Pylons. "We're fixing this and making it all simplistic, you hexagonal redcap!"

Dev bounced back the first ruler strike with his oversized paddle, not interested in pretending the system had the kind of problems the Wisps were trying to sell him. "Make me! You glowy paddle ball!"

CHAPTER FORTY-FOUR

Pencil fumed, his demeanor regally enraged. His mousy tone seethed as he prepared his spells. "You blithering fools! Stop trying to sate your claws. You're all flailing about like mindless imbeciles. Use your mana and blast it. It's going to run out of stamina soon enough. Nothing can keep an effort like that up forever!"

The demon mouse's perception followed Artorian, keeping up with the moving death blur that dropped four of his council, and wounded six more in the span of five seconds. He'd watched the assailant zip about, traversing across several floors. His prey changed elevation with the ease of an angry squirrel, and moved at ludicrous speed.

There was a point where it seemed like gravity would get the better of their assailant, but a cube of light sprang into being where its feet would land. The platform was then used as a springboard for the zippy squirrel to alter an otherwise final movement vector.

Touching his tiny mouse paws against his own chest, he let free some roiling yellow energy, making it coat his now shimmering frame. He could have expended the mana to share this effect with his council, but they were expendable, and this effect was expensive. No reason to spoil the fun.

Like any proper demon, he enjoyed indulging in the observation of suffering. It didn't particularly matter who the suffering happened to. Only that it did.

The gargoyles got the hint. Either by being yelled at by Pencil, or by the personal discovery that arrows to the face was not a dish they wanted to receive a second serving of. The council had been of the mind that this was a minor assailant. Something to play with. A toy they could toss around to coat their claws in blood. That was something fun, and to the Torture Savants, it was even considered an opportunity for art. How they desired to climb to such prestigious heights! Yet those heights required practice, experience, and unwilling canvases.

With the newfound knowledge that this wasn't a good day for painting, the demons remembered that they did in fact have more than greedy claws at their disposal. For this gargoyle variant, it just happened to be the case that the claw option was the most satisfying one.

Black flame broiled around their digits. Rather than charge, stone wings spread and sought distance from the castle interiors and walls. Most of the council took to the sky, while some slunk away into the shadows within the castle's corridors.

Slank, Fifth of the Council, had survived her encounter with the shotgun porcupine. She winced as her claw ripped away the brittle thorns piercing her face. That hurt! She had twenty percent damage reduction in her gargoyle form due to Stoneskin, how had some measly glowstick ignored half? She vengefully hurled her Broil Fire spell at the blurred grievance, its black heat exploding on impact.

Other gargoyles followed Slank's lead. An area of effect spell was great for a target they couldn't perfectly pin down. It had speed, but that's likely all it had! Slank throatily yelled at the Ninth of the Council. "Waraka! It's fast and uses arrows, likely a dexterity build. Mana Burn it! It can't make those sticks glowy if it has no mana pool. I bet that's the only thing that's actually hurting us. We are long invulnerable to mere arrows!"

Waraka had also pulled the thorns out of his face, a blue variant of the broiling fire starting to course around his arms. His stone claws rose to the sky, an orb forming that shaped itself to look like the equivalent of some large beast. "Pooling Inferno!"

Ultramarine flame spewed from the beast's mouth, coating the eastward interior of the courtyard in fire that didn't burn anything that didn't have mana. It caught their nuisance just fine, given the wide conical effect Waraka had invested in his spell. An abyssal shame shaping was so horribly expensive. The cone shaping alone had eaten half his mana bar. "Got it. Slank, it burns!"

Slank snapped back. "If you're going to say I was right, spare the effort on sustaining your spell. The more Mana Burn you can apply, the quicker this farce will end."

Waraka cleared his throat angrily. "I don't see you helping! Keep throwing those Broil Fires! Pool Inferno isn't going to chip at his health, and if you're full on mana while the rest of us go empty, it will be you we choose for the Ripping Festival!"

Slank hissed back. More Broil Fire was already building on her claws as other council members were busy throwing their own explosive attacks at the blur. Most blasts were blocked by quickly crumbling or dissolving infrastructure as their prey escaped. The assailant had taken to running through the castle's interior. Hunting down the council members that hadn't been smart enough to take to the sky.

Artorian's butt was on fire. He patted it in the middle of his run, failing to put it out as he followed the rules of combat. Never stop moving. Never stop attacking. He couldn't risk the glance at his status sheet, since he was already running on the walls from the sheer velocity he was going when he turned a corner. His footfalls left indents with each step, but Artorian couldn't be worried about being tracked right now.

It was all about the offensive, and his active abilities were putting in work. Electrosense warned him of hidden foes, outlining them in a landscape of wavelengths made purely out of wobbly lines. Once a foe was detected, Impeccable Focus updated the outline for that enemy to red. That the gargoyle around the corner was hidden, obscured by shadows, and using some manner of haze ability to further prepare for a sneak attack didn't matter.

Artorian aimed his bow at what ordinary eyes perceived as empty space, and released while the hallway behind him went up in smoke, fire, and explosive blasts. He heard crashing rock rather than the twang of his bowstring, and didn't linger to see one arrow become ten. Most of his shots found their mark based on the screams, and to him that was enough of a tell. The collapsing hallways and what he guessed were evil fireballs that followed in his wake did the rest.

While he'd been playing stalker in the nearby forest for a few days, Artorian had figured out that so long as he did the majority of the damage, he would receive experience for the kill even if he didn't land the final blow.

That thought wasn't a particularly important detail at this juncture, given his robe was still ablaze. So he dismissed it, and saw to the task of putting this strange fire out. More patting did nothing, but he had long run out of the mana needed to clean himself up with an obliterator. When it came to enemy projectiles, he was playing an elaborate game of dodge! The downside being that he could see neither the ball, nor the explosive radius those attacks would cause. The only solution was to go faster and hope his stamina and mana regenerated faster than he was using it.

They didn't.

Artorian spared a rare under his breath curse at this game and its oddities. There was just too much to pick up in short order. He was strongly considering kicking the cheating into gear when a small mouse with bright green eyes appeared before him, stopping him dead in his tracks with a kick right to the gut.

Artorian's thoughts were promptly thrown out of the window. The mouse followed up with a roundhouse that packed enough strength to make his body follow right after his lost thoughts. Artorian broke through the stone wall, his bow kept close to his chest as he hit the burning courtyard ground like an unenthused sack of potatoes. "Ow."

"Had that been a *mouse*?" He didn't have time to dally and question. It was up and at 'em to avoid a volley of very unfriendly looking explodey boys. The spot he'd laid became an earth-cracked crater soaked in fire so thick that the flame looked like a new form of liquid at an over-the-shoulder glance. The damage calculation screen hissed and spit, barely managing to tell Artorian that little pitstop via mouse cost him fourteen hundred health. No wonder that had hurt so much!

"How did that tiny thing manage to avoid Electrosense?" Artorian hadn't noticed the tiny-eared bugger at all! His momentary question made him miss the trajectory of a Broil Fire. Artorian took the burning attack squarely to his face. It knocked his feet up in the air while his head tumbled downwards. Mid-explosion, he managed to shove the bow under his robe so he would take the brunt of the boom instead of the tool, even if the pressure wave mashed him into the ground. The dang thing was brittle!

Three hundred health shaved off from his green bar, the explosion of a second one sending him hurtling towards broken ground where another Broil Flame waited for him. That one exploded and flipped the script, sending him skywards with force as another three hundred health vanished. Abyss, those things hurt! Like sticking your head into the oven while at the same time running your whole body into a glass door.

Artorian opened an eye when Breathe the Air and Flow Like Water triggered. Two of the gargoyle council had lunged, claws at the ready to rend and slash. Impeccable Focus punted the disorientation debuffs trying to populate onto his status panel away like tiny Gnomes that needed disciplining. Soul of

Zen thankfully gave him twice as much time to discern the gargoyle's attack trajectories.

Forming a platform above his head to regain control of his momentum, he pushed off with his hand to send him straight downwards. More spells had been shot up at his impending spatial position, and he didn't want to be there when they went off. The gargoyles were nearly on him when he'd managed this stunt, so he grabbed one by the lower leg on the way down, but was holding his bow with the other. To bring that second enemy along, he bit it in the ankle!

Hand-gargoyle was thrown to the earth with force. The other was merely dragged along. Artorian spit the ankle-gargoyle out so he could grab it, turn it, and slam the opponent already on the ground with his compatriot. That was enough to break the gargoyle already smashed to the ground, but not enough to crack the nobody in his grip. A glint in his eye caught the new volley of spells coming in, so ankle-gargoyle became an improvised shield. The demons must have been starting to run low on mana, as that caustic spellspear emanation looked directed rather than one that went boom.

Stepping back, he twisted in place, turning his hips while Flow Like Water helped to adjust his positioning. The struggling shield-gargoyle in his grip was used as a batting implement. Though rather than nun-chuck knocking the spear off course like he wanted, the demon instead took it to the chest, acid dissolving it on the spot. This left Artorian with a measly dismembered stone leg in his hand.

He tossed it straight at one of the flying casters, conking them in the face and knocking them from the sky. "Ha! Gotcha!"

Artorian noted that the spells were coming slower. The gargoyles had taken to charging them up before hurling them out. Waraka howled at him, finally having charged his Pooling Inferno enough for the mouth on it to open again.

Artorian would have chided the use of such an obvious notification to a source of danger, but he had better things to do. Breaking the burned earth under his feet as he took off, he ran across the length of the courtyard purely to build up speed. So that when he came to the mostly intact inner wall, he scaled it rather than come to a sudden stop, going up in a straight vertical before breaking a crenulation by pushing off from it. His redirected jump arc brought him right above the stationary Waraka, whose spell direction wasn't turning nearly as quickly as the target it was meant to engulf.

Waraka's blind spell movements did cause two of his brethren to become engulfed, but that was considered unimportant collateral as far as the spellcaster was concerned. As a bundle of ten thorns peppered his sternum, Waraka suffered catastrophic spell failure. A spell that large and mana-invested didn't just end when the caster suffered temporary setbacks such as sudden death. Pooling Inferno wasn't satisfied to just sputter and call it a day.

In a blaze of glory, Pooling Inferno consumed its caster outright, pulling Waraka's body into itself as fuel for an extra few seconds of activity. Rather than direct out its Mana Burn effect in a cone, Pooling Inferno sucked inwards and condensed to the size of an average pea. Artorian had seen an effect like this before, and moved his feet without thinking. Ember may or may not have broken some tectonic plates with an effect like this back in the day. "Nope!"

If it was anything like what he remembered, Artorian knew there was not going to be a good escape from this thing. Walls were going to do nothing, so Artorian got his still-burning keister into gear and hastily began platform bunny-hopping up and away to put distance between him and the inferno pea. During his hurried escape, spells still whizzed by his hips and ears. Two caught him right in the back, including one of those nasty caustic spears. "*Ahfw*. Ow! Those hurt!"

That spear alone was going to eat five hundred points out of his health bar over the course of ten seconds, while the biting hex just took twenty points out of his health, but two hundred points out of his stamina. It was fine! This was nothing so long as he managed to get out of the pea's radius in time.

On cue, the inferno pea burst, causing all the world below to become swallowed up by mana consuming fire. Artorian jumped once more, and was safe. "Aha!"

CHAPTER FORTY-FIVE

"Going somewhere?" Artorian swiveled his head around, surprised at the sudden voice speaking scree-scree. It was that blasted mighty mouse! How had it snuck up on him again? Without platforms no less! Oh… it had just used his. Huh… he should be careful about that in the future. Much as Artorian had done to the gargoyle, the mouse grabbed him by the ankle and hurled him earth side. Right into the still-roiling Pooling Inferno spell as Pencil activated an ability of his own. "Dispelling Smash."

Artorian hit the ground painfully hard, coughing from impact as his Monk skills cleared up some of the demerits he was struck by. Unfortunately, they didn't clear out all of them. He heard one of the gargoyles shriek out as the Mana Burn spell fizzled out, having consumed all of its invested energy. "I can't regenerate any mana!"

Artorian groaned and pushed himself to his feet, realizing that Soul of Zen was no longer active since he was moving at normal speed along with everything else. He was also covered in fire. Fire that wasn't burning him? Aside from making him annoyingly visible, it didn't seem to be doing him any harm.

That was, until he felt the pit in his stomach when his mana pool bottomed out. *Oof*. "Not a pleasant feeling."

The magic attacks had ceased for the moment, the pea having been rather indiscriminate. Artorian took the moment to look at all the gargoyles above him. They weren't casting, or were trying to charge their spells only to visibly get nowhere. Another yell went out that mana wasn't regenerating, and that worried Artorian enough to check his own sheet as he broke into a run. He stumbled from the sudden change of available statistics and frame of reference dilation. Swapping back and forth was never seamless, but he made it into the castle.

A castle that was becoming more rubble than proper structure, but there was no time for nitpicking. He pulled up his sheet and nearly squealed at the results. He had two thousand-ish health left, and a grand total of zero mana that didn't seem to be recovering. Stamina was tip-top though. He quickly glanced at his demerits, and wished he'd thrown the stone leg at the pool-caster instead. There was a very ugly entry present, which also explained why he was still on fire.

Mana Burn: Afflicted targets lose 5% mana per second. Dropping the target to 0 mana replaces this demerit with Advanced Mana Burn.

Advanced Mana Burn: The afflicted loses a percentage of their mana regeneration, burning the gained mana immediately. So long as mana continues to burn, this effect will sustain itself. This effect will slowly increase the amount of mana regeneration affected, turning into Endless Mana Burn when the meter reaches 100%.

Endless Mana Burn: Afflicted has been affected by 100% Advanced Mana Burn, and will continue to burn all gained mana in perpetuity.

Artorian was completely covered in the ultramarine flames, though checking his hands and arms revealed a lack of wounds. His mana pool being stuck at zero may as well have been just as bad of an injury. Interestingly, his sustain abilities hadn't deactivated? Well, if he had no mana, he might as well use them to the fullest that he could.

No mana meant no Ki Arrows. Actually, no mana meant no arrows at all. He'd been feeding the wispwood effect in order to get the ammunition he needed. How had he run out of mana so fast? "A drain of fifty per second shouldn't... *Oooooh*. Platforms took a thousand mana, riiiight."

"Poison Prison!" The mousy voice thundered outside, causing Artorian to miss the gargoyle that sped past him just to get out of the building. His knees bent, the first reaction being to give chase. Artorian stuttered in his steps as a lime green wall of fog burst through all available openings he could see. On second thought, going the other way was just fine!

He turned and ran deeper into the castle, breaking down doors with his shoulder while the cloud became ever more pervasive. He did not want to get caught in that thing! One moment. Didn't he have something against this? It was a poison cloud, so... wasn't it inhaled?

Artorian tried to activate Omnibreath, hoping it wouldn't shunt him out from lack of mana. He saw his maximum mana bar tighten up and shorten right before the buff populated on his status sheet. "Celestial Feces! *Yes*! We're back in the fight boys!"

Another eight percent maximum mana got used up, but that was fine!

Stopping in a room that looked like an abandoned larder, he turned to face the broken door that billowed with poison on the other side. Even without the buff, this was the end of the road unless he wanted to chance breaking through a stone wall. "Well... it works for water."

When the cloud engulfed him, he closed his eyes and exhaled before taking a fresh hopeful breath. The poisonous air tingled on his tongue, like he'd eaten some truly sour candy. Which then scrubbed a lemon across his taste buds after. All in all, once he peeked open an eye to look at his status sheet, there was no health damage! Win!

Since he had a second before the problems were going to come look for him, he expanded his status sheet to look over his options. No mana caused a lot of problems. "Alright. New plan. What do I still have to work with?"

Going down his abilities list, only the Empowerment option from Monk seemed like it could be applicable. It would eat up the rest of his maximum mana if he invested it all, but that seemed like a good option when he didn't have a drop of mana regardless. Also that Mana Burn fire wasn't going to help him hide, or land sneak attacks. He might as well be a torch!

"Let's see. With Omnibreath on, that is fifty-two percent of my mana bar used up. That leaves forty-eight for Empowerment." He could just give it a go? Steadying himself by taking a horse stance, he lowered his center of gravity and stabilized his core. Pulling his fists to the sides of his hips, he sustained a powerful yell as he applied the Monk skill one percentage point at a time.

A transparent mesh of mana billowed around him, the thin field sticking to his skin as it formed an effect Artorian found similar to inhabiting a Mage body. His form was still one of flesh, but something more had intermingled with his physical makeup to improve his capabilities. He flexed his hands as the power around him condensed and solidified. It felt like C-ranker empowerment, if some spice had been added to the soup to make it just that much better.

If anything, it was the ease in effort to sustain this added might that surprised him. No C-ranker would be able to pull this kind of fine control off. Well… maybe Irene? He missed Irene. A glance at his status sheet made him loudly whistle.

New Strength: 1084
New Dexterity: 1083
New Constitution: 1086

Artorian rolled his shoulders, exiting his stance since it just wasn't necessary. "*Ohohohoo…* A thousand in each? Shame that threshold bonus I heard about isn't in effect. I would have loved to see what breaking a thousand would have done. Maybe next time? Yes. Let's make it to the next time."

He was about to dismiss his ability screen, but noticed Echolocation didn't have a cost listed. Was that a flub? He smirked and gave it a try while doing some basic stretching. Had to regain that flexibility!

Outside of the wrecked castle previously known as Triplicate, Lord Pencil kept his tiny paws outstretched, sustaining his poisonous cloud cast until he was certain he'd suffused every last inch of his abode. Nothing was going to survive that. Any demon that had slacked, or council member thinking it was safe to hide, was now taking a stacking health-loss demerit that increased in strength and potency the longer that they remained in the cloud.

There wouldn't be survivors. Pencil was so sure of that that a tiny smirk curled on his face. Until the moment that a sharp *wub* whistled out from the interior. Like it was some kind of *taunt*. A taunt that mockingly asked: 'Is that all you've got?'

Pencil stopped his casting. His cloud was being beaten back? Nonsense. Shifting his power so it fueled his specialization rather than his base class, the Psychomancer mouse could see a waking, living mind present in one of the castle larders. How had that nuisance gotten around the poison cloud effect? That spell was as costly as it was effective. Just to check, he pulled it up.

Ability: Poison Prison

This ability enshrouds a large area in a cloud of poison. This cloud will remain so long as the caster sustains the mana cost, after which it will slowly dissipate. This ability was gained via the consumption of a 'Frailty Frog,' a creature which lives in a swamp perpetually filled with this spell effect. Casting Poison Prison has no initial cost. Poison Prison has a sustain cost of 200 mana per second, and a size limitation equal to one-

hundred square feet per skill rank. For each size rank used, Poison Prison will cost an additional 200 mana per second.

Poison Prison deals 5 points of damage per second, for every breath any living creature takes within its area of effect. One instance of this damage is counted as a 'tick.' Each damage 'tick' will last for 1 minute. A single tick of Poison Prison should do 300 damage by the time of that tick's conclusion, if the afflicted target has no appropriate protections or defenses.

Note: This ability is an inhaled poison. Unlike contact, injury, or ingested poisons, this ability must be repeatedly inhaled for its effect to function. Creatures native to a swamp, related to the Frailty Frog, or entities able to breathe in any environment will not be affected by this ability.

The mouse gritted his teeth, noticing that his mana also wasn't recovering. At all. If anything, his pool sputtered and gave him a single digit now and again, but the majority of mana filling the area just seemed to be burning away to nothing. "Infuriating. I blame Waraka for this."

Slank mumbled nearby. "He's dead, sir."

Pencil sneered at the comment. "I don't care. Get in there and drag what's left of the body out. Kick it a few times if it puts up a fight. Hold back on spells or pricey abilities until this strange mana entropy effect ends, so I suppose your claws may once again be the better option."

This order pleased the gargoyles greatly. Slank slunk herself towards the door, her stony tail swaying behind her as she waited for the green cloud to fade. She cocked her head as a slowly repeating sound reached her ears. They sounded like... footsteps? A hand burst from the opaque cloud, grabbing her face and pulling it into the deadly green depths. Slank's screams were cut short with a stony *snap*.

Pencil looked down when Slank's head, just the head, was tossed back out from the cloud, landing nice and neat at his feet in a pile of burned earth. The voice that followed unsettled him. It was human in nature, but the depth of it betrayed the beast hidden within. "I see you."

The lord lifted his nose into the air, silently listening to the footsteps recede as he momentarily flicked power to his eyes once again, watching the mind retreat. The cloud in the doorway began to fade, revealing the rubble that was left of Slank's stone body. Pencil didn't like that he was down to a measly four council members, so he decided numbers weren't a limitation he was going to be done in by. Lifting his paw to the air, a lime green beam pierced the sky. "Call of the Savant."

Pencil received a notice from the Voice of the World he wasn't expecting. The words within only made his expression all the more viciously toothy. The lost forces in the wood saw the signal pierce the sky, and knew it was a call of action. They were to return! That meant their foe had finally been found. They'd been aimlessly searching the wet verdant growth only to come up dry.

That side-effect was not the purpose of Call of the Savant. The call ability was a summoning, one that demanded demonic attention rather than sweetly beckoning it. As a round green gate opened into being next to Lord Pencil, a diminutive bat wobbled out. Dressed in only the most expensive finery and cobalt jewelry. Pencil bowed to the Archwizard equal. The bat then acted in turn, greeting a fellow savant. The bat's eyes shared the same lime green glow that the mouse possessed, as Pencil initiated another ability. Their conversation became entirely mental when their gazes connected.

Soni, a Torture Savant hiding away in the form of a tiny bat, swiftly understood the issue once the mental conversation concluded. "You are having such problems with a single nuisance that you call upon assistance by gate? What manner of joke are you playing on me, Pencil? You heretical pariah."

The mouse snapped its nose toward the remains of Tripli-cate. "It's as I showed you. I'm convinced it's the outsider that we're dealing with. The Devourer would never let us live it down if we didn't take care of the first wave. Though it seems the assault is one of an individual, rather than a group. Our predictions that they would send a strike force were false. They sent but one man."

Soni cackled with high-pitched shrieks. "One man? What can one man do against an army? I hear your call, fellow savant, and I find it to be justly hateful. I will send my demonkin through. Merely point them to the Devourer's meal. I will inform my troops that the remaining body is flesh to be offered."

Pencil and Soni shared their savant greeting once again before the bat went back through the swirling gate he'd come from. The mouse pointed sharply at the castle doors, addressing his council. "Tell the vermin pretending to be butchers to assail the outsider. We must find a way to restore our mana pools while softening our foe up. Reinforcements will be here soon."

The lord glanced at the castle, biting his thumb as his eyes managed to cycle another moment of mind-sight. "I don't like that it's so quiet. He's just sitting in the middle of the grand hall. *Waiting for us.*"

CHAPTER FORTY-SIX

Artorian meditated. He was still on fire, but with the lack of health loss and his mana bar otherwise expended, that wasn't a high priority. It didn't occur to him that he was burning up all the mana in the region; he was busy trying to make something that could get him out of this.

Oberon's music had changed from drums and sticks to chime and string instrumentation. He didn't want to leave, but he had to remain fully hidden while outside. So changing the music was his way of conveying his presence. He knew Artorian couldn't hear him for the moment, but he didn't mind. Oberon had deeply enjoyed the demon trashing, and more was soon to come!

A notification popped up next to the meditating man, vanishing soon after as it was read.

Event Notice: Negative Karmic Luck event triggered. The relevant attribute has been set to 0. A demon invasion has occurred in your local area. A nearby demon lord has used 'Call of the Savant' to call in more forces. Due to the karmic event, the number of forces called forth from other realms has been multiplied by twenty.

Artorian opened his eyes, exiting meditation just to evoke his distaste. "Twenty times? What? Oberon! What gives?"

The orange light checked to see if any wayward eyes might be prying at this location, but he found none. Making himself visible, he hovered off his musical throne to leave his noise-maker behind. Artorian could feel the smirk on the orange ball's expressionless face. "Isn't it great! More demons to squish!"

The man frowned in reply. "Buddy, if they were going to bring a thousand troops in, a hefty multiplication just happened. I do not have the spare health to take wayward damage, nor do I have the ability to recover any. This is a terrible time to play the attrition game. I'm also not making headway on ability making! I didn't know I needed mana to put things together."

Oberon quieted, scanning over his friend's character sheet. "Oh. That looks less pleasant than I thought it was. Well… there is a mysterious rock covering a patch of dirt next to your left foot. Just, uh… before you pick it up and go wiping, what do you need?"

Artorian fell back, flopping on the ground with his arms still crossed. "Any way to put this awful fire out?"

His orange friend made a peeping noise of uncertainty. Artorian waved it off. "Never mind. I don't need to be told from the dissuading complaint in your voice that there's some hidden benefit here I'm not seeing. I don't know then. I didn't expect to be in this corner. The bow you gave me is great if I have mana, but currently it's in massive danger of breaking. I took the harm for it where I could, but I'm not going to be able to keep doing that. I have nowhere to safely put it."

Oberon brightly illuminated with an idea, shining like a nixie tube. "I got it. Go ahead and turn the rock over."

Artorian didn't know what strange plan his friend had just enacted, but he knocked the rock away and brushed at the broken ground. Clearing some rubble away, he found an awkwardly placed storage cube. Might as well see for himself what his floaty friend was up to. He clicked the button and tossed it a few feet away. A ring was all that popped out, falling harmlessly to the ground.

He blinked at it, quirking a brow to look over his shoulder at Oberon. The orb was staying strangely quiet. Artorian got up and went to pick it from the ground, moving it between his fingers. The ring didn't seem particularly special. He shrugged and put it on.

Notice: You have found a spatial ring! This item functions similar to spatial bags from the old world, except that, unlike those, this actually works here! You may mentally store and take items from this spatial inventory at a whim. Current available space of this ring is twenty slots! Two slots are currently taken.

Well that was neat! He lifted the bow and looked at it. "Uh... store?"

Nothing happened, so he re-read the prompt. Mentally? He looked at the bow again and thought about the directive. The item promptly vanished from his hand, the weight of the ring increasing just a hint. It felt like three slots out of twenty were now in use. He wasn't sure how he knew that. Out of curiosity, he called for the items that had been in the ring to begin with.

Two Iridium tonfa appeared in front of him and fell to the ground, embedding themselves several inches into the broken floor. He hadn't known what to expect, so didn't think to catch them when they appeared. Unsure of what to think, he inspected the armaments that had a familiar looking emblem on them.

Name: Ten Ton Tonfa
Material: Gravity Iridium
Rarity: Special
Damage: 1–1
Special Quality: Graviton

A weapon from Jotunheim. Used by the most powerful Daimyo in the realm's history, Halcyon. These tonfas have a strength requirement of 500 each. Not meeting this strength threshold makes a person entirely unable to lift a single tonfa. A strength of 1000 is required to wield both tonfas. If wielded as a set, their special quality activates.

Gravity Iridium is a variant of the base metal that quintuples in weight when they strike an opponent. The tonfas may seem deceptively light if you meet the strength requirement. That is because to the wielder they feel five times as light regardless of being at rest or in motion. This comprises the basic function of the special quality: Graviton.

A graviton weapon does not cost stamina to swing. Repeated attacks will still incur the normal stamina strain penalties. On impact, a weapon with this quality doubles the base damage resulting from the strike. While their base damage is negligible, this calculation includes the strength bonus that is added to the weapon's raw damage.

Notice: Tonfas are considered a Monk weapon. Martial arts maneuvers can be used in conjunction with this weapon.

Artorian pressed his hand to his heart. Of course he knew this emblem! He'd passed hundreds like it on his fly-through realm checks. "Special? You dare call these heavy sticks merely special?"

He picked the near-weightless tonfas up by their grips, one in each hand. "These are irreplaceable, Oberon. I know of few other things I would call unique or Legendary, save for the worn tools used by my precious chosen."

The music increased in stringed instruments as the green cloud lessened. Oberon had another look around before replying. "It's not unique because she had a few. Went through a pair in a week. That's just the pair she didn't break."

Artorian was impressed! Breaking sticks like these? From overuse? He thumbed over the wear on the handles, feeling the small tears in spider silk fabric used as wrapping. "Cy… you beauty. Look at you. Filling your days with your passions."

A hint of loving pink energy rose from Artorian's hands when he squeezed his eyes closed. Gritting his jaw when flashbacks of events long past plagued him. He didn't see the crackle of static as some automatic error notices appeared around his grip, only to fizzle out when the color faded. "I'll call them... Halcyon Days."

Oberon said nothing about the error messages, or their brief life. He didn't want that to go in the log, even if he was already kicking the shin of the log's limitations. The other Wisps shouldn't have put restrictions on him. It would only make him more obstinate. "Instead of the original name for the tonfas?"

Artorian blinked, snapping out of his fugue. "Hmm? The...? Oh. No, I wasn't talking about the weapons, though yes. How delightfully fitting. Please change their names. While you're at it, how did Cy use these? Personally I'm wondering if these can cause critical hits. That's what saved my bacon with the arrows."

Oberon laughed loudly at that, merrily pulling up the tonfa's properties and altering the name. "It's always a surprise to just how similar chosen tend to think on the same lines as their Dreamers."

Artorian's interest could have broken the roof. "Do go on!"

The orange ball was suddenly in too good a mood to deny that request. "Halcyon asked that exact same question when she got a hold of her first pair. After her trident got bent. The build she made ended up being something we've come to call a Critfisher. She was focused entirely on making the numbers not as big as possible, but be counted as criticals as often as they could. Possibly because we made custom sound effects each time she succeeded on one, which let us live cast a rolling commentary. It was amazing."

Oberon snickered. "Much like you, she also used the well-fed and well-hydrated buffs to keep going at maximum capacity non-stop. Though I don't believe you actually know what those buffs do, since they currently have no referenceable entries."

Artorian beamed. He was going to need to prod Cy for stories when she woke up properly. Or he could run to Yuki! She was the story lady, even if it came with a cold shoulder. He patted his own cheeks with his hands to get himself back on track. "I, in fact, have no idea what they're supposed to do, but I like the idea of always being well nourished."

Oberon tried to pull up the information, but the entries from the sustenance boons were blank. "Still need more Pylons, but the side effects still work. So in our game mechanics, we have a system in place that simulates the strain you feel when throwing your weight around. Anything physical takes stamina. For the most part, the stamina regeneration has you sorted, and patches that right back up without you ever being the wiser. Unless you really start going for repetitive strain."

Artorian made the tonfas vanish into the spatial ring, and had a seat. There was still some lingering poison, so he figured they had a minute.

Oberon continued. "Making an unending set of attacks increases the strain counter, which adds how much extra stamina it costs to make an action. If you chop a hundred blocks of wood in succession, your arms would be significantly more tired than if you had done ten, right?"

His human friend nodded, so he just kept talking. "As you use stamina, we decrease your hydration and food gauges, which are hidden from you entirely. If those get too low, you start incurring demerits and penalties to any stamina actions, and stamina recovery, as your body doesn't have the resources to replenish itself. While well-fed and well-hydrated have effects of their own that are currently not working. Having them as a constant effect, by itself, means you will never hit those penalties, and are instead getting hidden bonuses to your stamina usage. The bonuses aren't numerically represented, so don't bother trying to pry it out of the status screen."

Artorian nodded again, hungering for knowledge as he wanted to hear more about this crit-fishing bit. Was fishing perhaps Halcyon's version of keeping sane, like his was archery?

He just listened further. "You will be able to fight and gather significant strain without a penalty, as your body will always have what it needs, when it needs it. Your cells are fed, and will remain fed so long as you keep that sustenance effect up. Also, I know the sleeping system is broken. Please don't mention it. We need more Pylons before we can implement that properly. We have it in the log that you have never really needed to sleep once. You've been here a while."

Artorian waved that away, wanting his orange friend to get back to the good stuff. "Right. So you are able to fight effectively… forever. Without pausing. Unless you use other things that bottom out your stamina bar. As a minor mention that I'm saying to the wind: Empowerment is the only thing allowing a certain friend of mine to lift heavy sticks, and using Soul of Zen would mechanically drop him below the limit where he could pick up both of them. Just thinking out loud."

"Crit-fishing, Oberon. Tell me about crit-fishing! You were talking about Cy and then you started talking to yourself." The human winked at his friend, but did want the juicy details.

The orange light shifted to a soothing blue on the edges. That was the first time Artorian had seen his friend become dual-toned. So he could do it too! Oberon spoke quickly to distract from the color, which he quickly fixed, but Artorian had his dastardly question out first. "Are you *really* an orange Wisp?"

Oberon hung silently in place, then sighed. "I can be any color I want. Orange is just my favorite. So about that crit-fishing!"

CHAPTER FORTY-SEVEN

Artorian scratched his head when Oberon finished his explanation. "So, in short, crit-fishing requires an entire fighting style which I don't have, that I basically would need to learn from Halcyon in order to properly get the skill for. That's a pain. Can I even have multiple fighting styles? Currently I have a denial one active."

Oberon went invisible, but still spoke. His physical body vanishing told his human friend they were out of time. Company was here. "You can have as many as you can learn. Most of the time their effects don't overlap, and the stamina costs keep everything fair. There's generally still only so many things you can do in any given round or second. Why? Do you know more?"

Artorian looked at his hands, making the tonfas appear and disappear on his open palms. At whim! "This spatial ring is great. Stuff just comes and goes as I need it. *Hmm?* Yes. I know several, now that I think about it. In the Phoenix Kingdom, back in the old world I mean. Their ways were drilled into me. Didn't matter how many roofs I tried to nap on to escape, the lessons got in there. Private drill sergeants are no fun. But... the style I think I need today comes from elsewhere."

Oberon hovered back up to his throne, settling back into it so he could kick off the music when the demons were at the great hall's big doors. "Does it have a name?"

Artorian made the tonfas appear on his hands. This time, he gripped them firmly. "Yes. I learned only parts of it, but had one pyroclasm of a teacher. It's called *Pantheon Style*, and it is meant for use against armies. For that is what I will make them believe they are fighting."

The human warrior rolled his shoulders, hearing the first axe crack slash into the large doors. Any of those gargoyles from earlier would have broken such a thing down by sneezing too hard. That meant these were the grunts. Grunts were fine. Grunts were practice. Wooden splinters littered the ground when the door finally came down. The first of the horde raged and howled, charging in only to stagger and slow at the sight.

A man made of muscle, clad in ultramarine flames that coated his simple robes and clothes, stood ominously before them. He took a deep breath, a foot moving forwards to prepare a launch as he whispered under his breath. His old students had done this silliness, and perhaps it was time to join them. "Halcyon Days. First breath. *Sunrise.*"

The grand hall exploded in debris as the floor turned to gravel from the downward force applied. Dust and rock shattered the windows, peppering and denting the walls as the entire floor gave way. Opening the chambers below them to the open air as a foe the demons knew only as the 'outsider' shot into the thick of them.

The staggered grunts at the front had been certain of an easy win. All of them against one nobody? Overkill. The front line exploded by the sheer effect of a dense, fast object moving past them. The enemy hadn't even attacked, and just ran right through them. The aftershock of which was bending, breaking, and snapping the bones of any Artorian passed. Including both armor, and creatures within.

Artorian surrendered his need to be clean. Pantheon Style was dirty. It was unkind. It was the culmination of using everything you had to destroy all in your wake in as quick a way as possible. Even if that meant resorting to unconventional means.

He had issues with it when Dawn first tried teaching it to him. She was just too powerful as a practice partner. Pantheon Style needed numbers to plow through, as the real purpose of the fighting method was to instill fear, terror, and horror on a mass scale. Pantheon Style was an all-out-aggression way of fighting that should make your enemies hope they wore their yellow and brown pants that day.

The style completely threw out the idea of defense in trade for pure devastation. Artorian recited a mantra containing a list of 'don't's rather than 'do's. "There is no block. There is a counter. There is no dodge. There is a reaction. Do not stop moving. Do not stop attacking. Do not give your enemy time to breathe. Do not give them time to plan. Do not give them space to move. Do not let them succeed in their attacks. Do not let their commanders speak. Do not let any live. Do not hold back. *Do not stop.*"

Artorian's first upward tonfa smash was followed by a whirlwind of colors. His first swing, true to the name he had given it, copied the colors of sunrise. A shining yellow source that blossomed to oranges and reds, finishing in a haze of blue and purple.

He ignored the notice that came up, snapping out an order. "Silence all these noises!"

Oberon knew it was for him, and so muted all notifications Artorian would otherwise be getting throughout this fight. The rest of the audience that laid eyes on Artorian after he broke the castle open had an entirely different interpretation. The chunk of the army waiting nearby to storm the gates saw the grand hall explode from within. The demon rabble needed to lift their shields to prevent being pelted by rock and glass.

Shortly after, the entire right side of Triplicate blew open with force. All of that rock was flung away as well, which they equally needed to raise their shields for, lest they be crushed by a catapult-projectile sized hunk of masonry. When the last of the dust and debris fell, the bodies of their dead brethren followed. Raining down in chunks as few of them remained in the single piece they started as.

Then the outsider stood in the opening, yelling at them to be quiet.

A reply would have been forthcoming had the outsider not vanished in a blur. More rock pelted those that survived the speedy path carved out by what they thought had been a weak man. The outsider had entirely ignored the structure of their ranks, their shields, and their spears. The spears may have mattered had he run into one, but it was impossible to tell as bodies just went flying to the air. If they were lucky. Those that went up weren't the ones crushed underfoot, dismembered, destroyed outright, or sent hurling through the ranks to harm others as improvised ammunition.

Wub. Artorian sent out a strong Echolocation. Something he knew he wasn't going to keep getting away with. The ability populated his overstuffed minimap, which he whispered to, wanting it to show only tokens that could be commanders or better. The minimap shimmered a momentary pink, updating to reflect the information he needed. According to the topography and dots, the closest commander could be reached just by going in a straight line.

Lorkhan the Griefer snapped his hand to his war horn when he realized the projectile of doom was coming right for him. He fumbled the horn to get it to his mouth so he could call for—

Artorian buried the short business end of a tonfa into the commander's chest, ignoring minor annoyances such as elevation or terrain obstacles. The landscape just tore itself to pieces at his passing, and the troops on it didn't fare much better. The troops, much like the land, were mostly Midgard-quality, and that just wasn't going to cut it against a person who should be tromping around in Asgard for a proper challenge.

Lorkhan took to the skies. Or what was left of Lorkhan did

after a four thousand damage impact to the chest. His blood and remains rained upon the fields of terrified grunts behind him. A field that Artorian moved through like a reaping scythe in order to beeline to the next commander. There was no reason to attack the common crop. Yes, they could hit him and do damage, but in a battle with numbers like this, getting bogged down in a spot would only get him killed.

Pantheon Style was strict, and no amount of being easily noticed as an ultramarine blur was going to be something that helped the twenty thousand strong demon force.

Pencil and his four remaining council members stood on top of a surviving tower in the wrecked remains of Triplicate. His eyes narrowed, annoyed. "I'm no longer amused. Who is this creature? At first I believed who or what they sent was a scout at best. This is ridiculous. This may not be The Master we were told to look out for, but this surely is just as bad. We've been poorly determining the threat assessment. I don't believe anyone other than at minimum an A-ranker stands a chance here."

The B-ranked council shared unpleasant glances. Their one hundred and twenty statistical attribute bonus across the board was great, but if their superior with a seven-twenty bonus was saying someone like him was needed just for it to be an even fight, then they felt glad to have so much as survived.

Pencil looked down to the courtyard, studying. "He tried to trick us. Making us believe he was a high-dexterity build. An archer. Such beautiful lies. Look at this slaughter and convince me *that thing* is an archer."

His council was unable, so they said nothing. Pencil spat, knowing he'd summoned reinforcements that would act as little more than a distraction. Yes, he had incredible numbers, but he'd been wrong. What good were numbers against this? He didn't need quantity. He needed *quality*. The only plus was that the view was inordinately satisfying. All that death. All those glorious kills. All those chunks, parts, and blood. It nearly made him shiver. "I… want him. He would make an excellent demon."

His council looked at him funny, but weren't going to question a superior that delighted in their suffering, given even a slight opportunity. The First of the Council had more stones on him than the rest, and dared a few words. "You… want him captured. Sir?"

Pencil snorted. "Oh, nono. I want him killed! Thoroughly. I just want a Core close at hand when we do so, we can make sure what's left goes to the right place. Wouldn't want something as wonderful at slaughtering as that to go to waste by allowing it to… go where it would have. Besides, the current loss of troops is fantastic for the Devourer's plans. Enough dead, and we will know where to go. I shall speak of that no further. Do not mention the latter of what you just heard to anyone. Yes, First in my Council, I want him. Preferably before another does. Any savant that realizes the true value hidden away in this abyss candidate will crave it greatly. Go secure an opal Core, the four of you. *Go.*"

The council schemed, knowing this to mean hidden opportunities for growth. Presenting a Core with the outsider in it to a power higher than a savant may lift their own being to that rank. A desirable thing. Pencil must have been too enraptured with the sight, letting slip so much information. The First of the Council merely bowed to the mouse. "It will be seen to."

The others followed, not at all intending to see to Lord Pencil's wishes. Though going through the political actions regardless. One couldn't become a savant if they didn't have a head on their shoulders. Pencil wrung his paws together. "I'm going to go and handle that myself. I was trying to stay out of it before. I have changed my mind."

CHAPTER FORTY-EIGHT

Artorian glowed bright gold, suffused by energy when he tonfa'd his eighth commander in the spine. This specific strike shouldn't have reasonably killed the commander, as Artorian hadn't gotten a particularly good hit in. The jab had mostly shaved against armor, but the game considered the hit to do four thousand-ish damage regardless. Which was far more than the health the demon had, even with his armor reduction.

Leveling up meant his health was topped off. Yes! It also made him wonder why this hadn't happened... sooner? Just how much more experience was it actually taking for his level to keep increasing the way it was. Not important right now! There was cleaning to do, and his janitorial services were in high demand today.

His pleasantry ended when that same abyss-blasted mouse appeared from his blind spot and kicked him in the knee. Forcing his stride to end as he took a rough tumble. A tumble that destroyed easily a hundred grunts just from passing through them, but served as an unwelcome pause in his killing streak nonetheless. That single, tiny annoyance had caused him more grievances than any of these other demons. He needed to focus it down.

The mouse had also evaded his Electrosense a third time, and did not seem to exist on his minimap. Even Impeccable Focus had trouble locking onto the demon, and staying on him. The mouse must be jamming his abilities somehow. Artorian felt a momentary pain in his skull, but whatever skill the mouse had used must have been resisted.

A feat that visibly surprised his tiny assailant.

"How did you prevent my mind control?" The tiny mouse spoke with poise. His stature completely dwarfed by the aura of lilac energy he suddenly emanated in the shape of an oversized skull. "I knew it. You're an A-ranker. Nothing else would have such a guaranteed chance to so much as attempt to rebuke me. It also explains why inspection fails regardless of attempt. Do you know how rare it is for me to not know something, outsider?"

Artorian's response was to strike at Pencil, who grabbed his sleeve and casually tossed the human over his shoulder. As if he knew what Artorian was going to do before he did. The human immediately likened the counter to his version of predictive sight, shooting an Inspect at Pencil only for no information to come up. He didn't know if he had failed, or if the window was repressed by Oberon due to his earlier request.

"Crackers." He plowed through another line of grunts from the toss, the mouse appearing right back in his face when his footing stabilized. "And toast!"

This critter was as fast as him! The lilac skull around the mouse, rather than the mouse itself, snarled at him. "You will be mine!"

Artorian had a hunch that Psychomancer was the correct class at play, and that the mouse wasn't the true thing he was fighting. It was just a shell. How he wished he could use his field right now. The mouse burst forwards, but it was his turn for a counter as Artorian flowed like water and applied Deny the Blow. Pencil's lilac shortspear was turned onto itself, stabbing the mouse in the thigh before being hurled through the demonic ranks.

Just as Artorian had been thrown earlier.

The slaughter only delighted Lord Pencil, who built the rest of the human-shaped lilac skeleton around himself to get up. The mouse himself remained where a heart should have been, laughing maniacally the whole time. Like he was having fun. His paws moved towards his chosen enemy, the actions he performed mimicked by the oversized skull and skeleton. A lilac zone appeared before him, causing the demons caught within to panic and scatter as Pencil rumbled out a spell. "Doomsday."

Artorian knew better than to get caught in an area of effect spell, and ran for it. What surprised Pencil was that the outsider didn't run *away*. Artorian was in his face with a tonfa before his spell channeling had finished, Pencil couldn't hide his enjoyment when the determined enemy drew a large breath and spoke during his charge. "Halcyon Days. Breath Series. *Starfall*."

Oberon's orchestra came in with a full brass section when the effect of the attack arrived to play. To Pencil's psy-vision, the special ability he was using to predict the thoughts of his enemy and thus their subsequent attack, the incoming attack was visibly seen to have more weight behind it than one would expect. The end of Artorian's tonfa grew outwards, gaining the density of a falling comet traveling at celestial speeds. The trail behind it animated in slow motion, filtering through faster and faster until the impact of the strike struck Pencil's skeletal construct.

The protective lilac sternum cracked while the ribs in the way of the tonfa shattered outright. Unable to provide enough defense or damage resistance to block the momentum-filled 'oomph' of the outsider's strike. Unlike before, Pencil couldn't dodge it, and took Starfall right to the cheek. The impact sent the demon lord hurtling out of his own construct. Pencil broke the middle of the lilac spine when he crashed through, causing the entire skeletal structure to crumble into itself before vanishing in a puff of black dust.

Artorian knew he had failed to score a kill when laughter broke out in the distance as the dirt plume mellowed out. "Finally! A challenge! How I have been so bored behind my papers! You're such a fantastic toy. You won't break quickly, will you? Come! More, I want more!"

Pencil ripped free from his mousy disguise, taking on his second form as a properly massive violet-skinned monstrosity that actually looked like an abyss-blasted demon. Heaving muscle, unguligrade posture, leather wings, several curved horns, growing green eyes, a snarling face, and claws for days. The works. As a bonus, with a new nasty bruise on his cheek!

Artorian grinned and got a move on the second he recovered his footing and stride. His strike had definitely done something, and that meant more were required as he bowled through a fleeing horde of scared, frightened grunts that did not want to be collateral. Nor be caught between area of effect attacks or uprooted chunks of the environment. The problem was that they were so numerous, fleeing was difficult. There was no free room to maneuver, save for a spot on the field that gained vacancies as the previous occupants were blown up.

The commanders of the troops were faring no better as the brawl between a Torture Savant and outsider began. The duo ripped through fields of their supposed best warriors as if they were little more than stalks of grain, ready for reaping. Most commanders couldn't even keep track of the blows the two were exchanging unless one managed to counter the other and send them hurtling away. What was worse was that the dueling duo were both getting faster as they fought, increasing the difficulty for commanders to shout out correct orders to make troops rally and get away.

The portal that the demon troupe from Alfheim arrived from had long closed, and their own lord had not come with them. The story may have ended differently for them had Lord Soni been here to help them with their escape. The sudden addition of a demanding voice in the commander's head who was considering this problem, dropped his heart into his stomach. "Fight for me, minion!"

The commander stopped all other activities, his eyes turning bright green as Lord Pencil mind controlled the battle leader. Through him, the rest of his troops became affected. The fleeing remnants stopped in place only to turn and charge the other way. They wanted to cut into outsider flesh when their minds and wills left them, weapons gripped tight and held at the ready. Reason was a tool of the intelligent, and these troops had none left. Reduced to nothing more than a mindless horde to do the Psychomancer's bidding.

The academic in Artorian noticed the change in local coloration, even if the musical ambiance was starting to become a distraction. His skills shut the demerit out, and that allowed him to fight smart rather than fight like a hungry bonfire. The pink glow glistened around his grip, and this time he noticed that as well.

Patterns were lovely. Patterns were great. Patterns that repeated were something the universe adored, and no **Law** was immune to that preference. He squeezed the spidersilk grips on the tonfas, seeing the pink fade before another attack went into the demon lord's ribs. He was missing something, but a Nixie Tube flickered above his head. He smirked, and yelled at the previously mousy demon when it got upright. "That's all you got? Don't think I don't see you redirecting the troops. You can't even get all of them! Ha! You must not be the class of demon I thought you were."

Pencil took this as a personal affront. Him? Seen as a nobody because he hadn't shown the true capacity of his reach? The gall! "Foolish mortal! I shall have your soul and feast upon your screams like the sweetest of mulled drinks. I am a Torture Savant! Demon Lord and overseer of Midgard. This realm is mine, and so is every creature upon it! Come, my minions, rise for your master!"

Seeing Pencil increase the strength of the connective tissue between himself and the other demons made the pink glow return to Artorian's hands. An idea flickered in his mind, and he grasped it as it attempted to fly away. He understood! Much as Eternium was beholden to his **Law**, **Love** desired him to do the same. Even if it could not influence him on quite as significant a level. He spoke to nobody in particular, but was convinced his words reached the ears of who it was for. "Sympathy, for those who have none."

Not looking at Pencil for a moment caused him to miss the tail whip that caught him underfoot. Swiping his feet out from under him as a follow up wing strike smacked Artorian all the way back into the mortar of the crumbled Triplicate. Taking direct hits was terrible! He felt that one. An easy three thousand damage to his everything from that double-combination strike, plus hard impact. Yeowch!

He'd been taking far too much damage in the brawl, so Artorian quickly checked his status while rolling over so he could more easily get up from the rubble.

Eight hundred. He had eight hundred health left.

"Crackers!" That was incredibly bad without a way to heal! That meant a change of tactics was necessary. He couldn't just carelessly go in and attack anymore. Pantheon Style was useless if his enemies were immune to fear and intimidation. Even now he could see the horde swarm towards the broken castle. "Abyss!"

His personal style wasn't going to cut it; that was a one-on-one type deal. Pantheon was anti-army, but no good here since he needed to survive. Phoenix Kingdom tactics were a hard sell without a shield and phalanx line, and he was alone. Getting to his feet, he saw a whole slew of grunts just fall over, dead.

That couldn't be a good sign, and then it occurred to him just how often he'd gotten successful hits in on the mousy demon nuisance. That thing should be dead. Was it sapping health from other living things to patch itself up? That was unhelpful! This needed a resolution, and fast. He was going to lose any attrition-based brawl at this point, and he bloody well knew it.

How was he going to skip that entire horde, and get in that mouse's oversized face? Not that much mouse was left, but Artorian enjoyed thinking of the savant as such. It was for similar reasons that he called their language scree-scree. He cocked his head, wondering. Could he just… jump over it all?

Well, he wasn't coming up with any better ideas, so once properly up, he ran down the rubble to the mostly intact side of Triplicate. He needed to build up speed if he was going to pull this off, and the burst he got from rapid launches wasn't going to be enough. He wanted to recreate the orbital drop experience, since turning or stopping in mid-air was not happening without platforms.

Pencil howled, enraged at seeing the outsider *run*. "You dare flee? You miserable insect! You shall learn to kneel at the foot of your lord, when my gasp comes within reach!"

His wings spread, flattening demon grunts underneath via the sheer downwards pressure-gust that his upwards momentum required. Pencil was in the air shortly after, once again getting a clear view of the outsider. Though his psy-vision showed a loop rather than a straight line. The miscreant was planning to double back and ambush him? Ha! Fat chance now that he had seen the surface thoughts of the human's plan. It was over! Victory was his.

CHAPTER FORTY-NINE

The demon lord dove towards the remains of Triplicate, planning to cut Artorian off as he took the predicted turn that Pencil's psy-vision outlined. Looping around, the human picked up speed at a frightening pace while aimed straight at a ramp. If an angled wall that was failing to fall over could be called as such.

Pencil smirked when the outsider solidified his trajectory, jumping from the top of the ramparts with a mighty leap in an attempt to come right for him. The demon could not help but boast. "Too bad, human! Your trajectory is going to drop off and land far below!"

To Pencil's growing amusement, the outsider must have noticed this as well as he desperately hurled both of his tonfas at the flying demon. The savant couldn't help but cackle. No matter the velocity of those sticks, he could catch them with ease! "A gift! For me? You shouldn't have! I shall see to your demise with your own tools!"

The savant did as he planned, snatching both weapons right out of midair before they could strike him. The follow up event did not go according to Pencil's plans, as he suddenly and inexplicably plunged towards the ground. Pencil did not know that the graviton weapons didn't have their condition met, and that he thus suffered their penalty. The savant's strength score was not nearly one thousand, and he was holding onto both weapons. Rules as written, he could not lift them. Therefore, the tonfas shot straight down to the ground and took the confused, screaming demon with them.

The Iridium sticks embedded themselves into the Midgard ground with the force of a small meteor. Causing a rumbling impact crater to form before the weapons pinned Pencil's claws beneath their overbearing weight. Pencil cried out when he attempted to wriggle free, only getting himself dragged into a deeper hole.

Psy-vision was a wonderful thing… except when a trajectory that previously would have missed suddenly showed an arc in a violet-green line right to his head. The outsider couldn't possibly have planned that!

Attempting to jerk free and dodge the impending strike, Pencil realized that he was well and truly stuck. Knowing he failed, he looked up, seeing an ever encroaching attack blaze with bright pink light. Tugging harder past the point of pain, he roared, but found his claws thoroughly pinned as the tonfas just wouldn't budge. One sort of did, but one was not enough. Moments before impact, Torture Savant Pencil became paralyzed by horror. Hearing his final words as the outsider's voice boomed.

"Sun's Love. *First Kiss*."

Artorian threw his fist forwards on the way down, punching Pencil squarely in the face. The attack was hard enough to make the demon's horned skull crack audibly. Artorian's mighty strength within the strike was secondary. Before any damage was tallied came Artorian's clever little ruse. A throwback to a trick he'd pulled in Ziggurat. Rather than strike only the body, Artorian struck with one of **Love**'s higher functions. Decking the sympathy connections that the demon himself had aggregated and activated.

Pink lightning crackled around his knuckles, then his fist, eventually coating his entire arm before the blow drove home as Artorian finished his journey with an outcry of effort. He'd relied on his luck to carry him through as the full force of his attack sunk into the demon's forehead. The green in Pencil's eyes flashed with electric pink before the demon's health hit zero, mind cooked from the inside out as Artorian's **Law** went about its grisly work.

Starting from Pencil's position, mind-controlled demons in close proximity were affected first. Regardless of the hierarchy connections Pencil's Psychomaster class had in place between all the commanders. Though those soon followed after when **Love**'s sympathy effect looked for where to go next. The pink electricity thundered into the Pylon system, bouncing between all Cores affected to apply a blanket 'punch it in the schnozz' effect to all entities of similar type. Just like Artorian had done in Ziggurat.

With glorious fanfare and the spectacular effect of a sparking pink force in the form of a fist, all commander demon heads simultaneously exploded to the well-timed crescendo of a musical piece. The troops under their direct command followed suit right after, falling like limp noodles to the ground as that impact was more than enough to kill them outright. Their skulls were crushed and minds were freed, but only for them to officially die and be mass Cored as their souls were trapped by the system.

After performing his feat, he was forced to eat the cost. Artorian collapsed to his knees next to a dead demon lord, only to flop over as a very angry metric appeared in red next to his stamina bar. "*Ow…*"

His body hurt when he fell prone to the ground, all his muscles seizing painfully. He couldn't move an inch, and the very attempt hurt. Moving so much as a pinky simultaneously burned and stabbed his nerves, as the system had awkwardly compensated by taking the attack's cost from his stamina pool instead of his mana pool. Given he currently didn't have the latter.

Now he didn't have much of the former either.

Oberon brought his orchestra to a satisfied culmination, leaving his Wisps to play their own music while going home as he became visible. Except that it wasn't in the form of an orb. Artorian saw some lanky man with an orange glow sitting on his haunches next to him, and he didn't recognize the person. The attempt at a greeting went as far as a pained *glurk*.

Oberon clapped slowly, his gaunt face wearing a cheeky grin. "Nicely done, my friend! I can't say you look too good right now, and I'm sorry to say I can't help. I will, however, say that you're a scant few digits away from a level up. That mouse was worth a lot of tasty numbers. I wish I could stay and help, but you gave my dungeon a migraine with that stunt just now. Using your **Law** while in here? *Tsk tsk.*"

The human-shaped Wisp stood up. "I'm turning your notifications back on. Be glad you didn't see the amount of broken error messages you caused. Lie there for a while. You'll feel better in a few hours! That's what it's going to take for that red number in your stamina to not be so unpleasantly negative. Thank me later for the mysterious malfunction in the Pylon that otherwise makes the excess drain from stamina below zero be taken from your health instead. Toodles!"

The lanky man vanished along with his remaining orchestra. Leaving Artorian half-buried in a battlefield of his own making. Unable to comment as the exertion to try just hurt too much. He couldn't speak, couldn't cry, couldn't jump for joy. A weak whimper was the best he had.

The strain from his active abilities was palpable now. A heavy weight felt on his chest when he desperately needed to breathe. Since for some reason his abilities hadn't turned off when his capacity to power them ran out, Artorian turned them off one at a time to relieve some pressure. Turning most of his active abilities and skills off had not helped remotely as much as he wanted. In hindsight, he shouldn't have let Empowerment go, as that helped him regain stamina faster. Too little too late now. That left him with Sustenance and Omnibreath.

Artorian had plenty of time to think while immobile and glued to the ground. He was unable to pull up his own status or talk, as he had neither the concentration nor the resources. He felt kind of pathetic after such a big win. Was it a big win? He wanted it to be a big win. There were a lot of demons that just got a love tap! He would laugh, but nobody was around to share in the joke.

He wanted to be angry at Oberon for just leaving him behind as a crumpled mess, but couldn't really blame the orange boy. Instead, he was angry at whatever was poking him in the ribs a few hours after the battle had ended. It was the middle of the night! What was out here bothering him? Granted, he was still on fire. Bright ultramarine fire. So that he was a target of interest didn't surprise him.

A rabbit with a horn on its head jumped over his prone form, just to fuff around and turn to face its punching bag. Was that a basic Basher from Cal's original dungeon? How cute! Except that he had found the culprit of the poking pain. He tried glaring the creature down to make it go away, but it was to no avail. The Basher performed its namesake, and bashed him right in the head, doing an impressive twenty damage. He needed that health! *Go away, you fluffy pain!*

The rabbit bashed him again, eliciting a pained grunt that did him more harm than the nubby horn on the rabbit's forehead. *You tiny rascal!* This was humiliating! All of that, and he was going to be done in by a mere, basic, level one rabbit? Now he knew what the people going into Cal's dungeon must have felt like. Cal, you miser!

Several unpleasant slams to the forehead later, and the rabbit had still not left him alone. Artorian was scrambling for options. Anything he could do while completely out of… options. If it needed mana or stamina, it was a choice currently drowning in the sea.

He heard the swipe of a blade, or the zipping of an arrow.

He wasn't sure, the sound was intermixed as if it were neither. Though he did hear a voice. "Unexpectus has arrived! By arbitration order of the Red Inkquisition, I shall take you into custody! Foulest of fiends! Stand, and face your justice!"

Artorian bit through the pain in order to squint. Who…? He didn't stir, very much unable to move a muscle. "Insult to injury! You dare step on my face, and then ignore an arbiter when he is talking to you? I, Unexpectus, shall not stand for this. Not with any of my tentacles! I will have you dragged to the Authority! No matter the kind of protective blue flames you employ!"

Several misunderstandings were at play here, but Artorian was just glad that the bruise on his forehead stopped growing. That bruise had a bruise, and that bruise had a bruise as well. He remembered the octopus now, not particularly happy that everyone was finding him so easily. Again, that ultramarine mana burn effect which didn't seem to be going away was biting him in the ass.

He needed help!

Notice!

You have requested help. As a rank 5 Divine, you may call upon some of your followers to help you. As your beacons are currently on Mana Burn fire, they will not be able to come to your aid swiftly. You may use this call for assistance once a month. Would you like to send out a call for help?

Artorian mentally slammed the yes option, causing the notification to vanish. Nothing else happened, so he hoped it had worked. The arbiter had discovered that the fire didn't actually harm anything. So like a fish out of water, Artorian was picked up and flung over the equivalent of Unexpectus's shoulder. One of the eight. Hard to tell with an octopus. One moment, had that notice said he was at deity rank *five*? How many followers did that require again?

With Unexpectus dragging him off, he was sure to have

plenty of time to figure it out. Though he was silently lamenting the loss of the Halcyon Days. He'd have to come back and get them, not to mention the racer hidden away in the woods. Otherwise they might become landmarks. Crackers! He'd have to do it all on foot too. He wanted to sigh, but that hurt too much.

Oberon had undershot his recovery time, apparently not having seen that extra zero at the beginning of all the digits which obscured yet another number. He wasn't going to be out of commission for hours. He was going to be out of commission for days. Greaaat. Off to the Octoid Authority brig? *Toast!*

First was getting there. That was going to take a while, given the speed he was being lugged about with. To his great misfortune, he also easily had about a thousand notifications to catch up on. Had the arbiter walked this entire way? Surely there must have been a quicker method to get around. He smiled a moment, distracted by a memory. How did it always happen that he got carted off after a big fight? This was like leaving the Ziggurat after whacking the Vizier, except with fewer poultices and rides on a bed of gold.

His pained expression of mischief, no matter how much it ached to do, was not lost on the Arbiter. "You dare scheme in the presence of Unexpectus? Heathen! I shall not allow this!" *Conk*!

The arbiter smacked him on the head with an oversized conch. Artorian didn't want to know where he'd pulled that out of. Maybe the creature had his own spatial ring? Since he was sitting at an uncomfortable below zero stamina, that small hit did enough damage to knock him out. Unfortunately for Unexpectus, that also undid Artorian's control over his human form. Subsequently flattening the octopus under a three-hundred-plus-foot-long dragon.

Unexpectus was furious, but his loud tirade amounted to little more than bubbled froth and wriggling mumbles under all the weight. It was going to take him hours to get free from under this fat noodle!

CHAPTER FIFTY

Unexpectus had company when his last tentacle snapped free from underneath the immobile living wall. The gathered group was an odd mixture. A muscled Red Panda, one fiery ferret, and a human man named Oswan. "Begone, onlookers! You gaze upon the catch and prisoner of the Red Inkquisition. Disperse post haste! Or I shall hold you in contempt!"

The trio looked to the arbiter, then to the ultramarine fire-covered noodle which to their eyes was made of milky galaxies. They didn't need an explanation of what they saw. They knew they'd found who they needed to, having paid for the beacon costs with their own mana.

Oswan stepped forwards, pointing at the wide-brimmed hat of the octopus. "No. You're the one that's going to leave. We can tell you're not aligned with us."

The exact meaning of those words were lost on Unexpectus, but he did not care. Oversized needles appeared in two of his eight tentacles as he armed himself. "Silence! I shall not be dissuaded from my task. I judge you with enmity!"

The arbiter attacked without warning, but had to immediately dodge an alligator mouth-shaped energy-construct that manifested when the ferret bit at him. He starfish-rolled over the ground as the panda lunged and threw a heavy swing, resulting in a quick miss. As if an arbiter would be struck by a blow so sluggish and slow!

Oswan attempted to cast the only spell he knew, but was no match for a seasoned arbiter. An oversized needle stabbed through his shoulder, causing him to groan and drop to the ground. Failing to further build up his spell as the magic died on his fingertips. A string of ink connecting the back of the needle to Unexpectus was used to pull the weapon back. He didn't like that the wound on the human was visibly healing. How was this frail creature regenerating health?

His curiosity would need to wait as a glowing hot claw swung above his head. Or it did when he dropped to the ground in order to dodge. Countering with practiced ease, a swift needle to the kidney dropped the ferret right away. These foes were weak! A paltry opposition. The octopus was getting ahead of himself, not noticing the panda's furious farmer fist until impact.

With a squelch, Ruffle's fist sank deep into the seaborne creature. He realized afterwards that his punch had accomplished little, as Unexpectus replied by stabbing his weapons into both of Ruffle's knees. Ruffle the Red Panda fell with a whimper, leaving the trio downed and out of the fight as their wounds slowly recuperated. "I'll have no more of this. I judge you guilty. *Stasis*!"

The trio stopped moving as they were affected by the arbiter's ability, locking them in place. It didn't prevent their wounds from healing, but they were unable to bother him further. Unexpectus believed that was just, and left them to their fates. He angrily bubbled when he saw his mana wasn't recovering.

Making it back to the unconscious noodle, he realized there was no way he was going to transport this wall-sized grievance to the Authority. That meant it was time to rifle through his sizable inventory and find other solutions. Even if it meant using costly ones that would end the stasis on the other three early. Priorities had to be adhered to.

After an hour of shuffling through his card catalogue of options, he found an unusual Inkquisition-appropriated unguent that may work for his purposes. He pulled up the properties just to be sure.

Name: Unguent of Youth.

This Unguent is a potion of Tonic quality. It must be applied as a creme. Originally considered a cursed item, this is a salve used by older ladies of Noble birth who did not desire to have their wrinkles foul the mood of the day. Rather than merely remove their wrinkles, it removed their age entirely. Turning them into toddlers. Regardless of their desires, they still very much fouled the day.

This potion will return any creature to a state of helpless youth, with appropriate modifiers to both statistics and mechanical effects. This unguent left circulation due to its... unfortunate side-effects.

Unexpectus had never seen a use for this, but uncorked it without concern, using the flat side of his needle to apply it to the noodle's scales. He wondered if he'd had enough salve, but once the entire potion was applied the effect was immediate. The Long's massive form turned to sparkles and glitter. A gentle breeze breaking the tiny flecks of matter apart to act as a coating across the demon body-littered battlefield.

All that remained behind of Artorian's prior massive form was a noodle maybe a foot in length. Extremely easy to carry! Unexpectus threw the flopped thing over his shoulder, and resumed his journey home. It was time to put this deviant into the brig! There would be a long trial for what he'd done to the pontiff.

Unexpectus was long gone by the time the stasis effect wore off on Ruffle, True, and Oswan. They each heaved a deep breath, feeling dehydrated and painfully hungry. They huddled together with an unpleasant groan, uncertain how to proceed. True was the first to speak. "So much for that plan. I thought you were a village elder."

Oswan grunted in pain. "I am. Doesn't mean I knew we were going to be facing an eight-legged wide-brimmed hat wielding sharp sticks."

Ruffle nodded, taking his sweet time getting up. "I know a thing or two about sharp sticks. Those were extra sharp. My knees still hurt, even if they're all better. I don't like to brag about my sturdiness, but those stabbies went straight through me. Didn't get stopped by bone."

The other two couldn't disagree. They'd all felt the incredible pain those massive needles had caused. True cut in. "Didn't know he could pull them back using a string either. I thought we were doing good rushing to aid, but I don't think we helped any."

Oswan looked to the woods, noticing a milky swirl hiding beneath a smattering of branches and leaves. "All might not be lost."

The other two glanced at him, and he pointed at the edge of the forest. Specifically, he was pointing at a shoddy mass of grass and leaves that could easily be mistaken for a compost heap. True and Ruffle stood and walked up to squint their vision in that direction. "I see the divine colors under it, but I have no idea what it might be."

Oswan was helped by Ruffle. Too tired to walk alone as the panda moved towards it, his enthusiasm recovering. "Let's go find out."

When the trio finally pushed enough greenery away to uncover what was hidden, only Oswan had a clue about what they were looking at. "It's the cart. He got in this, and sped away… incredibly quickly."

True ran his paws over it, trying to inspect the racer. "To my village, probably? Given the timeline we've pieced together from talking during our short travels together. What do you think he needed this for?"

Ruffle stuck a hand in the air. "Uh… to turn those beacon things on? It's what he did in both of your villages. Maybe this just helped him get there faster?"

True shrugged. "My call to defend the beacons activated when the one in ours burst into fire. It didn't hurt me any, but my requirements to stay in place fell away. Maybe he just didn't activate enough of them in time?"

Oswan motioned at the battlefield next to the wrecked castle. "I think there's more going on here than meets the eye, but you may be right. We've no way of telling without asking him directly, and I don't think finding him again is going to work. The call led us here, and the marker pulling me vanished on arrival. I have no idea where to go looking."

A shiny light caught True's attention, followed by a *tink*. The sound of an item that wasn't there before, now dangling from one of the racer's control handles. "Was this round thing always there?"

Ruffle leaned in and picked it up, moving it around in his hand while looking it over. "I don't know. It has moving needles in it. Not sure what they point to."

He handed it to Oswan, whose eyes widened in recognition. "It's a compass! As for what it points to… This might be a long shot, but wouldn't our Divine need to have a way to find these beacons somehow?"

He turned the compass around to show the others, as the navigating needle firmly pointed the same direction without fail. "Worth a shot? We could try to make this cart take us."

"There's an Inscription on the back." Ruffle pointed at the words on the small tool, noticing them when Oswan turned the compass in his fingers. "What's it say?"

Oswan pulled the compass close to his eyes to read the tiny scribble, reading it out loud. "For the fruits of labor."

He scratched his head after. "I have no idea what that means."

True hopped into the racer, accidentally bumping a lever that made the platform thrum loud. Right after, the platform hovered up from the ground by a full foot, displacing the majority of foliage used to hide it. "*Whoa!*"

Ruffle wasn't far behind, hopping into the strange carriage. "Nice going! So the levers make it work. Let's pull a few!"

Oswan knew this was a terrible idea, but snapped the compass shut between his fingers. There hadn't been a vote, but it looked like the three of them had settled on the same outcome regardless. "It's decided then. We look for the other beacons and try to turn them on."

It took them another hour to get the racer to work in a meaningful way. Oswan and True's mana pools weren't doing too well, given how much it took to operate the monstrosity. That was small potatoes in comparison to the prize, which was that they got the racer to work! Their perseverance was rewarded when they were greeted by a quest from the Voice of the World.

Quest: A Labor of Love.
Finish what your Divine started.

They all smashed the accept prompt before ever seeing the full description.

EPILOGUE

Artorian groggily woke up deep underwater, accosted by an annoying headache. It was wet, which was his first clue that he was somewhere new. The dark was his second, and the cell he was locked in his third. Bickering salmon guards swam nearby, keeping tabs on the prisoner trapped in the brig shell.

No reason to get their attention, as there was something odd with his perception. He was seeing things from the viewpoint of something tiny. A quick glance at his status sheet told him why. He failed to grimace as he read the effects of the salve, which didn't seem to have a duration. The potion applied to him was just a flat reset. What swindling cauldron-swirler sold bad products like this?

In addition, he was still on fire, had no mana to speak of, and his stamina was still so deep in the red that he closed the status sheet on principle. He didn't want to look at it that badly. From what he could tell, he was lying on something soft. Artorian couldn't discern what, but who cared. Soft was good! Great even when prone and entirely stuck in place. He couldn't move so much as a flipper. Not that he had any, but the metaphor was fitting since he was clearly back in the Octoid Authority.

Welp. Not much to do now. Might as well go through the notifications.

Sweet celestial mercy, that was a lot of messages which just yelled 'Error.' The result of his sympathy strike, no doubt. He cleaned most of those out over the course of a day, and scanned over the prompts that had some actual useful information in them. Those that did not include the level ups or small mentions his specialization level had increased. Prompts like that weren't that pressing, since they clearly didn't help right now.

Power Launch:
This skill is the result of combining the Run and Jump skills. By paying a stamina cost equal to quintuple the cost of the desired speed in feet per second, you may set your starting speed to the launch speed paid for. For example, setting your launch speed from a standstill position to one hundred feet per second has an immediate cost of five hundred stamina. At the Beginner rank, this cost is reduced by 5%. Each subsequent rank reduces the cost by another 5%.

Notice: If the stamina cost paid exceeds your maximum HP, Power Launch will fail and damage you. The same is true for your surroundings, as they may shatter or break from the exerted force.

Monk Weapon Mastery:
This skill gives a small boost to the use of all Monk Weapons in combat, or other weapons that qualify. Accuracy, damage dealt, and damage blocked increases by a bonus of $+10n\%$, where n equals your rank level. Monk Weapon Mastery also determines how many attacks you can make over the course of five seconds, equal to one attack per rank. Time between attacks decreases based on a Monk's Body Mastery skill.
Attacks have a flat cost of 10 stamina.

Body Mastery:
Unlocked by having a skill that requires this as a prerequisite. This is a Monk skill that focuses on wholeness of body, and using all that you are, all

the time. While this causes strain, it allows a Monk to bring out their full inner force.

Body Mastery changes base game mechanics. Rather than relying on your strength for damage or dexterity to determine successful hit chance, this skill combines your strength, dexterity, and constitution. Bundling them together as one. The average of these becomes the new floored number that is considered for health, damage, hit change, and other related mechanics.

Each rank of Body Mastery lessens the strain that sustaining this skill causes by 10 stamina per second. Using Body Mastery costs 60 stamina per second.

Tonfa Weapon Mastery:
This skill applies specifically to tonfas; providing an additional boost to Monk Weapon Mastery, focused on improving damage dealt and damage prevented. This skill stacks with Monk Weapon Mastery. Tonfa Weapon Mastery adds an additional 10% damage dealt and damage blocked per rank. Having Tonfa Weapon Mastery allows for named maneuvers, as this is not an umbrella skill comprising multiple weapons.

Tonfa Maneuver: Sunrise
Style: Halcyon Days, Breath series
The first attack in this series. This upwards strike condenses the user's focus into an air element-aligned attack meant to displace enemies or matter. Succeeding in this maneuver causes the visual of a sunrise to appear in the affected area. The area affected is determined based on energy investment. Sunrise uses chi to accomplish its special effect. If chi is not available, this cost will be drained from stamina instead. Sunrise costs the user five stamina to affect a five-foot cubic space in front of them. Each size increase multiplies the cost by nine, but also affects nine cube-shaped sections of space rather than one. The space affected must remain a cube, regardless of upscaling. This effect can be upscaled so long as the cost can be paid.

Artorian mentally *oooh'd* at this. So he had affected around seven hundred and thirty of these cubes? No wonder so much debris and chunks of castle were knocked out of his way. It didn't tell him how much force was applied, but based on the result he could remember. It was plenty!

Martial Arts: Pantheon Style
Specific style: Oppressive Offense

This method of fighting has no regard for the user's own health, seeking to maximize damage done and terror caused. Using Pantheon Style applies a damage bonus and fear demerit that builds in tiers, depending on how long an opponent has seen the user fight. Pantheon Style also decreases your chance to block or dodge by 30%. Pantheon Style makes the fear, dread, terror, and horror status demerits stack.

This school's color theme is red mana.

Your rank in this style determines how quickly the terror bonuses apply. At the Novice rank, the rate at which an enemy's fear track progresses builds by 10%. This bonus increases by an additional 10% every subsequent rank. At the Beginner rank, any attacks made while Pantheon Style is active causes the damage result to be rolled twice. Of which only the higher result is taken into account. Each subsequent rank increases the amount of times that raw damage is rolled by one.

Martial Arts Maneuver: Phalanx Breaker
This maneuver relies on the skill: Power Launch
An opponent can only react to an attack they can perceive. Phalanx Breaker plays on this limitation and ignores an opponent's readiness and static protection, allowing you to break right through their planned defenses and set formations. Readied attacks have a 40% chance to be ignored outright, increasing by 10% per rank.
Phalanx Breaker costs one hundred stamina to attempt.

Martial Arts Maneuver: Land Breaker
This maneuver relies on the skill: Phalanx Breaker
Unsatisfied with just bowling your enemies out of the way? Why not include the rest as well. Who cares about structures and small details such

as terrain? Wreck it all and make your own roads with Land Breaker! This maneuver applies charge damage. Calculated as the combination of your movement momentum, and damage as if you had made an unarmed melee attack.

Damage to structures and the environment increases by 10% per rank.

Land Breaker costs one hundred stamina to attempt.

Martial Arts Maneuver: Sky Breaker

This maneuver relies on the skill: Land Breaker

A finishing move that ends the chain. Sky Breaker transfers all charge damage back as momentum into the first actual attack the user applies while Land Breaker is in effect. Note that this does not apply extra damage. This maneuver will send an enemy, or what's left of them, flying out into the world as velocity is transferred. This maneuver is meant to send the recipient skywards, but is not penalized should the direction be otherwise.

Sky Breaker costs one hundred stamina to attempt.

Martial Arts Maneuver: Reap

Clear fields with a single swing! Regardless of that field being made of wheat or people. Reap allows the creation of a line that extends from a weapon or hand, which deals damage to all valid targets on a swing. The farther out the effect goes, the less damage this maneuver will do overall. Reap uses chi to accomplish its special effect. If chi is not available, this cost will be drained from stamina instead. Reap costs the user five stamina to affect a five-foot cubic space in front of them. Each added cube adds another five stamina as cost. The space affected must remain a line, regardless of upscaling. This effect can be upscaled so long as the cost can be paid. Each added cube reduces the total damage done to all targets by 5%. Each rank of this ability negates this damage penalty by 10%. Meaning that as a Novice, you may use Reap out to ten feet without suffering a damage penalty.

Reap costs one-hundred stamina at base to attempt, plus five per cube.

Artorian was amused that he was reliving the battle through the order in which he read these prompts. He hadn't thought about creating actual abilities since he needed mana to make them himself. That didn't seem to apply if he was earning them through discovery and use. Was this about the part where he decked that demon lord in the face with the business end of his punchy stick?

Tonfa Maneuver: Starfall
Style: Halcyon Days, Breath series

The second attack in this series. This downwards strike condenses the user's focus into an earth element-aligned attack meant to pierce or break armor. Succeeding in this maneuver causes the visual of a falling comet to appear around the affected weapon.

Starfall uses chi to accomplish its special effect. If chi is not available, this cost will be drained from stamina instead. Any amount of chi can be applied to Starfall. This paid cost translates to durability damage on a 1:1 basis.

Notice: Durability is a hidden item statistic, as we lack the Pylon resources to properly implement this feature. Durability values will be guesstimated.

Notice: This ability currently does not scale by ranks or levels, see the reason above.

Tonfa Maneuver: Hurled Sympathy
Style: Halcyon Days, Breath series
The third attack in this series. Enemy too far away? Throw your weapons at them! With kindness. Hurled Sympathy requires the user to take a deep breath, and have line of sight to their intended target. This maneuver throws your tonfas at your opponent. On impact, this will do damage as if the foe was struck directly. Damage falls off by 10% per 100ft of travel.
Hurled Sympathy requires no additional stamina for use, only the normal cost for an attack.
Notice: This ability currently does not scale by ranks or levels, see prior skill.

Artorian found some error messages he'd skipped before. Dismissing them as he went, he was surprised to see just how many he'd missed. Error this, error that. Did applying his **Love Law** really cause that big a disruption for Eternium? Based on the notifications alone, it was a higher caliber of headache for the dungeon to deal with. Perhaps... **Love** was something that didn't fit easily with **Order**?

Imported abilities made him snappy and sneak in those snarky notices. Cheating made Eternium irritated, but he worked with it. Did applying his **Law** directly have a different outcome? Cleaning out the last errors, he found the relevant prompt. Unlike the others, this one had a rainbow sheen to it. It also seemed to be cobbled together via pieces of stained glass. As if other prompts had to be broken for this one to get glued together.

Deity Maneuver: First Kiss
Style: Sun's Love
Description: Null.

Personal Notice: Artorian. I have no idea what you did. I only know that it gave me a migraine for a whole year. You did something strange to easily seventy Pylons. While they didn't break, they now act oddly. I had to break up a feud between a host of Wisps and Gnomes to have this matter seen to.

*From guesses and damage reports, your **Law** intervention caused a kind of sympathetic link to be attacked, rather than any kind of physical target. Not only did the demon you struck perish due to various factors, but every demon he was directly linked to perished as well. Each suffered an impact identical in all values to the power of the original. It even had some electric-pink visual effects.*

*Based on my personal discomfort, I know your **Law** intervened using your personal Mana. The reservoir contained within your Seed Core. This influx of Mana caused your deity title to temporarily toggle while the Pylons over-*

charged. As such, I'm keying this attack to your deity status so I can prevent it from happening again unless that title is active.

*More than mere cheating by importing knowledge, this is something I really can't abide, nor let happen to my **Order**. As such, I'm docking you a flat stamina penalty equal to the amount of energy you used to fuel that strike. I have just noticed that the Pylon responsible for shunting excess stamina loss to health damage doesn't work. I'm blaming you for this. You will be operating with negative stamina for at least a year.*

This means any actions that require stamina are denied to you. I find it fitting that you would remain out of action for an amount of time equal to which you put me out of action. I am aware that this will hamper your personal quest progress. I hope that your exploits so far have offered you a method to survive.

While there are currently no demon forces left on the entire Midgard continent, and a significant chunk is missing from another, they will return to retake the lands. For your information, I have successfully blocked the influx of any further demons. No new forces can be summoned from the Abyss. What exists in Eternia is all there is, or the balance would tip.

In addition to your existing penalties, I have applied the negative Karmic Luck you gained from all of this immediately. The next prompt should answer your questions on those effects.

Notice: Please understand that I despise mincing words. I hate what you did to me. It has been eons since I have felt pain.

Artorian mentally grumbled. He figured that Eternium was going to be a snooty little… *Bah!* That attack was just a little love tap! His grumbles then turned into snickers. Moving on to the next prompt while worried about being stuck like this for a whole year, and a bit.

Event notice!

You have been affected by the Unguent of Youth. Your current form will revert to its baby equivalent. While in this age category, you will be affected by the appropriate statistical penalties. The penalty for the baby category is a 90% reduction in all attributes. This penalty improves to 80% once you age up into the toddler category.

Notice: You are too large to be affected by the unguent. This limitation has been ignored via the use of a negative karmic event. Your current Karmic Luck is 0.

Event notice!
Current race: Long (baby)
As a baby Long, you are roughly the size of a stuffed sock. No other mechanical changes save for the ones mentioned will occur. Your age category will increase over time.

Event notice!
Your followers have answered your call, and will attempt to work in your interests. Due to your inability to continue several of your chosen tasks, a quest has been developed and offered to all your followers.
Quest: A Labor of Love
Finish what your Divine started.

Information: Your Divine has suffered a terrible fate, and is currently helpless. While the Divine is afflicted by the demerits from eradicating all current demons from the Midgard realm, his beacons will not properly function. Your boon remains unaffected, but your Divine can no longer pay the mana costs for your travels within the beacon network.

What exactly the Divine was working on was shared with none. Followers who accept this quest will have to discover for themselves what tasks require completion.

Artorian could kick himself. So in short: No mana. No stamina. No ability to talk, move, or complain. He was stuck underwater, in an Inkquisitorial prison, awaiting a trial that may spell the end of his painfully small health bar. He didn't seem to be able to make his Additional Nature title work, and already felt boredom creeping in. It didn't take more than a few minutes for him to sink into a sad mire.

Well, this was no fun...

The sound of salmon guards hurriedly swimming away caught his attention. He could see what was going on outside the front of his shell prison without moving, so that was something. A squid wearing a minnow chasuble addressed the local forces. "Changing of the guard, fishies. Off with you, this murderer requires a higher category of oversight. You are all excused from your positions here."

Artorian was interested in seeing who the replacements were. Had he been able to smile, his smirk would have been all teeth. Rip and Tear swam to his door, turning their backs to him. He didn't miss Tear's well-timed wink. Aha! Not all was lost!

The squid spoke with deep nasal inflection. "Shadow sharks, you will both see that this prisoner remains under shell and key. Regardless of how innocent and on-fire they may seem. This creature is a criminal, and reviled by the Octoid Authority."

A sound they both made counted as assent, the squid leaving so the troublemaking, coral-breaking duo could attend to their new dead-end jobs. Rip cleared his throat when they were alone, leaning to Tear. Though not addressing Tear when he spoke. "So we went back to that cavern, thinking you might have been hiding out there while a legion of arbiters attempted to chase you down."

The other shark picked up the conversation, making it seem to those looking from afar that they were just chatting to one another. "All we found was that beacon. We, of course, touched it. Why wouldn't we?"

Rip tried not to give away his amusement. "We couldn't resist. All we got was this prompt. Fantastic offer, really. We thought all was well until we suddenly received a quest notice.

So Tear and I went back to the cavern, and the beacon was on fire. A very specific color of it too."

Tear pretended to be surprised, as if freshly realizing something. "Why, Rip, would you say that the color of fire is similar to what our inmate is afflicted with?"

Rip turned to have a pretend look. "I would say so, Tear. Strange how the inmate also happens to look like a milky version of the depths. Look at all those swirls."

His friend sagely nodded. "Many swirls indeed, Rip. Though you know what catches my attention?"

Rip mused, just to be coy. "What would that be?"

Tear smirked, his smile the kind of toothy Artorian wished to convey. "This rather bright golden quest marker above his head. Really makes one wonder if keeping this alleged inmate imprisoned aligns with our best interests."

Rip pressed his fins together, pretending to be stuck in deep concentration. "I think you might have stumbled into a reef of truth there. It would be very bad for the Authority if this inmate wasn't here when the arbiters came to fetch him for their trial."

His hunting brother agreed. "A terrible event indeed. Especially if it happens as soon as those salmon guards rotate shifts again."

Rip and Tear shared their toothy grin, showing off all their shiny teeth. Artorian knew he was grinning like a fool right there with them. The tiny Long felt right at home in their scheming enjoyment. The game was on! A step-by-step solution made for a fantastic algorithm.

"Time for a prison break."

ABOUT DENNIS VANDERKERKEN

Hello all! I'm Dennis, but I go by a myriad of other nicknames. If you know one, feel free to use it! I probably like them more. I'm from Belgium, and have lived in the USA since 2001. English is my 4th language, so I'm making due, and apologize for the inevitable language-flub. I still call fans ceiling-windmills. The more shrewd among you may have noticed some strange sayings that may or may not have been silly attempts at direct translations! Thank you all for bearing with me.

I started writing in the The Divine Dungeon series due to a series of fortunate circumstances. I continue writing because I wanted to give hungry readers more to sink their teeth into, and help them 'get away' for a while. If you have any questions, or would like to chat, I live on Dakota's Eternium discord. Feel free to come say hi anytime! Life is a little better with a good book.

Connect with Dennis:
Discord.gg/8vjzGA5
Patreon.com/FloofWorks

ABOUT DAKOTA KROUT

Associated Press best-selling author, Dakota has been a top 5 bestseller on Amazon, a top 6 bestseller on Audible, and his first book, Dungeon Born, was chosen as one of Audible's top 5 fantasy picks in 2017.

He draws on his experience in the military to create vast terrains and intricate systems, and his history in programming and information technology helps him bring a logical aspect to both his writing and his company while giving him a unique perspective for future challenges.

"Publishing my stories has been an incredible blessing thus far, and I hope to keep you entertained for years to come!" -Dakota

Connect with Dakota:
MountaindalePress.com
Patreon.com/DakotaKrout
Facebook.com/TheDivineDungeon
Twitter.com/DakotaKrout
Discord.gg/8vjzGA5

ABOUT MOUNTAINDALE PRESS

Dakota and Danielle Krout, a husband and wife team, strive to create as well as publish excellent fantasy and science fiction novels. Self-publishing *The Divine Dungeon: Dungeon Born* in 2016 transformed their careers from Dakota's military and programming background and Danielle's Ph.D. in pharmacology to President and CEO, respectively, of a small press. Their goal is to share their success with other authors and provide captivating fiction to readers with the purpose of solidifying Mountaindale Press as the place 'Where Fantasy Transforms Reality.'

Connect with Mountaindale Press:
MountaindalePress.com
Facebook.com/MountaindalePress
Twitter.com/_Mountaindale
Instagram.com/MountaindalePress

MOUNTAINDALE PRESS TITLES
GameLit and LitRPG

The Completionist Chronicles,
The Divine Dungeon, and
Full Murderhobo by Dakota Krout

King's League by Jason Anspach and J.N. Chaney

Arcana Unlocked by Gregory Blackburn

A Touch of Power by Jay Boyce

Red Mage and
Farming Livia by Xander Boyce

Space Seasons by Dawn Chapman

Ether Collapse and
Ether Flows by Ryan DeBruyn

Bloodgames by Christian J. Gilliland

Threads of Fate by Michael Head

Wolfman Warlock by James Hunter and Dakota Krout

Axe Druid and
Mephisto's Magic Online by Christopher Johns

Skeleton in Space by Andries Louws

Chronicles of Ethan by John L. Monk

Pixel Dust by David Petrie
Necrotic Apocalypse by David Petrie

Henchman by Carl Stubblefield

Artorian's Archives by Dennis Vanderkerken and Dakota Krout

APPENDIX

Abyss – A place you don't want to be, and a very common curse word.

Adam – A celestial elemental from Dale's original party as a cleric. Now he serves as an embodiment of the celestial plane.

Adventurers' Guild – A group from every non-hostile race that actively seeks treasure and cultivates to become stronger. They act as a mercenary group for Kingdoms that come under attack from monsters and other non-kingdom forces.

Affinity – A person's affinity denotes what element they need to cultivate Essence from. If they have multiple affinities, they need to cultivate all of those elements at the same time.

Affinity Channel – The pathway along the meridians that Essence flows through. Having multiple major affinities will open more pathways, allowing more Essence to flow into a person's center at one time.

Affinity Channel Type – Clogged, Ripped, Closed, Minor, Major, and Perfect. Perfect doesn't often occur naturally:

- Clogged – Draws in no essence, because the channel is blocked with corruption.
- Ripped – Draws in an unknown amount of essence, but in a method that is unpredictable and lethal.

- Closed – Draws in no essence, because the channel is either unopened, or forcibly closed.
- Minor – Draws in very little essence.
- Major – Draws in a sizable amount of essence.
- Perfect – Draws in a significant amount of essence. This affinity channel type cannot occur naturally. It is very dangerous to strive for, as the path to this type leads to ripped channels.

Aiden Silverfang – The new leader of the Northmen, this Barbarian turned Wolfman holds deep grudges easily. He is one of the many supervisors of Midgard.

Alhambra – A cleric that lives in Chasuble. Kept down for the majority of his career, he remains a good man with a good heart. His priorities for the people allot him a second chance, one derived from an old man's schemery.

Amber – The Mage in charge of the portal-making group near the dungeon. She is in the upper A-rankings, which allows her to tap vast amounts of Mana.

Artorian – The main character of the series. If you weren't expecting shenanigans, grab some popcorn. It only gets more intense from here on. He's a little flighty, deeply interested, and a miser of mischief. He is referred to by the Wood Elves as Starlight Spirit. In Cal's Soul Space, he takes the position of head administrator, and supervisor of Jotunheim.

Assassin – A stealthy killer who tries to make kills without being detected by his victim.

Assimilator – A cross between a jellyfish and a Wisp, the Assimilator can float around and collect vast amounts of Essence. It releases this Essence as powerful elemental bursts. A pseudo-Mage, if you will.

Astrea – The Nightmare. Infernal Professor at the Phantom Academy. She is a daughter of the Fringe, and one of Artorian's grandchildren. Even as an Infernal Cultivator, she finds herself in the most unlikely of company. Including her best friend, Jiivra.

Aura – The flows of Essence generated by living creatures which surround them and hold their pattern.

Barry the Devourer – A powerful S-ranked High Elf with the ability to turn all matter within a certain range into pure Essence and absorb it. Like his appetite, his desire for power is ever growing and seems to have no sign of stopping in Cal's soul space.

Basher – An evolved rabbit that attacks by head-butting enemies. Each has a small horn on its head that it can use to "bash" enemies.

Baobab – A wood elf with innate fire resistance. Strong-willed, this woman can handle the heat.

Bard – A lucrative profession deriving profit from other people's misery. Some make coin through song or instrument, but all of them love a good story. Particularly inconvenient ones. This includes Kinnan, Pollard, and Jillian.

Beast Core – A small gem that contains the Essence of Beasts. Also used to strip new cultivators of their corruption:

- Flawed – An extremely weak crystallization of Essence that barely allows a Beast to cultivate, comparable to low F-rank.
- Weak – A weak crystallization of Essence that allows a Beast to cultivate, comparable to an upper F-rank.
- Standard – A crystallization of Essence that allows a

Beast to cultivate well, comparable to the D-rankings.
- Strong – A crystallization of Essence that allows a Beast to cultivate very well, comparable to the lower C-rankings.
- Beastly – A crystallization of Essence that allows a Beast to cultivate exceedingly well, comparable to the upper C-rankings.
- Immaculate – An amalgamation of crystallized Essence and Mana that allows a Beast to cultivate exceedingly well. Any Beast in the B-rankings or A-rankings will have this Core.
- Luminous – A Core of pure spiritual Essence that is indestructible by normal means. A Beast with this core will be in at least the S-rankings, up to SSS-rank.
- Radiant – A Core of Heavenly or Godly energies. A Beast with this Core is able to adjust reality on a whim.

Blanket – The best sugar glider. Blanket defends. Blanket protects.

Blight – A big bad. Also known as a Caligene, this entity can take many forms. Widespread and far-reaching, this thing has been around for over a millennia, and enjoys scheming to play the long game.

Birch – A friendly set of wood elves, of the Birch-tree Variant. They're friendly and well meaning, even if limited in what they can do. They like scented candles, particularly vanilla. They now spend their days with Mahogany, preparing to raise the next generation of Wood Elves.

Blooming Spirit – The Wood Elven equivalent of Aura. See Aura.

Bob – Cal's original goblin shaman. Remade to the best of his species. Bob becomes a Mage bound to the Death Law. Due to the myriad of tasks Cal set before him, several copies were made of Bob to complete them. Several then became several thousand. Bob is both a coding reference, and a small nod to the fantastic 'Bobiverse' series.

Boro – A trader in exotics, this man allied himself with the raider faction. He assists in swindling deals, and robbing villages blind after flooding them with gold that they will not keep.

Brianna – Having begun as princess of the dark elves, she is now both queen and supervisor of Niflheim. She is known by many names, such as the Hidden Blade, the Empress of Niflheim, and the Pinnacle. She has spies everywhere, and you never know what she's planning until she's already done steps one through six. Be wary of the Lady of Mists.

Cal – The heart of the Dungeon, Cal was a human murdered by necromancers. After being forced into a soul gem, his identity was stripped as time passed. Now accompanied by Dani, he works to become stronger without attracting too much attention to himself. Oops, too late.

Cataphron – One of the Skyspear headmasters. Uses the Imperius body technique of the Iron-Shelled Mastodont Kings.

Cats, dungeon – There are several types:

- Snowball – A Boss Mob, Snowball uses steam Essence to fuel his devastating attacks.
- Cloud Cat – A Mob that glides along the air, attacking from positions of stealth.
- Coiled Cat – A heavy Cat that uses metal Essence. It has a reinforced skeleton and can launch itself forward at high speeds.

- Flesh Cat – This Cat uses flesh Essence to tear apart tissue from a short distance. The abilities of this Cat only work on flesh and veins and will not affect bone or harder materials.
- Wither Cat – A Cat full of infernal Essence, the Wither Cat can induce a restriction of Essence flow with its attacks. Cutting off the flow of Essence or Mana will quickly leave the victim in a helpless state. The process is *quite* painful.

Celestial – The Essence of Heaven, the embodiment of life and *considered* the ultimate good.

Center – The very center of a person's soul. This is the area Essence accumulates (in creatures that do not have a Core) before it binds to the Life Force.

Chandra – A ranked mage who is a masterful cook. She has prior history with Ramset (Occultatum), and runs the 'pleasure house' restaurant establishments. She has an affinity for all things plants and nature, finding comfort within the green, more-so than with people. In Cal's world, she is stationed as one of the many supervisors on Midgard, and is responsible for all the basic flora and fauna in the soul space.

Chants – Affect a choir-cleric's growth, and overall fighting ability. A Choir war host in action matches the chant of every other. Each voice added to the whole increases the power and ability of each person whose voice is involved, through celestial and aural sympathy. Church officials get very upset when interrupted by half-naked men.

Chasuble – The name of both a particular type of scarf worn loosely around the neck, and the name of a major church-controlled city. Chasuble scarves are marked to show the rank of the person wearing them.

Church – 'The' Church, to be specific. Also known as the Ecclesiarchy, is one of the few stable major powers active in the world. It has several branches, each operating under different specifications:

- The Choir – The Face of the church, they carry to torch and spread the call far and wide. Operates as exploratory force and functions on heart and mind campaigns. The Choir's special function is to use harmonizing sound to buff and empower every member included in the group-effect.
- Paladin Order – The Fast-Attack branch, these mounted warriors function as cavalry would. The mounted creatures in question vary greatly, and most members employ a high-ranked beast for these purposes.
- Phalanx Sentinels – The Siege or Hold branch, the Sentinels are a heavy-armor branch that specialize entirely on securing locations. They are well known to be notoriously slow, and just as notoriously impossible to uproot from a position.
- Inquisitors – The Information gathering branch. This branch remains secretive.

Church Ranks – There are multiple Ecclesiarchy ranks, stacking in importance mostly based on cultivation progress.

- Initiate – A fresh entry to the church faction, the lowest rank. Generally given to someone still in training.
- Scribe – An initiate who failed to become a D-ranked cultivator, but was trusted enough by the faction to remain.
- Acolyte – Achieved by becoming a D-ranked cultivator. The second lowest rank in the church faction.

- Battle Leader – A trusted acolyte who shows promise in the fields of leadership and battle.
- Head Cleric – A high D-ranking cultivator, or a person who has been a Battle Leader long enough for their achievements to grant them their personal unit. Head Clerics are trusted to go on missions, excursions, and expeditions that differ based on the specific church faction.
- Keeper – Ranked equal to a Head Cleric. People who specifically keep administrative records, and interpret ancient texts. Keepers famously do not get along, and hold bitter rivalries due to said interpretations of the scriptures. Keepers tend to be Head Clerics who failed to enter the C-ranks.
- Arbiter – Achieved upon becoming a C-rank cultivator. An Arbiter is a settler of disputes of all kinds, whose authority is overshadowed only by those of higher rank. Otherwise, their say is final.
- Friar – A B-ranked cultivator in the church faction. Friars are glorified problem solvers.
- Father – An A-ranked Cultivator in the church faction. A Father may be of a high rank, but has fallen out of favor with the upper echelons of church command.
- Vicar – An A-ranked Cultivator in the church faction. The de-facto rulers, movers, and shakers of the church faction.
- Saint – An S-ranked Cultivator in the church faction. They do as they please.

Choppy – The prime woodcutter in the Salt Village. A very good lad.

Chi spiral – A person's Chi spiral is a vast amount of intricately knotted Essence. The more complex and complete the pattern woven into it, the more Essence it can hold and the finer the Essence would be refined.

Cleric – A cultivator of celestial Essence, a cleric tends to be support for a group, rarely fighting directly. Their main purpose in the lower rankings is to heal and comfort others.

Compound Essence – Essence that has formed together in complex ways. If two or more Essences come together to form something else, it is called a compound Essence. Or Higher Essence.

Corruption – Corruption is the remnant of the matter that pure Essence was formed into. It taints Essence but allows beings to absorb it through open affinity channels. This taint has been argued about for centuries; is it the source of life or a nasty side effect?

Craig – A powerful C-ranked monk, Craig has dedicated his life to finding the secrets of Essence and passing on knowledge.

C'towl – A mixture between cat and owl. Usually considered an apex predator due to the intermingling of attributes and sheer hunting prowess.

Currency values:

- Copper – One hundred copper coins are worth a silver coin.
- Silver – One hundred silver coins are worth a gold coin.
- Gold – One hundred gold coins are worth a platinum coin.
- Platinum – The highest coin currency in the Human Kingdoms.

Cultivate – Cultivating is the process of refining Essence by removing corruption then cycling the purified Essence into the center of the soul.

Cultivation technique – A name for the specific method in which cultivators draw in and refine the energies of the Heavens and Earth.

Cultivator – A cultivator is a silly person who thinks messing with forces they don't understand will somehow make life better for them.

Dale – Probably not important.

Dani – The most important. Wisp to Cal, and the sole reason the entire Soul Space is still standing. Many mental notebooks have "don't cross Dani" underlined no less than nineteen times. Surely there's a reason for that.

Daughter of Wrath – A ranking female servant to the Ziggurat, that showed promise and was given troops to lead.

Dawn – The name taken by Ember as her S-ranked incarnation. A full perspective change from her original self, new options and a new life have opened before her. While the way of being Ember espoused still exists within her, room for the new is now possible. Even though she is stuck in an A-ranked body for now, there's no way she's letting that stop her. Dawn is the supervisor of the fiery realm Muspelheim.

Decorum – A Morovia Liger who, through some meddling, has gained new life as the snazzy and mysterious Gomez. His rebirth gave him the opportunity to be the ultimate apex predator, but after a life of hunting and being hunted on Midgard he is pulled to move onto a greater stage. A true gentleman, or well, gentletiger.

Deverash Editor Neverdash the Dashingly Dapper – Also called Dev, or Dev Editor. A gnome that retained his intelligence, and may have quite the impact on adventures to come.

Duskgrove Castle – A location within the Phantomdusk Forest. It is the primary hideout for the Hakan's group of raiders.

D. Kota – An initiate in the choir, who has grand aspirations of becoming a scholar; and does. His works span the great ages. Known for all time.

Distortion Cat – An upper C-ranked Beast that can bend light and create artificial darkness. In its home territory, it is attacked and bound by tentacle-like parasites that form a symbiotic relationship with it.

Dimitri – Also goes by Dimi-Tree, due to his size. A mix between a dwarf and a giant, this brash and brazen mountain loves to dabble. Doing a little bit of everything, he has a reputation that there's nothing he can't fix.

Dreamt Ones – Creatures made of Liminal Energy, having manifested through dreams:

- Caliph – Dawn's dreamt one. Manifested as a Djinn and baby. Deemed relevant for reasons pertaining to the blocks in her continued growth.
- Scilla – Artorian's dreamt one. Manifested as a mixture of the small child he met in Chasuble and the bane of the Phantomdusk Forest. She withholds Artorian's Liminal Energy from him, at least, until he can work through his many, many regrets.
- Items – Cal's specific difficulty resulted in objects and challenges rather than creatures, as his Liminal Energy deemed that he needed to learn the lesson of

how to rely on others, rather than perform all tasks himself.

Dregs – A dungeon Core that has limited intelligence. It was installed into Cal's dungeon to control floors 1-4 so Cal could focus on other things.

Dungeon Born – Being dungeon born means that the dungeon did not create the creature but gave it life. This gives the creature the ability to function autonomously without fear that the dungeon will be able to take direct control of its mind.

Dungeon Cores – Curators of wild Essence.

- Gold/Pale Yellow – Celestial affinity dungeons who tend to be a tad on the lazy side. These dungeons are notorious for ignoring their work and simply kicking back and letting others bring the Essence to them.
- Blue – Water affinity dungeons tend to be the type that go with the flow. Since Cal's existence this theory has been debunked.
- Lapis – Air affinity dungeons are unable to build their own dungeons. They rely on their wisps to build the dungeon and often are the type to give up projects quickly from being discouraged.
- Red – Fire affinity dungeons are lazy. Unlike celestial dungeons, they would rather play in their sandbox of toys. Raging and destroying as they please, rather than build or keep their dungeon squared away.
- Green – Earth affinity dungeons are perfectionists. They focus on sheer quality and often ignore quantity without a wisp keeping them on track. These dungeons exemplify how the term "tunnel-vision" came to be.
- Opal-Black – Infernal affinity dungeons are gluttons

for knowledge. They lust for more information constantly, even to the point of destroying all who enter their dungeon in favor of new tidbits of data.

Dungeon Wisps – Beings made to balance out dungeons in the world. A very secretive group led by an all-affinity wisp. Each base color corresponds with an effect to match their dungeon:

- Blue – Celestial affinity wisps whose ability is to convince their dungeon that they are useful, and should use other Essence types beyond celestial.
- Pink – Water affinity wisps who are best known for reducing mind altering effects, and are incredibly skilled at keeping these dungeons on task.
- Purple – Air affinity wisps. These wisps must shape the world around them for their dungeon, as air affinity dungeons cannot do so. They provide the homes for the air affinity dungeons and constantly encourage the Cores like cheerleaders.
- Green – Fire affinity wisps are excellent taskmasters who keep their childish dungeons from breaking all of their toys, and assure they continue to improve and build out their dungeons.
- Orange – Earth affinity wisps are naturally soothing. They help alleviate the tunnel vision which earth affinity dungeons suffer from, and encourage their dungeon to value quantity as well as quality.
- Silver – Infernal affinity wisps remind their dungeons that patience is a virtue, and make sure their knowledge hungry dungeons do not destroy everything that enters their doors.

Don Modsognir – Goes by Big Mo. Leader of the Modsognir clan. Responsible for trading and caravan operations. Known to be a troublemaker, he has an impeccable link of loyalty to his family. He enjoys finery, nice suits, and better company. He's got the heart of a king, and the trouble-making penchant of a feisty five-year-old.

Dwarves – Stocky humanoids that like to work with stone, metal, and alcohol. Good miners.

Dwarven Traditions – Complicated unspoken rules that exist purely to protect the core dwarven heritage and ways of life. Specifically used against anyone deemed a non-dwarf or outsider, to sustain a public image that is of benefit to all clans as a whole.

Eucalyptus – A Wood Elf skilled in defensive and protective Essence techniques.

Ember – Secondary Main Character - A burnt-out Ancient Elf from well over a millennia ago. She's lived too long, and most of it has been in one War or another. She finds a new spark, but until then suffers from extreme weariness, depression, and wear. Her sense of humor lies buried deep within, dry as a cork. Ember enjoys speaking laconically, getting to the point, and getting fired up. She will burn eternal to see her tasks complete. No matter the cost, and no matter the effort. She becomes Dawn upon graduating to the S-ranks.

Egil Nolsen – Known to the world as 'Xenocide,' he is a Madness cultivator. Ranked SSS. He is but a moment of good fortune away from entering the Heavenly ranks, and is responsible for a majority of the world's problems, in one way or another.

Electrum – The metal used as Chasuble's currency. These coins are collectively known as 'divines' due to the very minor essence effect on them that keeps them clean. Their worth and value differs greatly from the established monetary system many other cities use, specifically to undercut them.

Elves – A race of willowy humanoids with pointy ears. There are five main types:

- High Elves – The largest nation of Elvenkind, they spend most of their time as merchants, artists, or thinkers. Rich beyond any need to actually work, their King is an S-ranked expert, and their cities shine with light and wealth. They like to think of themselves as 'above' other Elves, thus 'High' Elves.
- Wood Elves – Wood Elves live more simply than High Elves, but have greater connection to the earth and the elements. They are ruled by a counsel of S-ranked elders and rarely leave their woods. Though seen less often, they have great power. They grow and collect food and animal products for themselves and other Elven nations.
- Wild Elves – Wild Elves are the outcasts of their societies. Basically feral, they scorn society, civilization, and the rules of others. They have the worst reputation of any of the races of Elves, practicing dark arts and infernal summoning. They have no homeland, living only where they can get away with their dark deeds.
- Dark Elves – The Drow are known as Dark Elves. No one knows where they live, only where they can go to get in contact with them. Dark Elves also have a dark reputation as Assassins and mercenaries for the other races. The worst of their lot are 'Moon Elves,' the best-known Assassins of any race. These are the Elves that Dale made a deal with for land and protection.
- Sea Elves – The Sea Elves live on boats their entire lives. They facilitate trade between all the races of Elves and man, trying not to take sides in conflicts. They work for themselves and are considered rather mysterious.

Essence – Essence is the fundamental energy of the universe, the pure power of heavens and earth that is used by the basic elements to become all forms of matter. The six major types are named: Fire, Water, Earth, Air, Celestial, Infernal.

Essence Cycling – A trick to move energy around, to enhance the ability of an organ.

Eternium – A dungeon core who can hold all of Cal's soul space, aligned to the **Law** of **Order**.

Faux High Elf – A person who has the appearance of a High Elf, but is not actually one. It is a 'Fake' Elf, who takes the position in name only. A mockery and status-display rolled into one.

Father Richard – An A-ranked Cleric that has made his living hunting demons and heretics. Tends to play fast and loose with rules and money.

Fighter – A generic archetype of a being that uses melee weapons to fight.

Fringe – The Fringe region is located in the western region of Pangea. It has been scrapped from maps and scraped from history, by order of the Ecclesiarchy.

Gathering Webway – A web of Essence created around one's center. For the purpose of gathering and retaining Essence. This was the first method concerning Essence refining techniques. It should never be sticky.

Gilded Blade – A weapon, status title, occupation, and profession all in one. A Gilded Blade is a weapon of the raider faction. They are brutally efficient at a single thing, and terrible at everything else.

Gomei – Brianna's right hand and general. He despises humanity with extreme contempt. For no reason other than that they deprived him of his favorite condiment. Wars will start over this. Again.

Grace – Offspring of Cal and Dani. Adorable sm0ll wisp. All the energy of Dad. All the smarts of Mom. Was a wisp's color important again? Grace's color is purple~

Gran'mama – Ephira Mayev Stonequeen is Grand Matron of all the centralized Dwarven clans. She goes by Matron, or Gran'mama. While not a royal, she tends to be treated like one due to the vast respect she holds. She also keeps the great majority of land contracts. Beware of the dreaded chancla.

Hadurin Fellstone – Supposed Head Healer of the motley Fringe expedition crew.

Hadurin Fellhammer – Grand-Inquisitor Fellhammer. Executor of the Inquisition, Lord of the Azure Jade mountain, and slayer of a thousand traitors. While not fully of the dwarven race, he is short, portly, jovial to a fault, and as sly as a certain old man. I hear him with a thick Scottish or Irish voice.

Halcyon – The second of Artorian's chosen, granted the Blessing of Aurum. An uplifted Orca Matron, Halcyon shrunk into her shell as her sapience grew. Shy demeanor aside, a natural leader lurks within. Halcyon has multiple forms just like Zelia, such as fully human, fully Orca, and a hybridized state of flux.

Hakan – A gilded blade, she is the main antagonist of AA1. Her personality is as unpleasant as her fashion sense. She's snide, cuts to the chase, and speaks abrasively without much poise or respect to anyone else.

Hans – A cheeky assassin that has been with Dale since he began cultivating. He was a thief in his youth but changed lifestyles after his street guild was wiped out. He is deadly with a knife and is Dale's best friend. Now Rose's husband.

Hawthorns – A set of Wood Elves that has taken it upon themselves to guard and patrol the edges of the forest. They are generally abrasive, as the threats they come home with aren't taken seriously enough. Or abundantly happy to see you, with matching Southern cadence and happy reed-chewing style. Rules are actually guidelines. Make no mistake. In any other setting, Hawthorne would be a dastardly set of troublemakers.

Henry – Previously the prince-turned-king of the Lion Kingdom, he is now one of the several supervisors of Midgard. Henry is childhood friends with Aiden Silverfang.

Hulk – Odin's greatest nemesis, best squirrel friend to Yuki.

Incantation – Essentially a spell, an incantation is created from words and gestures. It releases all of the power of an enchantment in a single burst.

Infected – A person or creature that has been infected with a rage-inducing mushroom growth. These people have no control of their bodies and attack any non-infected on sight.

Infernal – The Essence of death and demonic beings, *considered* to be always evil.

Inscription – A *permanent* pattern made of Essence that creates an effect on the universe. Try not to get the pattern wrong as it could have… unintended consequences. This is another name for an incomplete or unknown Rune.

Irene – A Keeper in the Choir. There is more to her than meets the eye, and is far more powerful than she initially appears to be. Do not argue with her about scripture. This world-weary Keeper plays with subterfuge like children play outside. Though when able, she speaks with her fists. Her rage meter is tiny, and fills with a swiftness.

Jiivra – A Battle Leader in the Choir, she aspires to be a Paladin. She has the potential to become truly great, if only given the opportunity. Young, and full of splendor. She's hasty, sticks to order, dislikes surprises, and answers to them with well-measured responses.

Jin – The child of Tarrean and Irene, a Keeper in the Fringe.

Karakum – Only two things are certain: Death, and Taxes. Karakum is both. This fire-dungeon turned scorpion gained new life just as Zelia did. He's snippy, and can be a bit much to handle, but after becoming Dawn's chosen, he does what is required of him by the Lady of Flame. Karakum is based on Zorro.

Lapis – A mineral-mining town in the vicinity of the Salt Flats. They refine the color Lapis into varying shades of Blue, and are a prime exporter. Lapis is located in the Fringe.

Liminal – Also called Liminal Energy, or the energy of thought. It is the intermediary between Mana and Spirit. Liminal Energy is both sentient and sapient. It develops a mind of its own when the Mage reaches a certain point of progress. This energy can manifest itself in a variety of ways, but is difficult to control after it gains sapience. Sapient Liminal Energy frequently manifests as issues the Mage needs to tackle. Whether that be items, people, or challenges.

Maccreus Tarrean – Head Cleric of a Choir expeditionary force. His pride is his most distinguishing feature, next to that ostentatious affront known as his armor. Short and portly for non-dwarven reasons, this blundering, ego-driven voice blusters through life like a drunk through a tavern. Elbows first. His ability to craft schemes is as sharp as a dull, smooth rock. His Charisma unfortunately doesn't notice and charges on anyway.

Mahogany – Chosen leaders of the Phantomdusk Wood Elves. As a congregation of Sultans, they care deeply for their people. Forced to make difficult decisions on behalf of the people as a whole, they function with the full permission of the S-ranked council. Which is less active than they'd like it to be. A good soul, they speak with deep voices. Together with Birch they seek to rebuild Wood Elf society within Eternium.

Mages' Guild – A secretive sub-sect of the Adventurers' Guild only Mage-level cultivators are allowed to join.

Mana – A higher stage of Essence only able to be cultivated by those who have broken into at least the B-rankings and found the true name of something in the universe.

Mana Signature – A name for a signature that can be neither forged nor replicated, and is used in binding oaths.

Marie – Previously the princess-turned-queen of the Phoenix Kingdom. She is now one of the many supervisors of Midgard, establishing the human presence in Cal's soul space. A Mage of **Glory** and not afraid to use her trumpets to harken it.

Marud – Choir second-in-command Battle Leader, of the second expeditionary force to the Fringe.

Meridians – Meridians are energy channels that transport life energy (Chi/Essence) throughout the body.

Memory Core – Also known as a Memory Stone, depending on the base materials used in their production. Pressing the stone to your forehead lets a person store or gain the knowledge contained within. As if you'd gone through the events yourself. Generally never sold.

Minya – Ex-leader of the Cult of Cal. After entering Cal's Soul Space, she now presides over the research and development on the Moon with Bob. All she wants is peace and quiet. Maybe a small store.

Mob – A shortened version of "dungeon monster."

Morovia – A world region located in the south-eastern section of the central Pangea band.

Necromancer – An Infernal Essence cultivator who can raise and control the dead and demons. A title for a cultivator who specializes in re-animating that which has died.

Nefellum – Head Cleric of the second expedition force into the Fringe.

Noble rankings:

- King/Queen – Ruler of their country. (Addressed as 'Your Majesty')
- Crown Prince/Princess – Next in line to the throne, has the same political power as a Grand Duke. (Addressed as 'Your Royal Highness')
- Prince/Princess – Child of the King/Queen, has the same political power as a Duke. (Addressed as 'Your Highness')
- Grand Duke/Grand Duchess – Ruler of a grand duchy and is senior to a Duke. (Addressed as 'Your Grace')

- Duke/Duchess – Is senior to a Marquis or Marchioness. (Addressed as 'Your Grace')
- Marquis/Marchioness – Controls a section of land in a kingdom outside of the heartland. Is senior to an Earl and has at least three Earls in their domain. (Addressed as 'Honorable')
- Earl/Countess – Is senior to a Baron. Each Earl has three Barons under their power. (Addressed as 'My Lord/Lady')
- Viscount/Viscountess – Thought of as the lieutenants of the Earl in their region. Is senior to a Baron, if by just a small margin. (Addressed as 'My Lord/Lady')
- Baron/Baroness – Senior to knights, they control a minimum of ten knights and therefore their land. (Addressed as 'My Lord/Lady')
- Baronets – A member of the lowest hereditary titled order, with the status of a commoner. (Addressed as 'Sir')
- Knight/Dame – Sub rulers of plots of land and peasants. (Addressed as 'Sir')
- Esquire – A young nobleman who, in training for knighthood, acts as an attendant to a knight. (Addressed as 'Sir')
- Gentleman/Lady – Those of high birth or rank, good social standing and wealth, and who did not need to work for a living.

Oak – A set of Wood Elves that embody the purest spirit of flamboyance. Rules might exist, but Oak won't care to listen.

Oberon – Eternium's clever, cunning, orange wisp. Constantly finding new ways to con his dungeon to keep him on his metaphorical toes. Let's see how many times this wisp's name gets underlined by the end.

Occultatum – Previously known as the Master, he now resides on Hel as its supervisor. Cal supposedly stationed him due to the high Mana density, but in reality, it's to deal with those abyss-blasted swans and geese.

Odin – Elemental of Air and supervisor of Asgard. His ego is almost the size of the Valkyries stationed outside his baths; though, a certain frosty individual manages to keep him in line.

Olgier – A trader from Rutsel, whose greed greatly exceeds his guile.

Olive – A Wood Elf who is very down to earth. A little greasy, he likes to dig holes and hidden pathways.

Oversized Infernal Corvid – Really big raven with the Infernal channel. D-ranked creature. Intelligent. Moody.

Pattern – A pattern is the intricate design that makes everything in the universe. An inanimate object has a far less complex pattern that a living being.

Phantomdusk Forest – A world region that borders The Fringe. It is comprised of vast, continent-sprawled greenery that covers multiple biomes. Any forest region connecting to this main mass is considered part of the whole, if entering it has a high mortality rate.

Presence – In terms of Aura, this refers to the combined components that Aura encompasses. Ordinarily a Mage-only ability. Presence refers to the unity of Auras and them acting as one.

Ra – Lunella's first daughter, who causes an amount of trouble equal to the amount of breaths she takes. *Cough*, much like a certain grandfather.

Raile – A massive, granite-covered Boss Basher that attacks by ramming and attempting to squish its opponents.

Ranger – Typically an adventurer archetype that is able to attack from long range, usually with a bow.

Ranking System – The ranking system is a way to classify how powerful a creature has become through fighting and cultivation.

- G – At the lowest ranking is mostly non-organic matter such as rocks and ash. Mid-G contains small plants such as moss and mushrooms while the upper ranks form most of the other flora in the world.
- F – The F-ranks are where beings are becoming actually sentient, able to gather their own food and make short-term plans. The mid-F ranks are where most humans reach before adulthood without cultivating. This is known as the fishy or "failure" rank.
- E – The E-rank is known as the "echo" rank and is used to prepare a body for intense cultivation.
- D – This is the rank where a cultivator starts to become actually dangerous. A D-ranked individual can usually fight off ten F-ranked beings without issue. They are characterized by a "fractal" in their Chi spiral.
- C – The highest-ranked Essence cultivators, those in the C-rank usually have opened all of their meridians. A C-ranked cultivator can usually fight off ten D-ranked and one hundred F-ranked beings without being overwhelmed.
- B – This is the first rank of Mana cultivators, known as Mages. They convert Essence into Mana through a nuanced refining process and release it through a true name of the universe.

- A – Usually several hundred years are needed to attain this rank, known as High-Mage or High-Magous. They are the most powerful rank of Mages.
- S – Very mysterious Spiritual Essence cultivators. Not much is known about the requirements for this rank or those above it.
- SS – Pronounced 'Double S.' Not much is known about the requirements for this rank or those above it.
- SSS – Pronounced 'Triple S.' Not much is known about the requirements for this rank or those above it.
- Heavenly – Not much is known about the requirements for this rank or those above it.
- Godly – Not much is known about the requirements for this rank or those above it.

Refining – A name for the method of separating Essences of differing purities.

Rune – A *permanent* pattern made of Essence that creates an effect on the universe. Try not to get the pattern wrong as it could have... unintended consequences. This is another name for a completed Inscription.

Rose – Chaos cultivator and wife of Hans. She spent most of her life with her Aunt Chandra before making her way to Mountaindale and meeting her friends. She will happily slay a man with her speech or with her arrows. They decide.

Rosewood – Wood Elves with an unbreakable passion for fashion, and making clothes.

Rota – A sturdy and strapping Dwarf whose jokes latched him with the nickname "Otter," he once tried to scribe Runes onto a set of gambling dice. Beware of the explosions around this wily lad.

Royal Advisor – A big bad. Direct hand to the Mistress, the Queen and Regent in charge of the Ziggurat. Lover of the Cobra Chicken, and Swans.

Salt Village – The main location of Artorian's Archives One, where the majority of the story takes place. It is located in the Fringe, and is a day's journey from the Lapis Village.

Salt Flats – A location in the Fringe. The Salt Village operates by scraping salt from the Salt Flats, a place where the material is plentiful. It is their main export.

Scar – Known as 'The Scar.' A location in that Fringe that includes the Salt Flats as one of its tendrils. It is rumored to be a kind of slumbering dungeon.

Scilla – A small girl that lives in Chasuble. She is afflicted by an effect that caused her irises to permanently turn pink.

Sequoia – Wood Elves that will not be forgotten, even without them speaking.

Shamira – Scilla's mother. She is a resident of Chasuble, and not particularly happy about the conditions there.

Sproutling – A title for a child in the Fringe who has not yet been assigned a name, and thus is not considered an adult. Until a certain key event, this includes the famous five: Lunella, Grimaldus, Tychus, Wuxius, and Astrea.

Skyspear Academy – An Academy present on the world's tallest mountain.

Socorro – A desert in the central-band, eastern portion of Pangea. It used to be a place for something important. Now there is only sand, and ruin.

Soul Item – A construct made in a Soul Space that specializes the Mage to a certain set of ideas and concepts, allowing for advancement into the A-ranks and beyond.

Soul Space – A realm accessible by cultivators that exists outside of the self. Vastly important for Mages to keep increasing in rank. Soul Spaces are morphous in size, and tend to hold a Mage's 'Soul Item.'

Soul Space [Cal] – Cal's Soul Space is being designed to hold an entire world. Divided by several landmasses and unique locations:

- Midgard – The human, wolfman, and plant-people realm in Cal's soul space. This skyland supports anything in the G- to D-ranks, and is where a majority of individuals are decanted. Run by Marie, Henry, Chandra, and Aiden.
- Alfheim – The realm for the majority of Elves in Cal's Soul Space. This skyland supports anything in the C-ranks. Is built around having pill cultivation. Alfheim has no supervisor.
- Svartalfheim – The realm of the Dwarves in Cal's Soul Space. This skyland supports anything in the ranks. Is built on Aether cultivation. Svartalfheim has no supervisor.
- Vanaheim – The realm of the Gnomes in Cal's Soul Space. This skyland supports anything in the low B-ranks. Vanaheim is home to all the pylons that run Cal's bracket spells, and a land of many wondrous inventions. Beneath its shiny exterior, a civil war takes place. Deverash is Vanaheim's supervisor.

- Jotunheim – The realm of massive Beasts and gigantic Jotun in Cal's Soul Space. Home to many wonderful chosen and a door named Ellis, this skyland supports anything in the mid B-ranks. Artorian is the supervisor of Jotunheim.
- Niflheim – The realm of Mists and home of the Dark Elves in Cal's Soul Space. This skyland is set almost completely on its side, and supports anything in the upper B-ranks. Niflheim is run by Brianna.
- Muspelheim – The realm of fire, sand, and goblins in Cal's Soul Space. This skyland has many separate layers, from the floating triremes in the sky, to the paradise beneath the surface, and supports anything in the upper B-ranks. Many different races have found a home in Muspelheim; including Lamia, goblins, C'towl, Lizards, and a giant serpent named Jorm. This realm is overseen by Dawn.
- Asgard – The realm of elementals, heroes, and small party accidents. This skyland supports anything A-ranked; from minimum to apex. (As well as Odin's ego, if just barely.) This realm was having a swarm problem, but after some… suggestions, those were taken care of. Odin is the supervisor of this realm.
- Hel – The realm of all things S-ranked in Cal's Soul Space. This is the only spherical realm in Cal's world, and is made of all the corrupted ash from things dead and dying. Home to Gibble, the bone gazelle. Hel is supervised by Occultatum.
- Sun – Giant ball of interlocking rings and runes meant to provide light to all in Cal's Soul Space… Before the administrator caused it to explode. Home to Artorian's Archives.
- Moon – The place where most of the research and development takes place in Cal's Soul Space. The Moon's topside is a large area for the children to grow and enjoy themselves. Beneath the surface,

however, is the Rotunda of Holding, and a large laboratory where Minya and the Bobs work.

Soul Stone – A *highly* refined Beast Core that is capable of containing a human soul.

Surtur – Dawn's first chosen. A Lamia. She was granted a weapon made by Dawn, and uses it to lead her tribe to ever greater heights of prosperity. Even if her tribe keeps incorporating more and more races.

Switch – A village Elder of the Salt Village in the Fringe region. She croaks rather than speaks. Though that's only if she speaks. Usually she complains. Loudly, and in plenty. If forced to interact with Switch, consider stuffing one's ears with beeswax.

Tank – An adventurer archetype that is built to defend his team from the worst of the attacks that come their way. Heavily armored and usually carrying a large shield, these powerful people are needed if a group plans on surviving more than one attack.

Tibbins – An Acolyte in the Choir. He has a deep passion for all things culinary, and possesses a truly unique expression. He means well, but there's something about his poor luck that keeps getting him in someone's firing line. Sweet, loves to cook, and loyal to a fault. Tibbins is just in the wrong place at the wrong time. His voice tends to tremble when he is uncertain.

Tom – Former exiled Northman. Friend of Dale, and a general smashing success with his hammer: 'Thud.'

Vizier Amon – A big bad. Direct hand to the Mistress, the Queen and Regent in charge of the Ziggurat. Things will get better before they get worse. Unless maybe one can pull the strings of a few favors. Sang with serpentine tongue. His time as grand vizier was short, becoming more nope than rope.

Vol – A chosen one of Artorian who prefers his beastly Teslasaur form. He may not be the sharpest tool in the shed, but certainly has the speed and chompers of an apex predator.

Wuxius – Son of the Fringe and one of Artorian's five grand-children.

Wagner – Hel's premier goose of spite, gifted with the best pipes known to Eternium. Beware your ankles in his presence, they are prime targets for his rage-filled bites.

Yuki – A lady of snow and ice. Artorian's third chosen, gifted with an unaccepted blessing. Her cold countenance and sleety demeanor reflect her current perspective of the world.

Yvessa – An Elven name that means: 'To bloom out of great drought.' She is a Choir Cleric going up the ranks, and holds incredible promise. A girl of destiny. A demon-lord with a spoon. A caretaker who gains wisdom beyond her years from the kind of abyss she has to deal with. Her voice gains energy as she ages, as does her spirit.

Zelia – First chosen of Artorian, gifted with the Blessing of Argent. She is the mind of the Fringe Teleportation core, given life anew. A passionate artist, secretary, and seamstress. She is the sole peak of her spider family. Zelia is able to tap into her Dreamer's abilities and memories, and uses her Teleportation gifts with uncanny skill and efficiency. She grows to deeply care for her Dreamer beyond the constraints of what being a chosen forces, and has decided for herself to stick around. Zelia has multiple forms, including fully human, fully spider, drider (half and half), and a state of flux.

Ziggurat – Both the name of a region, and a large building central to it. Ziggurat is the current raider stronghold where all their activities are coordinated from. The hierarchies here are simple and bloody, but the true purpose of the place is to serve as a staging area for necromancer needs.